SUBSTITUTE SEDUCTION

CAT SCHIELD

A CHRISTMAS TEMPTATION

KAREN BOOTH

FSC FSC C007454

This book is produced from independently certified FSC™ paper to ensure responsible forest management.

For more information visit: www.harpercollins.co.uk/green

Printed and bound in Spain
by CPI, Barcelona

MILLS & BOON

First Published in Great Britain 2018
by Mills & Boon, an imprint of HarperCollinsPublishers,
1 London Bridge Street, London, SE1 9GF

Substitute Seduction © 2018 Catherine Schield
A Christmas Temptation © 2018 Karen Booth

ISBN: 978-0-263-93627-8

1118

MIX
Paper from
responsible sources

FSC

SUBSTITUTE SEDUCTION

CAT SCHIELD

Prologue

"We need to get back at all of them. Linc, Tristan and Ryan. They need to be taught a lesson."

When Everly Briggs had decided to attend the Beautiful Women Taking Charge event, she'd researched the attendees and settled on two women she believed she could convince to participate in a devious plot to take down three of Charleston, South Carolina's most influential men.

Each of the three women had shared a tale of being wronged. Linc Thurston had broken his engagement to London McCaffrey. Zoe Crosby had just gone through a brutal divorce. But what Ryan Dailey had done to Everly's sister, Kelly, was by far the worst.

"I don't know about this," London said, chewing on her coral-tinted lip. "If I go after Linc, it will blow up in my face."

"She's right." Zoe nodded. "Anything we try would only end up making things worse for us."

"Not if we go after each other's men," Everly said, pierced by a thrill as her companions started to look hopeful. "Think about it. We're strangers at a cocktail party. Who would ever connect us? I go after Linc. London goes after Tristan and, Zoe, you go after Ryan."

"When you say 'go after,'" Zoe said hesitantly, "what do you have in mind?"

"Everyone has skeletons in their closet. Especially powerful men. We just need to find out where the worst ones are hiding and let them out."

"I'm in," London said. "Linc deserves to feel a little pain and humiliation for ending our engagement the way he did."

Zoe nodded. "Count me in, too."

"Marvelous," Everly said, letting only a small amount of her glee show as she lifted her glass. "Here's to making them pay."

"And pay," London echoed.

"And pay," Zoe finished.

One

The party celebrating the ten-year anniversary of the Dixie Bass-Crosby Foundation was in full swing as Harrison Crosby strolled beneath the Baccarat crystal-and-brass chandelier hanging from the restored antebellum mansion's fifteen-foot foyer ceiling. Snagging a glass of champagne from a circling waitress, Harrison passed from the broad foyer with its white marble floor and grand columns toward the ballroom, where a string quartet played in the corner.

Thirty years ago Harrison's uncle Jack Crosby had purchased the historic Groves Plantation, located thirty-five miles outside the city of Charleston, intending to headquarter Crosby Motorsports on the hundred-acre property. At the time, the 1850s mansion had been in terrible shape and they'd been on the verge of knocking it down when both Virginia Lamb-Crosby and Dixie Bass-Crosby—Harrison's mother and aunt respectively—had raised a ruckus. Instead the Crosby family had dumped a ton of money into the historic renovation to bring it up to code and make it livable. The result was a work of art.

Although Harrison had attended dozens of charity events supporting his family's foundations over the years, the social whirl bored him. He'd much rather just donate the money and skip all the pomp and circumstance. Despite the Crosby wealth and the old family connections his aunt and mother could claim, Harrison had nothing in common with the Charleston elite and preferred his horsepower beneath the hood of his Ford rather than on the polo field.

Which was why he intended to greet his family, make as little small talk as he could and get the hell out. With only three races left in the season, Harrison needed to stay focused on preparations. And he needed as much mental and physical stamina as possible.

Spying his mother, Harrison made his way toward her. She was in conversation with a younger woman he didn't recognize. As he drew near, Harrison recognized his mistake. His mother's beautiful blonde companion wore no ring on her left hand. Whenever his mother encountered someone suitable, she always schemed to fix him up. She didn't understand that his racing career took up all his time and energy. Or she did get it and hoped that a wife and family might persuade him to give it all up and settle down.

Harrison was on the verge of angling away when Virginia "Ginny" Lamb-Crosby noticed his approach and smiled triumphantly.

"Here's my son," she proclaimed, reaching with her left hand to draw Harrison in. "Sawyer, this is Harrison. Harrison, I'd like you to meet Sawyer Thurston."

"Nice to meet you," Harrison said, frowning as he tried to place her name. "Thurston…"

"Linc Thurston is my brother," Sawyer clarified, obviously accustomed to explaining about her connection to the professional baseball player.

Harrison nodded. "Sure."

Before he could say anything more, his mother reinserted herself into the conversation. "Sawyer is a member of Charleston's Preservation Society and we were just talking about the historic home holiday tour. She wants to know if I'd be willing to open the Jonathan Booth House this year. What do you think?"

This was the exact sort of nonsense that he hated getting involved in. No matter what his or anyone else's opinion, Ginny Lamb-Crosby would do exactly as she liked.

He leaned down to kiss her cheek and murmured, "I think you should ask Father since it's his house, too."

After a few more polite exchanges Harrison pretended to see someone he needed to talk to and excused himself. As he strolled around the ballroom, smiling and greeting those he knew, his gaze snagged on a beautiful woman in a gown of liquid sky. Her long honeyed hair hung in rolling waves over her shoulders with one side pulled back to show off her sparkly dangle earring. In a roomful of beautiful women, she stood out to him because rather than smiling and enjoying herself, the blonde with big eyes and pale pink lips wore a frown. She seemed to barely be listening to her chatty companion, a shorter, plump brunette of classic beauty and pouty lips.

She seemed preoccupied by... Harrison followed her gaze and realized she was staring at his brother, Tristan. This should have warned Harrison off. The last thing he wanted to do was to get tangled up with one of his brother's castoffs. But the woman inspired more than just his curiosity. He had an immediate and intense urge to get her alone to see if her lips were as sweet as they looked, and that hadn't happened in far too long.

Turning his back on the beauty, he headed to where his aunt was holding court on one side of the room near a large television playing a promotional video about the Dixie Bass-Crosby Foundation. In addition to helping families with sick children, the foundation supported K–12 education programs focused on literacy. Over the last ten years, his aunt had given away nearly ten million dollars and her family was very proud of her.

Yet even as Harrison exchanged a few words with his aunt, uncle and their group, his attention returned to the lovely blonde in the blue dress. The more he observed her, the more she appeared different from the ladies who normally appealed to him. Just as beautiful, but not a bubbly party girl. More reserved. Someone his mother would approve of.

The more he watched her, the more he labeled her as uptight. Not in a sexual way, like she wouldn't know an orgasm if it reached out and slapped her, but in a manner that said her whole life was a straitjacket. If not for her preoccupation with Tristan, he might've turned away.

He simply had to find out who she was, so he went in search of his uncle. Bennett Lamb knew where all the bodies were buried and traded in gossip like other men bought and sold stock, real estate or collectibles.

Harrison found the Charleston icon holding court near the bar. In black pants and a cream honeycomb dinner jacket with a gold bow tie and pocket square, Bennett outshone many of the female guests in the fashion department.

"Do you have a second?" Harrison asked, glancing around to make sure his quarry hadn't escaped.

One of Bennett's well-groomed eyebrows went up. "Certainly."

The two men moved off a couple of feet and Harrison

indicated the woman who'd interested him. "Do you know who that is?"

Amusement dancing in his eyes, his uncle gazed in the direction Harrison indicated. "Maribelle Gates? She recently became engaged to Beau Shelton. Good family. Managed to hold on to their wealth despite some shockingly bad advice from Roland Barnes."

Harrison silently cursed at the word *engaged*. Why was she so interested in Tristan if she was unavailable? Maybe she was cheating on her fiancé. Wary of letting his uncle think he'd shown an interest in someone who was engaged, he asked, "And the brunette?"

"Maribelle Gates is the brunette." Bennett saw where his nephew was going and shook his head. "Oh, you were interested in the blonde. That's London McCaffrey."

"London." He experimented with the taste of her name and liked it. "Why does her name ring a bell?"

"She was engaged to Linc Thurston for two years."

"I just met his sister." Harrison returned to studying London.

Meanwhile his uncle kept talking. "He recently broke off the engagement. No one knows why, but it's rumored he's been sleeping with…" Bennett's lips curved into a wicked grin. "His housekeeper."

An image of the heavyset fifty-year-old woman who maintained his parents' house popped into Harrison's mind and he grimaced. He pondered the willowy blonde and wondered what madness had gripped Linc to let her go.

"He doesn't seem the type to go after his housekeeper."

"You never know about some people."

"So why is everyone convinced that he's sleeping with her?"

"*Convinced* is a strong word," his uncle said. "Let's just say that there's speculation along those lines. Linc hasn't been out with anyone since he and London broke up. There's been not a whisper of another romance on anyone's radar. And, from what I hear, she's a young widow with a toddler."

Harrison shoved aside the gossip and refocused on the object of his interest. The more Bennett speculated about the reason Linc Thurston had for ending the engagement, the less he liked London's interest in his brother. She deserved better. Tristan had always treated women poorly, as his recent behavior during his divorce from his wife of eight years demonstrated. Not only had Tristan cheated on her the entire time they were married, he'd hired a merciless divorce attorney, and Zoe had ended up with almost nothing.

"Now, if you're looking for someone to date, I'd like to suggest…"

Harrison tuned out the rest of his uncle's remarks as he continued to puzzle over London McCaffrey. "Is she seeing anyone at the moment?" Harrison asked, breaking into whatever it was his uncle was going on about.

"Ivy? I don't believe so."

"No," Harrison said, realizing he hadn't been paying attention to whatever pearls of wisdom his uncle had been shelling out. "London McCaffrey."

"Stay away from that one," Bennett warned. "That mother of hers is the worst. She's a former New York socialite who thinks a lot of money—and I do mean a lot—can buy her way into Charleston inner circles. Honestly, the woman is a menace."

"I'm not interested in dating the mother."

"London is just as much a social climber," Bennett said as if Harrison was an utter idiot not to make the connection. "Why else do you think she pursued Linc?"

"Obviously you don't think she was in love with him," Harrison retorted dryly.

He wasn't a stranger to the elitist outlook held by the old guard of Charleston society. His own mother had disappointed her family by marrying a man from North Carolina with nothing but big dreams and ambition. Harrison hadn't understood the complexities of his mother's relationship with her family and, frankly, he'd never really cared. Ever since he could remember, all Harrison had ever wanted to do was to tinker with cars and drive fast.

His father and uncle had started out as mechanics before investing in their first auto parts store. Within five years the two men had parlayed their experience and drive into a nationwide chain. While Harrison's dad, Robert "Bertie" Crosby, was happy to man the helm and expand the business, his brother, Jack, pursued his dream of running race cars.

By the time Harrison was old enough to drive, his uncle had built Crosby Motorsports into a winning team. And like the brothers before them, Tristan had gone into the family business, preferring to keep his hands clean, while Harrison loved every bit of oil and dirt that marked his skin.

"She pursued him," Bennett pronounced, "because her children would be Thurstons."

Harrison considered this. It was possible that she'd judged the guy by his social standing. On the other hand, maybe she'd been in love with Linc. Either way, Harrison wasn't going to know for sure until he had a chance to get to know her.

"Why are you so interested in her?" Bennett asked, interrupting Harrison's train of thought.

"I don't know."

He couldn't explain to his uncle that London's preoccupation with Tristan intrigued and worried him. For the last couple of years Harrison had increasing concerns about his brother's systematically deteriorating marriage to Zoe. Still, he'd ignored the rumors of Tristan's affairs even as Harrison recognized his brother had a dark side and a ruthless streak.

The fact that Zoe had vanished off his radar since she'd first separated from Tristan nagged at Harrison. In the beginning he hadn't wanted to get involved in what had looked to become a nasty divorce. Lately he was wishing he'd been a better brother-in-law.

"Do you know what London does?" Harrison asked, returning his thoughts to the beautiful blonde.

Bennett sighed. "She owns an event planning service."

"Did she plan this event?" An idea began to form in Harrison's mind.

"No. Most of the work was done by Zoe before..." Not even Bennett was comfortable talking about his former niece-in-law.

"I think I'm going to introduce myself to London McCaffrey," Harrison said.

"Just don't be too surprised when she's not interested in you."

"I have a halfway-decent pedigree," Harrison said with a wink.

"Halfway decent isn't going to be enough for her."

"You're so cynical." Harrison softened his statement with a half smile. "And I'm more than enough for her to handle."

His uncle began to laugh. "No doubt you're right. Just don't be surprised when she turns you down flat."

London McCaffrey stood beside her best friend, Maribelle Gates, her attention fixed on the tall, imposing man she'd promised to take down in the next few months. Zoe Crosby's ex-husband was handsome enough, but his chilly gaze and the sardonic twist to his lips made London shiver. From the research London had done on him these last couple of weeks, she knew he'd ruthlessly gone after his wife, leaving her with nothing to show for her eight-year marriage.

In addition to cheating on Zoe through most of their marriage, Tristan Crosby had manufactured evidence that she was the one who'd been unfaithful and violated their prenuptial agreement. Zoe had been forced to spend tens of thousands of dollars disproving this, which had eaten into her divorce settlement. A settlement based on financial information about her husband's wealth that indicated he was heavily mortgaged and deeply in debt.

Zoe's lawyer suspected that Tristan had created offshore shell companies that allowed him to hide money and avoid paying taxes. It wasn't unusual or illegal, but it was a hard paper trail to find.

"Heavens, that man cleans up well," Maribelle remarked, her voice breathy and impressed. "And he's been staring this way practically since he arrived." She nudged London. "Wouldn't it be great if he's interested in you?"

With an exasperated sigh, London turned to her friend and was about to reiterate that the last thing on her mind was romance when she recognized the man in question. Harrison Crosby, Tristan's younger brother.

A racing-circuit fan favorite thanks to his long, lean body and handsome face, Harrison was, to her mind, little more than a glorified frat boy. Zoe had explained that her ex-brother-in-law liked fast cars, pretty women and the sorts of activities that red-blooded American males went for in the South.

"He's not my type," London told her best friend, returning her focus to her target.

"Sweetie, I love you," Maribelle began, settling further into her native South Carolina drawl, "but you have to stop being so picky."

Resentment rose in London but she studiously avoided showing it. Since the first time her mother had slapped her face for making a fuss during her sixth birthday party, London had decided if she was going to survive in the Mc-Caffrey household, she'd better learn to conceal her emotions. It wasn't always easy, but now, at twenty-eight, she was nearly impossible to read.

"I'm not being picky. I'm simply being realistic." And since he wasn't the Crosby brother she was targeting, he wasn't worth her time.

"That's your problem," Maribelle complained. "You're always realistic. Why don't you let loose and have some fun?"

Out of kindness or sympathy for her longtime friend, Maribelle didn't mention London's latest failure to climb the Charleston social ladder. She'd heard more than enough on that score from her mother. When London had begun to date someone from one of Charleston's oldest families, her mother had perceived this as the social win she'd been looking for since the New York socialite had married restaurant CEO Boyd McCaffrey and moved to Connecticut, leaving her beloved New York City behind. And then, when London's father had been accepted for a better position and moved his family to Charleston, Edie Fremont-McCaffrey's situation grew so much worse.

When she'd first arrived, Edie had assumed that her New York connections, wealth and style would guarantee Charleston's finest would throw open their doors for her. Instead she'd discovered that family and ancestral connections mattered more here than something as vulgar as money.

"It's not that I don't want to have fun," London began. "I just don't know that I want to have Harrison Crosby's sort of fun."

Well, didn't that make her sound like the sort of dull prig who'd let the handsome and wealthy Linc Thurston slip through her fingers? London's heart contracted. Although she no longer believed herself in love with Linc, at one point she'd been ready to marry him. But would she have? London wasn't entirely clear where their relationship would be if he hadn't broken things off.

"How do you know what sort of fun Harrison Crosby likes?" Maribelle asked, bringing London back to the present.

She bit her lip, unable to explain why she'd been researching the Crosby family, looking for an in. There were only three people who knew of their rash plan to take revenge on the men who'd wronged them. What London, Everly and Zoe were doing might not necessarily be illegal, but if they were discovered, retribution could be fierce and damaging.

"He's a race-car driver." As if that explained everything.

"And he's gorgeous."

"Is he?"

London considered all the photos she'd seen of him. Curly black hair, unshaved cheeks, wearing jeans and a T-shirt or his blue racing suit with sponsor patches plastered head to toe, he had an engaging smile and an easy confidence that proclaimed he had the world on a string.

"I guess if you like them scruffy and rough," London muttered. Which she didn't.

"He looks pretty suave and elegant to me."

Maribelle's wry tone spiked London's curiosity and she carefully let her gaze drift in his direction. Not wanting the man to think she was at all interested in him, she didn't look directly at him as she took in his appearance.

The Harrison Crosby she'd been picturing looked nothing like the refined gentleman in a perfectly tailored dark gray suit that drew attention to his strong shoulders and narrow hips. Her hormones reacted with shocking intensity to his stylish appearance. He was clean-shaved tonight, appearing elegant enough to have stepped off a New York runway. Where she'd been able to dismiss the "rough around the edges good ol' boy" in racing attire, London saw she'd miscalculated the appeal of a confident male at the top of his game.

"Apparently he cleans up well," London remarked grudgingly, her gaze moving on before she could get caught staring.

"He's coming this way," Maribelle squeaked.

London's pulse revved like an engine as she took in his elegant appearance. "Get a hold of yourself," she murmured in exasperation, unsure if she was speaking to herself or Maribelle.

"Good evening, ladies." His voice had a deep, rich tone like the rumble of a cat's purr. "I'm Harrison Crosby. Dixie Bass-Crosby is my aunt."

"Number twenty-five," Maribelle responded in a surprisingly girlish tone that caused London to gape. "You're having a great second half this year. I'm Maribelle Gates."

A sexy half grin kicked up one corner of his mouth. "You follow racing?" he asked, echoing the question in London's head.

While his sea-glass eyes remained focused on Maribelle, London stared at him in consternation. Her body was reacting to his proximity in confusing ways.

"I do," Maribelle confirmed. "So does my fiancé. We're huge fans."

As her best friend displayed a surprising amount of knowledge about race-car driving, London began to feel like a third wheel. While the two girls had been best friends since their first day of the exclusive private girls' school they'd attended, certain differences had always existed between them.

Both were from wealthy families, but Maribelle's had the sort of social standing that had allowed her access to the inner circles that had eluded London and her family. And while each woman was beautiful, Maribelle had always fought with her weight and this had led to her feeling less secure about her appearance. But the biggest difference was that for all her lack of social standing, London had always been the more popular of the two.

Until now.

"Oh," Maribelle exclaimed, glancing toward her friend as if suddenly realizing they'd excluded London. "How rude of me to monopolize you. This is London McCaffrey."

"Nice to meet you," London said. Yet as miffed as she was at his earlier lack of interest, she wasn't sure she meant it.

"Nice to meet you, as well." Harrison's gaze flicked from one woman to the other. "Now, it seems as if you know all about me. What is it you ladies do?"

"I'm planning a wedding," Maribelle said with a silly little giggle that left London struggling not to roll her eyes.

Harrison's sculpted lips shifted into an indulgent smile. "I imagine that's a full-time job."

London bit the inside of her lip to keep from snorting in derision. "I own an event planning company," she said a trifle too aggressively. Hearing her tone brought a rush of heat to London's cheeks. Was she seriously trying to compete with her engaged friend for a man she wasn't even interested in?

"Are you planning her wedding?"

London shot her friend a glance as she shook her head. "No."

"Not your thing?" he guessed, demonstrating an ability to read the subtle currents beneath her answer.

"She mostly organizes corporate and charity events," Maribelle responded with a sweet smile that stabbed at London's heart.

"Oh, that's too bad," Harrison said, the impact of his full attention making London's palms tingle. "My brother's turning forty next month and I was going to plan a party for him. Only I don't know anything about that sort of thing. I don't suppose you'd like to help me out?"

"I…" Her first impulse was to refuse, but she'd been looking for an opening that would get her into Tristan's orbit. Planning his birthday party would be an excellent step in that direction. "Don't usually do personal events, but I would be happy to meet with you and talk about it."

She pulled a business card out of her clutch and handed it to him.

He glanced at the card. "'London McCaffrey. Owner of ExcelEvent.' I'll be in touch." Then, with a charming smile, he said, "Nice meeting you both."

London's eyes remained glued to his retreating figure for several seconds. When she returned her focus to Maribelle, her friend was actively smirking.

"What?"

"See? I told you. What you need is a little fun."

"It's a job," London said, emphasizing each word so Maribelle wouldn't misinterpret the encounter. "He's looking for someone to organize his brother's birthday party. That's why I gave him my card."

"Sure." Maribelle's hazel eyes danced. "Whatever you say. But I think what you need is someone to take your mind off what happened between you and Linc, and in my not-so-humble opinion, that—" she pointed at the departing figure "—is the perfect man for the job."

Everything London had read about him stated that he liked to play hard and that his longest relationship to date had lasted just over a year. She'd decided her next romance would be with a man with a serious career. Someone she'd have lots in common with.

"Why do you think that?" London asked, unable to understand her friend's logic. "As far as I can tell, he's just like Linc. An athlete with an endless supply of eager women at his beck and call."

"Maybe he's just looking for the right woman to settle down with," Maribelle countered. She'd been singing a different tune about men and romance since she'd started dating Beau Shelton. "Can't you at least give the guy a chance?"

London sighed. She and Maribelle had had this conversation any number of times over the last few months as her friend had tried to set her up with one or another of Beau's friends. Maybe if she said yes Maribelle would back off.

"I'm really not ready to date anyone."

"Don't think of it as dating," Maribelle said. "Just think of it as hanging out."

Since London was already thinking in terms of how she could use Harrison to get to Tristan, it was an easy enough promise to make. "If it means you'll stop bugging me," she said, hiding her sudden satisfaction at killing two birds with one stone, "I'll agree to give Harrison Crosby one chance."

Two

Harrison spent more than his usual twenty minutes in the bathroom of his penthouse condo overlooking the Cooper River as he prepared for his meeting with London McCaffrey.

A woman he'd dated for a short time a year ago had given him pointers on grooming particulars that women appreciated. At the time he'd viewed the whole thing with skepticism, but after giving the various lotions, facial scrubs, hair-care products and other miscellaneous items a try, he'd been surprised at the results and happily reaped the benefits of Serena's appreciation.

Still, as much as he'd seen the value in what she'd introduced into his life, his focus during racing season left little room for such inconsequential activities. Today, however, he'd applied all that he'd learned, scrutinizing his hands to ensure they were grease-free and giving his nails more than a cursory clipping, even going so far as to run a file over the edges to smooth away any sharpness. Although he didn't touch the high-tech race cars until he slid behind the wheel, Harrison often unwound from a race weekend by tinkering with the rare classics his uncle bought for his collection.

Today, however, as he surveyed his charcoal jeans, gray crewneck sweater and maroon suede loafers, Harrison decided that someone as stylish as London would appreciate a man who paid attention to his grooming. And in truth, his already elevated confidence was inflated even further when the receptionist at ExcelEvent goggled at him as he strolled into the King Street office.

"You're Harrison Crosby," the slender brunette exclaimed, her brown eyes wide with shock as he advanced on her desk. "And you're here." She gawked at him, her hands gripping the edge of the desk as if to hold herself in place.

Harrison gave her a slow grin. "Would you let London know I've arrived?"

"Oh, sure. Of course." Never taking her eyes off him, she picked up her phone and dialed. "Harrison Crosby is here to see you. Okay, I'll let him know." She returned the handset to the cradle and said, "She'll be out in a second. Would you like some coffee or water or…?" She trailed off and went back to staring at him.

"I'm fine."

"If you want to have a seat." The receptionist gestured to a black-and-white floral couch beneath the ExcelEvent logo painted in white on the gray wall. "She shouldn't be too long."

"Thank you."

Ignoring the couch, Harrison stood in the center of the room, wondering how long she would leave him cooling his heels. While he waited, he took stock of his surroundings, getting a sense of London's taste from the clean color palette of black, white and gray, the hint of drama provided by the silver accessories and the pop of color courtesy of the flower arrangement on the reception desk. On the wall across from him was a large-screen TV with a series of images and videos from various events that London had organized.

In his hand, his phone buzzed. Harrison sighed as he glanced at the message on the screen. Even though he took Mondays and Tuesdays off during the season, rarely an hour went by that his team wasn't contacting him as they prepared the car for that week's upcoming race. Each track possessed a different set of variables that the teams used to calibrate the car. There were different settings for shocks, weight, height, springs, tires, brakes and a dozen other miscellaneous factors.

For the first time in a long time, Harrison debated leaving the text unanswered. He didn't want to split his focus today. His team knew what it was doing. His input could wait until his meeting with London concluded.

A change in the air, like a fragrant spring breeze, pushed against his skin an instant before London McCaffrey spoke his name.

"Mr. Crosby?"

As he looked up from his phone, Harrison noted the uptick in his heartbeat. Today she wore a sleeveless peach dress with a scalloped neckline and hem, and floral pumps. Her long blond hair fell over her shoulders in loose waves. Feminine perfection with an elusive air, she advanced toward him, her hand outstretched.

Her fingers were cool and soft as they wrapped around his hand. "Good to see you again."

"I intend to call you London," he said, leaning just ever so slightly forward to better imprint the faint scent of her floral perfume on his senses. "So you'd better call me Harrison."

"Harrison." Still holding his hand, she gazed up at him through her lashes, not in a manner he considered coy, but as if she was trying to take his measure. A second later she pulled free and gestured toward a hallway behind the reception desk. "Why don't you come back to my office?" She turned away from him and led the way, pausing for a brief exchange with the receptionist.

"Missy, were you able to get hold of Grace?"

"I had to leave a message. Do you want me to put her through when she calls?" Missy glanced at Harrison as she asked the question.

"Yes. It's urgent that I speak with her as soon as possible." London glanced back at Harrison as she entered her office. Like the reception area, this tranquil space was decorated in monochrome furniture and accessories. "I hope you don't mind the interruption, but I'm organizing a fiftieth wedding anniversary for a client's parents in a week and some things have come up I need her to weigh in on. She's currently out of the country and not due back until just before the party."

"I understand." His phone vibrated with another incoming text as if to punctuate his point. "I'm sure you have all sorts of balls in the air."

"Yes." She gestured him toward a round table to their left and closed the door. "I always have several projects going at once."

"Are you a one-woman show?" His gaze tracked her as she strode to her glass-topped desk and picked up a utilitarian pad and basic pen. No fancy notebooks and expensive writing instruments for London McCaffrey.

"No, I have several assistants," she explained as she sat across from him. "Most of them help me out on a part-time basis, but I have two full-time employees plus Missy, my receptionist."

"I didn't realize your company was so large."

She acknowledged the implied compliment with a slight smile. "I've been fortunate to have expanded rapidly since I opened my doors."

"How long have you been in business?" Harrison leaned back in his chair and let his gaze flow over her slender shoulders and down her bare arms.

She sat forward, arms resting on the tabletop, the pen held lightly in her fingers. "Nearly six years. I started right out of college."

"Why an event planning company?"

Her eyes narrowed as if she'd suddenly noticed that he was interviewing her, but her voice remained smooth and unruffled as she answered. "My mother used to be a socialite in New York and has always been big on the charity circuit. I started attending events when I was in my teens and mostly found them tedious because I didn't know anyone. To keep myself occupied, I would spend my time analyzing the food, decor and anything else that went into the party. When I got home, I would write it all down and make notes of what I would do differently."

Harrison found himself nodding in understanding as she described her process. "That sounds a lot like how I got into car racing. My uncle used to let me help him work on the cars and, when I got old enough to drive, gave me the opportunity to get behind the wheel. I could tear apart an entire engine and put it back together by the time I was fourteen."

"I guess we both knew what we wanted to do from an early age."

"Something we have in common." The first of many somethings, he hoped.

As if realizing that they'd veered too far into the personal, she cleared her throat. "So you said you were interested in having someone organize a party for your brother's birthday?"

"Yes." Harrison admired her segue back to the reason for his visit. "He turns forty next month and I thought someone should plan something."

After meeting London the other night, Harrison had called his mother and confirmed that no one was in the process of planning anything for Tristan's fortieth birthday. In the past, events like this had been handled by Tristan's wife, Zoe, but she was out of the picture now.

She tapped her pen on the notepad. "Tell me something about your brother."

Harrison pondered her question for a moment. What did he know about Tristan? They were separated by more than just an eight-year age difference. They had different ideologies when it came to money, women and careers. Nor had they been close as kids. Their age differences meant the brothers had always attended different schools and Tristan's free time had been taken up by sports and friends.

"He runs the family business since our dad semi-retired five years go," Harrison began. "Crosby Automotive is a billion-dollar national chain of auto parts stores and collision centers in twenty states. We also have one of the largest private car dealership groups on the East Coast."

"And you race cars."

Her matter-of-fact tone carried no judgment, but Harrison imagined someone as no-nonsense as London McCaffrey wouldn't view what he did in a good light. No doubt a guy like Tristan, who put on an expensive suit and spent his days behind a desk, was more her cup of tea. On the other hand, she had been engaged to a baseball player, so maybe Harrison was the one guilty of being judgmental.

"I'm one of four drivers that races for Crosby Motorsports."

"Car twenty-five," she said, doodling a two and a five on her legal pad before encircling the numbers with a series of small stars.

He watched her in fascination. "Yep."

"I've never seen a race." She glanced up, caught him watching her and very quickly set the pen down atop the drawing as if embarrassed by her sketch.

"Well, you're in luck," he said. "I'm racing on Sunday in Richmond."

"Oh, I don't think…" Her eyes widened.

"It's my last race of the season." He made his tone as persuasive as possible.

London shook her head. "It's really not my thing."

"Then what is?"

"My thing?" She frowned. "I guess I don't really have one. I work a lot, you see."

"And that leaves no room for fun?"

"From what my friend told me about a racer's schedule, I'd like to know when you slow down for fun."

"You have me there. I'm on the go most of the year."

She nodded as if that put an end to the topic. "So, how many people are you looking to invite to your brother's birthday party?"

"Around a hundred." He'd secured a list from his mother after realizing he'd better not show up to a party planning meeting empty-handed and clueless.

"And do you have a budget?" London had relaxed now that they'd returned to familiar territory and flipped to a clean page so she could jot notes.

"Keep it under ten."

"Thousand?" She sounded a tad surprised, leaving Harrison questioning whether he'd gone too high or too low. "That amount opens up several possible venues. Of course, the timing is a little tight with it being the start of the holiday season. Did you have a particular date in mind?"

"His birthday is December fifth."

"I'll have Missy start calling around for availability." She excused herself and went to speak to her receptionist.

Harrison barely had a chance to look at any of the several texts that had come in while they'd been talking before she returned.

"Are you thinking a formal sit-down dinner with cocktails before and dancing afterward or something more casual?"

"My mother insists on a formal event. But I don't think dancing. Maybe a jazz band, giving people a chance to mingle and chat." Harrison was even more relieved that he'd checked with his mother because he was able to parrot everything she'd suggested.

"You were smart to get her input," London said, picking up on his train of thought. "I guess my last question for now is whether you had any sort of theme in mind."

Theme? Harrison was completely stumped. "I guess I was just thinking it was his fortieth birthday…"

"A color scheme?"

More and more Harrison wished he'd found a different way to connect with London McCaffrey. "What would you suggest?"

Her lips pursed as she pondered the question. "I'll pull together three ideas and run them past you. What are you thinking about for the meal?"

"Wouldn't it depend on the place we choose?"

"Yes, but it might help narrow things down if I thought you wanted seafood versus steak and chicken."

"Ah, can I think about it?"

With a slight shake of her head, she pressed on. "Give me your instant thoughts."

"Seafood."

She jotted that down. "There are several venues that do an exceptional job."

Although he'd never planned an event like this before, Harrison was finding that the process flowed easily with London in charge. She was proving to be both efficient and knowledgeable.

"You're really great at this," he said.

Her lips quirked. "It is what I do for a living."

"I didn't mean to sound surprised. It's just that I've never thrown anyone a birthday party before and you're making everything so easy."

"If you don't mind my asking, how did you come to be in charge of this particular event?"

Harrison doubted London was the sort who liked to play games, so he decided to be straight with her. "I volunteered because I was interested in getting to know you better and a friend warned me that you wouldn't be inclined to give me a shot."

"Get to know me better?" She looked more curious than annoyed or pleased. "So you decided to hire me to plan your brother's birthday party? You should know that I don't date my clients."

Despite her claim, he sensed she wasn't shutting him down entirely. "You said you usually work with corporate clients. Maybe this would be an excellent opportunity to gain some exposure with Crosby Automotive. And I get a chance to work with a woman who intrigues me. A win-win solution all around."

Interest colored her voice as she echoed, "A win-win solution…"

* * *

London's pen flowed across the legal pad as she randomly sketched a centerpiece and pondered Harrison's words.

When he'd called to set up this meeting, she'd been elated. Organizing his brother's birthday party would solve the problem of how she could get close enough to Tristan to figure out how to bring him down. The more she learned about Zoe's ex-husband, the more daunting her task. Frustration welled up in London as she considered the impulsive bargain she'd made several months earlier. What had she been thinking to agree to something that could lead to trouble for her in the future if she wasn't careful? But how did she back out now that Everly and Zoe had their plans in motion?

"Would you like to have dinner with me tonight?" Harrison asked.

The abruptness of his invitation combined with the uptick in her body's awareness of him caught her off guard, and London was shocked and dismayed by the delight blooming in her.

"I..."

She'd been so focused on her goal of helping Zoe that she hadn't considered the possibility of an interpersonal relationship between her and Harrison. Now, with his startling confession, the situation had grown complicated.

"Ever since meeting you at the party the other night, I can't stop thinking about you," he declared, his sea-toned eyes darkening as his voice took on a smoky quality. "You don't date your clients, but there's nothing that says you can't. Let me take you to dinner."

You made this devil's bargain. Now see it through.

"Tomorrow would be better," she responded a touch breathlessly.

"I'm heading to Richmond with the crew tomorrow. Tonight is all I have."

She was on the verge of refusing when his smile faded. An intense light entered his eyes and London found it difficult to breathe. The man's charisma was off the charts at the moment and London found herself basking in the glow of his admiration. At the same time she couldn't help but wonder if he was sincere or merely plying her with flattery to get her into bed. Worse, she wasn't sure she cared.

Maribelle's words came back to haunt her. London could use a little fun in her life and rebound sex with Harrison Crosby might be what enabled her to move on from Linc. If only she wasn't planning to use Harrison as part of their revenge plot.

"I don't want to have to wait another week to spend an evening with you," he continued as she grappled with her conscience.

"I'm flattered," she said, stalling for time.

His lips kicked into a dry grin. "No, you're not."

Harrison wasn't the sort of Southern gentleman she was used to. One she could wrap around her finger. He had a straightforward sex appeal that excited her and made her feel all needy and prone to acts of impulsiveness. The urge to grab his sweater and haul him over for a kiss shocked her.

"Really—" Her instincts screamed at her to retreat. Her susceptibility to this man could prove dangerous.

"You think I'm hitting on you because I want to sleep with every woman I meet."

"I wouldn't dream of thinking such a thing," she murmured in her most guileless drawl as she glanced down at her legal pad and noticed she'd been drawing hearts. She quickly flipped to a clean page and set down her pen.

"Don't go all Scarlett O'Hara on me," Harrison replied.

"I'm not going to lie and tell you I don't see us ending up in bed, but I fully intend on making it about the journey and not the destination."

Outrage poured through London, but there was a certain amount of amusement and curiosity mixed in, as well. Damn the man. His plain speaking was having the wrong sort of effect on her.

"You seem pretty sure of yourself," she said. "What makes you think I'm interested in you that way?"

"The fact that you're still here discussing it with me instead of kicking me to the curb."

"Do you honestly think you're the first client who has hit on me?"

"I'm sure I'm not." He didn't look at all concerned by her attitude. "But I'm guessing you're going to give me a different answer than all the others."

It pained her that he was right. Nor could she console herself with the falsehood that she would turn him down flat if it wasn't for this pact she'd made with Zoe and Everly.

"I'll have dinner with you tonight," she said. "But I get to pick the place and I'll meet you there."

"And I promise to behave like a proper gentleman."

She snorted. "There's nothing proper or gentlemanly about you, I think." A delicious shiver worked its way down her spine at the thought. "Do you agree to my conditions?"

"If they make you feel safe, then how can I not?"

His use of the word *safe* made her bristle. She hadn't set conditions because of any nervousness she felt around him, but to make him understand that she wasn't one of those women who flatter and swoon all in the hope of achieving that elusive five-carat sparkler for their left hand.

"How about we meet at The Front Porch at eight o'clock."

"That's perfect."

She then steered the conversation back to the original

reason for their meeting. "It would be a good idea if we could meet next week and check out a couple of the venues," she told him, already having a pretty good idea of the sort of elegant evening she intended to organize.

"I'll be back in town next Monday and Tuesday."

She picked up her phone and pulled up her calendar. "I'm open Monday afternoon, say two o'clock? The faster we book a location, the sooner we can start working on the details. And I'll pull some ideas together and send them along to you this week."

"Sounds great."

They'd arrived at an obvious end to their meeting and Harrison stood. As London escorted him to the front door, he asked, "Are you sure you wouldn't want to come watch me race in Richmond?"

London's eyes flicked to her receptionist. Missy was paying rapt attention to their exchange without actually staring at them. Heat bloomed beneath London's skin as she realized that word would soon spread about Harrison's invitation.

"I don't know…"

"You could bring your friend. Maribelle, wasn't it?"

"Yes." To her dismay, London's mood had dipped at the thought of sharing his attention. "I mean, yes, my friend is Maribelle. She's a huge fan. Both her and her fiancé, Beau."

"Bring them both along. I'll get you seats in our suite."

London considered how enthusiastic her friend had been after meeting Harrison. It surprised her that someone who had been trained from birth to epitomize a gracious Southern lady had an interest in such a loud and tedious sport. All the drivers did was go around and around in circles at high speeds for three hours. How could that possibly keep anyone interested?

"I'll see if she's busy and let you know." The words were out before London could second-guess herself.

She needed access to Tristan, and Harrison was the perfect way in. From the way her pulse triggered every time he smiled at her, acting interested wouldn't be a problem. She just needed to be careful that she kept her body's impulses in check and her mind focused on the revenge bargain.

Harrison looked a little surprised that she'd changed her mind, but then a grin slowly formed on his face. "Great."

"Wonderful," she murmured, reaching out to shake his hand.

She'd begun the gesture as a professional event planner, but as his long fingers enveloped hers, a jolt of electricity surged up her arm. The raw, compelling reaction left London wobbly. She couldn't let herself be distracted right now. Not when she had a mission and Harrison played an integral part in accomplishing it.

Capitalizing on his interest in her was one thing. Reciprocating the attraction would only lead to trouble.

"See you at eight."

Aware that they were still holding hands, London pulled her fingers free. "Eight," she echoed, glad Harrison had the sense not to gloat as she opened the front door and gestured him onto the sidewalk. "In the meantime, I'll keep you informed as we confirm availability on the potential venues."

After they said goodbye, she wasted no time watching him walk away, but immediately turned to her receptionist. Seeing that Missy was making a poor effort at busywork, London gathered herself to scold her and then realized if she'd been worried about the scene playing out in front of an audience, she should've taken him outside.

"Let me know what you hear from the venues," she said, heading for her office.

With a whoosh of breath, she plunked down on her office chair and ignored the slight shake in her hands as she jiggled the mouse to deactivate her screensaver. However, as she struggled to refocus on what she'd been working on before Harrison had shown up, peeling her thoughts away from the handsome race-car driver proved challenging.

Unsure what to make of his confessed interest in her and invitation to dinner tonight, she contemplated her legal pad and the mixture of notes and doodles. No fewer than ten hearts lined the margins and swooped across the page. What had she been thinking?

London opened a file on her computer for the event and typed in her notes before tearing the page into tiny pieces.

Going forward she needed to take a firmer grip on her subconscious or heaven only knew what might happen.

Once her initial work on the fortieth birthday party was done, London dialed Maribelle to give her a heads-up about all that had transpired and to extend Harrison's invitation to watch him race on Sunday.

"Beau will be thrilled," Maribelle said. "Do you think Harrison can get us into the pit on race day?"

"Maybe. I can find out what that entails." She traced her fingertips over the twenty-five she'd once again doodled on her legal pad. At least there were no hearts this time. "We're having dinner tonight."

Maribelle's squeal forced London to pull the phone away from her ear. "See, I knew he was interested in you. Where are you going? Is he taking you somewhere romantic? Are you going to sleep with him? I would. I bet he's great in bed. He's so sexy with that dark hair and those blue-green eyes. And that body. I read that he's in crazy great shape. What I wouldn't give to get my hands on him."

Maribelle's rapid-fire remarks left no room for London to speak. She really shouldn't sleep with Harrison Crosby, but any argument about what a bad idea it was would fall on deaf ears.

"Need I remind you that you're engaged? You better tone down your fan-girling," London warned. "Beau might not appreciate you heaping praise on another man."

"Don't you worry. My Beau knows while my eyes might wander my heart never will."

It was such a sweet and solemn declaration that London felt a flare of envy. Had she ever embraced that level of dedication to Linc? Not that she'd needed to. Once she'd settled on him as her future mate, she'd never looked at anyone else. And until the very end, she'd thought Linc felt the same. Her trust in him had never wavered despite all the women she knew must be throwing themselves at him while he was out of town during baseball season. She'd never imagined her competition would be someone so unassuming and close to home.

"You're lucky to have each other," London said and meant it.

"You'll find someone," Maribelle returned, her tone low and fierce. "And he will love you and make you feel safe."

Again that word *safe*. And again, London flinched. She was a strong, capable woman who didn't need a man to make her feel safe. Yet even as her thoughts trailed over this mantra, a tiny part of her clenched in hungry longing. What would it be like to be taken care of? Not physically or financially, but emotionally supported. To be part of a devoted team like Maribelle and Beau.

It was something she hadn't known growing up. Her parents had burdened her with huge—if differing—expectations. Her father was an autocratic businessman who'd impressed upon her that absolute success was the only option. London had spent her childhood living in terror that she would be criticized for not achieving high enough marks.

She'd undertaken a rigorous class schedule, participated in student government, women's soccer and debate club, and couldn't remember a time during her high school and college years when she wasn't worn out or anxiety ridden.

Nor was her mother any less demanding. If her father expected her to succeed professionally, her mother had her sights set on London's social achievements. To that end, there had been hours of volunteer work and social events her mother dragged her to. Becoming engaged to Linc had been a triumph. But even then it grew obvious that no matter how much London did, it was never enough.

"I just texted Beau," Maribelle said. "He suggests we fly up on Saturday and back on Sunday. So we can see the practice rounds. Will that work for you? Usually you have parties on Saturday night, don't you?"

As easy as it would be to use work as an excuse, she heard the excitement in her friend's voice and sighed in surrender. "All we have is a small anniversary party and Annette is handling that." To London's surprise, she realized she was looking forward to getting out of town. She'd been working like a madwoman since Linc had ended their engagement. Keeping busy was the best way to avoid dwelling on her failed relationship. "And since Beau is flying us up, I'll take care of the hotel rooms."

"We should go shopping for something to wear. In fact, we should go shopping right now."

London imagined her friend grabbing her purse and heading for her car. "What's the hurry?"

"I need to make sure you wear something on your date tonight that doesn't scream *I'm not interested in getting laid*."

"I'm not," London protested.

"Have you been with anyone since Linc?"

London winced. "You know I haven't."

"You need a rebound relationship. I think Harrison Crosby would be perfect."

That Maribelle had echoed what London herself had been thinking less than an hour earlier didn't surprise her. The two women had been friends so long they sometimes finished each other's sentences.

"Why do you say that?" London asked.

"Because he's the furthest thing from someone you'd ever settle down with, so that makes him a good bet for a casual fling."

London was warming to the idea of a quick, steamy interlude with the sexy race-car driver. Still, she'd never slept with anyone she didn't have feelings for. Yet with what she, Everly and Zoe were up to, maybe the fact that London wasn't going to fall for the guy was a plus.

"You might be right."

Maybe it would be okay to give sexual chemistry and a casual relationship a quick spin. They were both adults. What harm could it do?

Three

Harrison arrived at The Front Porch ten minutes early and parked himself at the bar in easy range of the entrance to wait for London's arrival. Since leaving her office that morning, he'd been half expecting she'd call to cancel. With each hour that passed, he'd grown increasingly confident that she wasn't going to fight their mutual attraction. Yet now, as he counted down the minutes until she walked in, he found his stomach tying itself into anxious knots.

Her effect on him should've sent him running in the opposite direction. Already he suspected that they were at odds on several fundamental issues. For one thing, she wasn't his type and it was pretty clear he wasn't hers. She was elegant and aloof. Completely the opposite of the fun-loving ladies who hung out at the track, enjoyed drinking beer and weren't afraid to get a little dirty.

He imagined she'd be bossy as hell in a relationship. Tonight was a good example. She'd chosen the time and place, taking control, making it clear if he wanted to play, it would be by her rules. Harrison smirked. She could make all the rules she wanted. He'd bend every one.

The restaurant's front door opened, and before Harrison had fully focused on the woman on the threshold, his heart gave a hard jerk. For someone accustomed to facing near collisions at ridiculous speeds and regularly operating at high levels of stress for long periods of time without faltering, Harrison wasn't sure what to make of the jolt London's arrival had given him.

For the space of several irregular breaths as her gaze swept the restaurant in search of him, Harrison had the opportunity to take her in. She'd changed her clothes since their earlier meeting and looked stunning in a navy dress with a broad neckline that bared her delicate shoulders and the hollows above her collarbones. The material hugged her upper body, highlighting the curves of her breasts, before flaring into a full skirt that stopped at her knees. The dark color contrasted with the creamy tones of her pale skin and highlighted her blue eyes. She'd pulled her hair back into a loose knot at the base of her neck and left long strands of gold waves to frame her face. Her only jewelry was a pair of simple pearl earrings.

When she spotted him, her uncertain smile hit Harrison like lightning. His nerves buzzed in the aftermath as he made his way through the crowded bar toward her.

"You look gorgeous," he murmured, cupping his fingers around her bare arm and leaning down to graze a kiss across her cheek.

Her body tensed at his familiarity, but her smile remained in place as he stepped back and looked down at her.

"Thank you," she said, her voice neither breathless nor coy. She took in his jeans, light blue shirt and oatmeal-colored blazer. "You look quite dapper," she said, reaching out to tug at the navy pocket square in his breast pocket.

"I'm glad you approve," he said and meant it. "And I'm glad you were able to join me for dinner tonight."

"You were kind to invite me."

Niceties concluded, Harrison set his hand on her back and guided her toward the hostess. They were led to a table by the front windows overlooking King Street.

"Do you come here a lot?" Harrison asked after they were seated. He scanned the menu, which specialized in farm-to-table fare, and settled on the scallops with smoked yogurt, beets and pistachio.

"Actually, I've never been, but it's one of Maribelle and Beau's favorite places. They had their first date here and... it's where he proposed." Her eyes widened as if she realized what she'd implied. "They're always going on and on about how good the food is. That's why I picked it."

"Can't wait to see if they're right."

"So, you've never been here before?"

Harrison shook his head. "I don't get out much."

"I find that hard to believe."

"It's true. I'm on the road so much of the year that when I do get home, I like to hole up and recharge."

"You do?"

"Most of my time and attention is focused on cars and racing. Analyzing my competition, studying the track, figuring out how I can improve."

"I did a little research on you and learned you're a big deal in racing." Bright spots of color appeared in her cheeks as he raised his eyebrows at her confession. "Lots of appearances and events."

"All to promote Crosby Motorsports. I'm actually an introvert." He could tell she wasn't buying it.

"You can't possibly be. You're a fan favorite with a huge following."

"Don't get me wrong, I do my share of press events and meeting fans, but it isn't what I enjoy. I'd much rather be tinkering with a car or hanging out with a few of my friends."

She made a face. "I figured you would be out in the public, soaking up the accolades, enjoying your stardom."

Her thorny tone made him frown. "You seem to have a very jaded view of me. Why is that?"

"It's not you." She moved her wineglass around in circles on the white tablecloth and seemed engrossed in the light refracted by the liquid. "I guess it's what you do. I've spent a lot of time around sports stars and most of them love being celebrities. The adoring fans. The special attention they get wherever they go. It makes them act…entitled."

Obviously her attitude had been formed during her relationship with Lincoln Thurston. As a professional baseball player, no doubt Thurston had enjoyed his share of the limelight. Harrison needed to convince her he and her ex-fiancé weren't cut from the same cloth.

"Not all of them," Harrison insisted.

"Most of them."

"Was Linc that way?" He'd asked, even knowing that it was risky to probe for details about what might be painful for her.

"I don't want to talk about him." London's brittle tone was a warning to Harrison that he should tread carefully.

Still, he needed to know where her head was at. "Because you're still not over the breakup?"

How could she be? He'd done his own bit of research on her and discovered only a few months had passed since their two-year engagement ended.

"I am over it." The bits of gold floating in London's blue eyes flashed.

"Are you over him?"

She exhaled in exasperation. "We were together for three years."

"So that's a no?"

London's expression hardened into a look that Harrison interpreted as *back off.* That wasn't going to stop him. This woman was worth fighting for.

"I can't imagine what having him break your engagement must have been like for you, but I am happy to listen if you want to dump on the guy." He paused and then grinned. "Or the male gender as a whole."

From her frown, he could see his offer had confused her. "Why?"

He shrugged. "Because I think too many men suck in the way they treat women."

"And you don't?" Her earlier tension faded into skepticism.

"I'm sure you can find plenty of women who would complain about me."

One corner of her lips twitched. "So what, then, makes you so different from all the other men out there?"

"Maybe nothing. Or maybe it's the case that I don't take advantage of people because I can. I'm not an entitled jerk like my brother can be all too often." Harrison brought up Tristan to see how London reacted. She'd shown far too much interest in him at the party and Harrison wanted to understand why. "Tristan treats women like they're his personal playground."

"But until recently he's been married. Are you insinuating he wasn't faithful?" London's interest intensified when Harrison shook his head. "I've never understood why men bother being in a relationship if they intend to cheat."

Harrison recalled what his uncle Bennett had told him about Linc Thurston's infidelity. London had every right to be skittish when it came to trusting any guy she perceived as having the same sort of fame and fortune as her ex-fiancé.

"It's a social norm."

London looked positively dumbstruck. "Is that what you think?"

"It's true, isn't it?" Harrison countered.

"What about love?"

"Not everyone believes in love. I don't think my brother does. Tristan chose to marry a very beautiful, very young, woman who was passive and pliable. For eight years she satisfied his need for a decorative and docile companion." Harrison recalled how Zoe's spirit dimmed with each wedding anniversary. "Her only failure was in her inability to make my brother happy."

"Why was that her responsibility?" London asked in surprise. "Isn't marriage a partnership where you support each other?"

"Mine will be." Harrison waited a beat to see how she absorbed that before continuing, "I think Zoe's dissatisfaction with her role grew too strong to be contained. One thing about Tristan—he likes having his way and becomes a bear if events run counter to his preferences. I imagine him perceiving Zoe's discontent as nothing he'd done wrong, but a failing on her part."

London absorbed his assessment for several seconds before asking, "How close are you with his ex-wife?"

"I like Zoe. She's quiet and subdued, but once you get to know her you see that she has a warm heart and a wry sense of humor." He could go on extolling her virtues but decided to keep to his original purpose, which was to make sure London understood that Tristan wasn't a good guy. "She deserved better than my brother."

"I hope she appreciated having you as her champion."

"I don't know about that. If I'd been a better friend, I would've steered her away from marrying Tristan."

"You might not have been able to do that. Sometimes we have to make our own mistakes. It's the only way we learn."

"Maybe, but some mistakes carry harsher consequences than others."

London sat back and let her hands slide into her lap. She regarded him steadily with her keen blue eyes. "You aren't what I expected."

"I hope that's a good thing."

"The jury is still out," she said, an enigmatic smile kicking up the corners of her lips. "So, Mr. Introvert, what is it you enjoy besides cars and racing?"

"The usual guy stuff. Outdoor sports. Spending time with my friends. How about you? What do you do when you're not working?"

She laughed. "Sleep and eat. Sometimes I get a massage or facial. I have a hard time unwinding."

"Sounds like we're both on the go a lot."

"Like a shark. Swim or die."

The phone in her purse chimed. She'd set the clutch on the table beside her plate and now made a face at it. "Sorry." The tone repeated.

"Do you need to get that?"

"No." She heaved a sigh. "I already know what it's about."

"That's impressive," he teased and was rewarded with a grimace.

"About this weekend…"

Something in her tone made him grin. "You've decided to accept my invitation to watch me race in Richmond."

"I spoke with Maribelle," she replied. "Both she and her fiancé are excited about your offer."

Her carefully worded statement left room for interpretation. "What about you?"

"I'm not sure what I'm getting into, so I'm reserving judgment."

"I guess that's something," he murmured, convinced he would win her over.

"We're flying up Saturday morning," she continued, ignoring his dry remark. "And Beau was wondering if you'd be able to get us into the pit. At least I think that's what he wanted to know."

"Absolutely."

She'd been seated facing the restaurant's entrance and suddenly her eyes went wide in surprise. Harrison drew a breath to ask what was wrong when she shifted her attention back to him and smiled brightly.

"You know…" she began, picking up her purse. "Maybe I should double-check the text to make sure nothing is amiss." She gave a nervous half laugh. "The pitfall of being the boss is that I'm always on call. Excuse me, won't you?"

And before Harrison could say anything, she'd fled the table, leaving him staring over his shoulder after her.

Everly Briggs strode along King Street, paying little attention to the restaurants, stores and bars clustered along the popular thoroughfare. Her entire focus was on the tall man she was following.

Linc Thurston appeared unaware of the stir he caused as he passed. Usually the professional baseball player paused to chat with fans he encountered, but tonight he seemed intent on reaching his destination.

Since Everly, London and Zoe had met at the Beautiful Women Taking Charge event, Everly had been actively pursuing whatever angle she could to take down Linc. From digging into all available gossip, Everly had gotten wind that the reason he'd broken off his engagement to London was that he'd started cheating on her with his housekeeper.

Once she'd determined that they weren't just involved in a fling, but a full-blown, secret relationship, she determined this would be the best way to get revenge on him. At the moment she had plans in the works to expose the woman's lies and sabotage her credibility. Linc would learn what it meant to be betrayed by someone he loved.

Of course, her plans would completely fall apart if she was wrong about the strength of his feelings for Claire Robbins, so Everly was doing a little spying to see if his cheating was a onetime event or if the man was a typical representation of his gender.

She was so caught up in her thoughts that Everly hadn't noticed Linc had stopped walking until she drew within arm's length. Jerking to a halt would be too obvious, so Everly was forced to sail on past. She did take note of what had captured his interest, however, and spotted London occupying a table beside the large window of The Front Porch. She was obviously having dinner with Harrison Crosby and the couple was engaged in some pretty serious flirting.

What the hell was London doing? She was supposed to be taking down Tristan Crosby, not dating his brother.

Everly's irritation spiked as she reached the end of the block. By the time she turned the corner, she'd pulled out her phone. Pausing, she typed a text and sent it. Although the three women had agreed not to communicate to avoid their plotting being discovered, Everly simply had to confront London.

We need to meet—E

She tapped her foot as she waited for a response. Meanwhile she kept her gaze on King Street, expecting Linc to pass by at any second. She'd intended to continue her surveillance and it annoyed her that London's behavior was forcing her to detour. When her phone didn't immediately chime with an answer from London, Everly rapidly typed a second message.

I saw you having dinner tonight. What r u doing?

When London still didn't answer, Everly knew she had no choice but to push the issue.

Linc had passed by while Everly had been typing her second text. Instead of following him, she doubled back to the restaurant. London sat facing the entrance and Everly made sure the woman noticed her enter. The two made brief eye contact before Everly headed toward the back, where the restrooms were located.

She entered the ladies' room and was relieved to find the stalls empty. She approached the sinks and pulled her lipstick out. Fury made her hands shake. While she was here dealing with London, Linc was getting away.

By the time London pushed through the door, Everly was more than ready to let her have it.

"Why are you having dinner with Harrison Crosby?" she snarled, barely restraining the urge to shout in displeasure. "You're supposed to be going after Tristan."

"What are you doing here?" London countered, pitching her voice barely above a whisper. "We agreed the way this works is to not have any contact with each other. We can't be seen together."

"I came to find out why you're going after the wrong brother," Everly said, ignoring London's objections.

London crossed her arms over her chest and glared back. "Did it ever occur to you that Harrison might be the best way for me to get close to Tristan?"

Everly let loose a disparaging noise. How could London possibly think she was buying that? It was obvious what was going on.

"It's more likely that you find him attractive and plan on sleeping with him." Based on the way London refused to meet Everly's gaze, she'd hit it square on the head. "Do you have any idea how badly that could backfire?"

"Look," London said, showing no sign of being convinced that her actions were flawed. "It's none of your business how I handle my end of the bargain. You and I meeting like this could become a problem if anyone sees us together and it's discovered that you were behind whatever happens with Linc."

"Give me some credit," Everly snapped. "No one's ever going to find out I was the one behind what happens to him."

"Regardless. We agreed this only works if we don't have any contact with each other. So leave me alone."

Before Everly could say another word, London flung open the bathroom door and exited.

For several long minutes Everly fumed. This situation with London and Harrison Crosby was a problem. Now she had to keep her eye on her own revenge scenario and make sure London stayed focused on their plan. And if London couldn't do the job, then Everly would show her what happened when you turned your back on your friends.

Four

With her heart pumping hard against her ribs, London smoothed her palms along her dress's full skirt and slowly wound her way back to Harrison. Everly's texts and subsequent appearance in the restaurant had been disturbing. What they were doing was dangerous enough. If they were caught in some sort of conspiracy, it could ruin all their lives.

Nor could she ignore the question front and center in her thoughts. Was Everly following her? The possibility made her skin prickle. How else could the other woman have known that London was having dinner with Harrison? And what sort of insanity had prompted Everly to confront London in public like this where anyone could have seen them? Had Everly contacted Zoe, as well? London was tempted to reach out to the third member of their scheme, but that was exactly what she'd railed at Everly for doing.

Anxiety danced along her nerve endings as she slid into

her seat opposite Harrison. London suspected her distress was reflected in her expression because after a quick survey of her face, he frowned.

"Is everything okay?"

"Fine." London forced a reassuring smile. "I just received a bit of bad news about an event I was going to organize." The lie came too easily, sparking concern over the person she was becoming. "The client had been on the fence about what they wanted to do and decided to cancel."

"You seem rattled. It must've been a big client."

"Not huge, but all my clients are equally important and I'm disappointed that this didn't work out." Even though London wasn't lying, the fact that she was deceiving Harrison left a bad taste in her mouth.

"Maybe they'll change their mind." His winning smile gave her heart a different reason to pound. "I'll bet you can be quite persuasive."

His attempt to make her feel better through flattery was turning her insides to mush and soothing away her earlier distress. She caught herself smiling at him in gratitude as pleasure washed over her. The man had a knack for getting under her skin.

"If by 'persuasive' you mean bossy," London said, recognizing that she had a tendency to stab directly into the heart of something rather than nibble away at the edges, "then I agree. I come on a little too strong sometimes."

"You want to get things done," Harrison said, nodding. "I get it. Winning is everything."

It struck London that maybe they had more in common than she'd initially thought. They shared a love of competition and a matching determination to get across the finish line. Maybe his way of doing things meant he slid behind the wheel of a car and drove at reckless and adrenaline-inducing speeds, making impulsive decisions in the moment, while she tended to be more methodical and deliberate in her approach.

"I don't exactly think of it as winning," London responded. "More like a job well done."

"Nothing wrong with that."

London toyed with her earring as she asked, "Do you win a lot?"

"I've had my share of successes over the years. Generally, I finish in the top ten drivers about two-thirds of the time. Except for the first couple years when I was still learning and a couple of seasons when injury kept me off the track."

"Is that good?" she asked, noting his amusement and figuring she'd just displayed total ignorance of what he did.

"It's a decent statistic."

"So winning isn't important?"

"Of course it's important, but with thirty-six races a year, it's impossible to be on top all the time. If I win four to six times in a season, that's good enough to put me in the top three for the year as long as my stats are solid."

As an event planner, London was accustomed to dealing with a lot of numbers. It was how she kept her clients happy while maximizing their budget and remaining profitable. She was interested in trying to understand the way driver standings were determined.

"How many other drivers are there?"

"Almost sixty."

"What was your worst year?"

"The year I started—2004. I finished fifty-eighth."

"How old were you?"

"Nineteen." Harrison's lips twisted in self-deprecating humor. "And I thought I knew everything there was to know."

London considered what she'd been like at nineteen and

couldn't relate. She'd been a freshman in college, away from her parents for the first time and struggling to figure out who she was.

"And now?" she prompted.

"Still learning," he said. "Always improving."

"Those seem like good words to live by," she said.

His blend of confidence and humility was endearing. London softened still more toward him even as she marveled at his gamesmanship.

The waitress approached to check on their meal and London watched the man across from her charm the woman with his friendliness. The contrast between the two brothers struck her again. During her brief introduction to Tristan, the way the man had looked her over had made London feel like running home and taking a shower.

"Did you leave any room for dessert?" the waitress asked.

Harrison glanced her way and London shook her head. "But don't let me stop you from ordering something."

"I hate to eat alone." And once the waitress had left with their plates, Harrison finished, "Besides, I'd much rather grab an ice cream cone at Swenson's."

"I haven't been there in years," London said, remembering what a rare treat it had been when her father had taken her there.

"Then it's time to go, don't you think?" He didn't wait for her answer before asking, "What is your favorite flavor? Please don't say vanilla."

"I don't know." She was struck by rising delight at the thought of enjoying such a simple, satisfying treat with Harrison. "Maybe strawberry."

"A few months ago they introduced a strawberry, honey balsamic, with black pepper ice cream. It's really good."

"You know quite a bit about the place." London's mouth

watered as she imagined all those delicious flavors harmonizing on her taste buds. "Do you take all your dates there?" She didn't mean the question to sound so flippant and flushed beneath his keen regard.

"You'd be the first."

"That was rude of me. I'm sorry."

"Are you skeptical of all men?" he asked. "Or is it just me?"

She took a second to consider his question before answering. "Not all men and not you. It's just that since Linc and I..." She wished she hadn't brought up her ex-fiancé's name again. "The breakup has left me feeling exposed and I lash out at unexpected moments. I'm sorry."

"He really hurt you."

"Yes and no." She really didn't want to talk about Linc over a first-date dinner with Harrison, but maybe it would be good to clear the air. "All my life I've achieved whatever I set my mind to. Except for one thing. Social acceptance in certain circles. In Charleston it's impossible to become an insider. You have to be born into it. When Linc and I got engaged, it opened doors I'd spent my life knocking on."

London sighed as she finished her explanation. She wanted Harrison to understand what had driven her. His own family was self-made, parlaying hard work into a booming automotive empire. Would he view her hunger to belong to a group of "insiders" as petty and shallow?

"Growing up, I attended the right schools," she continued, thinking back to the private all-girl high school she'd attended and the friends she'd made there. Friends who'd gone on to attend debutante classes and formal teas and to participate in the father/daughter skeet shoot. "But I was always on the outside looking in."

"And that bothered you a lot."

Despite his neutral tone, her defensiveness flared. "Shouldn't it?"

"Why did you think you needed the validation? In my opinion, you already have it all."

Delight set all her nerve endings alight and suddenly a lifetime of exclusion became less hurtful. "That's kind of you to say, but it never seemed enough." Seeing the questions in Harrison's raised eyebrows, London explained further. "My mother is constantly harping on how frustrating it is for her that no matter how much money she donates or how lavish her dinner parties are, she can't ever gain acceptance."

"So maybe it's your mother's issue and not yours."

If only it was that simple.

"She's pretty determined." London could've said more about her mother's unrelenting pressure on her to marry well, but decided further explanations would only put her family's flaws on display.

"It seems like a lot of pressure."

London shrugged. "I'm no stranger to that. After all, heat and extreme pressure turns coal into diamonds," she said, parroting her mother's favorite quote.

"That's not actually a scientific fact," Harrison replied.

"Fine," she grumbled. "But diamonds need heat and pressure to form."

His lips curved in a bone-melting smile. "True."

The exchange highlighted how easily Harrison could blow past her defenses and signaled to London that she might be mistaken about which Crosby brother presented the most danger to her.

Everly's words came back to London. Maybe the other woman's concerns weren't out of line. Did she have what it took to keep up her end of the bargain when already she was thinking of Harrison in terms of getting to know him better rather than someone she could use?

Fifteen minutes later Harrison opened the restaurant's front door, and as soon as they reached the sidewalk, he took her hand and threaded it through his arm. Already a warm glow filled her as a result of the wine she'd consumed and Harrison's stimulating company. Being tucked close against his body increased the heat beneath her skin and she inhaled the cool fresh air, hoping it would clear her head.

"Thinking about ice cream?" he asked, breaking into her thoughts. They'd reached the corner, and instead of continuing on to Swenson's, he pulled her onto the quieter thoroughfare. "Because I'm not."

"No?" she countered, trembling as he backed her up against the building's brick wall and leaned his forearm beside her head.

His gaze searched her features before settling on her lips. "The only dessert I want is a taste of your sweet lips."

If any other man had delivered that line, she would've had a cynical retort, but something about Harrison told her that he meant every word. Her muscles lost strength, making her glad for the wall at her back. She wasn't sure what to do with her hands. His hard body called to her, but letting her palms roam over his chiseled physique—while tempting—was a little too familiar for their first…dinner…date?

"Okay."

"Okay?" he echoed, his soft, firm lips grazing across hers with deliberate intent.

"Yes." She breathed the word and it came out sounding almost like a plea.

"Are you sure it's not too forward of me?"

He seemed determined to tantalize and torment her with what could be. The suggestion of a kiss did exactly what it was supposed to. It frustrated her and provoked curiosity at the same time. She reached up and tunneled her fingers into his hair.

"Kiss me like you want to," she urged, conflicting notes of desperation and command in her tone as he trailed his lips across her cheek.

"If I do that, we might get arrested." His husky laugh puffed against her skin, making her shiver.

Disturbed by the acute longing he aroused, London laid her palm against his chest. His rapid heartbeat caught her attention and bolstered her confidence. The chemistry she felt wasn't one-sided but sparkled between them, ripe with promise and potential.

"I don't know what to do with you," she murmured, trembling as his hand slipped around her waist and into the small of her back, drawing her tight against his hard body.

"Funny," he said. "I know exactly what to do with you." His fingers coasted over the curve of her butt and he punctuated his claim with a quick squeeze before setting her free. "You are temptation in high heels."

The heavy beat of desire pulsing between her thighs made it hard for London to utter her next words. "I think I'd better go home."

"I'll walk you to your car."

To her dismay, his words disappointed her. As they made their way to the parking lot where she'd left her car, she mulled several questions. How had she hoped the evening might end? That he would press her to extend their time together? Suggest that she come home with him?

He'd demonstrated that he was attracted to her…hadn't he? Wasn't that what he'd meant by his temptation-in-high-heels remark? He spoke as if he wanted her, but his actions hadn't crossed any boundaries she'd set for first-date behavior. His kisses hadn't been designed to blow past her defenses and set her afire. She had no doubt that would happen. The brief contact with him had demonstrated her body was dry kindling and his lips the spark that would set her alight.

"Are you okay?" he asked, breaking into her thoughts.

"Fine." Yet she was anything but. What if there was something wrong with her? Something that caused men to lose interest in sex. Could it be that she was the sort of woman who turned men off? Harrison had barely kissed her. Maybe he'd been uninterested in taking things any further.

London's skin prickled as she pondered her relationship with Linc. For months now she'd been plagued by the worry that the reason he'd broken off their engagement was her lack of desirability. Sure, sex between them had been good. Linc was a fantastic lover and she'd never gone unsatisfied. But there hadn't ever been the sort of rip-your-clothes-off passion Maribelle so often talked about having with Beau. In fact, London had grown surly with her best friend several times after Maribelle had shared stories about her and her fiancé.

"Remember I told you I was an introvert?"

"Yes."

"Aside from the negative impression we can give about being shy, aloof or stuck-up, we have a lot of really positive characteristics. One of those being our ability to take in a lot of information and process it."

Unsure what he was getting at, London asked, "What sort of information?"

"When I'm in the middle of a race, it can be tiny nuances about how other cars are moving that telegraph what their drivers are thinking. I'm also pretty good at reading micro-expressions. I can tell by tiny muscle shifts what someone might be feeling."

"You think you know what I'm feeling?" She disliked being like a bug under a microscope.

"I can tell you're not happy."

Rather than agree or disagree, she raised one eyebrow and stared at him.

"You can give me that face all day, but I'm not the one you're upset with."

"What makes you think I'm upset at anyone?"

"Not anyone. Yourself."

That he had read her so easily should've rattled London, but there was no judgment in his manner. "And I suppose you know why?"

"I could guess, but I'd rather wait until you're ready to tell me."

He couldn't have said anything better, and all at once London wanted to cry. She prided herself on her strength and resilience. That Harrison had whipped up her hormones, roused her insecurities and nearly reduced her to tears demonstrated just how dangerous he could be.

"What if I never do?"

To her shock, he wrapped her in a fierce, platonic hug that left her body tingling and her nerves raw.

"Everyone needs someone to talk to, London," he whispered and then let her go. Before she could untie her tongue, he continued, "I'll call you later this week with the details about Saturday. I'm looking forward to having you and your friends at the race."

London used the distraction of sliding behind the wheel to grab at her flailing control and reined in her wayward emotions. "Is there anything I should know beforehand?"

"We're looking at sunshine and midsixties for race day, so dress accordingly."

"Okay." London had no idea what to wear to a racetrack, but no doubt Maribelle would have plenty of ideas. "I'll see you Saturday."

"See you Saturday." With a wink, Harrison stepped back so she could close the car door.

"Harrison!" Jack Crosby's sharp tone brought his nephew back to the present. "What is going on with you? All week you've been distracted."

His uncle wasn't wrong.

It was early Saturday afternoon. The qualifying races had run that morning, and instead of revisiting his performance on the Richmond track, a certain blonde kept popping up in his thoughts, disrupting his ability to stay on task.

His usual hyper focus on the days leading up to a race had been compromised while he'd wasted energy regretting that he'd pulled back instead of making a definite move on her like she seemed to expect.

Yet her conflict had been plain. She'd made it clear that he wasn't the sort of man she saw herself with, but their undeniable chemistry tempted her. Based on how she'd begged him to kiss her, no doubt he'd gotten beneath her skin. Which was exactly why he'd retreated instead of wearing down her defenses. The woman was too quick to lay down the law. She had definite boundaries and ideas how courtship was supposed to transpire. He needed to set the foundation for new ground rules.

"I guess I've been a little off."

"A little?" His uncle crossed his arms over his chest. "I've never seen you like this."

"I'm sure it's not that bad."

"Since the day you showed up at Crosby Motorsports and declared that you were going to be our top driver one day, you've been the most focused member of the team. And that's saying something considering all the talent we've assembled. But not this week."

Harrison spied a trio headed their way along the alley between the garages and felt his lips curve into a giant grin. He'd recognized Maribelle right off. The lean, well-dressed man matching her brisk pace had to be her fiancé. And the leggy blonde trailing them looked like a fish out of water as her gaze swung this way and that, taking in the loud cars and mechanics that buzzed around the vehicles.

"Excuse me a second," he said to his uncle before stepping forward to meet the visitors.

"Welcome to Richmond," he said as he drew near enough to shake hands. "Hello, Maribelle. And you must be her fiancé, Beau. I'm Harrison Crosby."

"Beau Shelton." The man clasped hands with Harrison. "No need to introduce yourself. We're big fans." Beau tipped his head to indicate Maribelle and she nodded vigorously. "We appreciate this chance to get a glimpse behind the scenes."

"I'm glad you came," Harrison said, forcing himself to be patient when all he wanted was to push past the couple and snatch London into his arms.

Maribelle winked at him. "Thanks for the invite."

Harrison approved of her sassy demeanor, even as he noted once again how her outgoing personality differed from her friend's reserve. Given how close the two women seemed to be, Harrison hoped it boded well for his own chances with London. Obviously she liked—and definitely needed—someone in her life who encouraged her to have fun once in a while.

"Hi," he murmured to London after the couple stepped to one side to allow him access to their friend. He ignored her tentativeness and leaned down to brush his lips over her cheek. "I'm really happy you're here."

London peered at him from beneath her lashes. "You were kind to invite us."

"You look amazing."

She'd chosen dark blue skinny jeans with strategic tears that gave them a trendy appearance, an oversize fuzzy white sweater and a camel-toned moto jacket that matched the suede pumps on her tiny feet. She looked as if she'd worked hard to dress down, but hadn't succeeded in achieving her friend's casual weekend style. His fingers itched to slide into the low knot she'd fastened her hair into and shake the pins loose. She needed someone like him to mess up her perfect appearance.

"I like your suit." Her deliberate scan of his body heated his blood. "It's very colorful."

Fighting the urge to find a quiet corner where he could kiss that sardonic grin off her beautiful lips, Harrison stuck to polite conversation.

"How was the flight down?"

"It was a little more eventful than usual." Her blue eyes shifted past him and settled on her friends. "Beau is teaching Maribelle how to fly and today she did both the takeoff and landing."

"It was fine," Maribelle piped up. "Just a little windier than I was used to during the landing. I did a perfectly acceptable job, didn't I?" This last she directed to her fiancé, who nodded.

His heart was in his eyes as he grinned down at her. "You did great."

Envy twisted in Harrison's chest at the couple's obvious connection. The emotion caught him off guard. Over the last decade he'd watched most of his team and fellow drivers fall in love and get married. Many had even started families. Not once had he wanted to trade places. But since meeting London, he was starting to notice a pronounced dissatisfaction with his personal life.

"That's my car in the third garage stall on the left, if you want to check it out."

"I've never seen a race car up close before," Maribelle said, tugging at Beau's hand to get him going. "I have a hundred questions."

Harrison let London's friends walk ahead of them. The urge to touch her couldn't be denied, so he bumped the back of his hand against hers to see how she'd react. She shot him a questioning glance even as she twisted her wrist so that her palm met his. As his fingers closed around hers, a lazy grin slid over his lips.

"This is...really something." Her choice of words left him with no idea how she felt, but her gaze darted around as if she half expected to be run over any second. "There's a lot of activity."

Up and down the length of the garage, the crews swarmed their cars, making last-minute tweaks before the final practice of the day. Today was a little less chaotic for Harrison than race day and he was delighted to be able to give London and her friends a tour.

"If you think this is hectic, wait until tomorrow. Things really kick into high gear then."

"So, you look like you're dressed to get behind the wheel." She set her fingertip lightly on his chest right over his madly pumping heart. "What's going on today?"

"We had the qualifying race this morning and there are practices this afternoon."

She cocked her head like a curious bird. "You have to qualify before you can race?"

"The qualifier determines what position you start in."

"And where are you starting?"

"Tenth." He should've done better, but his excitement

at seeing London again had blown a hole in his concentration. It was unexpected. No woman had thrown him off his game before.

"Is that good?"

Based on the tongue-lashing delivered by his uncle, not so much.

"In a pack of forty," Harrison said with an offhanded shrug. "It's okay."

Nor was it his worst start all year. A month ago his car had failed the inspection before the qualifying race because of a piece of tape on his spoiler and he'd ended up starting in thirty-sixth position.

"So I'll get to see you drive this afternoon?"

"We have a fifty-minute practice happening at three." He took her hand in his and drew her forward. "Come meet my team and check out the car."

After introducing London and her friends to his uncle and giving them a quick tour of the garage, Harrison directed Beau and Maribelle to a spot where they could watch the practice laps. Before letting London get away, he caught her hand and stopped while they were twenty feet from the stall where his car sat.

"You know, I've been thinking about you all week," he confessed, mesmerized by the bright gold shards floating in her blue eyes.

"I've been thinking about you, too." And then, as if she'd given too much away, she finished with, "We have several venues to look at on Monday and I have lots of ideas to run past you for the decor."

He ignored her attempt to turn the conversation to business and leaned close. "I've been regretting that I didn't take you up on your offer."

Her tone was husky as she asked, "What offer was that?"

He pinched a fold of her suede jacket between his fingers and tugged her a half step toward him until their thighs brushed. At the glancing contact, she bit down on her lower lip.

"When you told me to kiss you any way I want."

"That was in the heat of the moment," she said, her voice soft and a trifle breathless. "I don't know what I was thinking."

"I was kinda hoping you weren't thinking at all."

"I guess I wasn't." She gave him a wry smile. "Because if I had been, I probably wouldn't have gone out with you in the first place." Her lighthearted tone took the punch out of her words.

"I'm gonna guess you think too much."

"I'm gonna guess you do, too," she said.

"Most of the time, but not when I'm around you. Then all I do is feel." Harrison cupped her face and sent his thumb skimming across her lower lip. Her eyes widened in surprise. "In fact, my uncle is annoyed with me because it's been hard for me to stay focused."

The temptation to dip his head and kiss her in full view of her friends, his uncle and the racing team nearly overcame him until she gently pulled his hand away and gave it a brief squeeze.

"You're quite the flirt," she said.

"I'm not flirting. I'm speaking one-hundred-percent unvarnished truth." He spread his fingers and entwined them with hers. "Will you have dinner with me tonight?"

"All of us?" she quizzed, glancing after her departing friends.

"Of course. You're my guests." He liked that she looked ever so briefly disappointed. Had she hoped to have dinner alone with him? "I have a press event at six. How about if I pick you up at eight?"

She glanced at the couple ahead of them. "That should be fine."

"Terrific." His gaze drifted to her soft lips. "A kiss for luck?"

"I thought it was just a practice," she retorted, arching one eyebrow. "Why do you need luck?"

"It's always dangerous when you get onto the track," he said, his voice pitched to a persuasive tone as he tugged her to him. "A thousand different things could go wrong."

"Well, I wouldn't want to be responsible for anything like that." Reaching up, she deposited a light kiss on his cheek.

It wasn't exactly what he'd had in mind, but Harrison's temperature skyrocketed in response to the light press of her breasts against his chest. He curved his fingers over the swell of her hip just below the indent of her waist, keeping her near for a heart-stopping second.

Too soon she was stepping back, the color in her cheeks high. Harrison wondered if his face was equally flushed because he appreciated the cool breeze blowing through the alley between the garages.

"Good luck, Harrison," London told him before turning to follow her friends. "Don't let that kiss go to waste."

With a rueful shake of his head, Harrison returned to the garage and wasn't surprised to find several of his pit crew ready to razz him over his obvious infatuation with London.

"She's obviously a great gal," Jack Crosby remarked flatly. "Now, can you please stop mooning over her and focus on the next fifty minutes?"

Harrison smirked at his uncle. "Jack, if you weren't so in love with your wife of forty years, I might think you were jealous."

Five

Anxiety had settled in by the time the clock on the night-stand in her hotel room hit seven fifty. London stared at her reflection, hemming and hawing over the third outfit she'd tried on.

She'd overdressed for today's visit to the racetrack. What might have suited a shopping trip in downtown Charleston had stood out like a sore thumb at Richmond Raceway. Was tonight's navy blue sheath and beige blazer another misstep? She looked ready for a client meeting instead of a date with a sexy race-car driver. Would he show up in jeans and a T-shirt or slacks and a sweater? Should she switch to the black skinny pants and white blouse she'd packed? London was on her way to the closet when a knock sounded on her door.

For a second her heart threatened to explode from her chest until she remembered that she'd agreed to meet Harrison in the lobby. He didn't have her room number, so there was no way he could be the one knocking on her door. She went to answer and spied Beau standing in the hallway. His eyebrows went up when he glimpsed her.

"You're wearing that to dinner?"

London had grown fond of Beau over the last three years, but having him critique her wardrobe choices was too much. She crossed her arms over her chest and glared at him.

"I am." Why did everyone find it necessary to criticize her appearance? "What's wrong with it?" She meant to sound hostile and defensive but the question came out sounding concerned.

"It's a dinner date," Beau pointed out, "not a business meeting."

"It's not a date," she argued, ignoring the fact that she wanted it to be. She just couldn't get attached to Harrison Crosby. Not when she was using him to get to his brother. "We're just four people having dinner."

"About that…" Beau began, his gaze sliding in the direction of the hotel room he was sharing with his fiancée. "Maribelle isn't feeling well, so we're going to stay in tonight and order room service."

London knew immediately that her friend was completely fine and that the engaged couple had conspired to set London up to have dinner alone with Harrison. Panic set in.

"But it's too late for me to cancel," she protested. "He's supposed to be here right now."

"I'm sure it will be just fine if the two of you go by yourselves." He offered her a cheeky grin and winked. "Just wear something else. And have fun. He's a great guy if you'd just give him a chance."

"Great," she grumbled, closing the hotel room door and pondering Beau's parting words.

Harrison was showing every appearance of being a really great guy. Certainly one who deserved better than what she was doing to him. Guilt pinched her as she went to fetch her purse off the dresser. As she passed the closet a flash of teal distracted her. She'd added the clingy fit-and-flare dress to her suitcase at the last second. The color reminded her of Harrison's eyes, a coastal blue-green she could happily drown in.

Growling at the impulses sweeping through her, London roughly stripped out of the blazer, unzipped her sensible blue dress and let it fall to the floor. A minute later she was sliding the soft jersey over her head and tugging it into place. Almost immediately London's perception of the evening before her transformed. As she turned to the dresser and the bag that held her jewelry, the full skirt ballooned and then fell to brush against her thighs, setting off a chain reaction of sensation.

The mirror above the dresser reflected a woman whose eyes glowed with anticipation. She tugged her hair free of its restraining knot and let it fall around her face before fastening on a pair of long crystal earrings that tickled her neck as she moved. A quick glance at the clock revealed she was now running late. London scooped her clothes off the floor and draped them over the bed before sliding her feet into nude pumps and snagging her purse.

It wasn't until she'd closed the hotel room door behind her and raced toward the elevator that she realized she was breathing erratically. Nor could she blame her agitation on the last-minute wardrobe change. She might as well face that she was excited to be having dinner alone with Harrison.

Since her hotel room was on the second floor, London had less than a minute to compose herself before the elevator doors opened. She stepped forward onto the smooth marble floor of the reception area.

At this hour the lobby was busy with people on their way to dinner or in search of a drink at the elegant bar. Suddenly she realized she hadn't specified a particular location in the large open area to meet Harrison. But even before her concerns could take root, he stepped into her line of sight, looking handsome, desirable and a little dangerous dressed all in black. She released a pent-up breath as he drew near.

"Hi," she said weakly.

"You look gorgeous." He leaned down and brushed her cheek with his lips.

Goose bumps broke out on her arms. "Thanks." London couldn't believe he'd reduced her to single-syllable words. "So do you." To her dismay, she felt her cheeks heat. "I mean, you look very nice."

"Thanks." He glanced past her. "Where are Maribelle and Beau?"

"She wasn't feeling well, so they're ordering room service and staying in."

He frowned. "I hope that doesn't mean they'll miss the race tomorrow."

"I think she'll make a miraculous recovery," London mused.

"Oh?" Harrison raised his eyebrows.

London cleared her throat. "She likes to play match-maker."

"I see."

Did he? When London peered at him from beneath her lashes, she caught him observing her in turn. His look, however, was bold and openly curious.

"She thinks you're a catch."

"I mean no offense when I say that I'm not interested in what she thinks." Harrison took her hand and led her toward the lobby doors. "I want to hear your opinion."

"Do I think you're a catch?" London knew her breathless state had nothing to do with their pace. It was more about the warmth of Harrison's fingers against her skin. "Of course you are."

He glanced at her as she sailed through the open door ahead of him. "You're a little too matter-of-fact when you say that."

"How else should I be?" Despite her earlier reservations, London was having a wonderful time bantering with Harrison. "Are you hoping I'll spill the beans and divulge that I'm infatuated with you?"

"It'd be nice." But his smile indicated he wasn't serious. "Especially given how much you've been on my mind these last few days. It's getting me into trouble with my team."

He'd recaptured her hand once they'd reached the sidewalk. Was he serious? They'd only met three times and been out once. Surely he was feeding her a line. It was tempting to believe him. The flattery gave her ego a much-needed boost. Heaven knew it had taken a beating since Linc had ended their engagement.

"You've gone quiet," he continued. "Don't you believe me?"

"We barely know each other."

"True, but I felt an immediate attraction to you. And I think you noticed the same pull. Why else would you agree to step out of your comfort zone this weekend and come watch me race?"

"Maribelle would've killed me if I'd turned you down." It was a lame cop-out and both of them knew it. London gathered her breath. He'd generously arranged this weekend for her and her friends. She owed him better. "And I wanted to see what you did. Watching you during the practice laps was really exciting."

His full smile nearly blinded her with its brilliance.

"Wait until you see the race tomorrow. It gets a lot more interesting when forty guys put it all on the line."

"I imagine it does." She found herself grinning back. His enthusiasm was infectious. "Where are we going?"

While they'd been talking, he'd directed her along the downtown street. Now, as they crossed another street, he gestured her toward a red canopy that marked the entrance to a restaurant.

"The food here is really good. I thought maybe you'd like to try it."

"Lead the way."

He'd brought her to a tiny French bistro with wood floors, a tin ceiling and white linens on the tables. Cozy booths were tucked against a brick wall while the opposite side of the room was lined with bottles of wine. The subdued lighting lent a warm, romantic vibe to the place and the scents filling the air made London's mouth water.

The hostess settled them into a booth near the back where it was quieter and London turned her attention to the menu.

"It all looks so good," she exclaimed. "I don't know what to choose."

"We could order a couple things and share," Harrison suggested.

It would ease the decision-making process, so London nodded. "Since you've been here before, I'm going to let you do the ordering."

"You trust me?"

She somehow sensed he had more on his mind than just meal selection. "Let's just say I'm feeling a little adventurous at the moment."

"I like the sound of that."

After the waitress brought their drinks and left with their orders, London decided to grab the conversational reins.

"So where are you staying?"

"In an RV at the raceway," he replied. "You're welcome to stop by and check it out later. It's pretty roomy with a nice big bed in the back."

"I suppose it makes sense to be close by," she said, ignoring his invitation. "I looked at the weekend schedule and they keep you really busy. I'm surprised you had time to have dinner with me."

"I snuck out," he said with a mischievous grin. "My uncle thinks I'm going over the data from today's laps before tomorrow's race."

"Really?" She was more than a little shocked until she realized he was kidding. "I'm learning there's a lot more to racing than just getting in a car and going fast."

"Sometimes the tiniest changes can make all the difference."

"So besides making sure you're super-hydrated," she began, referring to the fact that he was only drinking water and wasn't partaking in the bottle of wine he'd ordered for her, "what else goes into preparing for tomorrow's race?" In stark contrast to her earlier skepticism about being interested in a race-car driver, she was finding Harrison's occupation quite interesting.

"I make sure I eat a lot of carbs the night before. I hope you're a fan of chocolate mousse."

"I can always make room for chocolate of any kind."

"Tomorrow morning I'll have a big breakfast followed by a light lunch. In between I'll make sponsor-related appearances before checking in with my crew chief and team to run through last-minute strategy. After that there's a drivers' meeting where the racing association shares information about what's going on that day. If I'm lucky I'll get a few minutes alone at the RV to get my head on straight, but more likely I'll be doing meet and greets. Finally, after lunch, I'll suit up and head to the driver introductions."

"Wow! That's a packed schedule." She was starting to appreciate that his career wasn't just about driving. He was a brand ambassador for his sponsors and the league as well as being a celebrity. "You really don't have any time to yourself."

"Not really. It's all part of the job. And I wouldn't give up any of it."

"You call yourself an introvert, but don't all the public appearances and demands on your time wear you down to nothing?"

"It's not like I don't enjoy meeting my fans." He buttered a piece of bread and popped it into his mouth. "But when I have time off, I make sure I do whatever it takes to reenergize."

"I'm surprised you're out with me, then."

"Are you kidding?" His broad smile dealt her defenses a significant blow. "Being with you is quite exhilarating."

"That's sweet of you to say…"

"I mean it." He gestured at her with another hunk of crusty bread. "And this is where I should probably confess something."

London barely resisted a wince, thinking about her poorly conceived notion to get close to Harrison as a way of getting to his brother. She had yet to figure out what she could do to take Tristan down.

"Like what?" she prompted, hoping it was something terrible so she could feel better about her own questionable morality.

"I used my brother's birthday party as an excuse to see you again."

"Oh." Her pulse skipped. "Does that mean you don't need me as your party planner?" She considered the amount of time she'd spent working on the party and sighed. He wouldn't be the first client to change his mind.

"Not at all. My mother is thrilled that I've taken the project off her hands. My brother can be quite particular when it comes to certain things and it's better if I take the heat for his disappointment."

"You're assuming he'll be disappointed before you've heard any of my plans?" London frowned, but found she wasn't all that insulted. Neither Harrison nor his brother were the toughest clients she'd ever worked for. "That doesn't speak to your faith in my ability to do my job."

Despite the lack of heat or ire in her tone, Harrison's eyes widened. "That's not what I meant at all. I'm sure you will outdo yourself. It's just that Tristan is hard to impress. He's always been that way."

London remembered that Zoe had said something similar about her ex-husband and nodded. "Challenge accepted," she said, digging in where others might throw up their hands and quit.

Harrison nodded. "You thrive under pressure," he said, admiration in his steady gaze. "So do I. It's what makes us good for each other."

Although his words thrilled her, guilt shadowed her delight. Getting revenge on Tristan had prompted her to agree to work on his birthday party and go on that first date with Harrison. She simply had to get her emotions under control.

"You don't think two competitive people will end up ruining things because they're forever chasing the win?" she asked.

"Not if we do it together. I think if we became a team, there's nothing we couldn't accomplish."

Before she started nodding in agreement, London reminded herself of why she'd begun dating him. Getting close to Harrison was a means to an end. And if that made her a terrible person then that was something she'd just have to live with.

Harrison watched his car, number twenty-five, roll into the truck for the return to South Carolina. He was pleased with his second-place finish. With only one race left until the end of the season, he sat in third place for the year and, based on his points, he'd likely hang on to the spot unless he completely screwed up next weekend.

As the car disappeared, a familiar wave of exhaustion swept over him. Once the race was over and the media interviews finished, his body reacted to the long day by shutting down.

"Nice race," his uncle said. The two men were standing side by side while the team rolled Harrison's race car from one set of inspectors to the next. "I was a little worried about you in the beginning."

Today's race had been unusually challenging since at the beginning he'd had to work twice as hard to stay focused on the track and the cars around him while thoughts of London and their dinner last night dominated his mind. Things had gotten better once he'd passed his hundredth lap and settled into the race, needing to win so he could impress London.

"Just wanted to make it interesting," Harrison replied with a sly grin.

"You did that," Jack grumbled. "Let me know when you're ready to head back tonight. I'd like to get out of here by midnight."

"Actually, I've arranged a lift back to Charleston already."

His uncle raised an eyebrow. "Your new girlfriend?"

"She's not my girlfriend...yet." That last word slipped

out, revealing something Harrison hadn't yet admitted to himself. He had more than a casual interest in London McCaffrey.

What was going on with him? They'd only been out twice and he was already thinking in terms of a relationship? The only time he was quick to commit was on the track. But when he was with London, their connection felt right and his instincts had never failed him before.

"You sure she's the right woman for you?" his uncle asked, the question a jarring pothole Harrison didn't see coming.

Acid began churning in Harrison's gut. "You have some thoughts on why she isn't?"

While Jack had never commented on any of his drivers' personal lives, he was operating a business where each driver brought in hundreds of thousands to millions of dollars in sponsor revenue each year. That meant he couldn't afford for his team to operate at anything less than 100 percent. And anything that interfered with that would come under fire.

"I asked Dixie about her."

"And?" Harrison challenged.

"She's a social climber." Jack's expression grew hard. "Apparently she and her mother have been trying to access Charleston inner circles without much success."

"What does that have to do with us dating?" Although he already knew the answer, Harrison wanted to hear his uncle say it.

"I'm just concerned she's going to mess with your head if you're not careful."

"Because I'm not her type?" He'd already figured that out.

"Before Linc Thurston, she'd only gone out with executives and professionals," Jack said. "I don't think she'd have dated a pro ball player if he hadn't belonged to one of Charleston's oldest families. And I'm guessing the reason they're no longer engaged is because Linc figured that out before it was too late."

"I don't think she's as shallow as all that," Harrison said, hoping he was right. "And we're in the early stages of dating. Who's to say where things are going for us."

Jack grunted. "Make sure you figure it out one way or another before the season starts up again in February." His uncle frowned. "I don't need you distracted on the track."

"Hopefully it won't take that long."

Jack nodded and the two men parted ways.

Harrison headed back to the trailer, where he grabbed a quick shower. Even on cooler days like this one, the heat inside the car during the race hovered close to a hundred and thirty degrees. Since the sort of AC in a consumer vehicle weighed too much to be installed in a race car, drivers were cooled by a ventilation system that used hoses and a bag they sat on to blow air on their feet and head. With the average race lasting at least three hours, that was a long time to go without any sort of air-conditioning.

After getting dressed, Harrison slung his duffel over his shoulder and headed to the spot where he'd agreed to meet up with London and her friends. He was intrigued by the fact that Beau had his pilot's license and that Maribelle was learning how to fly. Harrison liked the couple, finding them an upbeat counterpunch to London's reserve.

On the heels of his conversation with Jack, Harrison reflected on his own concerns about what he was getting into with London. If all he wanted was sex, he wasn't going about it the right way given the chemistry that sizzled between them. Take last night, for example. He'd accompanied her back to her hotel room and once again she'd put out a vibe that welcomed physical contact. But instead of backing her into the room and doing all the things he'd been fantasizing about, he'd kissed her on the forehead—not trusting himself to claim her lips—and walked away with an ache in his chest and his loins.

Appreciating the cool night air against his skin, Harrison lengthened his stride, eager to see London and hear her opinion of the race. A silver SUV awaited him near the gate that led to the parking lot. The window was down on the driver's side and Harrison recognized Beau's profile. The easygoing fellow was smiling and gesturing as he spoke to the car's occupants.

"Hey," Harrison said as he approached. "Thanks for the lift."

"Are you kidding?" Beau glanced at his fiancée. "It's the least we could do after the weekend we've had. The behind-the-scenes access you gave us was incredible."

Harrison pulled open the rear driver's-side door and spied London sitting on the far seat. The sight of her made his chest go tight. *Damn.* The woman was beautiful. Today she wore black pants and a denim jacket over a cream sweater. Her hair was bound in a loose braid with long strands framing her pale cheeks. A welcoming smile curved her full, kissable lips and he glimpsed no trace of hesitation in her manner.

Heart thumping erratically, he slid in beside her and became immediately aware of her subtle floral scent. "So what did you think of your first race?" he asked, slipping his duffel into the SUV's cargo area. "Was it what you expected?"

"To be honest, I thought I'd be bored. Five hundred laps seemed like a lot. But it was really fun. It helped to have these two with me." She indicated the couple in the front seats. "They explained a lot of the ins and outs of the strategy. And congratulations on your second-place finish."

"The team had a good weekend," he replied, unsure why he was downplaying his success. Didn't he want to impress this woman? From everything he'd been told, only the best would do for her. "If all goes smoothly next weekend, Crosby Motorsports is poised to finish second this year."

"So next weekend is your last race? What do you do during the off-season?"

"Rest, play and then get ready for next year."

"How much time do you get off to do that?"

"Season starts again in February. I take a break in December to vacation and celebrate the holidays with my family. But even during the off-season I train. Both in the gym and with driving simulations to keep my reflexes sharp." Harrison reached out and took her hand in his, turning it palm up and running the tips of his fingers over her skin. He noticed a slight tremble in her fingers as he caressed her. "I had a really great time last night," he murmured, pitching his voice so only she could hear.

"It was fun. Thank you for dinner." Her gaze flicked from the hand he held to the couple in the front and back to him.

"I'm sorry we had to make such an early night of it."

"You had a big day today. I wouldn't have felt right if I kept you up too late." She sent him a sizzling look from beneath her lashes, banishing his earlier weariness.

Was she feeling bold because they weren't alone?

He toyed with her fingers, imagining how they would feel against his naked body. Yet, to his surprise, the rush of lust such thoughts aroused was matched by a strong craving to find out what made her tick. He lifted her palm to his lips and nipped at her skin. Her sharp gasp made him smile. He'd begun to suspect the route past her defenses might involve keeping her off balance by pushing her sensual boundaries. He would have to test that during tomorrow's hunt for the party venue.

"I think a sleepless night with you would've been worth doing badly today," he murmured.

"I'm sure your uncle wouldn't agree."

"He was young once."

"He's running a multimillion-dollar racing team," she countered, her tone tart. "And even if he forgave you, what about your sponsors?"

Harrison let loose an exaggerated sigh. "One of these days you're going to surprise me by not being so practical."

"You think so?" A faint smile curved her lips.

"I know so."

London subsided into reflective silence for several minutes and Harrison gave her room to think. At long last she said, "It's not part of my nature to be rash and spontaneous. My mother drilled into my head that I should think first and act second. She's very concerned with appearances, and growing up, I never had an opportunity to spread my wings, so to speak."

This bit of insight into her past intrigued him. "What would you have done if your choices hadn't been so restricted?"

"Run off and join the circus?" Her weak attempt at humor was obviously an attempt to deflect his probing. After a second she gave a half-hearted shrug and said, "I don't know. Sometimes I resent that my mother was so obsessed with advancing my position in Charleston society."

"Only sometimes?" he challenged.

London's fingers briefly tightened over his. "When I let myself think about it." For a long moment she sat in silence, but soon his patience was rewarded. "It's hard when your mother thinks your worth is defined by who you marry. That's something other people judge you by, not your own parent."

"Why do you care?"

His blunt question apparently surprised her. Despite the shadowy confines of the back seat, he could easily read the sudden tension in her expression.

She reacted as if he'd attacked some core value she lived by. "I want her to be glad I'm her daughter."

Harrison understood why this was important. Tristan had long sought their father's approval, especially since taking over Crosby Automotive. Harrison's brother seemed obsessed with matching the success their father had made of the company, yet profits had been mostly flat in the first few years Tristan had been in charge. Still, that hadn't seemed to affect his personal spending. Something Harrison had heard his uncle criticize more than once.

"You don't think she admires all you've accomplished?" Harrison asked, returning his thoughts to London's situation.

"I think my dad does." Pride glowed in her voice. "My company is very successful and that makes him proud."

"But not your mother?"

"She might've been happy if I'd married Linc and had several boys and one girl."

"Why only one girl?" Harrison suspected he knew the answer before she spoke.

"Obviously my mother's opinion is that women are worth less than men." London's tone was more matter-of-fact than bitter. "Still, she'd like to have a granddaughter who could do what I couldn't. Become a debutante."

Harrison knew his mother had gone through the classes and been presented at nineteen. But in this day and age, did that stuff even matter?

"Why is it so important to her?" he asked.

"My mother grew up in New York City and was never selected for the International Debutante Ball there, despite her family's connections and wealth. She took the rejection hard." London shifted in her seat, turning to face him. "And then she gets to Charleston and finds all the doors are closed to her. No one cared about her money. All that mattered was she was from *off*." London freed her hand briefly so she could form air quotes around the last word.

"You should talk to my mother," Harrison said. "She rejected becoming a debutante and married my dad, who was not only an outsider but poor by her family standards."

"I'm going to guess she'd tell me to follow my heart?"

"That was the advice she gave me when my dad hassled me about choosing racing over working for Crosby Automotive. If I hadn't, I'd be working for the family business and completely miserable."

"You don't see yourself as a businessman?"

"Honestly, not the sort who sits in an office and stares at reports all day. My plan is to take over for my uncle one day and run Crosby Motorsports."

"And in the meantime you're just going to race and have fun."

"Nothing wrong with having fun. I'd like to demonstrate that to you."

"What sort of fun do you think I'd be interested in?" she asked, her manner serious rather than flirtatious.

"Hard to say until I get to know you better." He had several ideas on the subject. "But would you have guessed that you'd enjoy today's race as much as you did?"

"No, not really. Maybe I do need to look outside my limited circle of activities."

"So that's a yes to new experiences?"

"As long as you're willing to balance adventure with somewhat tamer forms of entertainment," she said, "I'm in."

No sweeter words had ever been spoken by a woman.

Six

Shortly after lunch on the Monday following her weekend in Richmond, London sat at her desk, doodling on her notepad, her cell phone on speaker while Maribelle went on and on about how much she and Beau had enjoyed their time at the raceway. London's attention, however, was not on the race but on the man who'd invited her to it.

Almost as if her friend could read her mind, Maribelle said, "He's really into you. I think that's so great."

Maribelle's remark sent a little shiver of pleasure through London. "I don't know what to think."

But she wasn't being completely truthful. London was in fact thinking that she'd intended to use Harrison to get close to his brother, and the more time she spent with the race-car driver, the more troubling her attraction to him became.

Despite their closeness, London hadn't told Maribelle about the crazy plan hatched at the Beautiful Women Taking Charge event. London knew if she looked too deeply at why she'd kept it from her best friend of fifteen years, doubts would surface about her moral choices. Shame flooded her as London realized how far she'd strayed from the person she'd believed herself to be. Yet to stop now when others were depending on her...

"Are you worried what your mother would think of him?" Maribelle asked, breaking into London's thoughts.

Maribelle had been there for London during high school when Edie Fremont-McCaffrey's frustration with Charleston's society rules had made London's life hell. It wasn't her fault that she wasn't allowed to be a debutante, but that hadn't stopped her mother from raining criticisms down on her daughter's head. Blaming her mother gave London an excuse to be conflicted about getting involved with Harrison so that her real concerns never had to surface.

"She wasn't exactly thrilled with the fact that Linc was a professional baseball player, but he was wealthy and had the old Charleston social connections that she wanted for me." London toyed with her earring. "Can you imagine how she'd feel about Harrison? Not only is he a race-car driver, but his father and uncle are from off with no social standing."

"Why do you care?"

It wasn't the first time Maribelle had asked the question. Nor did it spark the familiar surge of resentment that was always just below the surface. About how easy it was for someone who had it all to downplay their advantages. Add to that how supportive Maribelle's family was about everything she did, and bitterness had often colored London's mood. Today, however, London was feeling less defensive than usual.

"Because fighting her is so much work. It's easier to give in." The admission flowed from London's lips, startling her.

And apparently surprising Maribelle, as well, because for a long few seconds neither woman spoke.

"Oh, London."

Sudden tears erupted in London's eyes. Shocked by the rush of emotion, she blinked rapidly, determined not to give in. Her mother had hounded her mercilessly all her life and London had always braced against it. For as long as she could remember, London had maintained a resilient facade while secretly believing that Edie was right and it was all London's fault.

She picked up the phone and took it off speaker. "My mother is a tyrant," she said in a barely audible whisper, almost as if she was afraid to voice what was in her heart. "She has criticized nearly everything I've ever done or said."

"She's a terrible person," Maribelle agreed, always London's champion. "But she's also your mother and you want to please her. It's normal."

But was it? Shouldn't parents want what was best for their children? That being said, Edie would claim that encouraging her daughter to marry well was the most important thing for London's future, but it was pretty clear that her mother didn't take London's happiness into account, as well.

"Maybe I need a new normal," London groused.

"Maybe you do," Maribelle said, her tone deadly serious. "What are you wearing right now?"

The question came out of nowhere and made London laugh. She dabbed at the trace of moisture lingering near the corner of her eye and found her spirits rising.

"Are you trying to get me to engage in phone sex with you?" London teased, pretending to sound outraged. "Because I don't think either of us rolls that way."

"Ha, ha." Maribelle sounded more impatient than

amused. "I'm only asking because I heard you making plans to get together with Harrison today to go venue shopping. I hope you're wearing something less…reserved than usual."

London glanced down at the emerald green wrap dress she wore. The style was more fun and relaxed than her typical uniform of conservative suits in understated shades of gray, blue and black.

"I'm wearing the necklace you bought me for Christmas last year." London had not previously worn the statement necklace of stone flowers in hot jewel tones, thinking the look was too bold for her. But today she'd wanted her appearance to make an impact and the necklace had paired perfectly with the dress.

"Is your hair up?"

London's fingers automatically went to the sleek side bun she wore.

"Forget I asked," Maribelle said. "Just take it down and send me a picture."

Feeling slightly ridiculous, London did as she was told, even going so far as to fluff her blond waves into a sexy, disheveled look, and was rewarded by her friend's joyful squeal.

"I think that means you approve."

"This is the London McCaffrey I've been waiting for all my life," Maribelle declared in rapturous tones. "You look fantastic and it's so nice to see you ditching those dull duds you think make you look professional."

"Thanks?" Despite her friend's backhanded compliment, London was feeling optimistic and excited about seeing Harrison again. Would he approve of her new look? Or was he a typical guy who wouldn't notice?

"You really like him, don't you?"

London opened her mouth, preparing to deny the way her heart raced and nerves danced whenever she was with

Harrison, but couldn't lie to her friend. "I do like him. More than I expected to. That being said, it might be that we have a lot of chemistry and there's no possible way we're compatible beyond that." She left an unspoken *but* hanging in the air.

It was getting harder and harder to make excuses for why dating Harrison would be a waste of her time. Unfortunately, the real reason was a secret London could never share with her friend and that made what she was doing all the worse.

"Say whatever you want," Maribelle said. "But I see things working out between you two."

"I don't know. We're so different. We have divergent points of view about lifestyle and the things we enjoy. How do we go forward if we have nothing in common?"

"That sounds like your mother talking. How different are you really? You both come from money. You may not run in the same groups, but your families share some social connections. Both of you are committed to your careers and highly competitive. If you're talking about the fact that he races cars for a living, he makes a boatload of money doing it and I think you'd be bored with some stuffy businessman who only wants to talk about how his company is doing. You need someone who gets you riled up."

"You keep saying things like that, but excitement has never been my criterion for finding a man attractive before."

"How's that worked out for you thus far?"

Before London could protest that she was quite happy with her life, her desk phone lit up with a call from Missy, likely indicating that Harrison had arrived.

"I think Harrison's here."

"Call me later to let me know how it went."

Instead of reminding her friend that this was a business meeting, London said, "I'm sure there won't be anything to tell."

"Let me be the judge of that."

London was shaking her head as she disconnected with her friend and answered the call from her receptionist. Sure enough, Harrison was waiting for her in the lobby.

Before she picked up her tablet containing all the information on the four venues she'd be showing Harrison today, London double-checked her makeup and applied a fresh coat of lipstick. She noted her sparkling eyes and the flush over her cheekbones put there in anticipation of seeing Harrison. The man had certainly gotten beneath her skin. Worse, she was glad of it.

Despite the fact that she'd seen him the night before, London's stomach flipped as she walked into the reception area and spied Harrison's tall figure. Although her primping had kept him waiting, he wasn't checking his phone or flirting with her receptionist. Instead he was focused on the hallway leading to her office. Their eyes collided and a shower of sparks raced across London's nerve endings, leaving her breathless and light-headed.

"Hi," she said, her voice sounding not at all professional. Cursing her body's longing to fling itself against his, she cleared her throat and tried again. "Sorry I kept you waiting." Flustered by his slow, sexy smile, she turned to the receptionist. "Missy, I'll be gone for the rest of the afternoon. See you in the morning."

"Sure." Missy brazenly winked at her. "You two have fun now."

London's mouth dropped open and her brain was scrambling to come up with something to reply when Harrison caught her hand and tugged her toward the door. She noticed how the man smelled delicious as he guided her to his Mercedes.

"Where to first?" he asked as he slid behind the wheel.

Although the entire afternoon's plans were already firmly in her mind, she cued up her tablet, needing something to do to avoid looking at him. After naming an address half a mile down on King Street, she began listing the positives and negatives of the space.

"The best part is their menu. They have an excellent chef. Unfortunately, there is no elevator, so the space is only accessible by stairs. I only mention it in case you have any guests who can't make the climb."

"That shouldn't be a problem."

Harrison found an open spot along the curb a half block up from their destination and parked. They then walked back toward the venue. As Harrison held the front door, allowing her to pass, she noticed his slight frown. The first floor of the narrow building was occupied by a wine bar.

"Don't let the size down here fool you," she said, waving at the manager. "Upstairs is fifteen hundred square feet and feels much more open and airy. There's plenty of room for all your guests and even an outdoor patio if the night is mild." She broke off to greet Jim Gleeson and introduced the manager to Harrison. "Jim has helped me with several corporate functions over the last two years," she explained.

The two men shook hands and then Jim led the way upstairs. "We can set up the space however you envision it," the manager said over his shoulder. "And the room is big enough that we can divide it into a cocktail setting with high tables or couches on one end and large round tables on the other for dinner."

"I think that would be nice," London said.

They'd reached the second floor and Harrison wasn't evaluating the space, but rather, his attention was focused on her.

"Since we'd talked about a jazz band," she continued,

determined to treat him like a client in this setting, "we could place them near the bar as people first enter."

At the moment the room was set up for a cocktail party with a freestanding bar at each end and high-top tables scattered along the perimeter.

Jim's phone buzzed and he excused himself, leaving the pair alone.

Somehow as soon as it was just the two of them, the massive room became oddly intimate. Or maybe it was the way Harrison was looking at her as if he intended to penetrate her professional mask and get to the woman beneath. London couldn't stop herself from recalling how disappointed she'd been on Saturday night that he hadn't tried to kiss her good-night. Or the way they'd leaned toward each other on the plane ride back, sharing the armrest as he'd shown her the camera footage from inside his race car.

"What I really like here is all the period details," she began, taking refuge in professionalism to avoid Harrison's hot gaze. She walked away from him, gesturing at the exposed brick and white wainscoting. Her heels clicked on the polished pine floor and echoed off the gleaming wood in the original coffered ceiling. "Isn't this fireplace fantastic?"

"I think you're fantastic."

"I'm picturing ten tables of ten. With big glass vases holding candles and filled with glass beads in the center. Since it's December, we could do evergreen centerpieces, but maybe that's too predictable." Aware that she was rambling, London continued. To stop meant she might give in to the longing pulsing through her. "Or we could do glass pillars with layered candies like peppermints and foil-wrapped chocolates in red and green. Unless you think he's too sophisticated and would prefer crystal with white and silver."

While she'd been going on and on, Harrison had been stalking after her, his expression intent, his gaze narrowed.

Now, as she approached the door leading out to the roof-top patio, he set his hand on the doorknob before she could reach it, halting her retreat.

"I think you're fantastic," he repeated, compelling her to stop dodging him. "Everything about you interests me."

"I like you a lot," she admitted, surprising both of them with the confession. "What you do is dangerous and exciting. I never imagined…"

Oh, what was she doing? It was on the tip of her tongue to spill everything about the riotous, treacherous emotions driving her actions. To share how disappointed she'd been Saturday night because he hadn't tried anything when he'd brought her back to her hotel room. Confessing her developing feelings for him was the absolute wrong thing to do. So how was she supposed to get out of the verbal corner she'd backed herself into?

Harrison watched a dozen conflicting emotions race across London's features. Most of the time she'd demonstrated a sphinxian ability to keep her thoughts concealed. Her need to keep herself hidden frustrated him. He wanted her to open up and share what made her tick.

"I've also had great success with hurricane holders filled with rice lights and Christmas balls," she stated in a breathless rush, returning to the earlier topic of centerpieces. "Or glass bowls with candles floating above holly sprigs."

"Never imagined what?" Harrison prompted, ignoring her attempt to evade the real subject.

She shook her head. "This really isn't the place for this conversation."

"Where would you like to go?" He hoped she'd suggest her place. Or his. It was past time he got her alone.

"I set aside my afternoon to help you find a venue for your brother's birthday party."

"London," he murmured, cradling her head in his palm, thumb caressing her flushed cheek.

"Yes?"

Her voice was equally soft and it seemed to him a trace of desperation colored her tone as if with each thump of her heart she was losing the fight to maintain control. It echoed how he felt when they were together. Each moment in her company tested his willpower. He knew better than to pressure her like this. As much as he wanted to go in with guns blazing, she needed to be coaxed. Wooed. Enticed. But damn if he didn't want to feel her surrender beneath his touch.

"I don't really care what venue we choose," he said. "The only reason I'm here today is to spend time with you."

He placed just the tips of his fingers on her spine. A tremor went through her an instant before she tipped her head back and gazed up at his face. The hunger glowing in her eyes transfixed him. Inching closer, he dipped his head until he could feel her breath on his skin. He grazed his nose against hers, ending the move with a slight bump that nudged her head into a better angle. Smiling at the sigh that escaped her, he slanted his mouth above hers, not quite making contact. Although he'd already kissed her on the street in downtown Charleston, that location hadn't offered him the privacy to do it right. Plus, it had been too soon to take things as far as he wanted to.

This time it would be different.

She made a soft impatient noise in the seconds before their lips met and his world stopped being ordinary. Then another sound erupted from her throat as fire flashed through him. Wildness sped across his nerve endings, setting his heart to pounding. Endless fantasies of her and him naked and rolling over his mattress in hungry, frenzied passion flashed through his mind.

Harrison didn't give a damn that the manager might return and interrupt them. The only thing on his mind was the woman making his heart pound and his body heat. Longing had gotten hold of him and wouldn't let go.

With one hand coaxing her forward, bringing her torso into contact with chest and abs, he cupped her cheek with the other and deepened the kiss. It nearly killed him to go slow when he wanted so much more. Her lips. Tongue. Teeth. All of her. And when her lips parted and a soft, helpless groan escaped her, he nearly lost his mind.

In the instant her body melted into his, they were both swept up in a way that Harrison found himself powerless to stop. Despite his best intentions, the kiss went nova too fast for him to rein it in. Instead he surrendered the fight, realizing while he desired this woman more with each encounter, she wanted him just as much.

This was how a kiss was supposed to be. A give-and-take of sweetness and lust. Pure longing and dirty intentions. He slid his tongue across hers, claiming her mouth and driving her passion harder. Her fingers clutched his hair and dented his leather jacket. It was all crazy, frantic fun with a poignant dash of inevitability, and he never wanted it to end.

The sound of footsteps on the wooden stairs behind him jolted Harrison back to reality. Cursing inwardly, he broke off the kiss and gulped in air. Without releasing his hold on London, he blinked several times in rapid succession, trying to reorient himself to their surroundings. When had he ever lost control like that? Who was this woman who could make him go crazy by relating details about square footage, color schemes and table layouts?

"How are we doing?" came a bright voice from the far end of the room.

London jerked in response to the interruption and pulled

Harrison's hand from her face. She took a half step back, her eyes stunned and wide as they met his. Her chest rose and fell as she put her hand to her mouth, hiding a dismayed *oh*. Harrison surveyed the hot color of her skin and her passion-bruised lips, unable to resist a smile.

Damn, she looked gorgeous with her vulnerability on display. All softness and submission. But even as this thought registered in his mind, he could tell she was rapidly regaining her poise. Her features shifted into the cool reserve with which she confronted the world. Only her eyes betrayed her in the second before her lashes dipped, concealing her confusion.

"It all looks great," he called to the manager. "I think we'll take it."

"Great," the man replied. "I'll get the paperwork started."

"You go do that," Harrison said. "We have a few more things to talk about up here and then we'll be down."

"I have three more properties to show you," London reminded him in a harsh whisper, regaining her voice even as the manager's footsteps retreated down the stairs. "You can't make a decision without seeing all of them."

He skimmed his fingertips over her cheekbone, admiring her delicate bone structure. "Do you really want to spend the rest of the afternoon pretending to look at properties while what we really want to do is get to know each other better?"

"I…" Her eyes narrowed. "If you think one kiss means I'm going to sleep with you, you're wrong."

No doubt she'd intended to make this declaration in tart tones, but her voice had lacked conviction.

"You have a dirty mind," he scolded, giving her an affectionate tap on her perfect nose. "I like that in a woman."

"I don't have anything of the sort."

"Really?" He raised an eyebrow. "I say I want to get to know you better and you assume that means sex."

"Well, sure." She gnawed on her lip and frowned. "I mean…"

"Table that thought," he growled, dropping his head and giving her a firm, brief kiss on the lips. "What I meant by getting to know each other better was more about how you came to Richmond this weekend to watch me race. I thought it might be nice for you to show me a little of your world."

It had occurred to him after being dropped off the night before that London McCaffrey had learned way more about him than he'd discovered about her.

Her gaze remained glued to him as she gestured toward the room. "This is it."

"What? Do you mean work? There has to be more to your life than just this." When she shook her head, Harrison nodded. Obviously they were two of a kind when it came to their careers. "So we'll continue to plan the party. We've chosen a venue. What's next?"

"The menu. Flowers. Invitations. A theme."

A theme? Harrison kept his thoughts hidden with some difficulty as he imagined the challenge in finding something that would appeal to his brother. Maybe his mother would have some ideas.

"So, let's go downstairs, sign the contract, plan the meal and then go buy some flowers."

She regarded him skeptically. "Really? You want to do that?"

"I want to spend time with you and see what you enjoy doing. If that involves flowers and invitations, so be it."

For several heartbeats she remained undecided, but instead of pushing, Harrison stayed silent and let her sort through whatever it was she was grappling with. At last she nodded.

"But first," he said, turning her around until they were both staring through the glass door leading outside. "Let's talk about this patio."

"Okay."

Her expression as she glanced back at him reflected her puzzlement. Keeping her off balance was part of his plan to discover all the little things she kept concealed.

"How do you see us using the space for Tristan's party?" As he spoke, he grabbed her wrists and slid her hands to the wood portion of the door before pushing her palms flat against the narrow panel. "Keep your hands right there. Now, tell me your thoughts."

She shivered as he ran his hands up her arms to her shoulders before moving aside her hair, exposing her neck. "They can string lights and put out couches."

"What else?"

He dusted a kiss just below her hairline, hearing her breath stutter as his lips continued to play over the fragrant flesh of her neck and run along the neckline of her dress. He dipped beneath the fabric with his finger, baring the top of her spine, claiming her shoulder, collarbone and nape with soft kisses.

She pushed back into his body and moaned as her backside came into contact with his erection. The sound inflamed his already fiery desire and he murmured encouragement as he kissed the shell of her ear and nipped at her earlobe.

"What else?" he repeated. "How do you envision the scene?"

"Um," she said, her breath coming faster. "We could have them set up a bar. Oh, that feels good."

This last was in response to his hand sliding over her

stomach and splaying as she rocked her hips, rubbing herself against him.

"How many people do you think could fit out there?" he quizzed, dipping his hand beneath the hem of her dress and running his fingertips up her thigh.

"A couple dozen. Oh." Her head fell back against his shoulder as he grazed the inside of her thigh. "What you're doing to me…"

"Yes?" he prompted.

Did she have any idea she'd parted her legs to give him better access? He raked her neck with his teeth, dying to touch her, to find out if she was wet for him.

"Don't stop."

"Besides the lights and couches, how would you decorate?"

He ran his fingers over the cotton panel of her panties, noting the damp fabric.

"Please." She was panting and rocking against his hand, making low, incoherent noises, trying to ask for more.

"How would you decorate?" he repeated, sliding his fingers beneath he elastic of her panties and cupping her for a long second before dipping his finger into her wetness. With a heartfelt groan he stroked her, absorbing her shudders as he discovered just how she liked to be touched.

"Candles." She ejected the word like a curse. "Lots and lots and lots of candles."

She was coming. Hard. Her hips rocked and bucked as her spine arched. The sounds emanating from her stopped being coherent. A storm was rising and it fed his own pleasure. In that moment they were no longer two people but one being, both focused on driving her into a mind-blowing orgasm. And then he felt the first wave of it rush over her. Felt her start to shatter against him.

"Give it to me, baby," he said. "Let me take care of you."

Her nails dug into his thigh. He'd been so focused on her he hadn't even realized she'd gripped him there. But now her touch, so close to his aching erection, caused him to harden to the point of pain.

"Oh, Harrison."

Her words ended in a shudder that seemed endless as she climaxed and he held on, easing his strokes as the last of her pleasure dimmed. Panting and limp, head bowed, she braced herself with one hand on the door frame and sucked great gulps of air into her lungs. The other hand eased its death grip on his thigh and she pushed a lock of hair behind her ear.

"God, I love making you come," he murmured, easing his hand from between her legs. He placed his palm on her stomach, keeping their bodies together while he dipped his head and kissed her neck.

"Not as much as I love coming," she retorted with a shaky chuckle.

He found his breath wasn't altogether steady as he said, "I've never known anyone like you."

"Really?" Her head swiveled just enough to give him a glimpse of her skeptical expression.

"Really."

Beneath her show of reserve—and he now realized that was all it was, a performance she'd played all her life— lurked a wild woman, unsatisfied with all the restrictions placed on her by society and expectations. He looked forward to coaxing her from hiding.

"You haven't gotten other women off in public?"

"Most of the women I've been with know the score. They're with me because of who I am and are willing to do whatever I'm into." He turned her around and put his hands on her shoulders, waiting until she met his gaze before continuing. "You are with me in spite of who I am.

What just happened was all about you. For you. I'm incredibly honored just to be a part of it."

"I can't believe I did that," she murmured, disbelief in her tone. "That wasn't at all like me."

"I think it was. You just don't want to admit it." He paused a beat, noted that she remained unsure and finished, "You were incredible."

"Don't expect that it will happen again."

But they both knew it wasn't the end. He recognized the truth in his gut and saw acknowledgment in her eyes.

"Whatever you want to happen will."

And as she frowned at him, trying to interpret what he meant, Harrison knew that party planning had never been so sexy.

Seven

Chip Corduroy was the sort of Charleston insider London had begun cultivating long before she'd started her event planning business because he knew everyone's dirty secrets and could be counted on to trade information for favors. The slender fifty-year-old had a proud pedigree and expensive taste. Unfortunately, that meant he mostly lived above his means, which was why he loved that London "treated" him to spa days, shopping excursions and dinners out at the best restaurants in exchange for leads and introductions.

"I heard you've been out with Harrison Crosby a few times," Chip said, shooting her a sideways glance.

They were standing in front of the hostess at Felix Cocktails et Cuisine waiting to be seated and London wasn't at all surprised that the sandy-haired man had caught wind of their dates.

"It's business," she responded, keeping her answers short. "I'm planning his brother's birthday party."

"Doesn't really seem your type," Chip persisted, obviously not believing her explanation.

"Because he's a race-car driver?" She heard the defensive note in her voice and inwardly winced.

"Because his family isn't old Charleston."

"There aren't many eligible men who are." London sighed, feeling disingenuous as she fed Chip what he expected her to say. "But from everything I've heard, it seems as if Tristan and I would be better suited." The lie tasted awful on her tongue, but she needed whatever Chip knew about Tristan.

"So you've given up on getting back together with Linc?" From the routine nature of the question, London suspected he already knew the answer. "I mean, you two were the golden couple."

"Maybe on paper."

In truth, the longer they'd been together and the more interest Linc had displayed in settling down and starting a family, the more she'd dragged her feet about setting a wedding date. Frankly, she'd been terrified at the idea that she'd be expected to give up her career and had struggled to imagine herself as a mother. Did she have the patience for children? Or the interest?

And yet none of those same questions or insecurities bombarded her when she imagined herself with Harrison. Not that she saw a future with him. Her mother would disown her if London married a race-car driver. And then there was the revenge plot against Tristan, something she'd have to keep secret from Harrison forever. What chance did a relationship have when the partners weren't truthful with each other?

No doubt the impossibility of a happily-ever-after with Harrison was what kept her anxieties at bay. Convinced they had no future, London was free to daydream about them settling into a house somewhere between downtown Charleston and the Crosby Motorsports complex. With her business growing ever more successful each year and thanks to the hard work of the fantastic staff she'd hired, she was in a position where she could delegate more. They'd have two darling kids. A boy and a girl. Both would have Harrison's sea green eyes and her blond hair. They would grow up to become anything they wanted to be with both parents encouraging their individual interests.

"Have you heard that he's taken up with his house-keeper?" Chip asked, dragging London away from her daydream.

She found herself reluctant to emerge from the satisfying fantasy. "Really?" She forced herself to sound aghast, knowing it would spur her companion to greater gossip even as her actions filled her with distaste.

"He's definitely sleeping with her."

When his mother had encouraged Linc to hire Claire Robbins, London's initial reaction had been to doubt Maribelle's concerns that the pretty military widow was competition and to ignore the fact that Claire and Linc had chemistry. In London's view, Claire was obviously still in love with her deceased husband and utterly focused on her darling toddler.

"Has he come out and said so?" London asked, breaking her promise to not dabble in unsubstantiated rumor about her ex. "Or is that just speculation?"

"They've been going out to dinner and he bought her a pair of earrings." Chip declared this as if it definitively proved his claim. "And the way he looked at her at his mother's party?" Chip fanned himself even as he rolled his eyes emphatically. "There's definitely something going on."

"That's all speculation," she insisted, hoping the gossip wasn't true. Something about Claire was off. She'd been too evasive when discussing her life before Charleston. "Plus, even if he's sleeping with her, it's not going to last."

Chip looked shocked. "Well, of course not."

As the hostess led them to a table, London shoved all thoughts of her ex to the back burner. Linc was Everly's project and London needed to give every appearance of having moved on to avoid any backlash after Everly's revenge plan came to fruition.

As London settled into her seat, she scrambled for a way to shift the conversation to what Chip knew about Tristan Crosby. When no smooth segue came to mind, she decided to be forthright.

"Harrison hired me to plan a surprise birthday party for his brother. What can you tell me about Tristan?"

Chip leveled a speculative look on her before answering. "Dresses well. Loves the finest money can buy. Gives to charities, but not because he cares, more so people will tell him how great he is. Several women have told me he's a sexual predator. Don't let yourself be alone with him or he'll have his hands all over you."

None of this was news, so she pushed for more. "Wasn't he married until recently?"

"Zoe. Nice girl. She had no idea what she was getting into when she married him."

"Girl?" London echoed, picturing the woman she'd met weeks earlier. "I thought she was in her late twenties."

"I'm speaking figuratively. He snapped her up when she was still in college and she always seemed to have a deer-in-the-headlights look about her. She barely spoke when they were out together. Just a decorative bit of arm candy that every guy in the room wanted as their own."

London shuddered as she pondered how it would feel to be valued for her face and figure alone. Although she'd barely met Zoe, their shared experience of personally being wronged by powerful, wealthy men had given her a sense of sisterhood that she hadn't felt with Everly, whose beef with Ryan Dailey had to do with his treatment of her sister.

"You can do better," Chip said, redirecting her attention. "Might I suggest Grady Edwards? Good family. Wealthy. A little obsessed with polo for my taste, but no one is perfect."

"I'll keep him in mind," London replied diplomatically, struggling for a way to return the conversation to Tristan. "Although I heard Landry Beaumont has been seeing him." This was a spurious remark. Rumor had it Landry was chasing Linc. "So what happened between Tristan Crosby and his ex-wife?"

"He dumped her. Something about her having an affair. Later I heard he fabricated the whole thing to get out of paying her anything. The man is ruthless," Chip said, leaning forward and lowering his voice conspiratorially even though no one was close enough to hear their conversation. "Magnolia Spencer told me in confidence that Zoe got next to nothing."

"Because of a prenup?"

"Because there's no money."

"How is that possible? Crosby Automotive does exceptionally well and, from what I hear, Tristan has been remodeling the Theodore Norwood house on Montague for the last five years. A client of mine has done some of the work and said Tristan has put nearly three million into the project."

Chip shrugged as he eyed the menu. The restaurant was known for its creative cocktails and small plates all done with a Parisian flare. "What looks good?"

As much as London wanted to keep the conversation alive, she decided more digging would only make Chip suspicious. Whatever Tristan was doing, his activities weren't spawning the sort of gossip that if it got out might harm him.

London stared at the menu, but her thoughts were far away. Finding an indirect way to take down Tristan seemed impossible.

Zoe had explained that Tristan was incredibly secretive about his finances. So much so that when her divorce lawyer had looked into his assets, it had become pretty obvious that Tristan spent far more than his annual salary from Crosby Automotive and the income he received from his investments.

"I think I'm going to have the tarte flambée," Chip said. "Or maybe the Spanish octopus."

Decisions made, London settled back and listened with half her attention as Chip filled her in on all the latest events. She let her troubling thoughts about Tristan drift to Harrison and the risky path she was following.

What had happened between them at the venue where his brother's party would be held was a perfect example of what a mistake it was to become involved with Harrison. The man held an unexpected and compelling power over her libido. She still couldn't believe she'd had an orgasm like that in a public place where at any moment they could be discovered.

Her cheeks went hot as she recalled how she'd rocked and writhed against him, greedily grabbing at the pleasure he'd offered. She'd never climaxed like that before, and recognized that some of her excitement had come from the danger of being caught with his hand up her skirt.

When London had shared what had happened with Maribelle, her friend had at first been shocked and then wildly encouraging. To say that London had stepped outside her comfort zone was a major understatement. What surprised her almost more than letting Harrison touch her like that was her lack of regret in the aftermath. She'd done something wicked and wanton and failed to hear her mother's voice rain scathing recriminations down upon her head. Maybe she was making progress.

London's phone buzzed. It was Thursday evening and Harrison had flown to Miami for the last race of the season. She was a little shocked the way her heart jumped in anticipation of hearing from him. Still, she left the phone screen down on the table.

Following that incredible encounter on Monday afternoon, Harrison had been a man of his word and accompanied her to choose flowers and pick out stationery.

In the subsequent days, even though he'd been preoccupied with pre-race preparations, he'd sent her several charming messages that made her body sing.

With each text she'd grown more and more impatient to see him again. She caught herself daydreaming about what she would do the next time she got him alone. In all-too-brief moments of clarity, London reminded herself that this behavior ran counter to her real purpose in getting to know him better. She was supposed to be focused on securing whatever information she could to take down his brother. The push and pull of regret and longing was making her question her character and decisions.

Unfortunately, it was too late to back out now.

Her phone buzzed again.

"Do you need to get that?" Chip asked.

Fighting the need to connect with Harrison was too much work and London nodded with relief. "It might be work," she said, hoping that wasn't the case.

It's hot in Miami. Thinking of you in a bikini.

Joy blasted through her, shocking in its power. Giddy with delight, she forgot that she was sitting across from one of Charleston's most fervent gossips.

Missing you.

She stared at the words she'd just sent. Despite the fact that it was true, she couldn't believe she'd opened herself up like that.

You're sure you can't join me?

She bit her lip as temptation raged within her. The corporate event she'd arranged for Saturday night could be turned over to Grace. It would be so easy to jump on a plane and be in the stands cheering him on Sunday afternoon.

Can't. How about dinner Monday? My place.

His response came at her in a flash.

Sure.

She sent a smiley face emoji and returned the phone to the table, aware she was smirking. Only then did she glance at her dinner companion and notice that he wore a bemused expression.

"That wasn't work," Chip said.

"What makes you say that?" she hedged, a flush racing over her skin.

"I've never seen you smile like that before." His eyes narrowed. "Not even when you were first engaged to Linc. You are glowing. Who is he?"

London shook her head. "What makes you think it was a he? It could've been Maribelle."

"It was Harrison Crosby, wasn't it?" Chip countered, displaying absolute confidence in his deductive reasoning. "You're interested in him. He's a catch."

"Is he?" London replied weakly. "I guess I haven't thought of him that way."

Lies, lies, all lies. She'd thought of little else these last few days. London was abruptly appalled at the person she was becoming. Nor did she have a plan to extricate herself from her pledge to take down Tristan even as her feelings for Harrison grew. More and more she was convinced that everything was going to blow up in her face and her actions would end up causing harm rather than helping Zoe.

At a table near the front window of the coffee shop across the street from London's ExcelEvent office, Everly sipped green tea and pondered her ever-deepening concern over London's relationship with Harrison. Stupid idiot. At least she'd picked the inconsequential brother to fall for. Everly would have to kill her if she'd fallen for Tristan.

Her cell buzzed, indicating an incoming call from her assistant. Annoyed with the distraction, she sent the call to voice mail. She refused to make London's mistake and lose focus. A second later her phone buzzed again. It was Nora again.

Blowing out a breath, she unclenched her teeth and answered. "What?"

"Devon Connor is here for your four o'clock meeting," Nora said, unruffled by her employer's sharp tone.

"What four o'clock meeting?"

Everly handled the branding for his numerous golf resorts up and down the coast. In the year since Kelly had been arrested, his account had become the bulk of her business.

"The one I texted and called and emailed you about yesterday and this morning. Where are you?"

Everly silently cursed. "Tell him I've been delayed."

"How long?"

A quick glance at her watch showed it was a quarter past four already. London usually left work by now.

Earlier today Everly had secured a little bit of tech that could help them all out. After deciding London was neither computer savvy enough nor equipped with the right tools to get dirt on Tristan Crosby, Everly had taken matters into her own hands.

The USB drive in her purse had come from a source connected to a friend of her sister's. In college Kelly had run with a group that hacked for fun. Everly hadn't known about it at the time or she'd have warned Kelly away from such recklessness.

The drive contained software that, when plugged into a computer and with a few commands, could bypass passwords and copy everything on the hard drive. The question remained if London was up to the challenge of gaining access to Tristan's computer.

"Reschedule him for tomorrow," Everly said, calculating how much work remained on the presentation for his newest acquisition. "Or if you can push him to next week that would be even better."

"He's not going to be happy."

"Make something up. Tell him I'm dealing with an emergency." Everly spotted London exiting her office. "I have to go."

Hanging up on her assistant, Everly exited the coffee shop and followed London, doing her best to behave like an unremarkable woman window-shopping along King Street.

London walked briskly. Obviously she had some place to be. Rushing off to another date with Harrison, no doubt. The thought made Everly grind her teeth.

Honestly, what did London think she was doing? Did the event planner imagine she and Harrison had any sort of chance? Even if London was merely engaging in a bit of fun with the handsome race-car driver, her priorities were skewed. Irritation flared that Everly needed to remind her of this fact again.

London had almost reached her car. Everly lengthened her stride until she was jogging and her timing was perfect. As London pushed the unlock button on her key fob, Everly drew within several feet of her.

"Where are you running off to in such a hurry?" Everly demanded, speaking with a more accusatory tone than she'd planned, causing London to whip around.

"What are you doing here?" Eyes wide, London glanced from side to side, scanning the area to see if they were being observed.

"Relax. Nobody's going to see us." Everly crossed her arms and regarded the younger woman with disdain. "You've been spending a lot of time with Harrison Crosby. Have you been able to get any information out of him that we can use against his brother?"

Everly suspected she already knew the answer, but asked the question anyway. From the way London's gaze shifted away, it was obvious she wasn't taking their revenge pact seriously.

"Look," London quipped, "it's not as if I can just come out and ask Harrison about Tristan's secrets."

"Of course not." Everly reached into her purse and pulled out a USB drive. "That's why I got you this."

London eyed the slim drive for a long second. "What is that?"

"It's a USB drive with a special program on it. You just need to insert it into a port on Tristan's computer, key in a few commands, and it will get you all the information you need off his hard drive."

"Where did you get it?"

"What does it matter?" Everly snapped, her irritation getting away from her. "All you need to know is that it will work."

"How am I supposed to get access to Tristan's computer?"

London was worthless. She was letting her feelings for Harrison distract her from their mission. Fortunately, Everly had thought everything through and had a plan prepared.

"There's a charity polo event coming up at Tristan's plantation," Everly explained. "Make sure you're invited. It will be the perfect opportunity for you to get the information we need."

"That sounds risky."

Everly wanted to shake the other woman. "Do you think you're the only one who's taking chances here?"

"I don't know." London's gaze hardened. "And isn't that the whole point? That we cut off all contact? With each of us handling the other's problems, no one was supposed to be able to trace anything back to us. A onetime meeting at a random event between strangers. Wasn't that the plan? Yet here you are following me from my company. Giving me some sort of technology that I'm supposed to use. What if I get caught and it gets traced back to you?"

"Don't get caught."

London made a disgusted noise. "Can this be traced back to you?"

"No. The person I got it from is very careful."

"Couldn't that person get into Tristan's files? Isn't that what they do?"

"If I wanted to hire the hacker, you'd be unnecessary. And it would be pointless for me to ruin Linc's life on your behalf." Everly neglected to mention the hacker had already tried and failed to access Tristan's laptop remotely as she shoved the USB drive at London. "Just do your part and it will all work out."

Before London could reply, Everly turned on her heel and walked away.

Leave it to a spoiled princess like London McCaffrey to ruin everything. Of course, she wasn't the only problem. Zoe's progress in taking down Ryan Dailey had stalled, as well. At least Tristan's ex-wife wasn't likely to fall for her target. Crosby had done a number on Zoe during their marriage and subsequent divorce. Chances were Zoe would never trust any man ever again. That worked for Everly. These three men were the worst of the worst and each one of them deserved every terrible thing that would happen to them.

Eight

London spent the days leading up to her dinner with Harrison pondering how she wanted the evening to go. She'd already decided to sleep with him and had prepared her bedroom with freshly washed sheets, flowers and candles for ambience. He probably wouldn't notice any of those touches, but she was an event planner. Arranging the environment to enrich the experience was second nature.

Plus, she didn't want him to catch her off guard a second time. What had happened between them at Upstairs had been amazing, but a little more spontaneous than she was used to. Tonight would be different. She knew what to expect. Could Harrison say the same? Would he realize that she was ready to take things to the next level? After getting her off in a public space, shouldn't he?

By the time he showed up at her door, a bottle of white wine in his hands, she looked poised and pulled together without any sign that she'd spent the weekend cleaning and the last two hours exfoliating head to toe, changing clothes a dozen times, reapplying her makeup twice and generally behaving in a frantic fashion.

"Wow," Harrison said, his sea-glass eyes taking in her appearance.

London had chosen a silky wrap dress in blush pink that flattered her curves and made her feel both sexy and comfortable at the same time. She'd painted her toenails a matching pink and left her shoes in her closet, showing the different side of her personality that came out in her own space.

"Thanks," she murmured. "Come on in."

"Did you know that we're neighbors?" he asked, sliding his arm around her waist and bringing her body up against his. "I live in the building next door." He bumped his nose against her neck right below her ear and breathed deeply. "Damn, you smell good."

"Really?" Her toes curled as she draped her arm over his shoulder and tipped her head to give him more access. "I mean about you living next door."

"Crazy, right?" With a sigh, he set her free and brought up the bottle between them. "You said we were having seafood."

"Scallops with risotto."

"Sounds delicious." He accompanied her to the kitchen, glancing around him as he went. "This is nice. How long have you lived here?"

Her unit faced east, with large floor-to-ceiling windows that overlooked the Cooper River. She'd fallen in love with the condo's hardwood floors and small but high-end kitchen with its white cabinets and marble countertops.

"Three years." She wondered if he'd think the space too neutral. She'd painted the walls a crisp white and paired it with a pale gray sectional, accessorizing with crystal and silver. "How long have you owned your place?"

"Almost five years."

"I'm a little surprised you have a place downtown. You strike me as someone who would prefer a big garage and a lot of outdoor space."

"I've thought about selling, but with my schedule it's easier to live somewhere that I don't have to take care of anything." He was standing at the sliding glass door, looking past her wide terrace and the dark river to the brightly lit Ravenel Bridge. Now he swung around and stepped up to the broad kitchen island. "Need any help?"

She pushed the wine and a corkscrew in his direction. He filled two glasses and brought her one by the stove.

"You cook, too," he said, sounding pleased. "You're a woman of endless talents."

"I like trying out new recipes. I used to entertain a lot, but it's been a while since..." She stopped abruptly, remembering all the dinner parties she and Linc had hosted here.

"You had anyone to cook for?"

She nodded, wishing she hadn't summoned the specter of her ex-fiancé with her careless words. "Maribelle comes over once a week to update me on her wedding plans, but she's worrying about fitting into her dress and so I tend to serve her healthy salads with boiled chicken."

"You can cook for me whenever you want," Harrison said. "Most days during racing season I'm so busy that I live on protein shakes and takeout. Sometimes the racing wives take pity on me and drop by with a home-cooked meal."

"You poor baby," she teased as her phone began to ring.

London noted the caller and winced. She'd been dodging her mother's calls for a week now. Someone had filled Edie in on the new man in her daughter's life and the four voice mails she'd left London had been peppered with her disappointment and unwelcome opinions.

"Do you need to get that?" Harrison asked.

"No."

His eyebrows rose at her hard tone. "Is something wrong?"

"She likes to put her nose where it doesn't belong."

"And where's that?" Harrison leaned his hip against her kitchen island and kept her pinned with his gaze.

"Everything about my life."

"Has she heard you and I are seeing each other?"

"I really don't want to spoil our evening with a conversation about my mother."

"I'll take that as a yes." He sounded unconcerned, but London didn't want him to get the wrong impression.

"I don't care what she thinks. It's none of her business who I see."

"But I'm not the one she'd choose for you."

"It doesn't matter who she'd choose." A defensive edge shaded her tone. "I'm the one dating you."

"I'll bet she was happy you were marrying Linc Thurston."

For what she had planned later, London needed this dinner to be perfect. That wasn't going to happen if a conversation about her mother's elitist attitude ruined the mood.

"If it's okay with you, I really don't want to talk about my mother or my failed engagement."

"I understand."

Something about his somber response warned her he wasn't satisfied with how the conversation had ended.

"I think the risotto is done," she said. "Do you mind bringing the plates over?"

They moved to the dining table and sat down. Candle-light softened Harrison's strong bone structure and gave his sea-glass eyes a mysterious quality as they talked about his race the day before and she updated him on the jazz group she'd booked for his brother's birthday party.

While they ate, London devoured him with her eyes. He was a daredevil. And a competitor. The sort of man who set his eyes on the finish line and went like hell until he got there. Which was why she'd imagined the evening progressing a different way. She'd figured the sexual tension would build during the meal, leading them to fall upon each other before the dessert course.

Instead, Harrison kept the conversation moving from one topic to another. They discussed their parents and favorite vacations growing up. She discovered he hated any drinks with bubbles and she confessed that she was a French fry junkie. It was fun and easy. Yet as they finished the white-chocolate mousse she'd made, and then worked together to fill her dishwasher, London couldn't stop her rising dismay.

Had she made a mistake when she'd assumed they would end up in bed tonight? Harrison seemed as relaxed as she was jumpy. Each brush of his arm against hers had sent her hormones spiraling higher.

Now, as the dishwasher began to hum, she turned to face him. They stared at each other for a long, silent moment. Hunger and anxiety warred within her as she waited for him to make a move. When the tension reached a bursting point, London lifted her hand to the tie that held her dress closed.

It was time to be bold with him. With a single tug, her dress came undone. Harrison remained silent, watching her as she shrugged the material off her shoulders, letting it fall to the floor.

Standing before him in a silk chemise and matching thong, she gave him a sweet smile. "I thought we might watch a movie," she said, toying with a strand of her hair. "Unless you have something else you'd rather do."

He expelled his breath in a half chuckle, one corner of his mouth kicking up. "We are going to be good together," he declared.

"I know." She twisted a handful of his warm shirt around her knuckles and tugged. "Kiss me."

He obliged, but not in the way she'd hoped. She needed him to claim her mouth and stir her soul. Instead he tormented her by drifting gentle, sweet kisses over her cheeks, eyes, nose and forehead.

"The things I want to do to you," he murmured near her ear.

Relief flooded London even as her breasts ached for his touch. "Like what?"

"Take you into the bedroom." His hand cruised up her side, thumb gliding beneath her breasts, inciting her to arch into his caress with a wordless plea.

If only he'd sweep that thumb over her nipples. Instead he shifted his palm to her back.

"And then?" she prompted, frustration apparent in her voice.

"Strip off your clothes."

Oh…hell…yes. Now they were getting somewhere.

"And…then…?"

"Lay you on the bed and spread your gorgeous legs wide open for me."

"Oh…"

His erotic words made her quake. And she suspected that what this man could do to her with his words wouldn't begin to compare to what would happen when his hands and lips met her skin.

"How does that sound?" he asked.

She nodded, excitement momentarily taking away her voice. "What else?" she asked in barely a whisper.

But he'd heard her and smiled. "I'd kiss you everywhere until you were writhing in pleasure."

"Yes, please."

"I'm going to warn you right now," Harrison said. "I'm going to talk during sex."

"What?" Heart thumping madly, London stared at him in helpless delight. "What sort of things are you likely to say?"

"I'll definitely be discussing how beautiful you are and how much you turn me on."

"Do you expect me to answer?" At this point in their relationship London wasn't sure she was ready to crack open her heart and divulge all her thoughts and feelings.

"No expectations. Just relax and listen."

"Relax?" Was he kidding? Already her muscles were tense and nerves twisted in agonized anticipation of his touch. "I feel as if I'll shatter the second you touch me."

"That's not going to happen," he assured her, easing his lips onto hers.

The contact made her sigh. With the release of her breath came a shift in her emotions. Anxiety diminished, replaced by eagerness and undulating waves of pleasure. Instinctively she knew Harrison wouldn't do something that would break her heart. In fact, he might just heal it. If only she could let him.

Except she couldn't.

A giant lie hung between them, casting a shadow over every beautiful emotion that swelled in her chest. Her subterfuge ate at her more and more each day. She longed to be with Harrison even as she recognized that one day her guilt would destroy everything good between them.

Butterflies whirled in her stomach as he grazed his palm

up her arm and brushed the strap of her chemise off her shoulder. She pushed all thoughts of the future away as the silk dipped low on her breast. The slide of the soft material tickled her skin and turned up the volume on her eagerness. A tremor shook her as his mouth skated down her neck and into the hollow of her throat. She wanted him. Wanted this. It was simple and at the same time complicated. But mostly it was inevitable.

His fingertips grazed the lace-edged neckline, sweeping the fabric downward. The material momentarily snagged on her sensitized nipple, drawing a sharp gasp from her lips before it fell away, exposing her warm skin to the cool air.

"Your breasts are perfect," he murmured, sliding his lips over their upper curves.

His words sent desire lancing straight to her core. She sank her fingers into his thick curly hair, her throat aching as she held back a cry of protest when his lips glided away from her aching breasts and returned to her shoulder.

With her free hand she slipped the other strap off her shoulder and bared both breasts. "I need your mouth on me. Please, Harrison."

Instead of doing as she'd asked, he leaned back and regarded her expression. Hunger darkened his eyes, strengthening London's desire and bolstering her confidence.

It wasn't as if she was an innocent. She'd known passion, had given herself over to lust and fast, desperate sex.

But what she felt for Harrison wasn't just physical. She genuinely liked him. Appreciated his wry sense of humor, his ability to read her moods and even his fondness for pushing past her boundaries. Deep in her soul she recognized they'd be good together. Better than good. Fantastic.

She and Linc had been together for three years, and with all the time they'd spent apart, she had rarely pictured them making love and grown so horny that she ached for release. Yet almost from the start Harrison had awakened unstoppable cravings. Cravings that on one occasion, all alone in her bed late at night, had compelled her to take matters into her own hands or go half mad.

"Are you wet for me?" He crooned the words, driving her hunger even higher.

"Yes." She gasped the word as his fingers moved between her thighs and grazed across the narrow panel of her thong, sending pleasure lancing through her. She rocked her pelvis in search of more.

"So you are," he purred, stroking her again. "Can you get even wetter?"

"Keep that up—" Her voice broke as he applied light pressure to the knot of nerves between her thighs. A blissful shudder left her panting. "And see."

He gave a husky little laugh.

"What if I bury my face between your thighs and taste you?"

Her legs had been on the verge of giving out before his offer. Now yearning battered her, making her achy and needy. But mostly it made her impatient.

"Harrison," she blurted out.

Every part of her was shaking. Her knees were threatening to buckle. But instinctively she knew he'd take care of her. She wouldn't crumple to the ground. He'd be there to lift her and carry her into pleasure unlike anything she'd ever known.

"Yes, London?"

His clever fingers slipped beneath the elastic of her panties and stroked her so perfectly she thought she might die from it. She clenched her eyes shut and struggled to draw enough breath into her lungs to tell him what she wanted.

"I don't want our first time to be here," she said, though

she was on the verge of not caring that she'd spent hours setting the stage for a perfect evening. "Take me," she gasped with what air his skillful touch hadn't stolen from her, "to the bedroom."

Harrison didn't care where their first time was as long as she was happy.

Without a word, he bent down and lifted her into his arms. She gave up a joyous laugh as she roped her arms around his neck and dropped soft kisses along his jawline while directing him down a hallway.

Her bedroom was like the rest of the condo. Cool and refined with a few decadent touches like a fuzzy throw rug, a vase of pink roses on the dresser to scent the air and a dozen flickering candles casting wavering light over the gray walls.

She'd planned this, he realized. Invited him for dinner with the purpose of sleeping with him. What a woman.

He set her on her feet inside the door and pulled her into his arms for a long, sexy kiss. Electricity jolted through him as she drove her tongue into his mouth and let him taste her desire. Rich and vibrant, the kiss promised fantasies he hadn't yet dreamed up.

Tonight was about finding out more about London. And something told him she was going to surprise him.

"I'm obsessed with your mouth," she said when he broke off the kiss and set his forehead against hers. Trembling fingers skimmed over his lips. "I can't stop thinking about all the places I want you to kiss me."

He answered her with a smile, letting his eyes speak for him. Gaze locked on his lips, she sighed.

"I've tried to fight this," she continued. "Tried to remain sensible, but just hearing your voice gets me hot."

Harrison smoothed his palms along her spine and across

her hips. He didn't want to say or do anything that would stop this confession. She made him feel things he'd never known and it was heaven to hear her echoing his own needs and desires.

"How hot?"

"My skin burns. My nipples ache. I want you to take them in your mouth and suck hard."

His groan was ragged and rough. "Keep going." The command was nearly incoherent as he set his lips against her shoulder.

She looped her arms around his shoulders and tipped her head, baring her long, white neck to his determined seduction. Taking advantage of what she offered, he lowered his lips to her skin and brought both tongue and teeth into play. Her muscles jerked as he nipped and a low moan rumbled up from her chest.

"Oh, Harrison." Her husky voice hitched, betraying how turned on she was, and despite the almost painful ache below his belt, he grinned.

He backed her toward the bed, divesting himself of shirt and shoes as he went. Hooking his fingers into her thong, he pulled the bit of silk and lace off her hips and down her thighs. She shivered as he knelt at her feet and helped her step out of the fabric.

While she scooted onto the bed, he stripped off his pants and underwear. As soon as it was free, his erection pointed straight at her. London reclined on the mattress, propping herself up on her elbows, her eyes gobbling him up.

Seeing that she had his full attention, she let her knees fall apart, opening herself to him. The sight of her so pink and wet and perfect made Harrison want to shout in jubilation. Grinning, he prowled onto the mattress.

"You are beautiful." He trailed his fingers across her

skin, lingering over her neat strip of hair that led straight to where he longed to go. "Especially here."

"Really?" She stared at herself and frowned.

"You can't appreciate it the way I can." He grazed his finger through her slick folds and her eyes popped open as a throaty cry burst from her lips. "I love how you're so sensitive."

"You bring that out in me," she murmured, her words coming in soft pants.

Grinning, he lowered his face between her legs and stroked his tongue through her heat. Her hips bucked while a sharp curse escaped her.

"Warn a girl," she gasped, pressing toward his mouth.

His breath puffed out in a chuckle. "I'm going to put my mouth on you and drive you crazy before I let you come."

"Better." She moaned as he went back for a second taste.

Her scent and sweetness made him smile as he devoured her. Each movement of his tongue caused her to moan. Her fingers dived into his hair, digging into his scalp as he drew her pulsing clit between his lips and gently sucked. She gave a half shriek before calling his name. Her hips twisted as she took her pleasure against his mouth.

"Oh, Harrison," she cried, her voice raspy and broken. "That's so good."

He gathered her butt in his palms and opened his eyes to watch her every response as he continued to ply her with lips and tongue. As in everything she did, her body moved with perfect grace. Yet her usual reserve had vanished. She was completely caught up in the moment, her hips rotating like she was dancing for him. It was so incredibly sensual that he just knew he had to push her pleasure still higher.

Harrison redoubled his effort, plying her with every trick he knew. She wouldn't know what hit her when she climaxed. But first, he had to make sure she was thoroughly familiar with the joys he could bring her.

"Harrison, it's too…" She grabbed a handful of the quilt and pulled hard enough to cause her knuckles to go white.

"Touch your breasts," he commanded, wondering if she was too far gone to hear him. "Show me how I make you feel."

To his shock, she released his hair and the quilt and gathered her beautiful breasts into her hands, kneading and rolling her nipples through her fingers, displaying an abandon he never imagined he'd see.

"Oh," she groaned. "More. More. Yes."

Her impassioned cries made him harder than he'd ever been before. But this moment wasn't for him. At least not directly. He took great satisfaction in driving her wild. Recognizing how badly she wanted to come, he slid two fingers inside her. Her head came off the bed and an incoherent noise tore from her throat.

"That's it, baby. Give me all you've got." He squeezed her butt cheeks and drove his mouth hard against her clit, grinning as her body began to shudder. "Let go."

"It's…it's…incredible," she exclaimed and then, with one long keening cry, started to come apart.

Harrison watched it all unfold. There was nothing so perfect in the whole world as London McCaffrey so aroused she became utterly lost in her pleasure, rocking and arching as she drove herself against his mouth. A powerful orgasm moved through her and he savored each wave as it battered her.

When her body grew limp, he eased his mouth off her and tracked butterfly kisses across her pelvis and over her abdomen. Her chest heaved as she labored to recover her breath. She lay with her hands plastered over her eyes as a series of incoherent noises tumbled from her lips.

"You okay?" he asked, gliding his lips up her body and noting the glorious glow her skin had taken on in the wake of her climax.

"What did you do to me?" she mumbled, sounding shaken and utterly spent.

"I'm pretty sure I gave you an orgasm." He made no attempt to hide his smugness and hoped she wasn't feeling overly sensitive about how she'd let go. It had been sexy as hell and he didn't want her to retreat from him. "A big one."

She spread her fingers and peered at him. "What am I going to do with you?"

A second later she answered her own question by dropping her hand to his erection, making him moan. "Just give that a stroke or two." His voice became a croak as she followed his instructions, demonstrating that she was eager to please him in kind. "No need to be gentle. It's not going to break."

"Like that?"

A series of provocative strokes made him groan. "That works."

He bent and kissed her deep, showing her how much he liked having her hand on him.

"This is nice," she murmured when they broke apart. "But it would be better if you'd slide on a condom and make love to me."

He didn't need to be asked twice. In seconds he'd located the foil packet and rolled on protection. She watched his actions through half-lidded eyes, lower lip trapped between her teeth. He paused a second to appreciate her tousled blond hair and passion-bruised lips. Then sliding between her thighs, he guided himself to her tight entrance, the tip dipping in, testing her acceptance. The feel of her, so open and receptive, made him want the moment to be perfect for her.

Brushing a strand of hair off her flushed cheek, he kissed her softly. "You ready?"

"Do you really have to ask?"

It took all his concentration to take it slow and let her adjust to him. What he hadn't considered was his equal need to adjust to her. Her breath shuddered out in a long, slow exhalation as he filled her. It was as if she'd liberated something she'd been holding on to for a long time.

As the long, slow thrust came to an end, she opened her eyes and met his gaze. The trust he glimpsed there made him feel like the most powerful man alive.

"Babe, you feel incredible," he murmured, making good on his promise to talk. "So tight and hot. I love the way your muscles grab me. Like you want me there."

"I do." Her palms coasted down his back and over his butt. She gripped him with surprising strength, fingers digging into his muscles, pulling him hard against her. "I love having you inside me."

"It's not too much?"

She shook her head. "I think we're a perfect fit."

"So do I."

And then there was no further need for words. It was a blend of hands, lips, tongue, breath and skin as they rocked together, discovering each other on a whole new level. To say being inside her felt good was a massive understatement. She was all heat and hunger and intensity as she wrapped her legs around his waist and clung to him.

He thrust into her, finding a steady, pounding rhythm she seemed to like. Her hips moved in time with his, matching his intensity and even taking the wildness up a notch.

"Harrison, please," she begged, inner muscles clamping down on him. "Make me come again. Now. I need you."

Harrison had never been one to disappoint a lady. He

slid his palm beneath her, lifting her off the mattress. Gripping her firmly, he went to work, watching her beautiful face for every nuance, adjusting his thrusts to bump her clit each time he plunged into her. And plunge he did. Over and over, gritting his teeth, a growl burning in his throat as he held back his own pleasure.

And then her back arched and a strained cry erupted from her lips. She drove her nails into his shoulder and summoned his name from some endless depth. Her body bucked against his, driving into his thrusts. Seconds later she was shuddering in a long series of ripples that drew him right over the edge after her.

With a final thrust, he collapsed onto his forearms, head falling to the mattress above her shoulder. She shifted so their sweaty cheeks pressed together. His chest heaved as he labored to draw breath into his lungs. It took effort for him to open his eyes. More still to lift his head. But he needed to look into her eyes to see for himself that the world-stopping sex had been just as amazing for her.

To his dismay, her eyes were closed. She was equally winded, but her features were relaxed into an expression of satisfaction.

"London?"

"That was way better than I expected." Her eyes flashed open. A possessive look blazed there for a moment before she let her lashes fall. "And I expected a lot."

He levered himself to one side, coming to rest beside her, his head propped on his hand. A strand of hair clung to her forehead. He brushed it off, delighting in the quiet moment. She lifted her hand and cupped his cheek. Her thumb grazed over his lower lip.

"Now I'm not just obsessed with your mouth," she said, sounding drowsy, "but with your dick, as well."

Harrison's jaw dropped. Had she really just said that?

Did her society friends have any idea this woman existed? He didn't think so. In fact, if he had to guess, he'd say that London hadn't realized the depth of her wantonness until recently.

"It's happy to hear that," he murmured, sliding his arms around her and pulling her firmly against his body. "And so am I."

Nine

With her left hand firmly clasped in Harrison's right, London's heart picked up speed as he angled the Mercedes onto the driveway and streaked through the Crosby Motorsports entrance gate. Above them, the company logo flanked by the four Crosby team car numbers welcomed employees and fans alike.

London had been silent through most of the thirty-minute car ride, content to listen to Harrison narrate the history of his uncle's rise to being number three on the all-time winner's cup victories list for the racing league. And number two in modern-day wins. His teams had won at least one championship-level race each season since 2000 and Jack had ten owner's championships.

Tonight they were heading to an end-of-the-season party for the six hundred employees who'd assisted Crosby Motorsports in achieving its third-place cup finish. It was London's first official appearance as Harrison's girlfriend and all day she'd been queasy as she grappled with the potential repercussions of how far she'd let things go.

The flash drive Everly had given her was a psychological burden bearing down on her heart. Each day she didn't use it was another day she hadn't betrayed Harrison. The woman who'd agreed to take revenge on Tristan was someone she no longer identified with. And what did she really owe Everly and Zoe?

Fifteen buildings made up the four-hundred-thousand-square-foot state-of-the-art facility that supported four full-time Ford teams. Walking hand in hand, London and Harrison neared the company's heritage center. The site of the original race shop when the company was founded in 1990, the building housed Jack Crosby's extensive car collection.

The flow of guests swept them into the building and past several exhibits, which Harrison explained were popular fan destinations. Freestanding bars had been placed in strategic locations so the guests could get a drink ahead of the dinner being served in a giant tent erected outside.

"Some night I'll bring you back here and give you a proper tour," he promised as they strolled hand in hand past rare cars.

"What's wrong with now?" she asked him.

"I misspoke. I meant an improper tour. Have you ever wanted to make out in the back of a rare 1969 Chevy Camaro?" He hooked a thumb at the bright orange car beside them.

She shot him a droll look even as her cheeks heated. "Do I seem the sort of girl who'd ever have that sort of fantasy?"

Even as she spoke, however, the place between her thighs tingled. She imagined herself grinding on him in one of these vehicles, steaming up the windows and watching his face as he came. What was he doing to her? London shivered in pleasure while his fingers pulsed against hers as if he'd read her mind.

"I suspect you've already done things with me you never imagined."

He wasn't wrong and she gave a little shrug. Before she could figure out what to say, however, a young man approached them asking if Harrison would come meet his grandmother. She was a huge fan and hampered by arthritic knees.

"Go ahead," London said. "I'm going to find the ladies' room."

"Meet you back here?" He glanced toward the Camaro. "You can consider my offer while I'm gone."

"I'll be waiting," she replied.

Ten minutes later she returned to the spot to await Harrison, unsurprised that he hadn't made it back. From what she'd seen of him at the track and when they'd encountered his fans out and about, he was always happy to sign autographs and take photos.

The blend of adrenaline junkie, focused athlete and all-around good guy had slipped through London's defenses. His daring and honed reflexes were remarkably sexy, yet the fact that every second behind the wheel could result in disaster somehow made Harrison relaxed and calm.

His composure was a complete contrast to the emotional minefield London found herself in. Happiness. Guilt. Responsibility. Selfishness. She wanted to bask in the joy of her growing connection with Harrison, but worry and obligation tormented her. Allowing herself to blissfully date Harrison while Zoe waited in limbo for Tristan to suffer couldn't last much longer. Time was nearly up. She had to act even if that meant she would be compelled to end things with Harrison.

As if summoned by her thoughts, Tristan appeared in her

line of sight. He strolled through the swarm of people as if he was the most important person in the room. He didn't radiate confidence as much as blare it. Several women and some men followed his progress and London couldn't blame them. The perfection of his strong, chiseled features, styled hair and powerful build made it hard to remain immune.

In his elegant charcoal suit, he looked broader-shouldered than Harrison, although she suspected his bulk wasn't all muscle. London knew firsthand the strength in Harrison's lean body. He was honed and sculpted by hours of mental and physical training.

Tristan looked less like a hungry cheetah and more like a sated lion. Either way he was dangerous. Which was why she felt that she'd been punched in the solar plexus when he caught her staring at him. Almost immediately he shifted direction and made a beeline for her. Cursing her lack of subtlety, she slapped a pleasant expression on her face as he neared.

"We meet again," Tristan said as he entered her space, eyeing her with an interest he hadn't shown during their first encounter. He held out his hand. "London, isn't it?"

"Yes." She gave him her hand and resisted the urge to yank it away as his fingers slid over hers in a way that was overly familiar. "I'm surprised you remembered me. We met so briefly at your aunt's charity function."

"You're a stunning woman." There was no mistaking the sensual glow in his eyes. "I remember thinking I'd like to get to know you better."

She doubted that. He'd barely given her the time of day before moving on to a woman with an impressive cleavage. So why the sudden interest now?

Confusion reigned as she forced a polite smile. "I'm flattered."

"You don't look as if you belong here any more than I

do," Tristan said, echoing what would've been London's opinion a few short weeks earlier.

She glanced away from him and surveyed the party guests, noting the difference from the charity event where she'd first met Harrison and his brother. That evening the women had been dressed in expensive gowns and dripping with jewels. They'd navigated the room dispensing sugary phrases in droll tones.

Tonight's assembly wore jeans, team apparel and the occasional blazer or party dress. London recognized that she stood out in the leopard pumps she'd borrowed from Maribelle and her classic little black dress. As when she'd gone to the racetrack in Richmond, her styling choices highlighted that she didn't have much in common with these unpretentious people. No wonder Tristan had approached her. He wore a gorgeous custom suit in dark gray more appropriate to the yacht club than a tent.

"I have to admit this isn't exactly my regular crowd," London said, hating the way that sounded even though it was true. "I take it you don't have much to do with Crosby Motorsports?"

"Hardly." Tristan glanced around before leaning down as if to share a confidence with her. "My brother is the one who likes to get his hands dirty." His sneer made his contempt for Harrison clear and the contrast between the brothers grew starker. "The fact that he races cars has made him an embarrassment to our family."

London wondered if Tristan had any idea she and Harrison had been seeing each other. "He's quite successful at it."

"Successful…" Once again his gaze moved over her, this time lingering at her neckline. "Don't tell me you're one of those racing groupies. You appear to have a little too much class for that."

The man's prejudice was so blatant that London found

herself momentarily speechless. And as she grappled with a response, it occurred to her that she'd been equally snobbish in the beginning, before she'd gotten to know Harrison. Shame brought heat to her cheeks.

"Feel like getting out of here?" Tristan's fingers curved over her hip, lingering for a few seconds as if to test her reaction. When shock kept her from pulling away, he must've taken that as encouragement because his palm slid over her backside and he gave her butt a suggestive squeeze. "My house is twenty minutes away."

London thought about the flash drive she'd taken to carrying in her purse. What excuse could she give Harrison that would let her slip away with Tristan and get the information off his computer? Her mind spun as she conceived and discarded a dozen justifications for leaving the party with Tristan. None of them made any sense.

"I—"

She never got to finish her refusal because Harrison emerged from the crowd and spied her standing with his brother. His brows came together in a frown that was half annoyance and half confusion as he noticed where Tristan's hand had gone. With an inaudible gasp, London stepped away from Tristan and tried to catch Harrison's gaze as he approached them, but his attention was firmly fixed on his brother.

"What are you doing here?" Harrison demanded, his expression and tone unfriendly.

"I am the head of Crosby Automotive."

"That doesn't answer my question."

"This is a family business," Tristan pointed out.

"And you've made it pretty clear you want nothing to do with us." Harrison's eyes narrowed. "Or at least that's been your attitude before your profits started to dip. What? Are you hoping to convince Jack to help you out financially?"

Tristan's expression darkened. He obviously didn't appreciate his younger brother pointing out his shortcomings.

"I don't need his help or yours," Tristan said. "And this little shindig of yours is a complete bore. I've got better things to do." With an elaborate sigh, he glanced at London and gestured toward the door. "Shall we?"

Harrison turned stunned eyes her way and London opened her mouth to explain, but her scrambled brain produced no words. Why hadn't she come straight out and told Tristan she was dating Harrison? Scheming was not her forte.

"She's not going anywhere with you," Harrison said.

"Why don't you let the lady decide?"

"Ah, actually I came here with Harrison," London said, cringing as she realized it was too little, too late.

She now understood that balancing her growing affection for Harrison against taking down his brother wasn't possible. It was either one or the other and the moment for her to choose was now.

"You two are dating?" Tristan asked, laughter in his voice.

"Well…" she hedged.

Harrison suffered none of her hesitation. "Yes."

While Tristan laughed at their diverging answers, London stared at Harrison. She found herself short of breath as their gazes clashed. In his sea-glass eyes she saw her future. The beauty of it struck her and suddenly she wanted to cry. She'd ruined everything.

"Sounds like you two need to sort out what's going on." Tristan squeezed London's arm. "If you get tired of slumming, give me a call."

She remained silent, biting the inside of her lip as Harrison's brother walked away. Words gathered in her throat but a lump prevented them from escaping. On the heels of the realization that she'd let the encounter with Tristan get away from her came the recognition that by falling for Harrison, she'd put her emotions in direct conflict with her promise to help Zoe.

"I thought we were on the same page," Harrison said. "If we're not dating, then what are we doing?"

"I don't know." As much as she wanted to escape his questions, he deserved honesty and openness. "This wasn't supposed to get complicated."

He frowned. "Because I'm not the man you think you want?"

"What?"

She was starting to believe he was the only man for her. And she'd made a mess of things.

His eyes flicked in the direction his brother had departed. "Are you thinking he could make you happy? Because he is incapable of putting anyone's feelings above his own."

"I'm not interested in your brother." At least not in the way Harrison was insinuating. How could she defuse this argument without committing herself one way or another? "In fact, I was in the process of defending you when he hit on me. You interrupted us before I could react."

Harrison assessed her for a long moment and whatever he glimpsed in her expression caused him to relax. "I don't need you to defend me."

"I know." Yet she could see he appreciated it. She took his hand in both of hers and stepped into his space, waiting until the tension seeped from his body before she finished. "But there was no way I was going to stand by and let him criticize what you do."

"It seems to me that you felt the same a couple weeks ago." He snaked his arm around her waist and pulled her tight against him.

"All the more reason for me to have your back. I was ignorant and shortsighted. You're doing what you love and no one has the right to judge you for it. Not even your brother."

"Fine. I forgive you," he said, cupping her cheek while his lips dropped to hers.

His kiss was romantic and intoxicating. She threw herself into the embrace, shoving her worries aside for the moment. Later she would delve into the ever-deepening mess she was making of things.

How long they stood in the middle of the crowded party, lost in each other, London had no idea. But when Harrison eventually set her free, London returned to her body with a jolt.

What magic drove all thoughts of propriety and decorum from her mind whenever he took her in his arms? She'd never acted like this before and loved every second of it.

By contrast, her relationship with Linc had always been so proper. She'd certainly never thrown her arms around his neck and kissed him with utter abandon in a public place. She'd always been hyperaware of how things looked and who might be watching. With Harrison, even though he was also a celebrity, she never considered appearances before showing affection with him.

"I'm sorry," she murmured when he ended the kiss.

"For what?"

So many things. "The way I feel when I'm with you is thrilling and scary all at once and way more intense than anything I've known before."

He kissed her forehead. "For me it's the exact opposite. Being with you calms me down. When we're together, it feels right."

Tears burned London's eyes. The man was just too perfect and she didn't deserve the happiness he brought her. Dabbing at the corner of her eye in what she hoped was a surreptitious manner, London took his hand in hers and exhaled heartily.

"You always say the right thing," she told him, wishing he'd demonstrate some of his brother's villainy. It would make using him to her advantage easier to swallow.

"Ready to go find our table?"

"Lead the way."

"This is quite a place," London remarked, taking in the state-of-the-art barn, paddocks, polo field and sprawling home with views that overlooked the horse pastures all belonging to Harrison's brother.

She'd started scoping out the house as soon as it had come into view, needing to find a way in so she could use the USB drive in her purse. The task terrified her. What if she was caught? Or the drive didn't work? Or the information they needed wasn't on his computer? So much could go wrong.

As Everly promised, Harrison had invited her to the charity polo event hosted at Tristan's property outside Charleston. She'd attended functions like this often with Linc. He'd loved giving back to the community. In fact, this particular charity was a pet project of his.

No doubt she could look forward to running into her ex. Would he be surprised that she was here with Harrison? Given what she'd heard about his relationship with his housekeeper, would he even care?

"I can't imagine how much it costs to maintain all this," she continued, anxiety making her remarks clumsy. "And he has a house in the historic district, as well? Crosby Automotive must be doing really well."

Harrison gave her an odd look.

Was she being too obvious in her interest again? "It's quite a bit of real estate," she added nervously.

"I guess. I've never really thought about it."

"And all these horses, it must cost a fortune to maintain them."

"Look, you really suck at beating around the bush," Harrison said, his tone slightly aggrieved. "Is there something you want to ask?"

"I'm being nosy, but I heard that his ex-wife ended up with next to nothing in the divorce settlement because Tristan wasn't doing all that well financially."

Harrison shrugged. "That might be what she's telling people. But what she got in the divorce might have more to do with something that triggered certain clauses in her prenuptial agreement."

"Oh."

London already knew what Harrison was referring to. Zoe had been accused of infidelity, a charge Tristan trumped up. There had been photos and hotel room charges. She'd disputed the accusation and proved her innocence, but the fight had racked up legal fees, eating up her small settlement. Meanwhile Tristan had cheated on her to his heart's content with no repercussions.

"You don't believe that?" Harrison asked, his ability to read her proving troublesome once again.

"I guess that makes sense."

All too aware she'd really put her foot in it, London cast around for a distraction and spied Everly in the crowd. Every encounter with the woman had driven London's anxiety higher and she tensed. Beside her, ever sensitive to her reactions, Harrison sent his palm skating up her spine in a soothing caress.

"Something wrong?" he asked, regarding her with concern in his sea-glass eyes.

What excuse could she give him? London's brain scrambled for anything that sounded reasonable but came up empty. At her lack of response, his gaze swept the crowd. Not far from Everly, Linc and his sister were strolling side by side through the crowd. He looked happy. Moving on had obviously been good for him.

In contrast, London's nerves were twisted into knots and her stomach felt as if she were on a small boat tossed by stormy seas. In the month since she and Harrison had first gone to dinner, the pain of her broken engagement had faded to a distant memory. She had Harrison to thank for that. Since that night at her condo, they'd been together almost every night. Sometimes at her place. Sometimes at his. Occasionally she wondered at her lack of interest in going out to dinner or in joining Maribelle and Beau for drinks. Having Harrison all to herself was addictive and she'd noticed herself almost constantly basking in the warm glow of contentment that he was in her life.

"Ah," Harrison said, bringing her back to the present. He'd noticed Linc and assumed that was why she was acting so strange. "Are you going to be okay?"

"Sure. Fine." London shook her head. "It's all good."

"Are you sure?"

Although he sounded concerned, his expression had gone flat. He'd obviously misinterpreted the reason for her dismay. London imagined how she'd feel if Harrison had an ex-fiancée and she was attending the same party. Not that Harrison could ever be described as insecure.

"Of course." London gave the declaration an extra punch to reassure him all was well. "It's water under the bridge."

"Is that why you're so tense?"

Damn the man for being so perceptive. London noticed her shoulders had started climbing toward her ears and made an effort to relax them. Usually only her mother had such a strong effect on her, but London had to admit Everly Briggs scared her.

"I haven't seen him since our engagement ended," London said. "It just takes a little getting used to." Pleasure suffused her at the concern in Harrison's eyes. As accustomed as she was to being strong all the time, it was a welcome change to lean on someone else. "Thank you for worrying about me."

And then, because actions spoke louder than words, she grabbed a handful of Harrison's bright blue blazer. Throwing propriety to the wind, she tugged him to her. Her high heels put her lips within kissing distance of his and Harrison obliged her by dipping his head. The kiss electrified her, sensation racing through her body with familiar and joyful results. She grew light-headed almost immediately and was glad for the strong arm he wrapped around her waist.

Thanks to him the kiss didn't spin out of control. If left up to her, London would have tugged him into a private corner and let her fingers find their way beneath his crisp white dress shirt. As it was, they were both breathing a little unsteadily when he lifted his head.

"Damn," he murmured in wonder. "You do surprise me sometimes."

"That's good, right?"

"Absolutely." He dropped a light kiss on her nose and relaxed his arm, letting her draw a deep breath. "Let's go claim some seats."

They found a spot near the center of the field and sat. Harrison hadn't relinquished her hand and London found herself having a difficult time concentrating on the match as he toyed with her fingers. It made her thoughts return to the morning and revisit how his caresses had danced over her skin until she'd begged him for release.

Her musings were interrupted by another glimpse of Everly. To London's dismay, the woman caught her eye and frowned at her. After she'd made her displeasure known, Everly glanced significantly in Linc's direction. London's ex-fiancé was chatting with several of his friends, but his attention was obviously not on the conversation. He was watching a slender brunette set up the picnic baskets for lunch.

London recognized Claire Robbins, Linc's housekeeper. All the gossip and speculation circulating about those two coalesced into reality and London felt…nothing. No regret. No jealousy. No shame. It was as if she'd gotten over Linc. Or she'd realized there wasn't anything to get over and that he'd been right to end their engagement.

Smiling, she glanced Harrison's way, but saw that his attention was on the polo match. As much as she wanted to share her epiphany with him, she kept silent. Everly's presence at the event reminded London that she had an ulterior motive for being here today.

The need to get into Tristan's house and plug the USB drive into his computer preoccupied London through the second match of the day and into the lunch break. The picnic-basket lunches for two that had been created by Claire were a delightful surprise to London. She had no idea how Linc's housekeeper had come to cater such a function or that she'd had any culinary leanings. The food was fantastic. There'd been a sandwich sampler made with beef, ham and salmon. The basket also contained an artisanal meat-and-cheese tray with a fabulous kale salad, fresh fruit, a bottle of Txakoli, and homemade aguas frescas made from melons, strawberry and mango.

London did little more than sample everything, but the sheer volume of food left her feeling thoroughly stuffed and a bit sleepy.

"That was amazing," she murmured, settling back in her chair with a groan.

"There's still dessert." Harrison gestured toward the food tent and the tables filled with trays of triple-layer chocolate cake, mini cheesecakes, tiny tortes, mousse and chocolate-covered strawberries.

"I couldn't possibly," London said, deciding this might be the opening she'd been looking for. "You go ahead. I'm going to take a quick walk and find a ladies' room."

With all the people milling around, it was surprisingly easy to gain entrance into Tristan's home. She was almost disappointed that the doors weren't locked because then she'd have a perfect excuse to turn around. What if someone caught her sneaking in? London lifted her chin and settled her nerves with a calming breath. The best thing to do would be to get it over with as quickly as possible.

It took her less than five minutes to locate Tristan's study. Heart pounding, London moved into the room and eased the door shut behind her. If she was caught in here, she had no explanation for sitting at his desk and perusing his laptop computer. This was madness. Was any of this worth the damage to her relationship with Harrison?

The question shocked London to her toes and made her chest ache. She craved more time with Harrison. More hours of conversation. More minutes holding his hand. More mornings sharing breakfast with him. More nights making love. More weeks to let their intimate connection grow and flourish. More years to build a life with him.

All of it was a foolish fantasy. There was no future with Harrison. The fact that she was standing in his brother's study on the verge of stealing the contents of Tristan's computer established where she'd placed her loyalty.

Fighting a sudden rush of helplessness, London pressed her back against the wall, letting her gaze roam the space. It was a typical masculine study with two of the walls lined in dark paneling, the others sporting hunting scenes and bookshelves. Heavy hunter green drapes framed the single window. An expensive Oriental rug stretched from her toes to a large, ornately carved wooden desk.

Move.

The longer she stayed in place, questioning her judgment, the more likely she was to get caught. Barely discernible above the thundering of her heart came the cheers from the crowd watching the polo match outside. She didn't have a lot of time. If she was gone too long, Harrison would start to wonder what was keeping her.

Tiptoeing across the rug to Tristan's desk seemed a bit ridiculous, but since London was breaking into the man's computer, she might as well act like a thief. Her hands shook as she rounded the enormous mahogany desk and approached his computer. She opened the laptop and the screen came to life. Unsurprisingly, the desktop displayed an image of Tristan on one of his polo ponies, looking suave and ruggedly masculine as he stared down the photographer.

Shivering with foreboding, London quickly found where to plug in the drive but hesitated before inserting it into the slot. Her heart raced, keeping pace with the rumble of hoof beats on the polo grounds. If she was going to do this, it needed to be now. Yet she continued to flounder.

And then the sound of approaching voices reached her: a woman's high-pitched laughter followed by a man's deep baritone. London jerked away from the computer, bumping into the desk chair and sending it thumping back against the wall. The noise seemed to explode in the quiet room and she glanced around wildly, looking for a place to hide before the couple entered. The long drapes caught her eye. In seconds she slipped behind the voluminous fabric, hoping she was out of sight.

Pulse jumping erratically, she waited. And waited. Expecting the door to open at any second, she tried to calm her rapid breathing but alarm had her firmly in its grasp. Had it been Tristan in the hallway? London recalled their encounter at the Crosby Motorsports end-of-season party. No doubt he had a string of women he entertained. The man's insatiable appetites weren't just gossip. He'd cheated on Zoe almost from the beginning of their marriage.

London wasn't sure how much time she spent behind the curtain before she realized no one was coming into the study. She eased out and glanced at the desk before making her way to the door. After straining to hear if anyone occupied the hall, she gathered a bracing breath and opened the door a crack. There was no one around, so she slipped out of Tristan's study and made her way back outside. Not until she reached sunlight and fresh air did she take a full breath. A second later the air whooshed out of her lungs in a squeak as someone spoke.

"Did you do it?"

London whirled around and spied Everly standing beside the side door. Her eyes gleamed with feral intensity.

"I couldn't."

"The program didn't work?"

London gripped the flash drive tighter. Would she have gone through with it if not for the near interruption? It was a question she'd be asking herself for a long time. How far was she planning to go to hurt someone she didn't know just to take revenge on Linc for ending their engagement? Especially when she no longer felt hurt and betrayed.

When she, Everly and Zoe had first concocted the plan, London had been reeling from the shock and hurt, and was feeling vengeful. But since Harrison had come along, she'd realized that Linc wasn't the only man in the world for her. Maybe he never was.

"I didn't try it," London admitted.

"Why not?"

"I'm not sure we're doing the right thing."

"Why? Because you're dating Harrison? Suddenly it's okay for you to back out on our agreement because you're happy? Is that fair to Zoe? She's living in the back room of the boutique she opened and can't pay her rent because the divorce lawyer got all her savings."

Because they weren't supposed to be in contact with each other, London hadn't had any idea Zoe's situation was so dire. "I'll give her some money to get by."

Everly ejected an exasperated snort. "You can't help her like that. The point of what we're doing is to not have any contact with each other."

"And yet you're here talking to me," London pointed out, glancing around and seeing that they were completely alone. "And apparently you've been keeping tabs on Zoe to know her current situation."

"I'm doing my part," Everly said, not responding to London's accusation. "If you don't do yours, then Zoe has no reason to go after Ryan. That man destroyed my sister and I intend to make him pay."

"I don't know," London hedged, unnerved by Everly's savagery. "This is all just so much more than I signed on for."

"Listen up," Everly said, leaning close, her manner intimidating. "We made a deal and you're going to see it through."

"Deals can be broken."

Abruptly, Everly's demeanor changed and she became cool and collected once again. "I wondered if this might happen with you. This is one deal you're not going to break."

"What are you going to do to stop me?" London asked, sounding more confident than she felt.

Everly's quicksilver mood change intensified London's concerns. What sort of unbalanced person had she gotten mixed up with?

"I've set things in motion that are going to ruin Linc's life. That was what I promised I would do. You need to do your part. You owe me and you owe Zoe."

"I'm out." London started to slide past Everly. To her surprise, the other woman grabbed her arm in a tight vise. "Let me go."

"If you don't go through with this, I will reveal to Harrison what you've been up to."

Panic flooded her and London scrambled for what to say to defuse the situation. The only way she knew to limit Everly's blackmail potential was to deny her feelings for Harrison.

"You'll only blow up this whole scheme if you do. I've used Harrison to get to Tristan. He means nothing to me except as a means to an end. If you tell him what I've been up to, we all go down."

That said, she yanked her arm from Everly's grasp, feeling the rake of the woman's nails against her skin as she pulled free. It wasn't in London to shove the woman before escaping, but if anyone deserved to be knocked around in that moment, it was Everly.

London walked away as swiftly as she dared, conscious that she'd already been away from Harrison for too long. Heat surged beneath her skin as her heart and lungs pumped adrenaline through her whole body. She couldn't go back to Harrison in this emotionally heightened state. He would want to know what was wrong. What could she tell him?

And then her gaze fell on a small group and the one individual who was utterly familiar to her. Lincoln faced Claire Robbins, and from her devastated expression and the anguish on his face, London realized whatever Everly had set in motion between Linc and the woman he loved had just come to a head.

Grief and rage hit her already raw nerves and London sped away from the crowds as her stomach pitched sickeningly. What had they done? What had she done? Linc didn't deserve to have his life ruined because he'd broken off their engagement. He'd been right that they didn't belong together. Only she'd been too busy wallowing in what she'd perceived as her failure to see it.

Tears blinded her as bile filled her mouth and anguish twisted her heart. She was well and truly stuck now that Everly had exacted London's revenge on Linc. Her chance to escape the situation long gone.

London made her way toward the refreshment tent where the lunches had been available earlier. She needed some water and a quiet moment to herself. What a fool she'd been to make such a terrible pact. Her fingers tightened over the flash drive. The moment to use it was gone. And London was relieved.

Everly's threat filled her mind. London had no doubt that Everly would tell Harrison what was going on even if it meant ruining everything for all of them. The woman was crazy. Or maybe it was London who'd lost it. She was still trying to figure out how she could get the incriminating information on Tristan and not let her actions destroy what she was building with Harrison. Talk about being stuck between a rock and a hard place.

Harrison had finished a full plate of desserts without London reappearing and wondered where she'd gotten herself off to.

The day had started out cloudless and warm for late November. Harrison's optimism had been sky-high. He'd

considered their first appearance in Charleston society as
a couple to be a statement about their relationship.

It had been.

Just not in the way he'd expected.

Ever since London had spied Linc Thurston, Harrison
had noticed a nagging disquiet. No, that wasn't quite true.
He'd been troubled since the first night he and London had
slept together after she admitted her mother didn't believe
Harrison was the sort of man London should date.

Normally he didn't care about anyone's opinions, but the
closer he and London grew, the more he wondered when
her mother would put pressure on her to find someone more
suitable. Harrison had no idea if she'd fight for them or cave
to her mother's will and that bothered him a lot.

Harrison had assumed he'd come to know London quite
well during the last couple of weeks. And he believed he'd
seen a change in her. Where she'd been reserved and even
a bit prickly toward him at first, once he'd gotten to know
the woman beneath the impeccable designer suits, he'd
found complicated layers of ambition, passion and vulnerability that intrigued him but also made him leery of
moving too fast.

Her walls went up and came down in ever-fluctuating re-
sponses to ways he behaved and how deeply he plumbed her
emotions. Yet now as he wondered about London's views
on the future of their relationship, Harrison accepted he
couldn't walk away from what they'd begun. He wasn't a
quitter. And she was a woman worth fighting for.

"There you are." London's overly bright smile couldn't
hide the shadows darkening her gold-flecked blue eyes.
"I've been looking all over for you."

"I'm glad you found me."

Harrison put out his hand and smiled as London slipped
hers into it. Ten days earlier she would've resisted doing

something this simple and profoundly intimate. Her level of comfort with him had come a long way in a short period of time. Yet he couldn't shake the feeling that things were ever on the verge of swinging back.

"Did you have fun?" he asked.

"I did. Makes me want to take up polo."

"Really?" He'd like to see her barreling down the field, mallet swinging. "Do you ride?"

"I used to when I was younger. My dad taught me. He loves to hunt." A girlish smile curved her lips. "You know, ride to the hounds."

"They still do that?"

"Tuesdays, Thursdays and Sundays during season."

Harrison shook his head in bemusement. "Who knew?"

"Can we get out of here?" she asked, catching him by surprise. "I want to be alone with you."

"Nothing would make me happier."

But a nagging thought in the back of his mind left him questioning whether she was eager to be with him or just looking to escape an event where her ex was with someone else.

It didn't help that she seemed unusually preoccupied during the return trip to Charleston.

"Anything in particular you want to do?" he asked, breaking the silence as the car rolled along King Street. "It's not too early to grab a drink."

"Sure. Where do you want to go?"

"The Gin Joint or Proof?"

"The Gin Joint, I think."

Fifteen minutes later they'd settled into one of the booths in the cozy bar and ordered two quintessential Gin Joint drinks. The bar prided itself on its craft cocktails, seasonally updated, with clever names like Gutter Sparrow, Whiplash, Whirly Bird and Lucky Luciano.

"Delicious," London commented after taking a sip of her Continental Army cocktail, featuring apple brandy, caraway orgeat, lime, Seville orange, falernum, sugar and muddled apple. "The perfect fall drink."

Silence fell between them as they sipped their cocktails and contemplated the snack menu. Harrison debated whether to bring up the topic of her ex and the issues bothering him.

"I'm just going to come out and ask," he said abruptly, causing London to look up from the menu in surprise. "Today after you saw Linc, you seemed distracted and upset."

Her eyes widened. "I wasn't."

She was a terrible liar, but he decided against pressing her. Instead, he turned to another burning question.

"Have you spoken with your mother about us?" Harrison winced at his blunt delivery. "I'm asking because I see a future for us." And he wanted to know what stood in the way.

"You do?" If it was possible, she looked even more stunned.

"I think about you all the time when we're not together and that's never happened to me before."

"But we barely know each other."

Concern lashed at him. Were they on the same page or not?

"I'm not saying I want to get married tomorrow, but I can't see an end to this thing between us and that's saying a lot." He leaned forward and fixed his eyes on her. "I need to know if you feel the same way."

"I…don't…know. That is…" She redirected her focus to the tabletop and an agonized expression passed over her features. "I do like you. A lot. But I haven't given any thought to the future."

Harrison sat back, unsatisfied by her answer. While he

had to give her props for being honest, it wasn't the ring-ing endorsement of their connection he'd been hoping for.

"Then you'd be the first woman I've dated who hadn't," he said, fighting annoyance that he'd opened up while she remained guarded. "Is it because of what I do?"

"You mean racing? No." When he snorted in disbelief, she reached both her hands across the table and laid them over his. "My engagement ended a couple months ago after I'd been with Linc for three years. I was just starting to fig-ure out who I am when you came into my life."

"I think that's crap. You know exactly who you are. The question is whether or not that woman can see herself with a guy like me. I'm not someone your mother would approve of. I don't have any interest in making the rounds of Charleston society. Our daughter would never attend a single debutante event. But I can promise I wouldn't ever make you regret a single day of our life together."

"Harrison…" She blinked rapidly and heaved a sigh.

"You have to decide what's truly important to you."

"You make me sounds like such a snob," she murmured, her high color betraying her inner turmoil. "I know what people say about me. That I wasn't in love with Linc. And that's probably true. There's a good reason why we were engaged for two years without ever setting a wedding date. But then there's the part where I think he was cheating on me." London's voice shook as she finished, "What if I don't have what it takes to keep a man interested long-term?"

Her words flattened Harrison against the booth seat. Was that what was bothering her? That she believed her-self undesirable? How was that possible when he'd shown her over and over how much he wanted her?

"You have what it takes to keep the right man interested long-term. You chose the wrong guy last time. Have faith in what you want and who you are." He turned his hands over so that their palms rested against each other. It wrenched his heart that she couldn't bring herself to meet his gaze. "You have what it takes to keep me interested forever."

Her breath caught. "You shouldn't say things like that."

"Why not? You don't think I'm being truthful?"

"I think you have a lot to learn about me and what you discover might change your mind."

He couldn't imagine what she was talking about and had no idea how to coax her out of this sudden funk she'd fallen into. "I guess that could be said of me, as well. All I'm asking is for you to be open to exploring who we could be to each other."

"I can do that." She gave his hands a brief hard squeeze and let go. After a large swallow of her cocktail, she fastened a bright smile on her face and said, "How about you and I go back to my place and do some of that exploring you were talking about."

Grinning, Harrison threw a hundred on the table and got to his feet, holding out his hand. "Let's go."

Harrison didn't know what to expect when they got to her condo. London had sent him smoking-hot glances the entire drive. Now the door was barely shut before she backed him toward the foyer wall and then gave a shove that sent the breath whooshing from his lungs. A second later she pressed her body against his, gripping his hair in a painful grasp while crushing her lips to his. She kissed him hard and rough, making his world go black and hot. Blood rushed through his veins, pounding in his ears as she ambushed his senses with teeth and tongue and ragged breath.

He was helpless to process the astonishing hunger that gripped her. All he could do was surrender to her feasting and let her set him on fire.

Sinking his fingers into her silky hair, he savored the soft texture while his other hand slid down her back and slipped over the curve of her butt, lifting her against his growing erection. The move caused her to shudder and suck his lower lip between her teeth. A searing nip, followed by the soothing flick of her tongue, made him groan.

"I'm going to make you come like you never have," she whispered in his ear while her fingers raked down his torso until they encountered his belt.

He was a fan of dirty talk, and her words slammed into him, sending blood rushing to his groin. He'd never expected to hear London speak so boldly or to want to be in charge. It turned him on.

"I look forward to it," he said, throwing her over his shoulder and heading to the bedroom so they could get the party started.

She squawked at the undignified carry, and from the expression on her face as he set her on her feet beside the bed, she intended to make him pay. Harrison stripped off his jacket and tie, and then went to work on his shirt buttons. He couldn't wait for her to do her worst.

By the time he'd kicked off his shoes, her clothes were in a neat pile on the dresser and she was naked. Hands on hips, she watched him drop his pants to the floor and step out of them. When her gaze dropped to the erection straining his boxer briefs, a little smile formed on her lips.

Harrison frowned as he tried to make out the significance of her expression. If he'd believed he had London all figured out, he'd been wrong. This was a new side of her. The woman who took charge when it came to her work was obviously capable of stepping up in the bedroom, as well. He found himself impatient to see what came next.

She stalked toward him and grabbed a handful of his boxers, tugging the cotton material over his jutting erection and down his thighs. He hissed as the cool air caressed his heated flesh, but the chill was short-lived as her fingers closed around him. The tight grip and firm stroke that followed felt out-of-this-world fantastic.

"On the bed, so I can get these the rest of the way off you."

"Yes, ma'am."

He did as she asked, admiring the way her breasts swayed as she stripped him bare. Like some sort of wild thing, she peered at him from between the glossy strands of hair that hung across her face as she tossed his briefs aside. Straightening, she put her hands on her hips, surveying him with a wicked half smile.

"Ready?" she asked, not waiting for his nod before bending over the bed.

"Drive me crazy with your delightful tongue," he growled, his voice a guttural rasp.

One corner of her lips kicked up in a smirk. She scraped her fingernails up his thighs and his mouth went dry. She obviously wanted to steer the ship and he was dying to see what happened next. Fortunately, he didn't have long to wait.

Lust blasted through him as her lips dropped toward the head of his erection, but instead of taking him into her mouth, she hovered millimeters above. The anticipation was almost too painful and it struck home that she intended to take her time with him.

A low curse passed his lips as she flicked her tongue out and swirled it over him. Harrison's hips came off the mattress as she followed that with a long stroke down his shaft and then back up. Placing her hands on his knees, she pushed them wider before crawling forward to set up between his thighs.

For a second his breath lodged in his throat as she gently cupped his balls and then her mouth swooped down again, sucking him into a hot, wet tunnel that made him groan and shudder. She swirled her tongue around his erection and pleasure detonated through him.

Speaking…was impossible.

Thinking… Incoherent chants filled his mind.

He was tumbling, falling into an upside-down world where his desire and pleasure were less important than the sheer bliss of catching her gaze and realizing she was enjoying watching his reaction.

Although he longed to close his eyes so he could better focus on the sensations pounding through him, the picture of her hair splayed over his stomach and thighs, her lips locked around him, was a sight to behold.

Her blue eyes sparkled as she glanced up at him. She was filled with naughty surprises. Tremors rolled through his body as he realized she was enjoying this as much as he was. He curved his fingers around her head as his stomach muscles tightened. Skin on fire, he fought to hold on, to make the moment last. But the flames licked him, spreading through his veins, consuming him. Her tongue swirled around his erection and the first shock wave washed over him. Then another. Her mouth felt so damned good.

"Coming." A curse ripped through his mind. "Coming hard."

And then a climax barreled through his body, crashing wildly into bone and muscle and nerves. The unleashed power of it obliterated words and stopped his heart. For several seconds he rocketed through supercharged joy while aftershocks jolted him.

He wasn't even aware that she'd released him until her lips trailed over his chest and slid into the hollow of his throat where his pulse slammed against his skin.

"Amazing." His voice cracked on the one word.

Enough strength had returned to his muscles to allow

him to gather her naked body against his. He drifted kisses along her hairline as he slowly recovered.

"Damn, woman," he murmured, cupping her cheek in his palm and bringing their lips together. He kept the kiss light and romantic, showing his appreciation. "You're good as your word. I think I blacked out for a second."

"You're easy," she told him. "You seem to enjoy everything."

He lifted his head off the pillow and regarded her in bemusement. "If by 'everything' you mean your gorgeous mouth on me, then you have that right. You make me come like I never have before," he told her, echoing her earlier promise. "It's different with you."

She looked shell-shocked, and even as he watched, she began withdrawing behind her emotional walls. "You don't need to say that…"

"Do I strike you as someone who says things he doesn't mean?"

"No."

"Then believe me when I tell you I'm in over my head here. I don't know what you do to me, but I like it."

"You do things to me, too," she replied, her long lashes concealing her eyes. "And I like it."

As she spoke, she stretched her lean body, making him keenly aware of her silky skin, renewing his desire. Harrison rolled her beneath him and tangled their legs, his lips finding that spot on her neck that made her shiver.

"Good to hear," he murmured, "because I'm going to spend the rest of the night doing all sorts of things to you. And I think we'll both like that."

It was nearly two in the morning and Everly sat in her car outside a twenty-four-hour drugstore, tearing apart the packaging to get to the prepaid cell phone she'd just purchased. It was important that the call she was about to make couldn't be tracked back to her.

She'd been thinking about this step for two days, weighing the options and debating if such a radical move would be beneficial to their plans. In the end, she'd decided that London needed to be punished. Her failure to use the flash drive to pull the information off Tristan's computer proved that not only her priorities had shifted but also her loyalty.

How was Zoe supposed to get her revenge if London didn't do her part? More important, what was the motivation for Zoe to take down Ryan if nothing bad happened to Tristan? And Everly really needed Zoe to enact some truly devastating vengeance on Ryan for what he'd done to Kelly.

Everly had kept to her part of the bargain. Satisfaction lay curled like a sleeping house cat in her chest. She was nearly purring with pleasure at the damage she'd caused.

In the midst of the charity polo event, she'd ruined Linc Thurston's life by showing him the truth about his housekeeper, ending their ridiculous romance.

No doubt by now, with Claire's past catching up to her in a big way, exposing all her lies and deceptions, Linc was feeling devastated and more than a little stupid that he'd been taken in so easily by an obvious opportunist.

In some way, Everly had actually done him a favor. Not that he'd thank her if he knew she'd been the one who'd contacted Claire's family and let them know where she was.

The look on Linc's face when he'd realized that Claire had lied to him about everything had given Everly such a thrill. She'd planned and executed a flawless plan and the results had been better than she could have imagined.

But not everyone had the strength of will to follow through. That had become crystal clear with the way London had chosen her romance with Harrison over loyalty to the plan. And now she would pay.

Everly keyed the play button on her phone and London's voice rang out with clear conviction.

I've used Harrison to get to Tristan. He means nothing to me except as a means to an end.

Everly dialed a number on the burner phone and waited for the call to roll to voice mail. She'd chosen the late hour, knowing Harrison would be occupied with London. The two of them had been spending all their time together, and after watching them at the polo event, it was pretty clear Harrison was falling for the event planner. And she for him.

Well, falling in love hadn't been part of the plan. London should've kept her clothes on and her focus on what they were trying to achieve.

"You've reached Harrison. I'm not available right now, but leave me your name and a brief message and I'll get back to you."

Smiling, Everly hit Play.

Ten

London woke to a soft morning light stealing past the gauzy curtains of her bedroom. She loved that her windows faced east. Waking up to the sunrise always boosted her optimism. The soothing palette of peach, pink, lavender and soft gold offered a tranquil beginning to her day. She often took a cup of coffee onto her broad terrace and sucked in a heady lungful of river breezes.

Stretching out her hand to the far side of the bed, she found the space empty and the sheets cool. Sighing, she pushed to a sitting position and ran her fingers through her tangled hair. Usually she braided it at night, but Harrison said he loved the spill of her satiny locks over his skin and she adored the way he tunneled his fingers through it.

She slipped from bed and donned a silky robe before following her nose to the kitchen, where the smell of coffee promised a large mug of dark roast. But as she neared the kitchen, the sound of her own voice reached her ears.

I've used Harrison to get to Tristan. He means nothing to me except as a means to an end.

She stopped dead, a malignant lump of dread forming in her chest as she remembered when she'd made that declaration. What did Everly think she was doing?

In her kitchen, Harrison stood at the island, one hand braced on the marble countertop while he stared at the phone. He looked like he'd been told he could never race again.

It was the same devastated look Linc had worn at the polo event during the brutal incident with Claire.

A rushing noise filled her ears as the edges of her vision grew fuzzy. She must've made a sound because his gaze whipped in her direction.

"What is this about?" he demanded, holding up his phone. "Why did you say those things?"

Even if she could speak, she had no words to explain.

"Damn it, London." His voice broke on her name. "I thought we had something."

She had to reply. He deserved an explanation. But would he listen? London doubted she'd be open to it if their situation were reversed.

"It isn't like it sounds—"

"Don't lie to me. I want to know what's really going on."

Gathering a huge breath, she stepped up to the kitchen island and set her hands on it, leaning forward. "I'm trying to find out if your brother is hiding money."

"Why?"

She bit her lip. They'd promised not to tell anyone about what they were doing. Yet hadn't Everly broken their pact when she'd sent that audio clip to Harrison? What more could the woman do? Taint London's reputation? Bad-mouth ExcelEvent?

In the end, cowardice ruled. "I'm not at liberty to tell you."

For long, agonizing seconds he stared at her in silence, confusion and annoyance chasing across his features. "Why?"

"Because it's not my story to tell."

"So, us…?" The unformed question drained all animation from his eyes. "Was I a means to an end?"

She could try lying to him, but he knew her well enough by now to see right through it. "At first."

He took the hit without reacting. "I suppose you want me to believe that things changed."

"They did. I would never have…" She hesitated, unsure what came next. Thanks to the revenge bargain she'd become unrecognizable to herself.

"Never would have…?" He prompted. "Slept with me? Led me to believe your feelings for me were real?" Although his tone remained neutral, the tension around his eyes and the muscle jumping in his jaw displayed what was really going on inside him.

"I do have feelings for you."

But even as the claim left her lips, London saw it was too little and too late. Harrison's eyes hardened to flint, and her heart stopped.

"You don't understand," she protested.

He appeared impervious to her desperate plea. "Then tell me what's going on."

"I can't." Trapped between her mistakes and her longing to come clean, London closed her eyes and wished herself back in time to that fateful women's empowerment function. How had she believed that doing something wrong would make anything better?

"You mean you won't," Harrison countered.

"It's complicated."

The lame excuse bought her no sympathy. Harrison crossed his arms over his chest and regarded her in disgust.

"Can you at least explain to me why you're doing this?"

Maybe it would help if she did. She couldn't tell him everything, but she could say enough that maybe he'd understand.

"I'm helping a friend. Your brother hurt her and I'm trying to…" This is where her story got murky. London no longer believed that what she, Zoe and Everly were doing would make any of them any better off.

"Hurt him back?" Harrison guessed.

London found it hard to meet his gaze. "That's the way it started."

"And things are different now?"

"Yes and no. There's no question that Tristan is a bad guy who did bad things. I'm just not sure doing bad things to a bad guy is the answer. How is it helping anyone to get back at him?"

"I'll be the first one to admit that my brother has not always been a decent individual and I turned a blind eye to a lot of his behavior."

For a second London thought that maybe Harrison understood and could forgive her, but there was no sympathy in his eyes. Only regret.

"Your comments about his spending habits at the polo match got me thinking. I'm not sure if he's been engaged in questionable activities, and I sure as hell hope it has nothing to do with Crosby Automotive, but he's spending above and beyond his income." Harrison rubbed his hand over his eyes. "And I know he treated Zoe badly. She didn't deserve his abuse while they were married or to be discarded the way she was."

"She didn't have an affair. It was something Tristan trumped up to get out of paying her a fair settlement."

"I never believed she did and I should've spoken up on her behalf. She deserved better than she got."

London remained quiet as Harrison's eyes narrowed. His statements struck close to the heart of her motivation.

"Was Zoe the one you were helping?" Harrison asked after a long span of silence.

Her instincts urged her to trust him even as she doubted her purpose in doing so. Did she hope he'd forgive her if he knew what they'd been up to? And how would he feel about what Everly had done to Linc on London's behalf? And what if Everly got wind of the fact that she'd confided in Harrison? What insane stunt would she pull then?

"Talk to me," he said, softening his tone. "What the hell is going on?"

London chewed on her lip, fear of the consequences paralyzing her. At long last she sighed.

"All I can say is that I was trying to find out the truth about your brother's financial situation. It seems likely that he's hiding money because it's pretty common knowledge that Zoe didn't get anywhere near the settlement she should have."

"And how did you think you could do that?" Harrison asked.

"He has to keep track of things somehow. I thought by gaining access to his computer I could find everything I needed."

Harrison frowned. "That's absurd. Didn't you realize he'd have his computer and his files password protected?"

"I have something that's supposed to get past that."

"What?"

She went to her purse, pulled out the USB drive and held it up. "This. It's some kind of special program that was supposed to get me past his security."

Harrison came toward her, gaze fixed on the drive. "Where did you get it?"

With her eyes begging him to understand, London shook her head.

A muscle jumped in Harrison's jaw. "How does it work?"

She explained the process and he held out his hand.

"Give me the drive."

Meek as a lamb, London handed it over. "I'm sorry," she whispered. "Please don't tell Tristan. If he finds out, he'll make things worse for Zoe."

If her plea had any effect on him, nothing showed in his expression. He remained furious, but London hoped a shred of affection for her had survived and he wouldn't do anything to cause her harm.

Harrison turned the flash drive over and over in his hand, contemplating it. "My brother doesn't need to know about this. But I'm keeping this and you will stay away from him."

Relief flooded her. Nothing suited London more than backing away from the whole situation. Then she remembered that her problems weren't limited to Tristan. Everly had sent Harrison the snippet of their conversation as a warning shot. London still had to contend with her.

"What are you going to do with the drive?" she asked.

"I don't know." He dropped it into his pocket. "The only thing I'm sure of at the moment is that you and I are done."

Harrison drove the familiar roads to Crosby Motorsports, seeking comfort in what he knew and loved. Cars and racing had always been his go-to when things got hard. He'd lost track of how many hours he'd spent as a kid with a wrench in his hand, learning how to tear apart something and then putting it back together. There was security in the logic of how the pieces fit together, each with a particular purpose. As he'd reached an age when he spent more time behind the wheel than under the hood, his appreciation had grown for a perfectly functioning car.

Unfortunately, in the racing world, as much as they strove to have everything work smoothly, that rarely happened. Bolts loosened. Suspensions failed. Brakes gave out. Drivers trained for when things went wrong, when systems failed or other drivers made mistakes. Situations didn't always have to spin out of control.

The other side of the coin from preparation was luck. Harrison considered himself fortunate that during his career while he'd been involved in several wrecks, he'd walked away from all but one of them. Yet despite the danger inherent in his sport, he never questioned getting behind the wheel of number twenty-five.

Too bad life wasn't equally easy to prepare for and navigate. Nothing he'd ever experienced could've enabled Harrison to see the wreck between him and London coming. She'd completely blindsided him. One second he was in his lane, thinking that he had everything in hand, and the next he was spinning out of control on a trajectory that sent him crashing into the wall.

Ahead of him the entrance gate to Crosby Motorsports came into view. As he sped onto the property, the peace he'd always gathered from being there eluded him. The facility had been more than his home away from home for nearly two decades. It was the center of his world. Yet tonight as he pulled up in front of the engine shop, his heart wasn't here.

He expected the building to be empty. With the season done, the team had headed home for some much-needed rest and family time. Harrison used his keycard to access the engine shop and easily navigated the familiar space in the dim light. Of all the various components that went into the cars, he had a particular fondness for engines since his earliest memories were of working beside his uncle, learning how all the complicated parts came together to move the vehicle forward in breathtaking speeds.

Of course, the engines designed and built by the Crosby Motorsports team were far more sophisticated than the engines Harrison had learned on. These days the engines were customized each week for the particular racetrack based on the speed and throttle characteristics and even the driver.

"What are you doing here?"

Looking past the neat row of engines lined up along one wall, Harrison spied his uncle headed his way.

"Just clearing my head."

"How's London? Things going okay?"

"Why do you ask?"

"She's the first woman you've brought around in a long time. I figured she was someone special." Jack removed his ball cap and ran slender fingers through his thick gray hair. "And with the hangdog look about you right now, it stands to reason that something went wrong."

With the season over, Jack became a lot more approachable, and Harrison decided to take advantage of his uncle's years of experience being married to a firecracker like Dixie.

"When London and I first started dating, I thought our biggest problem was going to be that she wouldn't give me a chance because I didn't have the sort of Charleston social connections she was looking to make."

"And now?" Jack asked, not looking a bit surprised.

"I think those issues are still there, but they aren't the biggest problem we have."

Jack shook his head in disgust and suddenly Harrison was an impulsive teenager again, eager to get behind the wheel of a car he couldn't handle.

"Do you think for one second if I hadn't fought for Dixie

that we'd be together right now?" Jack asked. "Your dad and I had empty pockets and big dreams when I met your aunt."

"But she married you," Harrison reminded him.

"You say that like there was never any question she would. Her dad chased me off their property the first time I made her cry."

Harrison regarded his uncle in shock, intrigued by this glimpse into Jack's personal life. Usually his uncle stuck to tales about the business or racing and Harrison sensed there was a good story waiting to be told.

"You made her cry?" He couldn't imagine his tough-as-nails aunt reduced to tears. "Why? How?"

"I wasn't the smooth operator I am today."

Harrison snorted. His uncle often told stories, and the more dramatic the circumstances, the better. Not everything was 100 percent true, but there was enough reality to provide a moral. The key was discovering what exactly to believe.

"So, what happened?"

"She was debuting and wanted me as her escort for the ball. We'd been going out for only a few months at the time and I certainly wasn't her parents' first choice."

"Did you do something to embarrass her at the event?"

"I never made it to the ball."

"Why?"

"Stupid pride." Jack's expression turned sheepish. "I turned her down. She and I were from different worlds. I believed if we went together, she'd be the target of ridicule and I didn't want to put her through that."

Harrison winced. That same thought had crossed his mind at Richmond Raceway when he'd glimpsed London there. It had been so obvious that she didn't fit in. And later when he'd seen her with his brother at the Crosby Motorsports party, he'd briefly wondered if she'd prefer to be with someone who shared similar business and social connections.

"If that's what you believed," Harrison asked, "why did you start dating her in the first place?"

"Because she turned my world upside down. I could no more stay away from her than stop breathing. She was my heart and my reason for getting up every morning."

Jack's words hit closer to home than Harrison would've liked.

"So what happened after you turned down her invitation to attend the ball?"

"I'd underestimated how strong she was. And how determined. She didn't give a damn what other people thought. She was proud of me, of the man I was, and wanted everyone to know it." Jack raked his fingers through his hair as regret twisted his features. Even now, after more than three decades of wedded bliss, Harrison could see his uncle wished he'd behaved a different way. "My actions made it appear that I believed her choices were flawed. And that I didn't trust her."

"But she married you, so she must have gotten over it," Harrison said.

"It took a year."

Harrison could imagine what those months must've been like for his uncle. He was experiencing his own separation angst at the moment.

"You must have been really hung up on her to have stayed in the fight that long," he said.

"You know, at the beginning of the year I don't believe I understood what I was feeling. Plus, if I'd been truly in love or, more to the point, been willing to surrender my stubbornness and give in to my emotions, I might have saved myself a lot of pain."

Harrison didn't want to ponder an entire year away from

London, so he asked, "Why did you keep going when she rejected you for a year?"

"Because to be without her hurt more than my foolish pride. I tried to stay away, but rarely lasted more than a week or two. Life got pretty bleak for me, pretty fast. It also made me more determined to be worthy of her. That's when Crosby Automotive really started to take off. I threw every bit of my frustration and fear and joy into making something I could be proud of. I thought if I was wealthy and successful that I could win her back."

"Did it work?"

Jack shook his head. "It made things worse. The better Crosby Automotive did, the more confident I became and the less she wanted to have anything to do with me."

Harrison wasn't liking where the story was going. "So what did it take?"

"She started dating someone perfect for her. A guy from a wealthy, well-connected family." Jack's expression hardened. "I fell into a dark well for a couple of weeks."

"How'd you come out of it?"

"I weighed being happy for the rest of my life against my pride."

"And?" Harrison didn't really need to ask. He saw where his uncle was going. "What did it take?"

"The most difficult conversation of my life. I had to completely open myself up to her. Fears, hopes, how she made my life better and that I wanted to be worthy of her love."

Strong emotion filled Jack's voice even after three and a half decades. The power of it drove Harrison's misery higher. His throat tightened, preventing him from speaking for a long moment.

Into the silence, his uncle spoke again. "Is what you feel for her worth fighting for?"

Could he live without London? Probably. Would it be any fun? Doubtful. For so long racing had been his purpose and passion. He'd never considered that he'd sacrificed anything to be at the top of his game. But was that true?

With London he'd started thinking in terms of family and kids, and there was no question that she'd pulled his focus away from racing. The telling part was that he didn't mind. In fact, he'd begun to think in terms of how he intended to make changes in his schedule next year to spend as much time with her as possible. He suspected that if this business with his brother hadn't gotten between them, he'd be well on his way to looking at engagement rings.

"For a long time I thought so." Harrison's chest tightened at the thought of letting her go, but he couldn't imagine how to get past the way she'd used him. He'd never been one to hold a grudge, but trusting her again seemed hopeless. "Now I'm not so sure."

Eleven

A subdued and thoroughly disgraced London entered the Cocktail Club on King Street and searched the animated crowd for her best friend. Maribelle had grabbed two seats at the bar. As London made her way through the customers, Maribelle was flashing her engagement ring at a persistent admirer.

These days because of the magic of Maribelle's true love glow, members of both sexes flocked to her. By comparison, London felt dull and sluggish. She couldn't sleep, wasn't eating and couldn't remember the last time she'd exercised.

"Holy hell," Maribelle exclaimed as London slid onto the bar stool beside her. "You look awful." She narrowed her eyes and looked her friend up and down. "Are you ready to tell me what happened?"

It had been ten days since that horrible morning when Harrison had received that damning audio clip from Everly.

As London filled her in, Maribelle's expression underwent several transformations from shock to dismay and finally irritation, but she didn't interrupt until London's story wound to its bitter finish.

"He's never going to speak to me again," London said, putting the final nail in the coffin that held the most amazing romance of her life.

"And well he shouldn't." Maribelle scowled. "I'm a little tempted never to speak to you again, either."

Knowing her friend didn't really mean that, London sat in rebuked silence while Maribelle signaled the bartender and ordered two shots of tequila.

"You know I can't drink that," London protested as the shots were delivered along with salt and limes. "Remember what happened the last time."

"I do and you are going to drink it until you're drunk enough to call Harrison and tell him the whole story, after which you're going to beg for his forgiveness. And then I'm going to take you home and hold your hair while you throw up." Maribelle handed her the shot. "Because that's what best friends do."

"I love you," London murmured, nearly blind from the grateful tears gathering in her eyes.

"I know. Now drink."

It took two shots in close succession and twenty minutes for London's dread to unravel. Two more and an hour before London found enough confidence to do the right thing.

"I'm going to regret this in the morning," London muttered, picking her phone up off the bar. The roiling in her stomach had nothing to do with the tequila she'd consumed. Yet.

"I know." Maribelle's voice was sympathetic, but she maintained the steely demeanor of a drill sergeant. "Now call."

Beneath Maribelle's watchful eye, London unlocked

her phone and pulled up Harrison's contact information. With her heart trying to hammer its way out of her chest, she tapped on his name. As his handsome face lit up her screen, she almost chickened out. Maribelle must have sensed this because she made the same chastising sound she used to correct the new puppy she and Beau had just adopted.

London put the phone to her ear and reminded herself to breathe. Facing Harrison after what she'd done to him ranked as the hardest thing she'd ever had to do. But she owed him the full truth and so much more.

"I didn't think I'd hear from you again."

She almost burst into ugly sobs as his deep voice filled her ear and suddenly her throat was too tight for her to speak.

"Hello? London, are you there?" He paused. "Or have you butt-dialed me while you're out having a good time? It sounds like you're at a party."

Someone behind her had a rowdy laugh that blasted through the bar right on cue.

"I'm not having fun." Not one bit. *I miss you.* "I have things to tell you. Can I come over so I can explain some things to you?"

He remained silent for so long, she expected him to turn her down.

"I'm home now."

"I can't tonight," she said, glancing at the line of empty shot glasses. "Tonight, I'm going to be very, very sick."

Again he paused before answering. "Tomorrow afternoon, then?"

"At two?"

"At two."

The line went dead and London clapped her hand over her mouth before making a beeline for the bathroom.

* * *

At a little after two the following afternoon, Harrison opened the door to his penthouse unit and immediately cursed the way his heart clenched at the sight of London. From her red-rimmed eyes to her pale skin and lopsided topknot, she looked as miserable as he felt.

To his dismay, instead of venting his irritation, his first impulse was to haul her into the foyer and wrap her in his arms. Her gaze clung to him as he stepped back and gestured her inside.

Due to the turn in the weather, she'd dressed in jeans, soft suede boots and a bulky sweater in sage green. From her pink cheeks and windblown hair, he suspected she'd walked over from her building along the waterside thoroughfare that ran beside the Cooper River.

With the front door closed, the spacious foyer seemed to narrow. Beneath the scent of wind and water that she'd brought into his home, her perfume tickled his nostrils. Abruptly, he was overwhelmed by memories. Of the joyful hours she'd spent here. The long nights they'd devoured each other. The lazy Sunday mornings when they'd talked over coffee, croissants and egg-white omelets.

"Thank you for letting me come over," she murmured.

Harrison shoved his hands into his pockets. He would not touch her or offer comfort of any kind, no matter how soft and sweet and vulnerable she looked. He would not let her off easy or tell her it was okay, because it wasn't.

"You said you wanted to explain about going after my brother," he growled. "So explain."

"I will, but first I need to say something to you." London's beautiful eyes clung to him. "When I'm with you, I feel…everything. I didn't expect all the things you make me want and need. I didn't understand that once we'd made love there would be no going back for me."

Harrison's muscles quivered and it took willpower to prevent his body from responding to what she was saying. Her every word echoed how he'd felt about her and the loss he'd experienced these last few days gripped him anew.

"All I want is to be with you." Her hands fluttered, graceful as a dancer's, opening and closing as she poured out her emotions. "You made me feel beautiful and fulfilled. You gave me a safe place to be open and vulnerable."

"That's not an explanation for why you used me," he said, his heart wrenching so hard it was difficult to keep a grip on his impatience.

Her expression was a study in consternation as she began again. "I was afraid to tell you what I was doing for fear that you'd hate me."

Her declaration shook him to the core.

"I could never hate you."

He loved her.

The realization left him stunned and reeling. For days he'd ignored the part of him that had recognized the signs.

"Harrison, I'm sorry," London said, her voice sounding very far away even though she stood within reach. "I did a terrible thing."

He loved her?

How was that possible given what she'd done?

She'd used him to get to his brother. Didn't she know he would've done anything for her if only she'd asked? His soul ached as he resisted his heart's longing for her. She would always be his weakness.

Needing to put some distance between them before he succumbed to the urge to back her against the wall and lose himself in her, Harrison marched back toward his living room.

It wasn't until he threw himself onto the couch that he realized she hadn't left the foyer. With an impatient huff, he rose and went to find her. She stood where he'd left her, pulling down her sleeves to hide her hands.

"I'm so deeply sorry that what I did hurt you," she said, her voice tiny and choked with tears. "And I want to tell you everything."

"You might as well come in and tell me the whole story."

Losing the battle to avoid touching her, Harrison towed London into the living room and drew her to the couch. Once they were seated side by side, she began her tale.

"It all started when I met Zoe and another woman, Everly Briggs, at a networking event a few months ago. We were all strangers and each of us was in a bad place. Linc had just broken off our engagement. Zoe's divorce was going badly. And Everly claimed her sister had been wrongly imprisoned."

London's fingers clenched and flexed in her lap. "I don't know who first brought up the idea of getting back at the men who'd hurt us, but Everly jumped pretty hard on it and her enthusiasm swept up both Zoe and me."

Harrison hated that London's pain from her broken engagement had driven her to do something reckless.

"Zoe was pretty scared of Tristan and I didn't want to go after Linc and damage my reputation by appearing vindictive. So..." She blew out a big breath. "Since we were strangers who met by chance, we decided to take on each other's men. Everly went after Linc for me. I went after Tristan for Zoe. And she's supposed to take down Ryan Dailey for Everly."

Despite his dismay at her story, Harrison could see the logic in their approach. "So who sent me the audio clip of you?"

"Everly. She wanted to make you hate me." London peered at him anxiously. "She saw how important you were becoming to me."

His treacherous heart sang as some of his hurt and anger eased at her confession. The longing to take her in his arms grew more urgent, but he resisted. Although it was clear that no matter what she'd done or why, he couldn't stop wanting her, he required a full explanation before deciding what to do next.

"So where do things stand now?"

"I don't know. Obviously, I wasn't up to fulfilling my part of the bargain and you can see how Everly reacted to that." London made a face. "I feel terrible for Zoe. Among the three of us, what happened to her was the most damaging."

"Didn't you say Everly's sister went to jail?"

"Yes, but from what I've been able to find out, she did something illegal. Maybe Ryan Dailey didn't have to go so far as to press charges, but his company lost several million dollars because of her and he was well within his rights."

London lapsed into silence, her gaze fixed on his chest, her downcast expression battering the walls he'd erected against her. Her genuine remorse left him grappling with her decision to take revenge on her ex-fiancé. What did that say about her?

Yet after suffering his own heartbreak, he was better able to sympathize with the pain she'd experienced. Dark emotions had taken him to irrational places unlike any he'd visited before she entered his life.

Harrison reached around to the sofa table behind him and picked up a manila envelope. The information it held put him square in the middle of London's trouble.

"Here," he said, handing her the envelope.

"What is this?" London's gaze flickered from his face to the envelope and back again.

"Open it up and see."

London unfastened the clasp and flipped up the flap to peer inside. "It looks like banking information."

"My brother's banking information," Harrison clarified. "Turns out Tristan had secret offshore accounts and shell corporations that he used to move money to the States. I don't know if the information will help Zoe, but it wasn't fair that Tristan hid these accounts from her."

While he spoke, she pulled several pages out and scanned them. "Why did you do this?"

"Zoe got a raw deal."

It wasn't his only motivation, but Harrison wasn't ready to say more. He'd done a lot of soul-searching before he'd betrayed his brother by using the flash drive and stealing these files. Although he remained conflicted about his decision, seeing the questionable legality of what Tristan had been up to had eased his conscience somewhat.

"This is a lot of money," London said. "I mean a lot of money. Way more than he should have been able to put away by regular means. Where do you suppose it came from?"

The question had been keeping Harrison up at night. He had yet to figure out what to do with the information he'd gathered, but knew a conversation with his father and uncle was in order.

"I think he's been laundering money," he said.

"Laundering money for whom?"

"Drug dealers. Russian mob." The more he'd reviewed the information, the more extreme his speculation had become and the more concerned he'd grown about the potential repercussions for Crosby Automotive. "It's hard to say."

Her eyes went wide. "You don't seriously believe your

brother is doing something illegal, do you? How could that be happening?"

"Crosby Automotive buys almost all its parts from overseas manufacturers and my brother is responsible for deciding which companies we buy from. It wouldn't be impossible for him to channel bribes into one of these off-shore accounts."

"But does he need more money than he has?"

"You've seen his homes and his spending habits. Tristan likes to live the life of a billionaire. 'Act like you're worth a fortune and people will be inclined to believe it,'" he quoted in his brother's lofty tones. "Instead it looks like he just went deeper and deeper into debt."

"Is Crosby Automotive in danger from what he's been doing?"

"I don't think so." Harrison hoped not. It would be something he'd need to address in coming months.

London shoved the pages back into the envelope. "How can I thank you for this?"

"No need. What Tristan did to Zoe was wrong."

She set her hand on his. The move sent a zing of excitement through his body. He set his teeth against the urge to pull her onto his lap and sink his fingers into her tousled hair. His gaze slid to her full lips. One kiss and he'd be beneath her spell once more. But...

"I'm so sorry for what I did," she said, forcing Harrison to rein in his lust-filled thoughts.

"Look, I've started to understand your motives."

"My motives in the beginning," she corrected him, turning his hand over so her fingers could trace evocative patterns on his palm. "Things changed when I got to know you."

Harrison's blood heated as she inched closer. The entreaty in her eyes undermined his willpower. "I get it, but I can't just go on as if none of this happened."

"I don't blame you." She peered at him from beneath her lashes. "But I just want you to know that you changed me in ways I never imagined possible."

"London…"

Before he knew it, Harrison found himself leaning in. Her feminine scent lured him closer still. He knew exactly where she applied her perfume. A dab on her neck, right over the madly throbbing pulse. Another behind her ear. The hollow of her elbow. Behind her knees.

"I know I have no right to ask, but could you ever…?" She bit her lip, unable to finish the question.

"Forgive you?" He was on the verge of forgetting everything except the driving need to delve into her heat as her palm coasted over his shoulder.

"I know it's not fair for me to ask. But if there's anything I can do." Her other hand found his thigh and Harrison almost groaned at the tornado of lust swirling in him. "If there's any way back to where we were," she continued. "Or forward to something better. All you need to do is tell me what you need me to do."

Harrison raked his fingers through his hair and blew out a giant breath while his craving for her warred with his shattered faith.

"My uncle told me a story about when he and Dixie were dating. He did something wrong and spent the following year trying to get back in her good graces."

"If you think it'll take a year for you to forgive me," London said, so close now that it took no effort at all for her to slide her lips over his ear, "I'm for doing whatever it takes."

Harrison shuddered as her husky voice vibrated through

him. "You'd make that pledge without knowing if I could ever trust you again?"

"I trust that the man you are will play fair with me." She tipped her head and let him see her conviction. "You are worth the risk."

With his ability to resist her unraveling, Harrison said, "You know, when we first started seeing each other I got the impression you didn't feel that way."

"That you were worth the risk?" She shook her head. "Maybe at the very beginning I judged you for what you did for a living. But you were willing to give me a chance anyway."

With a warm, willing woman sliding her hand farther up his thigh, Harrison couldn't figure out why he was still talking. But while his body was revving past safety limits, his heart hadn't yet recovered from crashing.

"You had great legs."

She shook her head at that. "I wasn't exactly your type, though, was I?"

"No. You were far too reserved."

They shared a grin at how much that had changed and more of Harrison's doubts began to fizzle and fade.

"If that was true, why did you approach me at the foundation event?" she asked, leaning more of her body against him.

"Truth?" He sighed as her soft breasts flattened against his arm. "Because you seemed interested in Tristan and I wanted to protect you from him."

"Seriously?" She eased back a fraction and shook her head in wonder. "So, if not for my ill-conceived plot against your brother, we never would've gone out."

"We might have." But he didn't really believe that.

"I don't think so," she said. "We were too different."

While she'd caught his eye at the event, he'd initially

dismissed her as not his type. Odd that they'd both nearly let their prejudices get in the way of something amazing.

"That means," she continued, "in a fateful twist, the revenge plot brought us together."

Harrison considered that for a long moment. "I guess it did."

"I'm glad. I don't regret a single second of the time I spent falling in love with you."

"You what?" Her admission was unexpected.

She looked surprised that he didn't know this already. "I've fallen in love with you." Her voice gained confidence as she repeated herself. Drawing her feet under her, she got onto her knees and cupped his face. "I love you, Harrison Crosby. You are strong and thoughtful and sexy and just the best man I've ever known."

Abruptly, she stopped gushing compliments and scanned his face, gauging his reaction. As their gazes locked, the last of Harrison's doubts washed away. This was the woman he was meant to be with. The proof was in the thunderous pounding of his heart and the exquisite openness of her expression.

This time, the impulse to put his arms around her was too strong. Harrison hauled her against him.

"I adore you," he murmured, burying his face in her hair. "You've shown me what's been missing in my life and I know now that I'll never be happy without you."

As their mouths fused, he felt as well as heard a half sob escape her, and then she was pushing into the kiss, her tongue finding its way into his mouth. He let her take the lead, enjoying the way his brain short-circuited as her hunger set him on fire.

His fingers dived beneath her sweater, finding bare skin. They groaned in unison as his thumbs brushed her tight nipples. He shifted their positions until she was flat on her back, her thighs parted and legs tangled with his. For a moment he ignored the compelling ache in his groin and smoothed silky strands of her hair away from her flushed face.

"I want to marry you," he said.

Her surprise lasted less than a heartbeat. "I'd like to marry you, too."

"You don't want to think about it?" He looked for some hint of doubt or hesitation in her manner, but only love and trust blazed in her eyes.

"I'm a better person when I'm with you," she said. "Why would I ever want to give that up?" She smiled then and it was the most beautiful thing he'd ever seen. "You're stuck with me."

"I'd say we're stuck with each other."

"And I don't want a long engagement."

"Lots of planes go to Las Vegas every day from the Charleston airport."

His suggestion briefly caught her off guard but then the most mischievous smile formed. "I'm feeling like the luckiest woman alive at the moment, so that sounds like a great idea."

He'd only been partially serious, but seeing that she was game, he nodded. In truth, he'd expected her to want to spend months planning an elaborate wedding to rival her friend's. "Just you and me?"

"Would you be upset if I invited Maribelle and Beau? I think she'd kill me if I got married without her."

"Let's give her a call."

"Later." London's lips moved to his neck even as she gave his butt a suggestive squeeze, pulling him hard against her. "Right now I want to make love with you."

Harrison nodded as his lips swept over hers, tasting her deliciously sweet mouth. As he wedged his erection against her, he could feel her smile and grinned in return as she rocked against him, inflaming both their desires.

Eventually he knew they would take things to the bedroom, but for now he was content to fool around on his couch like they were a couple of teenagers.

* * * * *

A CHRISTMAS TEMPTATION

KAREN BOOTH

For Melissa Jeglinski,
my amazing agent and friend.
I'm so thankful to have you on my side!

One

Eden's Department Store offered a dazzling array of merchandise, but in Sophie Eden's mind, everything started with the shoes. Thus, she always began her workday in the shoe department, surveying the latest and chitchatting with the salespeople as they prepared for the day's shoppers. Sophie often devoted ten or fifteen minutes to the pursuit before heading upstairs to her office. Some days she'd even try on something new. Not today. With less than a month until Christmas, and the vultures circling, getting right to work was the most pressing matter.

She bustled through the department down the wide center promenade, past the Lucite and chrome displays of sling-backs and stilettos, beneath the splendid crystal chandeliers that dotted the high coffered ceiling. Her delicate heels click-clacked on the gleaming white marble floor. Her shoes were particularly magnificent today—Manolo Blahnik pumps with a slim leather tie at the ankle, in Christmas red. The color choice was no coincidence. The holidays were Sophie's favorite time of year, and she was going to sneak in every second of cheer she could. She already knew Christmas would be difficult this year. This would be the first without Gram, her grandmother, the founder of Eden's.

Sophie rounded a turn as the aisle spoked off to the various sections of the department known to fashion editors all over the world as "shoe heaven." Tucked back in the far corner was the vestibule with the private elevator that would take her upstairs to the true guts of the Eden's operation. She sucked in a deep, cleansing breath as she took her short ride up one floor. Normally, she loved her job, but right now it was much farther from heaven than the number on the elevator door suggested.

"Good morning, Lizzie," Sophie said, greeting her assistant. She shrugged off her cream-colored wool coat and slung it over her arm. Considering the dirt and grime of the city, such a light color was a stupid idea, but Sophie loved the way it showed off her red hair. It was one of her best assets.

Lizzie popped up from behind her desk, all sunshine and raw energy. Her platinum pixie cut was extra spiky today. "Good morning, Ms. Eden. How are you?"

"Depends. How's my day looking?"

"You've already received three gift baskets from real-estate developers this morning."

"It's barely nine o'clock."

"The couriers start delivering at eight."

Sophie shook her head. This had been the drill for the last month, ever since her grandmother, Victoria Eden, had passed away. Everyone knew that Sophie and her sister, Mindy, would inherit Eden's. Their grandmother spoke of it often, at runway shows and cocktail parties and even to the press. Eden's was a business built for women, by women, and it would be run by women for as long as Victoria Eden could see it through.

The will was to be read the week before Christmas when the heirs could gather. It was viewed as a formality, though. Sophie and her sister, Mindy, would own the store. Thus the influx of gift baskets, flowers, phone calls and emails. It wasn't that anyone was particularly interested in Eden's as a business. They were after the building and the land. Everyone assumed Sophie and Mindy would want to sell. Mindy was desperate to do so. Sophie was diametrically opposed to the idea.

"Oh, and your sister called to say she will not be able to come by today after all," Lizzie said as she trailed Sophie into her office.

"Lovely." Sophie made no effort to disguise the unhappiness in her voice. She and Mindy were at odds right now. "I'll have to give her a call and see what her problem is." She got settled in her chair, which was custom upholstered in peacock blue velvet with gold nail-head trim. She pulled her laptop from her bag and set it on her sleek white glass-topped desk. "Anything else?"

"Everything's in your calendar. You have a meeting with the department heads at two this afternoon. Also, Reginald will be up to do the holiday decorations in your office soon. I tried to get him to come earlier in the morning, but it just wasn't possible. I think they're all still recovering from installing the holiday window displays."

Sophie waved it off. "Yes. Of course. My office is definitely the bottom of the priority list. And I'm glad they're coming while I'm here. I'd like to be able to pitch in." Sophie loved decorating for Christmas. It was one of her absolute favorite pursuits.

"Do you think Reginald will actually let you help? You know how he is." Lizzie bugged her eyes and whispered, "Control freak."

"And I'm about to be the president of Eden's Department Store. Plus, he loved Gram, and he knows how close we were." Sophie wasn't sure who had cried harder at her grandmother's funeral—her or Reginald. "I'm sure he'll be nothing but accommodating."

Lizzie made her way to the door but stopped before exiting. "Oh. I almost forgot. Jake Wheeler called again last night. Also, he sent the fruit." Lizzie pointed to the credenza behind Sophie's desk. Three elaborate cellophane-wrapped baskets sat atop it.

Jake Wheeler. How could one man's name send both a flash of anger and a flutter of delight through her body at the same time?

"Did he leave a message?"

"He did. He wanted me to remind you that it's very important he speaks to you."

"Of course he did. He's a man accustomed to getting everything he wants." Sophie picked up the fruit basket. "Put this in the employee lounge. Someone should enjoy it."

Lizzie held out her arms, which dropped a bit under the weight of the basket. "Don't you want to read the card first?"

Sophie didn't really want to read the card, but knowledge was king and she needed to know what Jake Wheeler was thinking. Otherwise, he was a mystery. He always had been.

Sophie grabbed the gold-trimmed envelope and ripped it from the plastic. "Thank you, Lizzie."

"Of course, Ms. Eden. You know where to find me if you need anything."

Sophie sat in her chair, her back straight and chin held high as she slid a manicured finger under the envelope flap. There was no telling what Jake had written on this card. When they were in business school together, everything out of his mouth was witty and warm. It was one of the things that first drew her to him. That and his unforgettable green eyes.

Dear Sophie,
You can't ignore my phone calls forever. Sooner
or later, I'll get through to you.
Best,
Jake

A zip of electricity ran along Sophie's spine. From somewhere deep in the recesses of her mind, the sound of Jake's sexy rumble of a voice had been set free. It was like a wild animal, pouncing on her. She'd forgotten the way it made her feel. A wave of warmth started in her chest and rolled back over her shoulders. She reclined in her chair and closed her eyes, recalling the magical moment when he'd first kissed her eight years ago, his insistent lips bringing every fantasy she'd had about him to life. He'd kissed her like he meant it, his arms tight around her waist, pulling her body into his. It was a dream come true in so many ways. She'd spent two years desperate for him to do that, trying so hard to be the kind of woman who would catch his eye. Finally, she'd done it.

Little had she known Jake Wheeler would break her heart and shatter her opinion of him in less than twenty-four hours.

Sophie's eyes flew open when there was a knock at her door.

Lizzie stood before her, plainly concerned. It was not like Sophie to sit at her desk with her eyes closed. "Ms. Eden? Reginald is here."

Sophie bolted upright and scrambled out from behind her desk. "Yes. Great. Good morning, Reginald. Please, come right in."

"Everything okay?" Lizzie asked under her breath.

"Just a slight headache."

"Good morning, Ms. Eden." Reginald, Eden's creative director, floated into her office and began surveying the walls and windows. "We're here to transform your office into a glamorous winter wonderland." Reginald was a bald, spindly man with thick horn-rimmed glasses who always wore a suit with a bow tie. His ensemble today was navy blue with a lavender pinstripe, the tie matching the stripes. Reginald did not do quiet, dull or subtle—precisely the reason Eden's window displays were one of the most popular Christmas attractions in the city.

Two young women rushed in behind him, lugging large boxes overflowing with sparkly silver and white garland. They set down their armfuls in the corner of Sophie's office and hurried back out into the hall, presumably for more supplies.

"What's the plan?" Sophie asked, filled with a mix of anticipation and sadness. Decorating one's office was Gram's tradition. She wanted Christmas oozing from every corner of Eden's. It helped to make the most arduous month of the year tolerable.

Reginald cast a doubtful look down at her, his glasses sliding to the tip of his nose. "You aren't planning on staying, are you? I work best unencumbered. And unsupervised."

Sophie frowned. "You used to let Gram help you when you decorated her office."

"That was different. She was the matriarch of the store. A queen. An unparalleled woman."

Sophie didn't need any more of this speech. She was well aware of the grand specter of her grandmother. She lived and worked under it every day. Sophie, along with her sister, would eventually fill the matriarchal role, but it wasn't right to claim it now. That was a position that must be earned, not inherited. "Got it."

Reginald patted her on the shoulder. "Trust me. It'll be stunning when you return." He made a grand gesture for the door. "Now shoo."

Sophie grabbed her cell phone from her desk and stepped out into the hall. Gram's office was right next to hers. The door was still open, and Sophie flipped on the light. It still looked so strange with no Gram. Sophie had no trouble sketching in what was missing—her grandmother, with her trademark strawberry blond bob with thick bangs, never a hair out of place. On a day like today, Sophie could imagine her in a tailored dress in a fun color, perhaps a bold floral, accessorized with gold bangles and diamond earrings. She was always glamorous perfection.

Gram's office was a similarly colorful and pristine place, with everything exactly as it was on the last day she'd worked, at the end of October. Sophie had a lot of regrets about the last time she'd seen Gram. Sophie's day had been horrible and she'd only waved goodbye to her grandmother when she left the office. If she'd known Gram would have a heart attack in her sleep that night, she would have taken one last time to say *I love you*. She would have run out from behind her desk, grabbed her and given her one last hug.

Sophie turned off the light. She wasn't ready to use Gram's office. She might never be. It would only make her feel sad and inadequate. She could just imagine the looks on people's faces when they walked into the room and realized that the woman sitting behind the desk did not possess the gravitas of her predecessor.

Instead, Sophie ducked into an empty cubicle hidden behind the reception area. She dialed the number for her sister, Mindy, who answered right away.

"Lizzie said you aren't coming in today. Why not?" Sophie asked.

"Because it's December and one of our high-production printers is broken and my team is struggling to fill orders. I don't have time to spend at Eden's." Mindy had her own successful business, By Min-vitation Only, an online shop that sold high-end custom cards and invitations. "Everyone needs their Christmas cards yesterday. It's a madhouse over here."

"Oh. Okay. I understand."

"Don't sound so disappointed, Soph. You knew this was going to happen. You knew I couldn't simply drop everything and take on new responsibilities. I appreciate that you're steering the ship at Eden's until Gram's will is read, but I need you to accept the reality of our situation."

"And what is that exactly?" Sophie crossed her legs and bobbed her foot, stealing a glimpse of her red pumps. God, she loved those shoes. Mr. Blahnik was a genius.

"Today is our reality. I am too busy to play a role in the

store. Today I'm dealing with Christmas, but after that is New Year's and Valentine's Day. There is no downtime for me. I've worked hard to build my business, and I'm not stepping away from it."

Sophie understood her sister's predicament and her argument. She did. She just wished it wasn't the case. Now that Gram wasn't around to offer advice and solve problems, Sophie was perpetually out of her depth. And alone.

"Eden's is a lost cause, Soph. You'll be much happier when you just admit it," Mindy said.

"It is not. Gram didn't think so, and I don't think so, either. We can turn it around. Our earnings were up two percent last quarter."

"And my earnings were up twenty."

Way to rub it in my face. "I get it, Mindy. But this is our family business."

"I'm family. And I have a business. I'm telling you, as soon as the will is read, you and I need to sell Eden's to the highest bidder, pocket the cash, and then you need to come work for me. Easy peasy. We'll both have it made."

Mindy made it sound so simple and obvious, but she hadn't made promises to their grandmother. She hadn't spent the last three years working for Gram, learning and growing and soaking up every drop she could of her genius. "I'm not prepared to talk about anything until after Christmas. It's in poor taste."

Sophie stepped out of the cubicle and tiptoed over to her office door to sneak a peek through the tiny gap between the door and the jamb.

Reginald rushed right over. "Oh, no you don't." He quickly closed the door, right in her face.

"Fine," Mindy said, sounding impatient. "But will you

at least call Jake Wheeler and listen to his pitch? The man
is ridiculously persistent. He's calling me twice a day."

There it was—that name again. "I know. He sent me
a fruit basket."

"He's got superdeep pockets, Sophie. And he sure
speaks fondly of you. You'd think you two were exes the
way he talks about you."

Sophie leaned back against the wall, her vision nar-
rowing just as her lips pinched together. "You know that's
not the case."

"Oh, I know. I know the whole story. He's the one
who got away."

Sophie shook her head. "He is not. He's the snake who
slithered away. And I hardly had him to begin with." *Just
one unbelievably hot night of abandon.*

"Regardless. Call him."

"I'll think about it." Sophie already knew there was
no way she would call Jake. There was a lot of wisdom
in the adage about not clawing at old wounds. He'd hurt
her. Badly. She would never, ever forgive him.

"Think harder. I'd like to cross him off my to-do list."

Sophie stifled a snort. Jake Wheeler had spent two
years on her "to-do" list.

Years later, she still regretted it like crazy.

Granted, expressing condolences was not Jake Wheeler's strongpoint. He'd found it much easier to get through
life by glossing over sad moments and enjoying pleasant
ones. But after three unreturned phone calls, a sympathy
card that garnered no response and an ignored charity
donation in her grandmother's name, he was certain Sophie Eden was not impressed with his efforts.

Jake's admin, Audrey, buzzed the line in his office. "Ms. Eden's assistant is on the line, Mr. Wheeler."

Jake picked up his phone. "Lizzie, I'm worried that if we continue to spend this much time on the phone, people will start to get the wrong impression of our working relationship."

"Sir? You remembered my name?"

"How could I not? Is this our fourth or fifth time speaking?"

"I'm not sure, sir. Probably the fifth."

"And I'm guessing you know why I'm calling." Jake rocked forward and back in his chair, watching out the window of his tenth-floor office in the luxury steel-and-glass tower of 7 Bryant Park. He had stunning views of the New York Public Library and other midtown Manhattan landmarks, but the one he enjoyed most was that of the building's namesake. Down on the street, a temporary Christmas market was set up with vendors, music and ice skating. The holiday disruption had been overtaking the normally peaceful green space every December in recent years. Jake couldn't wait for January, when it would all be gone.

"I do. And I'm very sorry, but Ms. Eden is not available right now."

"Can you at least tell me when she'll be back in the office?"

"She's here all the time, Mr. Wheeler. But her schedule is packed and always changing, as I'm sure you can understand. It's December. She runs one of the largest department stores in Manhattan. It's a very busy time."

"Of course." Jake tapped his pen on his desk. "Did she get the fruit basket I sent?"

"She did. And she was generous enough to share it with the staff. Everyone has enjoyed it greatly. Thank you."

Jake wasn't sure what more he could do to get her to return his phone calls, and he certainly couldn't arrive at a conclusion about why she was avoiding him. Their last interaction, years ago, at business school graduation, had been nothing but pleasant and cordial. They'd both agreed to let their shared history remain where it belonged—in the past.

"But she's not there right now?" He purposely added a heavy tone of suspicion to the question. It was the end of the workday. If Sophie was too busy to pick up the phone, she had to still be at the office.

"I'm sorry, but she's not available right now. No."

Jake wasn't sure what that meant, but he knew he was getting the runaround. "Fine. I'd like to leave a message. Again. My name is Jake Wheeler, and my number is—"

"Ms. Eden has your number."

Jake choked back a frustrated grumble. "Please remind her that it's very important. I need to speak to her."

"She knows, sir. I've delivered each one of your messages personally." Judging by the tone in her voice, Sophie's assistant was losing her patience. That much they had in common.

"Great. Thank you." Jake hung up the phone, more frustrated now than ever. He had to get Sophie to talk to him. He had to meet with her. Jake was a member of an exclusive investment group called the War Chest. It was run by financier Jacob Lin, and they tackled only the biggest of big deals—ones that required several sets of deep pockets. Jake had suggested Eden's when Sophie's grandmother had died. The other War Chest members, hoteliers Sawyer and Noah Locke and real-estate broker

Michael Kelly, along with Jacob, had all voted yes on the idea. Jake assured them with a great deal of confidence that he had an inside track with Sophie. Of course, until a month ago, he'd thought he did have an inside track. He and Sophie were best friends in business school. For a brief but memorable twenty-four hours, they'd been more.

"Audrey?" he called out into the void of his office.

In seconds flat, Jake's assistant snapped to attention in his office doorway. Audrey was fastidious, hyperorganized and very opinionated. "Sir, I really think it's too late for coffee. You'll get edgy, and caffeine is disruptive to sleep patterns."

"I don't need coffee. I'm wondering if you have any ideas on convincing a woman to call you back."

"Jewelry. Flowers. Chocolate. A profession of love."

Jake shook his head. "Not like that. I know *that*. I mean, in a professional setting."

"So nothing romantic?"

Jake didn't have to think about that one. He and Sophie were better off sticking to business. Of that much, he was sure. "Not intentionally romantic, but Ms. Eden does appreciate the finer things in life if that helps."

Audrey nodded. "Ah, yes. Your unromantic fruit-basket recipient."

"Precisely."

"And that didn't go over well? Who doesn't love a fruit basket?"

"I have no idea."

"Flowers?"

"Isn't that a cliché?"

"Not if you buy a ridiculous amount of her favorites and show up with them in person."

Jake raised both eyebrows at his assistant.

"That's what my husband did when he proposed."

"I'm not proposing marriage."

"But you are trying to talk a woman into selling her business when it's been only a few weeks since the family matriarch passed away. You might want to go big."

"Excellent point."

"Any idea what her favorite flower is?"

Jake had a recollection of a dinner at a professor's house and Sophie commenting about the centerpiece. "The ones that look like roses, but aren't actually roses. I think it starts with a *p*."

"Peonies?"

"Yes. That's it. Pink would be good."

"I'm on it."

"Thanks, Audrey." Jake sat back in his chair and turned his sights to the city again. The sky was dark, snow flurries starting to fall. Could it be as simple as flowers? Jake doubted it highly. Nothing was ever simple with Sophie. But he needed to mix things up or he would lose ground. He knew for a fact that other investors and developers were courting her and her sister. His pitch would work so much better in person, especially if he could get Sophie alone. She'd always dropped the tougher parts of her veneer when it was just the two of them.

Visions of Sophie flashed in his head—her lush red hair, her full lips, the way her brown eyes flickered with gold when she smiled. Each thought of her was more beautiful than the last. They'd been drawn to each other from the moment they met at a business school mixer. She laughed at his jokes and flirted like crazy with him, touching his arm and flashing her gorgeous eyes. They shared an immediate chemistry that was off the charts.

In any other scenario, Jake would have taken her home that very first night.

But he made a point of keeping their relationship platonic, even when there had been days where that required superhuman strength. He wanted her. There was no question about that. But he knew how brutal those two years of school were going to be. He couldn't afford to have a fellow classmate royally pissed at him for seducing her and then calling things off before they got serious, which was what Jake did every time. The panic when a woman started to get close to him was real. There was no erasing the part of his history that made him feel that way.

Still, the night they both gave in to their attraction had been magical. He couldn't deny that. Two years of waiting and wondering and resisting can make giving in that much more delicious. They'd been studying at the library for hours, preparing for one of their final exams. Exhausted, Jake had asked Sophie if she wanted to go get a beer. She then realized how late it was, and in a panic asked Jake back to her apartment.

"My roommate is out of town and I'm supposed to feed her cat. The poor thing is probably starving. Come to my place. Okay?"

"Yeah. Sure. I just can't study anymore."

When they got to Sophie's, after the cat had been fed, they sat on the couch and had a drink. To this day, he could remember the moment when he'd decided to finally kiss her. She'd put her gorgeous red hair in a pile on top of her head, and she'd laughed at one of his goofy jokes, quite possibly a little too hard, and her hair slumped to the side. She'd pulled at the tie, and it tumbled down onto her shoulders. Maybe he'd been tired. Maybe it was the

beer. He only knew that after nearly two years of waiting, he had to kiss her.

So he did.

No woman had melted into him the way Sophie did.
Her lips were pillow soft, her sweet smell truly beguiling,
and her hands were everywhere. Before he knew what
was happening, she was tugging his shirt up over his
head and pushing him down on the couch, her body settling between his legs and driving him crazy with desire.

The moment when she sat back up, took his hand and
led him to her bedroom was one of the most surreal. He'd
fantasized about Sophie plenty, but she was also one of
the only female friendships he'd managed to not only
build, but maintain. He'd thought about it for a second
that night, considered telling her it wasn't a good idea for
them to go to bed together, but once she took off her top
and her stunning red hair tumbled back onto her shoulders? He was a goner.

They'd made love three times that night. They even
took a shower together in the morning, which should
have been enough to convince him that Sophie might be
the one worth trying for more with. But when the time
came for him to think about going back to his place, and
it was clear that there were expectations for the two of
them to discuss where this next went, Jake panicked just
as he always had.

"You know, Sophie, last night was amazing, and I will
always remember it. But we're such great friends and we
both have so much we want to do in our careers. I think
it's best if we chalk this up to two friends blowing off a
little steam together."

He knew the instant he'd said it that she deserved better. Sophie had wrapped her robe around her tight and

nodded, forcing a smile. "Oh, yeah. Of course. A couple of friends hooking up, right? Happens all the time."

He'd heard the hurt in her voice, but he told himself that with time it would go away. Sophie was too special—too smart, too funny, too beautiful. Some amazing guy, somewhere, would meet her and snatch her up and treat her the way she deserved to be treated. Jake wasn't that guy. He didn't possess the trust to let someone in like that. He'd tried and failed. He was self-aware enough to understand this particular shortcoming.

After their one night together, his friendship with Sophie quickly returned to its previous state, or at least close to it. Neither of them mentioned what had happened, they helped each other study, and soon enough, it was time to graduate. They'd hugged for a very long time that day. They'd wished each other luck. It was all perfectly normal and uncontroversial, except for Sophie's parting words.

"I love you, Jake."

Stunned, he ignored what she'd said and simply let her walk away. A few times during the eight years since then, Sophie's words had resurfaced in his memory. He always fought them back. *I love you* was something a woman said right before she left forever. And sure enough, that was exactly what Sophie Eden did.

Two

Once again, Sophie had to start her workday by rushing through the shoe department, but she didn't make it far before she stopped dead in her tracks. A stunning pair of chartreuse-green Blahniks had appeared since yesterday. Perched on a tall pedestal, with small bundles of sparkly beads and intricate lacing up the front, they were like a phoenix rising from the ashes of the other, lesser shoes. They stole her breath. She had to have them. They were sexy as all get-out. If only she had a man to test them out on. Her dating calendar had been tragically light since coming to work at Eden's.

"Marie," Sophie called out to the department head. She was training a new salesperson. "Can you set aside a pair of these for me?"

Marie smiled generously. "I thought those might catch your eye. They're already in your office, sitting on your desk. Just have Lizzie buzz me if you don't like them and I'll have someone come by to pick them up."

"Do you really think I might not like them?"

Marie shook her head. "Not a chance."

Sophie grinned. Her job was sometimes overwhelming, but this was one of her favorite perks. Without another second to waste, she rushed back to the elevator and up to the top floor.

"Morning, Lizzie. What's the gift-basket count today?"

"Five, I'm afraid. I think people are trying to outdo each other now."

Sophie trailed into her office and set down her things, bypassing the baskets and zeroing in on the beautiful heels nestled in a box and tissue on her desk. She sat down and removed her pumps and worked her feet into the new shoes. "Did we at least get anything good?"

"How do two dozen gourmet caramel apples slathered in chocolate and sprinkles sound?"

"Like I need to skip lunch. Which is perfect because today is crazy." Sophie stood up and took the new pumps for a spin around her office. "What do you think?"

"Honestly? Sexy. Super sexy."

Sophie admired her feet again. Sure her toes were pinched and her arches would be screaming by the time the day was over, but she didn't care. Right now, beautiful shoes were the only things that were making her happy. "If Marie comes by, tell her I'm keeping them."

"Will do. Now, back to your crazy day. There's a long list of fires that need putting out all over the store."

"Great. Can't wait." Sophie gave the statement all the sarcasm it deserved.

"All six employees of the coat check have come down with the flu. We got someone from housewares to fill in, but you know how people feel about working the coat check. The ladies' lounge on the fourth floor flooded at some point late yesterday and nobody noticed. There's some water damage on three, but I have maintenance on it. Lastly, the perfume counter somehow managed to run out of Chanel No. 5, which seems like a problem at Christmas."

"A huge problem." Gram would've been horrified.

"Unfortunately, the distributor can't get us anything for a week."

"I'm on it. Can you call a temp agency to see if we can get somebody else to cover the coat check? People stay a lot longer in the store if they don't have to carry around their winter gear."

Lizzie left and Sophie wasted no time getting to work, first taking care of the more urgent matters, like the critical depletion of the Chanel No. 5 supply. After that, she pulled up the previous day's sales numbers, which, although good, weren't where they needed to be. This was one of those instances where she really needed Mindy to help her brainstorm on new marketing and store ideas for next year. But, of course, Mindy hadn't merely expressed her disinterest; she'd said she absolutely refused to help out.

Lizzie rapped on Sophie's door. "It appears that Jake Wheeler has taken things to the next level."

"What now? Giant gourmet fortune cookies?"

Lizzie shook her head. "No. He's here. With flowers. Lots and lots of flowers."

"Here? He's here?" Incomprehensible excitement rushed through her, followed quickly by a dizzying dose of jitters. She hadn't seen Jake in eight years. It had taken three of those to get over him, and even then she wasn't totally sure she'd managed to get him completely out of her system. Knowing what the mere mention of his name did to her made it seem that much more unlikely she'd accomplished the task. "What did you tell him?"

"He knows you're here. Sorry, but Marie stopped by to check on your shoes and he heard me say that you were wearing them right now."

"Lots of flowers?"

"Lots and lots."

Sophie sucked in a deep breath and decided it was best to just get this over with. She couldn't hide from him forever, even though she desperately wanted to. "Okay. I'm coming out." She straightened her clothes, admittedly happy she'd worn a sleek, curve-hugging black dress. Jake didn't need to know that it was one of the more comfortable work outfits she owned. All he needed to know was that she looked amazing in it, and unless he'd lost some visual acuity in the last eight years, he should have no trouble seeing that.

The problem was *she* wasn't prepared to see *him*, especially not as she marched into the reception area and was confronted by his face, somehow more handsome eight years later, poking out above an armful of her favorite flowers—pink peonies. It was as if her subconscious had constructed this scene to disarm her. To leave her as a puddle on the floor. Between the heady smell of the flowers and the mind-blowing sight of Jake, she was surprised she could still stand.

His dark hair was just as thick and unruly as ever. Good God, she'd spent an embarrassing amount of time fantasizing about running her fingers through it. And when she'd finally had the chance, it was even better than she'd imagined. "Hi, Sophie. It's been a long time."

His penetrating green eyes broke her down as he unsubtly checked her out from head to toe. His unforgettable mouth pulled into a self-assured grin, one that said he was greatly enjoying the fact that he'd made it into her office. They were finally face-to-face.

"It has been a long time, hasn't it?" Sophie stood a little straighter, but it was just a defense mechanism. She'd forgotten how vulnerable it made her feel to meet his appraisal. Aside from a beautiful pair of black leather wingtips and the hem of charcoal-gray trousers, every other part of Jake was obscured by the flowers. The war that raged inside her whenever Jake popped into her head, or now, her world, was reignited. He knew what he was doing. He knew exactly how weak she was for sweet gestures and sentimentality. This wasn't about expressing his feelings. This was about Jake Wheeler getting what he wanted—his hands on Eden's Department Store.

"I brought flowers."

"So I gather. First fruit, now this?" Sophie planted both hands on her hips, wanting to come off as powerful. Invincible. Certainly as someone who could never be hurt. She dug the heel of her shoe into the office carpet, noting that he couldn't resist the chance to look at her legs. Once again, Mr. Blahnik had done his job.

Jake laughed. "I'm working my way through all the best gifts that start with the letter *f.* Not sure I'm prepared to invest in a Ferrari, though, judging by your reaction to the flowers. I might just go with a ferret."

Sophie was trying to contain her smile. His quick wit had always gotten to her, but it was yet another of his considerable assets, one that he would likely use to soften her defenses. "You're terrible. You think you can just show up at my office with the world's largest arrangement of my favorite flowers and I'll just talk to you?"

"As a matter of fact, I do."

The heat was rising in her cheeks, making her all the more determined to keep this a short visit. She had a million things to do and Jake was nothing but trouble, however nice it was to look at him. "Ten minutes. That's all you get."

"How about ten minutes to catch up and ten to talk business?"

"This isn't a negotiation. We'll spend ten talking business and then you can leave." She wasn't interested in catching up or reliving old times. It was too painful to think about how over-the-moon she'd been for him and how effortlessly he'd rejected her.

"Okay. But what about the flowers? It would be nice to put them down somewhere. Or at least feel like you appreciate them. Peonies are not available in Manhattan in the winter. I had to have them flown in."

His words hit her in one fell swoop. This man she had once cared about deeply had been jumping through considerable hoops to get to her. His motives might be questionable, but perhaps she needed to stop being an ice queen about it. "I'm sorry. I do appreciate them. They're beautiful."

She took two careful steps toward him, not sure whether she should look at him or the peonies. With every inch closer to Jake, she felt herself fall under his spell a little more. She reached for the flowers, but they were so bulky that he had to lean unimaginably close to lay them in her arms. The penetrating gaze of his green eyes left her wondering if this was a dream. Somewhere behind the veneer of expensive gifts and grand gestures, the well-made wool coat and tempting five o'clock shadow, this man who had once been her entire world was still living and breathing.

"Thank you," she muttered. "They really are gorgeous."

Jake didn't step away. He didn't break the connection between them either, his warm hand on her bare elbow, his lips just as kissable as they'd always been, maybe even more so. "They're nothing on you, Soph. I have to say you look amazing. All this time apart has done you well."

Sophie's knees wobbled. His voice caused a deep tremor that resonated through her entire body. "You look great, too. But you were always handsome. You know that." *Handsome* was such an inadequate word for Jake, it was ridiculous. Perhaps it was because he was so much more than good-looking. There was the swagger. The easy confidence. The glint in his eye that made you feel like you were the only woman in his orbit.

"Doesn't mean I don't like hearing it."

Sophie held her breath. If this were a movie, this would be the part where he'd throw caution to the wind, take her into his arms and kiss her, crushing what might be a thousand dollars in flowers between them. She couldn't let herself get carried away with that particular mental image, so she cast her sights down at the arrangement in her arms and gave them a sniff. "I'd better get these in some water."

She hurried over to Lizzie and deposited them on her desk. "If you could put these in some water, that would be great."

"Absolutely." Lizzie looked past Sophie and eyed Jake.

It was easy to see how much she was appreciating the view. "Would you like me to hold your calls?"

A good interruption would make for an easier escape if she started to feel overmatched by Jake, but she had to get through this. She had to listen to his pitch, try not to let the past creep in and send him on his way. "I think I'll be fine." She waved Jake on to her office. "Come on. We'll meet in here."

A certain sense of pride hit Sophie when she stepped inside. Yes, this job was her birthright, but she worked hard and her office was impressive, especially now. Reginald and his team had really gone all out. Each of the six windows in her corner office had its own fresh wreath decorated with flocked pinecones and berries, tied with a wide white velvet bow. Sparkly white and silver garland framed the views of the city beautifully. But the tree was the real showstopper, decorated with silver glass balls, tiny white-and-red birds wired to the branches and more twinkle lights than Sophie had ever seen in a single application. Every time she looked at the holiday iteration of her office, her heart swelled.

"Please. Have a seat," Sophie said, offering one of the two upholstered chairs opposite her desk.

"It looks like Christmas exploded," Jake said, sounding a bit stunned.

"It's beautiful, isn't it?" Sophie stepped behind her desk, surveying the room and ignoring his poor choice of words. Surely he didn't mean it in such a crude way.

"Who did this to your office?"

"Reginald. Our creative director. He really outdid himself. I don't know how I'm going to get any work done at all. I just want to stare at it." She folded her hands in her lap, deciding it was no longer time for small talk. "Now, why don't you say what you came to say."

He slowly unbuttoned his coat and draped it over the back of one of the chairs, still admiring the room. Meanwhile, Sophie was trying not to stare at how incredible he looked in his impeccably tailored suit. He cleared his throat, crossed his leg and sat back in his chair, nothing less than pure, casual confidence. "As you know, you and your sister are in a very unique situation. You are not only set to inherit one of the largest commercial buildings in Manhattan, your grandmother had the foresight and the means to purchase the land, as well. You don't come across that every day. I'd like to buy the property. I've already told your sister that I'm prepared to pay 4.5 billion for the land and the building."

Sophie worked with a lot of numbers every day, but that one was a doozy. She knew how much the property was worth, and Jake had clearly done his homework. The offer was in line with market value, but just sweet enough to make her have to think twice. She drew a deep breath through her nose to calm herself enough to deliver her answer. "Thank you, but no."

"You can ask any appraiser in the city. It's a very generous offer. I'm willing to move quickly. I have a small group of partners on this deal and we're prepared to do an all-cash sale."

Sophie found a lump in her throat. That was more money than she could likely ever spend, but this wasn't about cash in the bank, at least not for her. This was about carrying out Gram's wishes. Still, it was a good thing Mindy wasn't here right now because she would strangle Sophie for what she was about to say. "Again, no. But thank you."

Jake smiled and nodded as if she'd just agreed to everything he wanted, a tried-and-true negotiation tactic. She wasn't surprised he was resorting to it. "Maybe it's best if I just let you think about it for a few days. Let that big, fat, delicious number tumble around in your head. Because I can guarantee you that any of these other companies and developers are not in a position to pay what I'm willing to pay." His voice held an edge of determination that betrayed the pleased look on his face.

Still, Sophie had to be firm. "I understand what you're saying, but the answer is no. My grandmother worked too hard for me to simply walk away from it."

Jake nodded slowly again. "I know. She was a legend. At one time, she was one of the most successful businesspeople in the city."

"In the country," Sophie interjected. "Quite possibly the world. There were seventy-six stores in twelve countries at the height of Eden's."

"Yes. And now you're back down to this one store. It was the 1980s. It was a different time. Retail isn't what it once was. Frankly, owning a store this big, at this time, is a disaster waiting to happen. You're going to die a very slow, painful death." He was no longer trying to butter her up. Now he was resorting to cold, hard facts, and Sophie didn't like it at all.

"Always the pessimist, aren't you? You know, I think I'll do just fine on my own. And if I don't, I'll just have to die trying." Sophie pushed back from her desk and stood, sucking in a deep breath. This wasn't how she wanted things to end between them, but end they must. She had to put him on notice that she would not waver. She would not sell to him. She would not allow herself to fall under Jake's spell. "Thanks for coming by. And thank you for the flowers."

He cocked his eyebrows and stood. "And the fruit."

"And the fruit. But none of that was necessary, nor is it necessary in the future. I don't need to come into my office to find a flamingo or feather boas."

Jake stood there looking at her, hands in his pants pockets. It felt like he was trying to tear down the invisible barrier she'd tried to build between them, and she didn't like it. "You know, Sophie. I have the distinct impression that this is about far more than your grandmother."

"What? My refusal to do the deal?"

"That and your general distaste for having me share the same air as you."

Sophie froze. All she could hear was the thunder of her own heartbeat in her ears. So this was how he was going to play this. He wasn't going to politely ignore their history as she'd done. He wanted to dredge it up. Sophie could do that. She didn't have to let him off so easy anyway. "The way things ended between us is difficult to ignore if that's what you're suggesting."

"The last time I saw you was on graduation day. I thought things were fine. We hugged. We wished each other well."

That moment was such a permanent part of Sophie's memories it was as if it was tattooed on her brain. It was still a bit raw, even after all this time. She could still feel the deep longing for him, a tug from the center of her chest that told her he was all she ever wanted or needed, but she'd never have him. *With my very beaten-up heart, I told you that I loved you, and you acted as though I hadn't said it.* "That's not quite how I remember it, but

I'm glad you can look back on it so fondly. I was still pretty hurt about the way things played out after our one night together."

Jake's forehead crinkled as his eyebrows drew together. "That was for the best. We both know that wasn't going to go anywhere. I wanted to save our friendship, and I thought I had. Now I'm starting to think I've been wrong all this time."

Sophie shook her head. "Of course you felt as though it was up to you to save us from each other. No need for discussion or a conversation. Just a few parting words to get you off the hook, right? It might take two to tango, but only one person has to call it off."

"If it upset you that much, you should've said something at the time. You seemed completely fine with it."

"I didn't really have time to absorb it. You practically broadsided me."

"Trust me. You're a happier woman right now than you would've been if things had continued."

Anger began to bubble under Sophie's skin. He had no way of knowing things would have ended badly between them. If he'd just given them a chance, they could have been happy. They could have had it all. "Ah, well, apparently your crystal ball works great. Mine is off at the shop. But thanks for watching out for me."

Again, he only looked at her, his mind clearly working hard. "You know, if it wasn't completely inappropriate, I would ask if I could kiss you right now."

Sophie's heart seized up in her chest. A kiss? Was he insane? "I thought you were supposed to be saving me from being hurt."

"I know, but I'm just thinking that the first time I

kissed you, you melted right into my arms. That was the moment I knew I could convince you of anything."

She dared to peer up into his dangerous green eyes. They swirled with such intensity it was hard to know whether she'd be able to remain standing or if they'd simply sweep her away. She couldn't believe he would so brazenly use her weakness for him against her. "Get out. Get out of my office right now."

"You won't kick out the guy who brought you a bushel of your favorite flowers."

"I'm serious, Jake. Don't make me call Duane from security. He's six foot six, three hundred and fifty pounds, and has a very short fuse."

"Soph, come on. I'm just kidding. You know me. I'm a kidder."

With a jab of her finger, Sophie directed him to her office door. The exit. "The problem, Jake, is that I do know you. I know exactly what you're capable of, which is the reason I have to ask you to leave."

In a daze, Jake stepped off the elevator on Eden's ground floor. He felt a bit like he'd been run over by a truck. His meeting with Sophie had not gone well, but even more than that, he'd forgotten what being around her did to him. Her sleek black dress was enough to make him sign over his entire business, hugging every gorgeous curve of her body, reminding him of everything he'd had and given up. And that was only the start—her trademark red tresses tumbling over her shoulders, her deep brown eyes blazing and her full cherry-pink lips tempting him into making an admittedly bold remark. It was a business meeting and he shouldn't have brought up kissing. But everything he'd said had been the absolute truth. She had melted into him that night. They were on the same wavelength, completely.

He'd really thought the flowers might do the trick. Sophie was sweet and sentimental. What woman like that doesn't appreciate that sort of gesture? He hadn't expected an immediate yes to his proposition, but he had hoped she would at least consider it. Instead, she'd done nothing more than try to create distance between them. If she'd been any more successful, she'd have had him on the other side of bulletproof glass. It was a real shame. There had been a time when Sophie would come running to him. Not anymore.

He met David, his driver, at the curb and jumped into the back of the black Escalade, his mind a jumble of thoughts of Sophie and business as the sights of the city whizzed by in a blur. He had to turn this around. His killer instinct, the one that had brought him success that surprised even him, wouldn't allow him to back off simply because of one bad conversation. His fellow members of the War Chest were eager to get the jump on this deal, and with each day closer to the reading of Victoria Eden's will, the more unlikely it would be that Jake's plan would work. Everyone in the city with a fat bank account would be pursuing Sophie and her sister by then. If Jake was going to bring this deal to fruition, he had to do it now. Wait and lose out. That was all there was to it.

By the time he reached his office, Jake knew that flowers and fruit baskets had been the wrong approach. He needed to go with reason. She and her sister were sitting on a fortune. All they needed to do was cash in their golden ticket. He needed to show Sophie on paper, in hard numbers, why it was in her best interest to sell. Eden's future was indeed grim. He was certain of it.

"Unless I get a call from Sophie or Mindy Eden, I'm in a meeting," he said to Audrey as he strode past her desk.

"Yes, sir, Mr. Wheeler."

He sat at his desk, pulled out a fresh legal pad, grabbed the folder of background materials Audrey had pulled together on Eden's and opened up a new browser window on his laptop. "Time to figure out just how bad things look for Eden's Department Store."

Hours later, Jake had pages and pages of numbers and notes. He'd read two dozen articles about the future of retail, made estimates as to how much space Eden's was using and wasting with some of their departments. Unfortunately for Jake, the most profitable department, women's shoes, only stirred up thoughts of Sophie in the ones she'd been wearing today. They were some of the sexiest shoes he'd ever seen. For a moment, he had a vision of them on his shoulders and Sophie at his mercy, an idea he immediately wrenched from his mind, although he might be forced to revisit it later.

He moved on to analyzing Eden's online presence and the amount of company resources they were devoting to everything from marketing and advertising to store security and, yes, decorating executive offices like the inside of a snow globe.

This was a bit like reading tea leaves, but he had to make do with what he had, and there was a great deal of satisfaction to take from the knowledge that no other money guy or investor was putting in this kind of work. Sophie would see that he was just looking out for her. He had her best interests at heart.

And himself, of course. This deal would be the talk of developer circles for years. Decades even. And he'd grow his bank account considerably.

But first, he had to call the one person who was on his side—Mindy Eden.

"Jake, I told you the last time we talked, I'm not the one you need to convince. It's all Sophie. I have zero interest in anything having to do with Eden's. I have more than enough on my plate."

Jake tapped his pen on his planner and looked out his office window. The holiday market down in the park was again bustling with people. He'd never understand some people's obsession with Christmas. "Okay. So then tell me how I get through to her. She's not only digging in her heels about the store, she refuses to have a conversation with me."

Mindy laughed. "You do know you broke her heart, right?"

Jake froze as Mindy's words worked their way through his head. "I did not break her heart. Sophie and I had a little too much to drink one night, we had some fun, and I ended it the next day so she didn't have to. Believe me, I was looking out for your sister. Any other guy would've strung her along for months." Did Sophie truly feel as though he'd broken her heart? He'd only tried to protect her.

"Or he might have fallen in love with my perfectly smart and beautiful sister and lived happily ever after."

Not this guy. Jake swallowed hard to stuff those words back inside him. It was one thing to get personal with Sophie, and quite another to talk about subjects like this with Mindy. "Something tells me she would've gotten tired of me real quick."

"Hmm. I don't know about that."

"Do you think it would help to try to talk to her outside of the office? Maybe catch up with her on the weekend when she's more relaxed?"

"You must know that Sophie doesn't relax. I'm not sure a weekend will help you. Plus, she's gone this weekend."

"To where?"

"Our grandmother's house in Upstate, near Scarsdale. It's where the family spends Christmas. She's heading up tomorrow morning."

The wheels in Jake's head were turning. Opportunity was in the air. "Is that the house where you and Sophie spent your summers?"

"That's the one. Eden House."

"Sophie used to talk about it all the time. She seemed to have a lot of great memories from being there."

"We both do, but yes, Sophie loves it. She goes every chance she gets."

"Are you going up this weekend, too?"

"I told her I'd drive up Saturday night. The weather's not looking good, but I think she'll kill me if I don't show up."

This might be perfect—drive up Friday and convince Sophie, Mindy arrives Saturday and they would work out the rest of the deal. The commotion of Eden's wouldn't be a distraction, and hopefully Sophie would be more relaxed and open to the things he had to say to her.

Also, it was clearly time to smooth her ruffled feathers. He hated that she might have been harboring ill will toward him all these years. He'd truly had her best interests in mind when he'd called off their romance before it had a chance to start. He wasn't about to delve into specifics or dig up his own past. There were too many unhappy memories to be found. But he could at least remind Sophie that they had once been very close. He could at least show her that they could, in fact, get along and find a way to help each other.

"So, Mindy. I'm wondering if you can help me with something."

"Sure. What?"

"I'm going to need the address for Eden House."

Three

The instant Sophie turned onto the winding private drive leading to Eden House, she felt more like herself. Her Bentley Bentayga SUV crept silently ahead as the family estate came into view—graying cedar shakes trimmed in crisp white, with three stone chimneys poking up from the gable roof, all of it surrounded by a maze of manicured hedges. Sophie had nothing but the happiest of memories here—endless sunny summer days in the pool, leisurely morning strolls through the rose garden with Gram, rainy days of gin rummy and evenings spent roasting marshmallows over the fire pit on the backyard terrace. Soon this house would be hers, bequeathed to her by her grandmother. Would it ever again be filled with love and laughter? This Christmas was the first big test, and she was terrified that she'd fail.

Sophie and Mindy had spent every Christmas of their

lives at Eden House. The family tradition went back to Gram's childhood when her parents had built the house, although it wasn't given the name Eden until Gram inherited it years later as a married woman. Her parents had done well for themselves in the 1950s, importing and wholesaling fabrics for the garment industry. The entire country was booming then, and if you were somebody, you had to have a vacation home. It was simply what you did to show the world that you were a success.

Sophie pulled around to the side entrance and parked her car under the porte cochere in order to ferry the groceries straight into the kitchen. As soon as she opened her car door, she was hit by a bracing cold, the wind whipping past her, picking up the tails of her coat and tossing her hair into disarray. The clean but icy smell of snow was in the air. The forecast was for a fast-moving system that would leave behind one to two inches. Sophie wasn't too worried. In some ways, it would be a dream to get snowed in at Eden House. The power lines were buried, so the electricity rarely went out. She had her cell phone and internet if she needed to get any work done, and there was more than enough wine in the family cellar. A day or two where she was forced to stay away from the store might do her good.

Sophie struggled with the house key, her arms loaded down with shopping bags and her fingers freezing from the cold. She nearly fell through the door and into the kitchen when the lock finally turned. She plopped her bags down on the large center island and opened the Sub-Zero fridge to put away her perishables. That was when the tears started.

The refrigerator was nearly empty, but there on the second shelf were three bottles of Krug champagne.

Gram adored champagne, especially Krug. She would've sipped it morning, noon and night if it were in any way socially acceptable. Sophie took one of the bottles from the shelf and smoothed her fingers over the familiar gold foil label. This was an iconic image from her childhood, when champagne was an exotic drink meant only for grown-ups. Gram had brought these bottles up in early October in anticipation of the family's Christmas celebration. And now she wouldn't be there to enjoy them.

Sophie carefully slid the bottle back into place, wiped her tears from her cheeks and put away her groceries. Countless memories of her grandmother would crop up this weekend, and she needed to pace herself. Gram would want her to unwind and not dwell too much on sadness. She'd had an unwavering belief in the power of positive thinking. Life was so much more enjoyable if you could just find a way to be happy. Bad things would happen, but the sun always came up the next day and, somehow, life went on.

Sophie grabbed her suitcase out of the car and lugged it inside. It was snowing now—fat, fluffy flakes. She'd better call Mindy. Her sister was not the type to pay attention to the weather.

"Are you there?" Mindy asked when she answered her phone.

"Just got here, and it's snowing. I checked the forecast and now it's saying at least four inches. Maybe more. I really think you should consider leaving earlier than tomorrow morning. I'm worried the roads won't be passable."

Several moments of background noise filtered through from her sister's side of the line. "There's no way. Things are crazy busy here."

"But you're the boss. You have to take a break sometime, and this is the weekend to decorate the house. There won't be another one." With every new word from Sophie's mouth, she started to feel a bit more panicked. She cared deeply about following through on the family tradition. "I can't do it by myself. I don't want to do it by myself. It's not right."

"First off, I have no doubt that you can do it yourself. Second, there's a chance you won't have to."

"So you'll knock off early and get your butt up here?"

"No. I'm sticking to my plan to leave tomorrow. But there's a chance you might run into Jake."

"Run into him? Where?" Sophie's heart leaped into her throat.

"I don't know. The kitchen? The sitting room?"

"What did you do? Did you send him after me?"

"As serious as you are about not selling, I'm just as determined to change your mind."

A swarm of conflicting emotions buzzed in Sophie's head—anger, frustration and the familiar flutter of anticipation that had become synonymous with seeing Jake. How Sophie wished that part of her brain would stop being so hard on her. "I can't believe you would do this to me."

"I wouldn't if it was a stranger. But you know Jake. You've known him forever. I just think he wanted the chance to talk to you alone."

The word echoed all around her—*alone, alone, alone.* "He won't come. He has too much pride to grovel."

"He showed up at your office with dozens and dozens of peonies, didn't he? Sounds to me like he'll do anything to make a good impression on you."

Sophie shook her head and started down the center hall, with its herringbone brick floor and wide white baseboards. She could already smell the fresh pine of the Christmas tree she'd asked Barry, the Eden House caretaker, to deliver. The fragrance alone lifted her spirits, all while the idea of Jake trying to make an impression aggravated her. He'd never really tried before now, certainly not eight years ago when she'd wanted it more than anything. So what had changed? The promise of a big deal. That was all Jake cared about. Any overtures he made were not only designed to manipulate her and pull at her heartstrings, they were solely prompted by money. She couldn't let him play with her like that. "I have to go."

"Are you mad, Soph?"

"Of course I'm mad. You put me in Jake's crosshairs. You know how badly he hurt me. He broke my heart."

"I know that. I reminded him of it when we talked."

"You did?" Sophie stepped into what Gram had always called the sitting room. The tree was in the corner, waiting to be trimmed, all while Sophie was overcome with the sort of embarrassment that haunts a teenage girl forever. "He already doesn't take me seriously as a businesswoman. Why did you have to bring our romantic past into it?"

"Because he's a clueless man. He couldn't figure out why you were giving him such a hard time."

"I don't want to sell. This has nothing to do with romance."

Mindy tutted as if she was scolding Sophie. "You really expect me to believe that? Because I don't. Your history with him is clouding your judgment, and you need to get past that. Not just for my sake, but for yours. I think it'll be good for you two to finally talk things through. Clear the air."

Sophie trailed over to one of the tall leaded-glass windows overlooking the sprawling yard. What she could see of the grounds was already covered in a thin blanket of white, with the storm steadily adding more layers. In the spring and summer, this was a lush green vista that had always seemed to go on forever—much like her feelings for Jake, the ones that she desperately wished would just end. "There's nothing for Jake and me to talk about. I already know how he feels about me."

"And how is that, exactly?"

"He sees me as sweet, gullible Sophie. The woman who would do anything for him. I'm not that girl anymore. I won't let him trick me into being her, either."

Mindy grumbled. "Just listen to him if he shows up, okay? That's all I ask."

"As long as you promise you'll still try to come up tomorrow."

"I'll do my best. I'll give you a call in the morning with an update, okay?"

"Fine."

"Love you, Soph."

"Love you, too." Sophie hung up and drew in a deep breath, blowing it out through her nose. She considered calling Jake and telling him to not come, but maybe Mindy was right. Maybe it was time for the two of them to really hash things out. Maybe that would finally let her forget him for good.

In the meantime, Sophie didn't dare start the decorating until Mindy arrived tomorrow. Plus, after her long drive, and her hellish workweek, she was simply exhausted. A nap wasn't merely in order; it was a necessity. She grabbed her suitcase and headed upstairs.

Eden House slept twenty people comfortably, which

meant that Sophie and Mindy had always each had their own bedroom. Sophie's was the second on the right in the upstairs hall, directly across from Gram's master suite. It was beautifully decorated in white and soft tones of gray and pink, with a cloud-like four-poster bed and the most picturesque view of the backyard and woods beyond. Sophie changed into comfy lavender silk pajama pants with a tank top and climbed under the fluffy comforter. Not bothering to set the alarm on her phone, she closed her eyes, let her head sink into the feather pillows and tried as hard as she could not to think about whether or not Jake was going to turn up on her doorstep.

When Sophie woke, the room was much darker. From somewhere beyond her door, she'd heard a banging sound. *Bang bang bang.* She bolted up in bed and clutched the covers to her chest, her brain slowly whirring to life. How long had she been asleep? She fumbled for her phone. Her nap had lasted for hours. *Bang bang bang.* Sophie jumped. Then she heard the more pleasant ring of the doorbell and she realized what all that banging was. Jake.

She grabbed a thick cream-colored cardigan, tucked her feet into her boiled-wool slippers and hurried down the hall. As she descended the staircase, clutching the banister, she craned her neck, trying to see through the sidelight. The snow was coming down so fast now it was impossible to make out much more than a dark jacket and a tall figure.

Was it Jake? Logic said yes, but what if it wasn't? Sophie was not a paranoid person, but if that was a strange man out there, she'd better be prepared. She was all alone in this house, practically a sitting duck. Frantically, she scanned the foyer for something to defend herself with.

Nothing too scary. She just needed a little insurance. Unfortunately, everything her eyes landed on was too bulky, like a lamp, or useless, like a book. Then she spotted the cast-iron fleur-de-lis doorstop next to the front door. It was heavy but fit into her hand nicely. It would have to do, although she couldn't imagine having the nerve to ever hit anyone with it. The threat was most important, she decided.

Gripping it tightly in one hand, she held it flat against the side of her leg. With her other hand, she flipped the dead bolt and unlocked the door.

Icy cold rushed in with a gust so fierce that she fell back on her heels. Before her stood the most handsome mirage she'd ever seen. Jake. In a puffy black coat and a gray stocking cap that made his eyes look even more intense, like he was seeing right through her. "Jake? What are you doing here?" Of course, she knew the answer. She just wanted to hear it from his mouth.

His shoulders were bunched up around his ears. The wind whipped, sending snow flying past him and into the foyer. "Can I come in?"

Her heart pounded in her chest. "Yes. Of course." She opened the door wider, watching as he stepped inside and stomped the snow from his feet. "What are you doing here?" Again, she waited for the answer. Jake was here because there was no way he was going to give up after their one conversation in her office. He had no problem walking away from Sophie the woman, but he couldn't leave Sophie the business deal alone.

Her hand dropped to her side. The doorstop plummeted, landed square on her foot and tumbled to the floor with a thud. "Ow!" Sophie's foot crackled with unimaginable pain. She jumped and raised her injured foot, hopping her way over to the staircase. Jake mercifully shut out the cold behind him.

"Soph. Are you okay?" He rushed over to her. His voice held enough true concern to make her feel lightheaded.

Sophie wasn't sure where to look. At her injured foot or at Jake. "Why did you have to show up and make me drop a doorstop on my foot?"

"Why are you walking around the house with a lead weight in your hand?"

"If you were an intruder, I was planning to knock you out with it."

"I guess I should have called first, huh?"

"That would've been nice."

He dropped to his knee and tugged off his gloves, setting them on the stair tread. He reached for her foot. He was so close now, his cheeks bright pink from the cold, but the rest of his face had its normal tawny tone, the one that looked so perfect with the dark scruff on his jaw. She had an irrational desire to touch it.

"Can you take off your slipper so I can look at it?" Impatient Jake didn't wait for her; he simply removed it himself.

"You still haven't told me what you're— Ow!" She recoiled from the pain.

He held his hands up in surrender. "Sorry. I just… I think we need to get some ice on this and get it elevated. There's a chance you broke your foot." He stood, tugging off his hat and rolling his broad shoulders out of his jacket. To her horror, he tossed them onto her grandmother's upholstered settee.

"Jake. That's velvet and there's snow on your jacket. The water will leave a mark on the fabric." She knew she was being a pain in the butt, but she couldn't help it. He was being thorough, determined Jake—the guy who never gives up on what he wants, no matter what it takes. She had to remind him that he was on her turf. If there was an upper hand to be had here, it was hers.

"We need to get your foot elevated. Can I carry you somewhere so you can lie down?"

The idea of lying down near him had her thinking all sorts of crazy thoughts—she nearly answered that her bedroom was right upstairs. Nearly. She needed to retrain her brain to stop thinking about him that way. There had been a time when she was skilled at keeping herself in the friend zone, but she was out of practice. "I can walk." She had no idea if that was true. Her foot was throbbing like it had its own heartbeat.

"I'm sure you can. But I'm not going to let you hurt yourself when I can stop it."

"So I'll sell you my two billion dollars in Manhattan real estate?" She might as well just put it out there. His true intentions would go far in reminding her that however gorgeous and sexy he was, Jake was a threat to the future she wanted for herself.

"No. So you'll listen to me when I say that I need to hide out here for a few hours until the storm passes." Placing his knee on the tread immediately below her, he reached out for her. "Come on. Put your arm around my shoulders."

Sophie was prepared to protest some more, but this close, Jake's heady scent filled her nose, and that switched her brain into a far too accommodating creature. She'd long ago developed a serious weakness for his heavenly smell of soap and sandalwood, and the years apart had *not* managed to dull her reaction to it. Sophie raised her arm and he came in closer, making the fragrance even more intense. He wrapped his hand around her waist and scooped up her legs with his other arm. She had no choice but to curl her other hand around his neck and turn her face into his chest as he straightened and picked her up from the stairs.

"Where to?" he asked.

Sophie was too mesmerized by the sensory delights of being this close to Jake to think of an immediate answer. He was wearing the softest black cashmere sweater, which was a delicious contrast to the way his facial hair scratched at her temple. His body radiated so much warmth, she just wanted to stay like this. Everything about him seemed designed to draw her in. "Across the hall. The arched doorway."

Jake carried her into the sitting room. "I'm going to set you down on the couch." His warmth quickly evaporated as he let go, a very real reminder of what a disappointment it was when he decided to step away. He grabbed a pillow for behind her back and another to go under her foot. "Now ice?"

"Kitchen. Straight down the center hall. You'll find it."

He sauntered out of the room while Sophie took the opportunity to watch him walk away. Talk about a man who looked good coming and going—that was Jake. It was as if his butt was made for those jeans. But now that she was alone, doubt and reality crept back in, reclaiming their stake on her. Jake had a motive for being here, and no amount of admiring him in those jeans or breathing his inebriating scent was going to change it. Jake wanted to buy her dream out from under her, and she wasn't going to let that happen.

* * *

Jake found the ice with no problem. It was his confidence that was escaping him.

"What am I doing here?" he mumbled to himself. "This was so dumb. How desperate could I possibly look?" No answers came—spoken or otherwise. He opened several drawers until he located a dish towel to wrap up the compress for Sophie. He found himself almost glad that she'd hurt her foot. It gave him a diversion so he didn't have to answer her questions, but he knew they were coming. She never let him off the hook.

"Here we go," he said, waltzing into the room as if this was a casual meeting of the minds and it wasn't strange that he'd driven hours to get to her. He sat at the far end of the couch and carefully slipped his hand under her foot. Touching her bare skin made a long-gone recognition flicker to life inside him. He looked up at her and their gazes connected, completing a circuit, or at least that was the way it felt on his end. He quickly looked away. He had no business feeling this way about Sophie. Whatever heat and desire that had once been between them might still be smoldering, but he couldn't allow it to burst into full flame. One time, however amazing, was history. Nothing more.

He gently placed the ice pack on what was now a bulging red bump.

She winced. "Do you think I broke it?"

"Can you move your toes?"

She managed a wiggle. "A little. It hurts, though."

"How much does it hurt?"

"I don't know. I've never broken a bone before."

"Seriously? I broke my left arm twice before my tenth birthday." As a kid, he was always getting into trouble while running around the neighborhood, but that was preferable to being in the house. His home life had been lonely and unhappy, especially after his mom left him with his grandmother and never came back. He didn't like to think about it too much, even when he fully owned that it had made him into the man he was today. Independent. Determined. Untrusting.

"I was not rough-and-tumble, Jake. I was the girl reading fashion magazines and thinking too much about boys."

"But then you ended up in business school."

"That was Gram's idea. It was always her plan to groom Mindy and me to run Eden's." Sophie shifted in her seat and looked right at him, chipping away at his resolve with her warm brown eyes. "I know that's why you hunted me down."

So much for small talk. At least he didn't have to sidestep topics or make excuses. "I wouldn't say I hunted you down so much as I used the resources at my disposal to find you."

"I talked to Mindy. I think she was hoping that sending the hot handsome guy to distract me might make me give in to the idea of selling."

A smile played at the corner of his mouth, but he tried his damnedest to suppress it. He shouldn't be happy that she'd called him hot or handsome. "I don't know what her thought process was, but I know she understands that the three of us can help each other. A lot."

Sophie frowned. "So that really is the only reason you're here. One more attempt to get me to give in to you."

The thought of Sophie giving in to him...well, it was too much to take. He'd never get any business done, or repair this friendship, if he was focused on that. "That was part of it. Sure. But I also hate the idea that I can't call your office and get you to pick up the phone. I don't like the fact that I went to see you and it was like our friendship had never existed."

"My grandmother died a month ago, Jake. Believe it or not, this is about more than you and me and our history."

"But we were close once, Soph. Really close."

"*Were*, as in past tense. A lot of years have gone by, during which I heard from you exactly zero times."

"The phone works both ways. I could say the same thing for you."

Sophie jerked her foot back from Jake's hand. "I had my reasons." She leaned on the sofa arm and attempted to stand up. "Ow." She slumped back down on the cushions. "I can't have a broken foot. I don't have time for it. I have too much stuff to do."

"Hey. Easy. It's Friday." He glanced out the window, where the snow was coming down even harder than it had been fifteen minutes ago. "By the look of things, neither of us is getting out of here anytime soon."

"Was it snowing when you left the city?"

"It was. Not too bad."

"And you kept going?"

He'd thought about turning back once or twice, but two things kept him from doing that—first, his promise to his fellow investors that he would close this deal this weekend, and second, he wanted to spend time with Sophie. That line about hating the fact that she wouldn't take his calls was true. He didn't want her to hate him. "The forecast said it was only supposed to be a few inches."

"There's practically a foot out there already."

"I'm sure it'll slow down soon."

Sophie sat back against the sofa cushion. "Do you mind starting a fire? It's a bit drafty in here."

Jake was perennially hot, but if memory served, Sophie got cold all the time. "Sure thing." He hopped up from the sofa. "Where's the wood?"

"Utility room off the kitchen."

He hustled down the hall, found the wood, a stack of newspapers and a carrier. Supplies in hand, he headed back to the sitting room. He stopped for a minute to look at a few of the family pictures in the hall. One in particular held his attention—Christmas morning. Sophie looked to be about thirteen, with spindly legs and a mouth full of braces. Also there were her sister and parents, as well as her grandmother. Each face was so happy Jake found it hard to believe it was real. His own memories of Christmas looked nothing like that. How fortunate Sophie had been to grow up with that in her life—something she didn't have to doubt or question. Jake would have done anything to have had that when he was a kid.

"I can't believe Mindy sold me out," Sophie said as he returned to the room.

He opened the flue and stacked the wood across the cast-iron grate. "I called her after our run-in at your office. I thought an in-person conversation was better than one where you're unbearably busy and a million people are running around." He crumpled newspaper and tucked it between the logs, then used one of the long fireplace matches to start the fire.

"So you wanted to separate me from the herd."

He slid the fireplace screen into place and joined her back on the sofa. "From where I sit, you're already separated from the herd. You're trying to steer a sinking ship all by yourself. And the one person who could help you, your sister, wants nothing to do with it. I don't see how you're going to do it. What happens if she demands a buyout?"

Sophie collected her long hair in her hand, draping it over one shoulder. Jake had always been so mesmerized by the color. He had a serious weakness for blondes and for redheads. Sophie's color was somewhere in between, and he'd never seen that particular shade on anyone, making her doubly alluring. "I guess I'll have to figure out a way to raise the money or propose a payment plan. She is my sister. I'm sure she'll work with me."

"I don't know. She could really use that money for her business. It's important to her."

"My business is important to me, too. Everybody acts like this is no big deal and it feels like life or death to me." Her tone bubbled over with desperation. It was clear that all she wanted was for someone to hear her. She must be awfully tired of Mindy's not listening.

Jake had come to Eden House prepared to show Sophie the problems with the sustainability of her business, but this might not be the time to share everything he'd learned. Plus, one could argue that pointing out the trouble spots would only help her turn things around. He had a loyalty to her, but his first responsibility was to himself and his fellow investors. "I'm sorry. I don't want to upset you."

"Look. Here's the deal. Nothing about Eden's can even be decided until the will is read on December 18. Can we just agree to not talk about the sale until after that day? I don't want to be stuck in a house with you if we have this hanging over our heads."

This was a clever move on Sophie's part, one he hadn't seen coming. He took a moment before responding. He had to cover his own butt. At the very least, his fellow investors expected him to get a leg up on any other potential buyers. "Make me one promise?"

"That depends." She cocked an eyebrow at him. "But I'm listening."

"Promise me you won't make a deal with anyone else without first talking to me. Please don't pull the rug out from under me. I shouldn't even admit this. I know I'm just showing my cards, but chances are that I will always be able to sweeten the deal."

She eyed him with an overwhelming sense of distrust. It felt as though she was peeling back his layers, which made him extremely uncomfortable. "I'll have your back as long as you have mine. Trust is just like the phone. It goes both ways."

Jake sensed this was as close as he'd get to a victory. At least for today. "Does that mean you're willing to mend fences?"

"I'm willing to try. I think champagne might help."

Four

Sophie was proud of herself. She'd found a way to get Jake to back down about Eden's, albeit only a temporary fix. As for their friendship, was it a good idea to repair it? Was it even possible? Her doubts mostly stemmed from the hurt she was still clinging to after eight years. She could admit that much to herself. But it wasn't as simple as forgiving and forgetting. Her attraction to him was still bubbling away inside her, and now that she was back in close proximity to him, there was no telling when she might just boil over and do something stupid like kiss him. Or beg him to take off his sweater. Maybe give her a naked back rub. Stuck together until Mother Nature stopped it with the snow and the road conditions improved, there was no telling what she might do.

"You stay put," he said. "I'll get everything from the kitchen if you just tell me what I'm doing."

"It might be easier if I go with you."

"You want me to carry you again?"

A fun idea, but she needed to maintain her independence. "Maybe you just let me put my arm around your shoulders and I'll hop along on one foot."

The corners of his mouth turned down in the most adorable way. "I'm not sure."

"I'm a grown woman, Jake. I think I can take the risk." Using the arm of the sofa, she pushed herself to standing, balancing on her one good foot. "Should I see if I can put any weight on the bad one?"

He shook his head. "No way. Let's save some excitement for tomorrow." Stooping lower, he wrapped his arm around her waist. His touch was tentative, as if he was recognizing the walls still towering between them. She hated that they were there, but she'd been the one who'd spent so much time and effort shoring them up. And they *did* protect her. There was no discounting that.

She followed his cue, gently draping her arm across his firm shoulders. She leaned into him, and they ambled down the corridor, Sophie traveling one hop at a time. She used a hand to steady herself on the wall, but otherwise depended on him. If this wasn't a metaphor for the first two years of their friendship, she wasn't sure what was. She'd always felt a step behind him, and as if he would always be more capable. One more reason to be glad they'd agreed to table any discussion of Eden's. She despised being at a disadvantage, especially when what was on the line meant so much to her.

"I noticed some of the pictures," he said, gesturing to the wall. "Looks like you had some nice times with your family here."

"The best."

Jake stopped right in front of the one of Mindy and her standing by the pool. This particular snapshot had always made Sophie cringe. She was thirteen and Mindy fifteen. The vast differences in development between girls at those two ages was so evident, it was like a before-and-after picture. Mindy had real hips and breasts, curves and confidence. Sophie was flat-chested and board-straight, incapable of filling out her pink two-piece.

"I love this one," he said.

"You would. This is the only one I hate. Gram thought it was cute."

"It *is* cute. You're adorable with your braces and those long legs."

"What? No. There's nothing adorable about it. I'm so awkward, it's painful to look at."

He shrugged, studying the photograph. "I don't think it's awkward. I can see the beginnings of the beautiful woman you eventually become." He traced his finger along the lines of her body in the photo. "I can see where every curve will eventually be. Knowing what you look like now, the transformation is remarkable."

It wasn't often that Sophie's opinion of anything having to do with herself could be changed or turned around, but he had a point. She'd always looked at the photograph and allowed herself to feel dragged back to the days when she wasn't confident in the way she looked, rather than taking stock in how far she'd come. "I never thought of it that way."

"Most people don't see themselves the way the world does, but I've always suspected you might be one of the worst at it."

"What does that mean?"

"You don't give yourself enough credit for anything. You never have."

"If you're trying to flatter me to get me to soften my view on selling Eden's, it won't work."

He looked down his nose at her, admonishing her with his piercing green eyes. "We agreed not to talk about it, remember? We're supposed to be on a mission for champagne."

"You're right. I'm sorry." He tugged her away from the photograph and they finished their trip to the kitchen. Sophie used the counters to help herself get around the room as she directed Jake to the refrigerator. "There's some amazing cheese in the fridge. Smoked Gouda and Camembert with truffles. Grab that while you're in there and I'll get some crackers."

"Sounds like dinner."

"That was pretty much my plan. It's not fun to cook for one."

Jake nodded. "I know that all too well."

Sophie had to wonder how it was possible that after all this time, they were both still single. She'd had a few near misses over the years, but no one who'd meant enough for her to be devastated that it hadn't worked out. No, she'd used up all her devastation and crushed feelings on the man standing in her kitchen. "The Krug is right on the shelf. It was supposed to be for Christmas, but it'll only be Mindy, myself and our mom this year. I doubt we'll drink three bottles on our own."

"Mindy said you usually come up for the weekend to decorate the house. Why go to that much work if it's such a small celebration?"

"It wasn't always small. When I was little, my grandfather was still alive, and it's only been five years since my dad passed away. Gram had friends who would come and visit, too."

"At Christmas?"

"Sure. You know, people who weren't able to celebrate with their own families, for whatever reason. She never wanted anyone to be alone, but especially not on that day." Sophie hopped over to the pantry and got a box of water crackers then took a small silver serving tray that was tucked back in a cabinet. "What about you? Do you still go home to San Diego?"

Jake brought his findings from the refrigerator. "I've never gone back."

"What? Never?"

"Aside from a business trip a few years ago, I haven't gone back."

Sophie leaned against the counter and stared at him, trying to understand what could possibly keep a person away from home. "But that's where you grew up, right?"

"It is. But I don't have deep ties to it. It's just a city."

"What about your family?"

He cast his sights down at the floor for a moment. "I don't like to talk about it. We should get you back to someplace where you can sit."

Sophie's brain and mouth were now engaged in a tug-of-war—she wanted to ask more questions, badly, but the tone of Jake's answer made it clear this was not a topic he cared to discuss. "Okay. The champagne flutes are in the bar in the sitting room."

Jake carried their impromptu meal on the tray, while Sophie improved her one-foot mode of travel, again using the wall for balance.

"How's the injury?" he asked.

"It's throbbing a lot less, so I guess that's good." Sophie

stopped at the bar, which was right inside the entrance to the room, and with both glasses in one hand, she hopped back to the couch. "This is really going to suck if I can't wear cute shoes to work. It's a big part of my look."

Jake sat next to her and peeled the foil from the champagne bottle. Sophie had forgotten what nice hands he had—large, but nimble. "I noticed. Those shoes you were wearing the other day were pretty spectacular." He popped the cork perfectly, leaving only a tiny wisp of fizz escaping the bottle.

"You noticed?" she asked as he filled her glass and handed it to her. Of course, she'd remembered the way he'd looked at her. She remembered every time he admired her so openly, mostly because it hadn't happened very often.

"How could I not? You have amazing legs. The shoes were the very sexy icing on the cake." With his own glass filled, he turned to her. "To Eden's. Come what may, I wish you nothing but success."

She was painfully aware of her own wariness as a smile crossed her lips. She found it hard to believe that he truly wished her business well. It was in his own interest for her to fail. She took a sip of champagne to dull the reality. The pop of golden bubbles tickled her nose, leaving her light-headed, although it might have been more the effect of Jake than the champagne. "You're smooth, Jake. No wonder you're so successful." She reached over and nabbed a cracker from the box, taking a bite.

"I am not smooth. I'm just me. And I didn't feel smooth in your office the other day. I felt like a bungling idiot."

She laughed quietly. "The flowers were a bit over the top. Beautiful, but a bit much."

He shook his head and pinched the bridge of his nose. "A big miscalculation on my part, but I was trying to get your attention." Jake reclined and draped his arm across the back of the sofa, tempting her to relax in a similar fashion, but that would only put her in a position to curl into him. She didn't trust herself.

"You got my attention with the sneak attack of the comment about the kiss. I never saw that one coming. You caught me completely off guard."

She could only imagine what the surprise on her face had looked like at that moment. It had been the very last thing she'd thought he would bring up, made all the more powerful by the sheer magnitude of the memory. That first kiss had been so momentous it was as if her entire world shifted. Since then, it had only become more cinematic in her head, a movie that clicked by frame by frame and filled her with both happy thoughts and bad memories whenever she revisited it. The jubilation when their lips had first met and she finally had her taste of the man she'd wanted for so long? She still couldn't wrap her head around how good that had felt.

"If it makes you feel any better, I never planned on saying that to you, especially not in your office. It was about the most unprofessional thing I've ever done. I guess that just shows you what a disadvantage I was at that day."

Sophie downed the last of her champagne. "You're never at a disadvantage. You knew it would put me off my game."

Jake finished off his first glass as well, then poured them each a refill. "I only said it because I was standing there trying to figure out how to remind you that there had once been a time when we got along great. And I looked at you and the instant I saw your lips, I thought about the kiss. You can't deny that was a kiss for the ages."

"I don't deny it. At all." The flood of warmth in her body that came from thinking about the kiss only made her angry. *And you threw it all away.*

"I still think about it sometimes."

Sophie narrowed her sights on him. Was that an actual blush of pink on his cheeks? "You do?"

"Well, sure." He took another drink and leaned forward, placing the glass on the coffee table. When he sat back, his hand brushed hers, which was planted on the sofa between them. He pulled his away, leaving her nothing but painfully aware of his effect on her. An instant of touching and he'd stoked the fire inside her, the one that had always burned brightest for him. "Don't you?"

Of course she did. How could he be so clueless about what it had meant to her? She still thought about that kiss and everything that had come after it. She'd thought about it more in the last few days than was probably healthy. "I know what you're doing. You're reminding me of the good and glossing over the bad."

"I'd like to think I'm taking advantage of a chance neither of us ever knew we would have. We're in this beautiful house together. The snow is coming down. There's a fire crackling away. We're drinking champagne and enjoying each other's company."

Was that all this was? What did he want from her? The truth of it, not just what he'd said to make himself look good. Her head was filled to the brim with contradictory answers to both questions. She wanted Jake just as much as she'd wanted him all those years ago. She wanted him as much now as the night he finally gave in. That night was sheer heaven—dozens of tightly held fantasies brought to life. She would have given anything to revisit that feeling, when the world and future felt wide open.

"I should go to bed." She steeled herself and got up from the couch. She had to save herself before she did something dumb and embarrassed herself. It would be too easy to give in to his touch and give away what little power she had.

"You sure? It's early."

"I'm sure."

"Let me help you up the stairs." Jake stood and offered his arm.

She should have refused it, but the truth was that she wasn't entirely steady. Mentally or physically. "Okay. But I need to get back on my own two feet tomorrow."

"There's no reason to push it. You have time."

As promised, he helped her up the stairs. Not a word was uttered. Jake was performing his duty and Sophie was too busy dying on the inside. Why did she have this weakness for him? And if she was meant to suffer with that for all eternity, why did he have to come waltzing back into her life? It didn't seem fair. Why couldn't she find a regular man, one to whom she was attracted a normal amount, one she could count on to stick around?

"Thank you," she said when they arrived at her bedroom door. "I can take it from here."

"I can help you to the bed."

Sophie closed her eyes and wished for strength. "I'm fine hopping my way around."

She let go of his arm, but his hand immediately went to her shoulder. "Sophie, wait."

Her eyes clamped shut again. "What?"

"Downstairs. I thought we were having a good time."

"We were." She swallowed hard and looked at him,

wondering if she had the guts to be truly honest and say what needed to be said. "But then your hand touched mine and I started to lose my mind."

"I wasn't trying to make a move, if that's what you're suggesting."

"Then why even bring up the kiss? Why mention it in my office the other day?"

"Because I have incredibly fond memories of that moment. I guess I don't see the harm in being open about the way I feel about it."

Sophie's knees wobbled. If she needed any evidence that she acted erratically when it came to Jake, that reaction was absolute proof. "I don't want you to hide your feelings. But it would be nice if you could acknowledge that when you're traipsing down memory lane, you're digging up an awful lot of painful things for me."

Jake nodded slowly, taking it all in. "I never want to make you feel bad. That's not my intention." His hand was still on her shoulder and his thumb brushed back and forth. "Maybe now is the time to talk about it. Were there things you wished you'd said to me then that you want to say now?"

Sophie unleashed a breathy laugh, if only to relieve some of the pressure built up inside her. How do you tell someone in a single breath that you're mad at them, but you still want them? How do you tell a man that if he wanted you, you were exactly dumb enough to forgive him? "I lied when I said it was fine that you wanted to go back to being friends. I wanted more then. A lot more."

"Oh." His forehead crinkled with concern and more than a bit of genuine confusion.

"Honestly, I thought you were being stupid. But I also wasn't about to argue with you. I didn't want to have to stand there and make a case for your liking me. That's not how it works."

"I've always liked you. I still like you. But it feels like you hate me." He inched closer, almost imperceptibly, but Sophie would have noticed if a single hair on his head had shifted. She was that hyperaware of everything he did.

"I don't hate you. I want to, but I can't."

Now it was his turn to laugh. "That bad, huh?"

She stared up at the ceiling. "Yes. I'm pathetic. I look at you and all these old feelings rush back like they never went away. I'm in the same room as you and I want you just as badly as I did before. Maybe more."

Jake slowly slid his hand from her shoulder down the back of her arm, stopping at her wrist. He rubbed the tender underside with the pads of his fingers. Back and forth in a lazy yet steady rhythm that made Sophie dizzy. The man's hands were magic. "So we're in the same boat. I wanted you the instant I saw you in your office the other day."

"You did?" Red-hot heat flooded Sophie's cheeks. Her breath caught in her chest.

Jake looked right at her with those intense green eyes of his. She felt a little like he was looking right through her. He cupped the side of her face with his hand. It took every ounce of strength not to smash her body against his.

"It's not just because you're beautiful, either. It's more than the big brown eyes and perfect skin and beautiful hair. It's more than your unbelievable body. It's the spark that's inside you. It's the crazy things that come out of your mouth." He swiped his thumb across her lower lip, sending want through her. He inched closer until they were standing toe to toe, now cupping the back of her neck, his fingers curling into her nape. "I loved being able to carry you. I loved having my hand brush yours and seeing the reaction on your face. It all made me want more."

Sophie stared at his full lips. Did she have the nerve to say what she wanted to? If she said something daring and it led them to bed, could she live with it if he rejected her again? Surely that was the path before them right now. She might get a night with Jake Wheeler, but she'd never get a lifetime. "Why should I believe you?"

He reached down for her hand and then did something Sophie never expected. He took it and threaded it under his sweater, holding her palm flat against the center of his chest. "Do you feel my heartbeat?" he asked.

Indeed, she did. She also felt the warmth of his skin and the firm muscles of his chest. She didn't have words, so she nodded, never taking her eyes off him.

"Good. Now feel how it changes." He raked his fingers through her hair and pulled her closer, planting his lips on hers. He took his time with the kiss, soft and sensuous, silently begging her tongue to tangle with his. All the while, he kept her hand pressed hard against his chest.

Sophie closed her eyes, leaning into him, wanting to keep her hand pinned between their bodies. She curled her fingers into his chest, but she never let her palm move. She felt what he wanted her to. His heart was thumping wildly. She was doing this to him. He really did want more.

"See what I mean?" He kissed her cheek softly, then her jaw and finally her neck.

"I do," she whispered, tilting her head to one side to grant him full access, thinking she might reach her peak from this alone. His mouth on her body felt so impossibly good.

He gathered her hair in his hands and pulled it to one side, leaning into her ear. "Told you I wanted more."

"That's what I want, too." It felt so good to say it.

Jake swept Sophie up into his arms and made the quick journey to her bed, laying her down on the buttersoft bedding, still rumpled from her nap. She scooted back and curled a finger, wanting him closer, wanting his body weight on top of hers.

He reached for the hem of his sweater and pulled it up over his head. Sophie sucked in a sharp breath. She loved Jake's chest, and after eight years she was not disappointed. He'd clearly spent much of that time at the gym. He was muscled and taut, with contours that just begged to be explored. He sat on the edge of the mattress and stretched out next to her, lying on his side, kissing her like this was everything he wanted. His hand slipped under her cardigan, pushing it from her shoulders. He rolled to his back, pulling her along with him. She straddled his hips and wrestled her sweater from her arms, tossing it to the floor.

"I love that you're already dressed for bed, but I want to watch you take off your top." Jake's voice shook Sophie to her core.

She crossed her arms and peeled the garment up the length of her torso. She hadn't been wearing a bra that whole time, and her nipples, already hard from the simplest of Jake's touches, became impossibly hard when the cool air of the room hit her skin.

Jake groaned his approval and had his hands all over her, cupping both breasts and squeezing. With a tug, he urged her to lower herself until he had one nipple in his mouth. His lips were soft on the firm bud, but his tongue was insistent, swirling in circles that made Sophie feel as though she was already about to burst. She rotated her hips back and forth, rubbing against the firm ridge in his pants. Another gravelly affirmation came from his throat, and Sophie closed her eyes as he moved his mouth to her other breast, repeating those same mind-blowing moves.

As amazing as this all was, she wanted him naked, and if she were being honest, these pajama pants she was wearing were getting in the way, as well. She slid back on his legs, unbuttoned and unzipped his jeans while he tucked his hands back behind his head.

"Feel like you need a rest?" she asked, only half joking.

"No. I just like watching you."

She smiled and tilted her head to the side, her hair falling across her shoulder. She peeled back his jeans and his black boxer briefs, until they were just past his hips. As soon as she wrapped her hand around him, she knew exactly how hard he was for her. She would have been lying if she'd said it didn't make her immensely happy to know that she could still have this effect on him.

His eyes were closed, his head fitful on the pillow and his back arching as she took long, firm strokes with her hand. "That feels so good," he muttered.

Another smile crossed her lips. She loved pleasing him. "Yeah?" She lowered her head and pressed soft kisses against the flat plane of his stomach, keeping her grip and caressing.

"I want you, Sophie. I want you now. But I don't have a condom with me. I didn't exactly plan for this."

She loved the subtle begging tone of his voice. "I have a few in my bathroom." She hopped down and traipsed into the bathroom, opening a drawer and getting what she came for.

"I'm not sure if I should be happy that you're so prepared," Jake called from the bedroom. He was sitting up on the edge of her bed when she returned. His jeans and boxers had thankfully landed on the floor.

"I hate to break this to you, but there were other men in my life after you."

He gave in to his adorable frown. "I'll pretend that you didn't say that. Now come here."

Sophie stepped between his legs, still wearing her silky pajama pants, but nothing else. Jake gripped her hip with one hand while untying the tie at her waist. He poked a finger beneath the waistband and loosened it until her pj's slumped to the floor.

Standing before him, totally naked, she was struck by how surreal this all felt. She'd never thought she'd ever have Jake again. Not once had she dared to truly believe it could happen. And yet here he was. Looking so handsome she could hardly comprehend it.

He lowered a hand to her knee and dragged his palm up the length of her thigh, turning inward as he went. When his fingers found her center, Sophie dragged in a deep breath and held it, waiting to see what he would do. His other hand pulled her closer until her knees were pressed against the mattress, while his fingers moved in determined circles and his mouth, wet and hot, traveled all over her stomach.

Sophie closed her eyes and let her head drop back, giving in to the sensation, letting Jake take her wherever he wanted to take her. She combed the fingers of one hand into his thick and silky hair, rubbing his scalp, wanting him to feel even a small measure of the pleasure he was giving her. The pressure was building in the most delicious way, but she couldn't deny that she wanted all of Jake, not merely his hands or his mouth on her body. She wanted them joined.

She tore open the foil packet in her hands and kissed the top of his head. "I want you, Jake. I want you inside me."

He smiled and leaned back, resting his elbows on the bed and watching as she rolled on the condom. She planted her hands on either side of his hips and kissed him. They both took that kiss as deep as it would go, mouths hungry for each other, tongues winding and playing. Jake scooted back on the bed. Sophie took the invitation and climbed onto the mattress, straddling him. Jake guided himself inside her. Sophie's eyes clamped shut as she felt him fill her completely.

Jake hummed his appreciation. "You feel perfect."

"You do, too." *So perfect. So unbelievably perfect.*

They were both already a little breathless, nothing more than soft moans and gasps. She lowered her torso and kissed him while rocking her hips forward and back. His thrusts were strong but careful, every pass hitting the right spot. Again, she was speeding toward release. His kisses, hot and reckless, only made the pressure coil faster.

Jake clamped his hands onto her hips, curling his fingers into her bottom like he couldn't get enough. It intensified the pressure, and that brought her right to the brink, her breaths now choppy and desperate.

"Are you close, Soph?" he asked, burrowing his face in her neck and kissing that sensitive spot beneath her ear.

"So close." She could practically see it in her mind, a swirl of intense colors she wanted to become a part of.

Jake took a thrust and flipped her to her back, straightening his arms and using his considerable strength to drive all the way inside her, then nearly all the way out. Sophie arched her back and gave in to the pleasure as it rocketed through her. She wrapped her legs around Jake's waist and muscled him closer with her feet, studying his incredible face while he, too, reached his peak. A smile stretched across his lips as the subtle tremors shook his body. He collapsed on top of her and rolled to his side, pulling her against his chest. He smoothed back her hair with his hand, gently and lazily.

Sophie relished the afterglow and tried so hard to stay in the moment. Was this really happening? Was she really in his arms? It was real, with no reason for her to feel anything but happy and satisfied. There was no reason to let doubt creep back in. There was no reason to wonder if he'd started things simply because he wanted to keep her under his control.

Five

Jake woke up the next morning wondering if he'd messed up. Sophie was not in her bed with him, and the disappointment registered square in the center of his chest, an emptiness that was deeply uncomfortable. That alone scared him. Had he made a mistake by taking her to bed last night? He didn't have the best track record. It was difficult for him to trust, especially a woman.

He'd allowed himself the pleasure of Sophie only after she'd promised not to cut a deal on Eden's with anyone else without first speaking to him. In that moment, he realized that she did still value their friendship. She was still loyal Sophie. And that made him want to trust her.

He rolled to his side and checked her side of the bed for warmth. Whatever had been there was gone, but her sweet smell wafted into the air when he rubbed his hand across the sheets. They'd had the most incredible night, making love for hours. They'd even managed to use up Sophie's condom supply. It had to have been nearly four in the morning before they drifted off in each other's arms, which made her absence this morning that much more confusing. How could she be up and about on so little sleep?

He decided to investigate, climbing out of bed and putting on his jeans and the T-shirt he'd been wearing under his sweater. Through Sophie's window, he saw the back of the property covered in virgin snow. The sun was out, and apparently the storm had passed. Surely the process of clearing the roads was already under way.

He was starting down the hall when he heard a terrible racket coming from what sounded like the kitchen. He followed the noise through the house, shuffling into the room. "Are you sure you should be walking around on that foot of yours?"

"It's fine. Swelling has gone down." Sophie glanced at him over her shoulder and smiled. Wearing formfitting black yoga pants with a pale blue sweater that dipped temptingly off her shoulder, she had a vast array of cooking supplies out on the counter.

"What are you doing?" he asked.

"Getting ready to bake Christmas cookies."

"Cookies? It's just the two of us."

"Not back at home it isn't. I'll bring a bunch back to the city. Take them into the office. I'll freeze some for Christmas Day, too. Want to help?"

Jake saw that the coffeemaker was on. He was going to need caffeine before grappling with the idea of holiday baking. He'd been hoping he'd talk Sophie into coming back to bed. "May I?" he asked, gesturing to the carafe.

"Oh, yes. Of course. I'm sorry. I should have offered.

I'm just scattered this morning." She handed him a carton of half-and-half from the refrigerator, watching him as he filled his mug and stirred it. "By the way, I spoke to Barry, our caretaker, and he said the driveway will be clear by night. He checked with the state highway patrol and they're expecting the roads to be fully passable by morning."

There was his answer about how long he and Sophie had together. Once they were headed back to the city, he'd have the unenviable task of telling Sophie that although this was fun, it probably wasn't a good idea considering their opposing viewpoints on a multibillion-dollar deal. "Thank you for the coffee."

"Good?"

"The best."

She smiled and cocked her head to one side. "Last night was the best."

He couldn't believe how relieved he felt to hear that from her. He really had been thrown off his game by her absence this morning. He set his mug down on the counter and pulled her closer, kissing only the tip of her nose since there was no telling how bad his morning breath was. With his hand, he swept tendrils of her hair from her face. "It was amazing. I was hoping for more. There must still be a few dozen positions we haven't tried."

A beautiful pink blush rose in her cheeks. "You sure? I'm pretty sure we went for a world record last night. Plus, we're out of birth control."

"There are other things we can do to make each other happy." He bounced his eyebrows at her.

She nodded. "I know. And that sounds awesome, but I have to get through my to-do list today. Cookies. Decorating."

He had to admire her dedication to upholding family traditions, even if it was getting in the way of what he considered to be a markedly better time. Plus, the entire idea of baking and cookies and decorating for a holiday was a foreign concept. The only long-held practice in his family involved cruel words muttered under one's breath. "Whatever you want to do, I'm good with."

"Really? You'll help? I would've pegged you as the guy who would much rather sit on his butt and watch football all day."

"Football is on Sunday. And I'd still prefer that, but we should probably honor your grandmother's traditions. I never met her, but I'd like to think she'd want us to."

A melancholy smile crossed Sophie's face. "She absolutely would want us to. She'd be horrified if she knew that I ended up going home without a tin of cookies in the back of my car." She drew in a breath that made her shoulders rise. "The butter is probably soft by now, so we can get started."

"Put me to work."

Sophie began the Christmas cookie operation by directing Jake to follow her into a large pantry at the far side of the kitchen. She handed him a stack of metal sheet pans, then piled flour, sugar, baking soda and baking powder on them. "One more second. I need to find the cookie cutters and the sprinkles." Sophie pulled out a small stepladder.

"Why don't you let me do that?" he asked.

"I'll be fine."

"So says the woman who dropped a ten-pound doorstop on her foot." Jake ducked back into the kitchen, put the supplies on the counter and returned to the pantry. Sophie hadn't listened. She was up on the ladder, reaching for items on the top shelf. "I really don't want you to hurt yourself again. I'll feel responsible this time."

"Just come here and let me hold on to you."

Jake stepped closer and Sophie placed her hand on his shoulder. He was facing her side, and if he looked up, he could see the lovely curve of her breasts as her top stretched tighter across her chest. It brought back some very hot memories of last night, and that only made his jeans start to feel much snugger below the waist. Looking straight ahead was no help—he either had to look at the rounded perfection of her backside in yoga pants or the sweet scoop of her lower back as her top shifted up and revealed her creamy skin.

"Here are the cookie cutters." Sophie handed him a large plastic jar filled with silver metal shapes.

Jake took it from her and set it on a lower shelf, returning his sights to her.

"And here are the sprinkles."

"Gotta have sprinkles."

"Lots and lots of them. There is no such thing as too much sugar in this scenario."

All Jake could think was that Sophie was the real sugar in the room. She was so sweet and mouthwatering, it would be a struggle to stay focused on the task at hand, especially when he didn't care about silly things like cookies.

They returned to the kitchen and Jake helped Sophie get out a large stand mixer. He studied her as she worked. She was still limping but otherwise getting around just fine. Her face was both happy and content, but there was something even more mesmerizing about her, something he'd just realized. She was comfortable in her own skin. That was the biggest change between now and when they'd first met. Back then, she'd had this coltish quality—all unbridled beauty. But she hadn't seemed to know that she was, in fact, beautiful. She was a wallflower of sorts, shying away from compliments and always deflecting.

Now was different. She owned her movements, much more comfortable with herself. When they'd made love last night, Sophie was confident in a way she hadn't been before. She wasn't shy about taking pleasure for herself, which he loved. Having her in his arms, her sweet taste on his lips—it was like revisiting the most perfect memory, only better. He and Sophie hadn't been perfect together all those years ago, but he had to wonder if it was all his fault that it hadn't lasted. He'd thought he'd been protecting her. He'd always thought it was so much better to have a little bit of something beautiful than ever risk it getting ugly.

"Have you talked to Mindy?" he asked as Sophie cracked eggs into the mixing bowl.

"She sent me a text this morning. She's not coming, but I get it. The roads are terrible."

Jake nodded. If he and Sophie hadn't come to their agreement, the news of Mindy might be disconcerting, since he'd counted on an audience with her to seal the deal. Now he was glad that she wasn't coming. It meant he had Sophie all to himself. At least for a little while longer.

She stared down into the mixer, then flicked the switch off. "I think that's good. We need to wrap up this dough and let it chill for an hour before we bake."

"We have to wait for cookies?"

She grinned so wide her cheeks were like little apples. "Afraid so. But you can help me with all of the house decorating until then."

"I was hoping to get cleaned up. Maybe take a shower? Together?" He tugged on Sophie's sweater until she was in his arms again.

She returned the embrace and settled her head against his chest. "That sounds amazing. But no." She straightened and patted his shoulder before returning her attention to the cookie dough, wrapping it up in plastic.

"No?"

"As tempting as you are, not right now. Later. I promise."

Grossly disappointed, Jake helped Sophie clean up the kitchen, and then they moved into the sitting room, where cardboard boxes and plastic crates were stacked against one long wall.

"When you come up here for a weekend by yourself, what do you do the whole time? Read? Watch TV? I think I'd go stir-crazy."

"This is actually the first time I've come by myself. Normally, either Gram and I would come or we might drag Mindy along or my mom, although she and Gram never got along."

"How is your mom?" Jake had met her at business school graduation.

Sophie shook her head. "Not well. Erratic. Losing it. Honestly, she just hasn't been herself since our dad died five years ago."

"I was sorry to hear about that."

"Thanks. It was so hard on Gram. No one wants to see their own child die before them."

"Of course not." Again, Jake was struck by how tight-knit her family was. He knew, of course, that many families were. He simply hadn't had such a bird's-eye view of it.

Sophie began opening the boxes and inspecting the contents. "We've always spent Christmas in this house. It's all Mindy and I have ever known. Gram always came up from the city one weekend in December to decorate the house, so it would be all decked out for celebrating. When Mindy and I got old enough to help, we came up with her."

"An entire weekend devoted to decorating for Christmas. Who does that?"

Sophie shrugged, fishing smaller boxes out of the large ones. Judging by the quantity of decorations, they were going to be busy with this for a while. "The queen of England travels to Sandringham Estate a week before Christmas just to prepare for everything."

"The queen of England and about fifty members of her staff. I realize you come from a lot of money, but unless I managed to miss something, you aren't royalty."

"Of course not. But it's still a nice idea, isn't it? The tradition. The devotion to getting the details right. And most important, wanting that family time to be special."

"I guess. But you're just going to have to take it down later. It seems like a lot of work for nothing."

Sophie turned to him with brows furrowed in confusion. "How do you accomplish anything with that attitude? You're a developer, Jake. You build things. You turn a piece of property into something better or different. How can you have that kind of vision and still be so pessimistic?"

He shrugged. "One person's pessimism is another person's practicality."

Judging by the look on her face, she remained unconvinced. "Let's get started. The sooner we finish, the sooner we get to take that shower."

As distracted as Jake was by the promise of soaping up Sophie's beautiful body, he still felt as though he had to come clean about his disinterest in this exercise. "There's something I need to tell you before we start. A confession of sorts."

"What's that?"

"I know you're going to think I'm crazy, but I hate Christmas."

Sophie could hardly compute what Jake had said. Honestly, it was crushing. How could she be so hopelessly attracted to someone who hated her favorite time of year? "You don't hate it. I don't believe that for a minute. Maybe you think it's too commercial or overhyped or something, but I don't believe that you *hate* it. That's such a strong word."

Jake held up his hands and shrugged. He was somehow extra handsome when he appeared defenseless, even when she knew it wasn't real. "Fine. Then don't believe me. But it's the truth."

"So you aren't enjoying this?"

He cocked an eyebrow at her. "I'm just here for the shower."

Sophie was excited by the prospect, but she couldn't fail at this family tradition. Plus, she was still sorting out how she felt after last night. It had been absolutely incredible, and Jake wasn't showing signs of retreat, which had been her greatest fear, but what would happen tomorrow when they left their snowy hideaway? She needed to prepare herself for the worst. He could easily tell her he wasn't interested and she'd have no choice but to accept his decision. After all, she'd known very well what the possibilities were. She'd known all along that Jake might hurt her.

But she couldn't allow herself to think about that now. It would ruin one of her favorite days of the year. She reached for one of the bins. "We need to put the lights on first. Before anything else."

"If you say so."

Sophie wrinkled her nose. It was as if Jake had never done this before. Perhaps he was merely letting his attitude and actions demonstrate his dislike for the holiday. She pulled out several strands of lights, which had all been carefully wound around pieces of sturdy cardboard. She handed Jake the plug end of one. "Let's test these before we put them on the tree."

"Good thinking." He crouched down near the outlet. One by one, he checked to make sure they all still worked.

"Gram was always adamant that only white lights went on the tree. What about your family?"

Jake didn't make eye contact. "I don't really remember."

Sophie decided to accept that Jake simply hadn't taken note of his family's Christmas preparations. Even with her admittedly persnickety placement, they had the tree strung with lights in no time. "You know, plenty of people say that stringing Christmas tree lights is the ultimate test of a relationship." As soon as the words crossed her lips, she knew she'd made a mistake. She and Jake had the strangest, most tenuous of relationships right now—a long-gone friendship only recently rekindled, an apparent weakness for the other, especially when naked, and a business deal Sophie didn't want waiting off in the wings.

"I'd say we did pretty well," Jake said. "But then again, we've always made a good team. We've always worked well together."

Was this one of his sales pitches? Or was it as innocent as it sounded? An admission that they did indeed work well together?

Jake reached for one of the boxes tucked inside the larger carton labeled Ornaments. "Maybe I should hand you these one by one and you can be in charge of placing them on the tree."

Sophie nodded. "Good plan. Less walking for me. But I'll need you to put up the high ones."

An hour later, the tree was trimmed. Jake built a fire while Sophie put out Gram's collection of musical snow globes on the antique console table in the hall. She then sent him into the kitchen to make hot chocolate while she carefully decorated the banister and the mantel, just as Gram had always done, with garland and ribbon. She was admiring her handiwork when Jake returned to the sitting room with the silver tray they'd used for champagne last night, this time topped with mugs of cocoa.

They sat on the sofa, and Sophie was overcome with a deep sense of accomplishment until she realized what was missing. "Oh, my God. Gram's gold star. We forgot to put it on top of the tree." Sophie sat up and hobbled over to the storage containers, rummaging through them, but there wasn't much left. Just some ribbons for the fresh wreaths, which the caretaker would put up next week after she was gone.

"I went through all of the boxes, Soph. I don't remember seeing a star."

"It has to be here somewhere. It has to." Her stomach sank as she reached for the last box and discovered that it, too, was empty. "I wonder if Barry forgot some of the boxes." She turned to look around the room. The only problem with that theory was that the other decor was all up. She didn't want to get unduly upset about a star, but this one was special. "I'm sure this sounds silly to you. What with you thinking Christmas is terrible to begin with."

Jake got up from the couch and went to her, pulling her into a reassuring embrace. She loved being in his arms, even when she knew that getting used to it was a dangerous proposition. "If it's important to you, it's important to me. I'm sorry you can't find it. Hopefully the caretaker can track it down and it can be the first thing you put up when you're here for Christmas."

Sophie gazed up at him. It was still three weeks until the big day, and two until Gram's will would be read. Where would she and Jake be by then? Anywhere? She would've considered inviting him to spend Christmas with her family, if her gut wasn't telling her to set aside expectations and take every bit of enjoyment she could out of her time with him. "You're right. It's got to be here somewhere. I'll let Barry worry about it."

Jake pressed a soft kiss to her forehead, leaving behind a lasting tingle. "That's the spirit."

She smiled. "As handsome as you are, you sort of look like hell, you know. Your hair is a disaster and we should probably try to find you some other clothes to wear."

Jake's eyes darted from side to side. "Was I not the person leading the charge on a shower earlier?"

Oh, yes. That. She took his hand and, even with her slight limp, started to lead him out of the room. "And I'm following through with my commitment."

Without warning, he scooped her into his arms and

pulled her tight against his chest. "Hold on, humming-bird." Like a man on a mission, he bounded up the stairs, determined. A few steps down the hall and he delivered her to the bathroom en suite, placing her on the cool white marble counter.

She watched as he opened the glass door and reached in to crank the handle for the water. The sight was exactly like a daydream she once would have readily whipped up in her head—enticing Jake, with two days of dark scruff on his face and a flicker in his eyes, happy and so clearly enthusiastic to be with her, taking off his T-shirt and letting her admire him in just his jeans. Was she, in fact, dreaming? "You haven't called me hum-mingbird in forever."

A clever smile spread across his face. "You know, you are the only person I've ever given a nickname. Ever." He stepped in between her knees, snaking his arms around her and leaning against the counter.

"Really?" Sophie remembered the day like it was yes-terday, but she hadn't thought about it in forever. It was a glorious late-spring day, warm and sunny, and they'd met at a café to study. On the side of the building was a patio with hanging baskets overflowing with pink and purple petunias. Nearly a dozen hummingbirds buzzed and flitted among the blossoms, drinking the nectar. Jake had said that they reminded him of her. "Busy and fun to watch" were his exact words.

"Yes, really. I am not a nickname sort of guy. But it suits you. It still does." With his thumb, he inched her top off her shoulder and kissed it with his mouth open. The bathroom was beginning to fill with steam. "Now let's get you out of these clothes."

Why Sophie was so touched by this revelation she

wasn't sure, other than knowing that she occupied any exclusive space in Jake's life felt very special. She eased off the counter to get undressed. Jake quickly had his remaining clothes in a puddle on the floor. She drew in a deep breath as she looked him up and down. The man was a stunning specimen—long, lean and defined from head to toe—shoulders, chest and abs were only the start. He had an impressive erection, too. She couldn't wait to please him again.

She pulled her top over her head and unhooked her bra while Jake studied her in turn. "Sorry. I'm still a little behind," she said.

He shook his head. "Don't be sorry. I'm enjoying every second of anticipation." Steam billowed out of the shower enclosure, making Jake look that much more like a god.

She shimmied her yoga pants and panties past her hips, taking her time and following his eyes as they traveled down the length of her body. Every subtle approving glance made her feel more special. And lucky. Jake tugged her into his arms and placed a firm kiss on her lips, then took her hand and led her behind the glass door.

The bathrooms had been remodeled six or seven years ago and Sophie's shower was magnificent—with gray and white hand-painted tile in a Moroccan pattern, a white honed marble floor, six multidirectional sprays and more than enough room for two people. Arguably the best feature was a bench at one end, which Sophie used for shaving her legs.

"Sit," Jake instructed. "I'm not taking any chances with you and that foot and slippery surfaces."

"Yes, sir." Sophie did as instructed, while Jake turned in the spray, slicking back his hair and providing her with an unparalleled view as water trickled down his body, following each muscled contour.

Sophie picked up a bottle of body wash and offered it to him. "Here. This will help."

Popping the cap, he gave it a sniff. "Mmm. Nice."

"Coconut. Not too girlie."

"It's perfect. But not yet. I don't want to get any soap in my mouth."

Sophie suddenly found it hard to speak or swallow. The anticipation of what might come next was too much. Jake descended on her, his mouth on hers as he knelt on the shower floor between her legs. He slipped both hands behind her knees and dragged her forward until her bottom was at the front edge of the bench. He kissed his way down her neck and to her breasts, taking her nipple into his mouth and swirling his tongue against the tight skin. Wet heat swirled all around her, while inside her, a fire that could be put out only by Jake had burst into full flame.

He took her breasts into his hands, squeezing and kneading and plucking at her nipples with his fingers while he kissed his way down her stomach. When he passed her belly button, he tugged her even closer to the edge, parted her tender folds with his fingers and nearly sent her off into space with a single pass of his tongue. Sophie's eyes fluttered shut and she dug one hand into his hair while her other hand was flat on the bench for support. Jake worked her apex with his tongue, winding in dizzying circles. He grasped the ankle of her good leg and raised her foot until it was on the bench. She leaned back, resting on her elbow, while Jake placed one hand on her inner thigh and with the other slipped two fingers inside her.

Sophie could hardly keep up with what was happening as he licked her center and his fingers glided in and out of her. The pressure was intense. Building. Doubling. Rising. Cresting. And then the pleasure broke through an invisible barrier, crashing into her with unbelievable force. Sophie gasped and her head jerked forward as she rode out each wave. Jake stilled both his hand and mouth, but he didn't lose contact until she began to come down from her heavenly high.

She grasped both sides of his face, raising his lips to hers and kissing him deeply. She felt as if she were floating in all that warmth and contentment. "That was unbelievable." She peppered his face with kisses, wanting him to know how much she appreciated his masterful effort. Reaching down with one hand, she took hold of his rock-hard length. She could feel the pressure beneath his smooth skin. He was just as turned on by pleasing her as she was by the idea of doing the same for him. "It's your turn. I want to make you feel good."

They switched places and she licked her lips in anticipation of taking him into her mouth. He surprised her by leaning forward for another soft and sensuous kiss. "You already make me feel good, hummingbird. And I can't wait for more."

Six

By Sunday afternoon, the snowplows had done their job. The roads had been cleared, which meant the Eden House caretaker had done the same for the private drive leading to what had become Jake and Sophie's weekend retreat. Their hiding place.

Standing in the foyer of Eden House, Jake dreaded saying goodbye. He didn't want to end things the way he needed to—neatly. He didn't want to hurt Sophie. Quite frankly, he couldn't afford to hurt her. He should have thought this through better, but he hadn't. He'd given in to desire when he knew he couldn't follow through and give her more. The professional relationship he hoped to form with her made his mistake markedly more complicated.

"I'd say thank you for the hospitality if it didn't feel so inadequate."

"It wasn't like I had a choice. You showed up on my

doorstep in the middle of a blizzard. I couldn't make you sleep in your car."

Sophie leaned closer and jokingly elbowed him in the ribs, but he took the chance to pull her into his arms and steal what could very well end up being their last kiss. *One more.* He closed his eyes and breathed her in, wishing things were different. Wishing he was different. When their lips parted, Sophie had a blissful smile on her face, her eyes only half-open. She looked like an angel. Meanwhile, Jake felt like the devil. Guilt was crashing down on him like that doorstop on Sophie's foot.

"It really was an amazing weekend. Thank you." He had to ease into this. He had to find the right words.

"You're welcome."

"Take care of that foot, okay?"

"It's much better today, but I still think I'm going to have to wear something sensible to work tomorrow." She jutted out her lower lip, and for a flash, all he could think about was sweeping her back upstairs and taking off every shred of her clothes.

But no. He had to return to work. Back to reality and responsibilities. He had to go back to the version of himself who didn't give in on a whim, the man who did not throw caution to the wind. "You know, it might be better for both of us if we keep this quiet. You know how people talk, and there's already so much gossip going around with you and Mindy inheriting the store. I wouldn't want my business partners to find any of this suspicious."

Sophie smiled, but it was pained. "Of course. Makes perfect sense."

"Are you sure? I don't want you to tell me one thing when you're thinking another. It nearly cost us our friendship the first time."

She nodded and started leading him toward the door. "I'm absolutely sure. It's not a good idea, especially when you want one thing for my business and I want another."

"Technically that's true, but I'd still like to find a way to hold on to our friendship. It's important to me. Truly."

"I know. Me, too. Don't worry about it. I guess I'll talk to you sometime after my grandmother's will is read?"

Jake knew that was the most sensible course of action. So why did the very idea of staying apart make his stomach sour? "I don't think we have to stay that far apart. We could have lunch one day. Maybe dinner."

"We'll see. December is crazy for me. The store. Christmas."

It wasn't quite the answer he hoped for. He wanted her to participate in this mini-negotiation. He wanted her to stumble through the dark with him, and help them arrive at a set of parameters that kept their roles and expectations clear. "I get it. You're a very busy businesswoman. Lizzie told me so every time I called and you weren't available."

Sophie planted a final, parting kiss on his cheek, then thrust a tin of Christmas cookies into his hand. They'd ended up baking them at two in the morning. Sophie had been that insistent and determined. Before that, they'd been equally occupied with each other. "Here. Don't eat all of these on the ride home."

"I'll do my best."

Out into the cold, he trudged to his car. For the entire ride home, his final exchange with Sophie tumbled around in his head. For someone who truly didn't want to hurt her, he sure had a talent for leading them both into situations where that was likely. He decided that the house had given him a false sense of security. They'd been tucked away from the rest of the world, and repercussions had been a distant thought. And then there was Sophie—she was too much for him to handle. He had to resign himself to this. She was the one woman who made him question his plans, both personally and professionally.

Very little was any clearer the next morning as he arrived at his office. He did know that it had been less than twenty-four hours away from Sophie and the notion of returning to work felt like a burden. All he really wanted to do was see her, or at least talk to her. He wanted to know that everything was okay between them. Could they remain friends after their weekend? Was that what she wanted? Or did she want more? Judging by her reaction when they'd parted, she was happy with the way things had ended. But Sophie had concealed her true feelings before. Was she doing it again? And if he managed to get through to her true feelings, could he live with the answer? Either she was fine with the noncommittal goodbye, which meant he hadn't left a mark on her the way she'd left one on him. Or if she wasn't okay with it, well, he'd gone and hurt her again. How could he have allowed himself to repeat the same mistake?

His email inbox was no help in trying to think less about Sophie. His voice mail wasn't much better. He had messages from each of his fellow members of the War Chest. They all wanted to know about Eden's and whether or not he'd been successful convincing Sophie. Yes, he'd made inroads, but not the sort of steps forward anyone had any business knowing about.

As he listened to voice mails, he wished he had more time to devise a different plan. Could he liquidate enough assets and make the Eden's purchase on his own? Or perhaps try to become her business partner? He'd done his research on the store. He knew where she could succeed and where she might fail.

Jake's assistant buzzed him. "Mr. Wheeler, Sawyer Locke is on the phone for you."

Sawyer was not only Jake's closest friend in the War Chest, he was one of the few real-estate developers in the city Jake enjoyed spending time with socially. "Sawyer. What are you up to?"

"Oh, you know. The usual. Happy to be back at the office after a weekend of changing diapers and getting almost no sleep."

"Sounds like fun." Jake laughed, although his own reality was so far from Sawyer's that he could hardly imagine it. Sawyer and his wife, Kendall, had a baby at home, a little girl named Violet, if memory served.

"Actually, it is fun. I love being a dad. But that's not why I called. You know I have to ask about your meeting with Sophie Eden. Did it actually happen?"

"It did. We talked quite a lot, actually."

"And so? What happened?"

Jake wasn't sure how he should respond. He was *not* about to kiss and tell. It wouldn't reflect well on him and it wasn't fair to Sophie, either. The fact that he had to couch his answer only confirmed to him that he had, indeed, made a mistake. "We discussed the state of her business. I expressed our eagerness to do a deal, but in the end, we agreed not to discuss anything until her grandmother's will is read on December 18. Anything before that would be premature. She's still grieving and she wants to wait until everything can play out as her grandmother intended. I had to respect her wishes. She holds all the cards here."

The other end of the line was painfully quiet for what

felt like an eternity. "I have to be honest, Jake. This makes me nervous. That's two weeks away. A lot could happen between now and then. You know as well as I do that Eden's has a lot of suitors. We're giving everyone else a chance, and I don't like it."

"She promised me that she wouldn't cut a deal with anyone without speaking to me first."

"She promised? Did you sign some sort of agreement?"

"I'd call it a handshake. I've known Sophie for a long time. I'm not worried about her sticking to a promise." Jake's stomach became more uneasy with every passing word. Would his initial plan to travel to Eden House and mend things with Sophie ultimately backfire?

"Okay, then." Sawyer's voice was pure exasperation. "I guess we have no choice but to trust your judgment. It still makes me nervous, though. This is a huge deal. I don't want us to miss out."

"I know. I know. I don't want us to lose it, either. Believe me, I'll do everything I can to keep that from happening." That much he could promise.

As soon as Jake hung up, his cell phone buzzed with a text. It was like Sophie knew that she was on his mind. Despite the tension of his conversation with Sawyer, it took only a few words from Sophie to put a smile on his face. What a pleasant surprise.

Work sucks.

He grabbed his phone and leaned back in his chair to type a response. It does.

I wish we were back at the house gorging ourselves on cookies.

All Jake could think about was what had happened after they'd done their baking, when Sophie started a powdered-sugar fight and they ended up making out in the kitchen. I wish we were doing the things we did after the cookies.

The blinking dots that meant Sophie was typing her response appeared on his screen. He waited expectantly, all the time wondering what must be going through her head. Was she feeling the same way he was? Or had he pushed it too far? Finally, he got a reply.

What are you doing tonight?

Bingo. Nothing. As in I'm available.

8:30? It's the earliest I can knock off.

Sure.

My place? Bring champagne?

What are we celebrating?

The end of the workday?

Good enough for me. See you then.

Audrey buzzed Jake's line, making him jump. "Sawyer Locke is on the line again."

Jake picked up, his body buzzing from his text exchange with Sophie. "Sawyer. Did we forget something?"

"I just got off the phone with my brother. He got his

hands on some information about Eden's. If what he heard is true, we could be in big trouble."

Sophie was fairly sure she shouldn't have sent flirtatious texts to Jake, but she wanted to test the waters. Just because he'd said he wanted to keep things quiet didn't mean he wanted to *end* things between them. It had been her mistake to assume that yesterday morning. The old Sophie, the version of herself from eight years ago, jumped to conclusions like that. The more seasoned Sophie didn't want to. It gave Jake too much power. She could steer this ship as well as anyone. She just had to hope it didn't capsize because of her choices.

The promise of seeing Jake again made it nearly impossible to focus on work. All she really wanted to do was reread their texts and fantasize about what might happen at her apartment later tonight. She was assuming a lot, based on only a few words that they hadn't even spoken to each other, but she wanted to go on her gut with this one. Their weekend together had meant something. To both of them. She'd heard the genuine appreciation in Jake's goodbye, and she'd also felt his hesitation at leaving.

But what if she was wrong? What if he'd tricked her into thinking they could have more? She wanted to think she could be satisfied with only this second taste of Jake. She was so much stronger than she had been eight years ago. She had more confidence, was more resilient and self-assured. Even then, she doubted it in herself. She would be hurt if and when he called things off. Her marshmallow-like insides were still there, even if her outer shell had hardened.

As for what that meant for this Eden's deal that Jake

was so desperate to make? The truth was that Sophie had only suggested they stop talking about it in order to give herself a break from saying no. It had conveniently come at a time when all she'd wanted to say to him was yes. Nothing about her plans for the future had changed. She would not sell the store. Not to Jake or anyone else who might come along. She would not let Gram's memory down. That was the top of her priority list, and she couldn't envision a reason why that would change. Not even the allure of pleasing Jake could make her set aside her family loyalty.

Sophie jumped when her cell rang and she saw Jake's name on the caller ID. Was he eager to chat? Was texting not enough? Or was he calling to cancel? The way her heart skipped and stumbled at the thought of each possibility should have told her that perhaps getting involved with Jake was not the wisest choice.

"Hey," she said. "This is a pleasant surprise."

"I have something I need to talk to you about."

"Oh. How nice." Just hearing Jake's voice made Sophie draw her finger along the edge of her desk and lazily lean back in her chair. Dreamy thoughts of what it was going to be like to see and touch him again flooded her brain. She could definitely get used to this feeling. "Do you want to wait so we can talk about it in person?"

"This can't wait. I'm calling because the word on the street is that there's another buyer in the mix for Eden's and I'm wondering what in the hell happened since I left Eden House yesterday."

Sophie sat up so fast her chair made a clunking noise. "Another buyer? What are you talking about?"

"Sam Blackwell. Wall Street guy. Real shark. He's going around telling people that the Eden sisters are in the palm of his hand. I thought I had the inside track here,

Sophie. We agreed to that much. You wouldn't lead me astray on that, would you?"

What in the world had happened while Sophie was away? "Jake. I don't even know this Sam Blackwell person, so he must have talked to Mindy. You do have the inside track. I told you that. But it's the inside track on nothing right now. I've been nothing but incredibly clear with you. I'm not ready to sell. I might never be ready to sell."

Jake grumbled. "You can't mess around with him, Sophie. Sam Blackwell is a player and he will not hesitate to resort to dirty tricks to get what he wants. We're talking employee tampering or choking off supply lines to kill your business. He has connections with the city that are downright scary. If there's a single thing out of whack with your deed to that building or the property, you could lose it."

Sophie's heart was pounding so fiercely she was afraid she might be having a heart attack. Was there really someone out there powerful enough to take the store away from her? "How could someone do that? It doesn't seem possible. I'll talk to our lawyers. I won't let it happen."

"That's not a bad idea. But first, you need to shut down Sam Blackwell. You need to let him know you have no interest in doing business with him."

"Are you making this suggestion as my friend or as the person who wants to be victorious when this is all said and done?" Sophie hated that she had to question his motives. Jake made no secret of how competitive he was with other investors, especially other men.

"Both. Either. I'm both of those people. I do care about you, Sophie. I don't want you to get ripped off or mixed up with the wrong guy."

Sophie sighed and pinched her lower lip. Was that true? Did he really care about her? Or was this all about business?

Lizzie poked her head into Sophie's office. "I'm sorry to interrupt, but Mindy's on the line for you."

Speak of the devil. "Jake, my sister is on the other line. Let me go so I can talk to her. I have a sneaking suspicion she can shed some light on the Sam Blackwell situation. I'll let you know what she says. Like I said, this is the first I've heard about this."

"Perfect. Yes. Call me back."

"Will do."

Sophie hung up and, for a moment, stared at the phone on her desk. She hated feeling so out of the loop, especially on a matter of which she made up 50 percent of the vested interests. She really didn't like the fact that Jake had caught her so off guard. Why did she always have to be the last person to find out these things?

"Mindy. Hey. I need to talk to you," Sophie said when she picked up the extension.

"Are you back in the city?" Mindy replied, ignoring Sophie's request. "I was worried about you. Or should I say I was worried about you guys?" A mischievous snicker followed the question. "How is Jake, anyway?"

"I got back last night. And it's not like we were in danger. You know that. It was just some snow and bad roads. It was all clear by yesterday afternoon."

"How did things go? Between you and Jake? Was it like old times? Or did he just want to twist the thumbscrews on Eden's?"

Any number of interactions could fall under the purview of old times for Jake and her—everything from hanging out like buddies to falling into bed. She was thankful the latter had happened, at least to know now that Jake was genuinely attracted to her. That wasn't the reason he called things off all those years ago. Something else had been at play, most likely a case of twentysomething male jitters. "It was nice. We have definitely rekindled our friendship, which is great." Sophie decided to stop at that. She wanted to keep some things to herself.

"Did you talk about Eden's at all? Because I have something I want to discuss with you."

"Jake told me there's another buyer in the mix? He's not happy about it, and quite frankly, neither am I. It's one thing to talk to Jake, and it's quite another to bring someone else in. Starting a bidding war doesn't do any good when I haven't agreed to sell in the first place. You're just going to end up making people mad."

"Will you slow down? I didn't plan for this to happen. It just happened. The guy's name is Sam Blackwell. I was out with some friends at a bar Saturday night and he approached me. He's a Wall Street guy. He does some real-estate investments, but it's not the only thing he does."

"Jake told me who he is. He hates him. He says he's a total snake. I can't believe you let some guy chat you up in a bar without first finding out who he was."

"Well, he is incredibly handsome. Who was I to send away a good-looking guy who wants to buy me a drink? And that's all it was. A Manhattan and a conversation. Perfectly innocent."

"From everything Jake said, there's nothing innocent about this guy at all. I don't like the idea of a person like this being within fifty feet of our grandmother's store."

"Hold on a second. Are you mad because I spoke to someone about selling the store and property or are you mad because that someone wasn't Jake? Did you two cut a deal over the weekend? Without me?"

"In fact, we agreed to the opposite. No talking about it until after the will is read. I can't believe you're even suggesting it."

"How am I supposed to know what went on between you two when you were stuck in that big beautiful house with nothing but a fully stocked wine cellar, a roaring fire and complete privacy?"

"Now what are you suggesting? That Jake and I are involved? Because we aren't." Were they? Her text conversation with Jake sure made her think they might be. Sophie buried her head in one hand, holding the phone to her other ear. Right now, she needed Mindy her sister, not Mindy her business partner. "At least I don't think we are."

"Sounds to me like somebody is confused."

"That's just Jake. He has that effect on me."

"Even after all this time? You need to get a grip, Soph. He's just a man."

Just a man. Easy for Mindy to say. She wasn't a hopeless romantic like Sophie. She didn't have a bad habit of holding out hope forever, like Sophie did. "Do you really not know what it's like when somebody has your number? When a guy could walk into the room for the five hundredth time and you're still just as bowled over by him as you were the first time you saw him?"

"No. I do not put men on a pedestal. If a guy is hot, he's hot. I don't sit there and think about how hot he is. I just go up and talk to him if I'm interested."

Yet more evidence that perhaps Mindy and Sophie should get their DNA tested someday. Sophie still wasn't sure they were truly related. "I don't put all men on a pedestal. Just some. And believe me, I would be much happier if he wasn't up there. It's just my stupid brain. I look at Jake and all I can see is everything I ever wanted." If that wasn't damning, Sophie didn't know what was. Jake's hold on her was just as strong now as it had been the first time. She needed to work harder at not giving him so much power.

"Wow. Seriously?"

Sophie sighed for what felt like the one hundredth time. "Yes. I can't help it. There's just something about him. Those green eyes and his mouth and the way he makes me laugh, especially at the most inopportune moments."

"Oh, my God. You really did sleep together."

Sophie's shoulders dropped. There was no point in hiding it. Mindy was smart. Sophie couldn't deny it forever. "We did." Sophie considered calling it inevitable, but it truly wasn't. Even when Jake had shown up at her door, even when she realized they were all alone, she never assumed he would want her.

"How was it?"

"Amazing. Completely incredible." Sophie didn't want to get too stuck in memories of her weekend with Jake, but everything was still so fresh in her mind—the way he smelled, the way it felt to be in his arms, the way it erased so much of the hurt and pain of the years spent apart. It was perfect. A little too perfect. Things with Jake and Sophie did not have a habit of working out.

"I want to be happy for you, Sophie, but this could put us at a huge disadvantage. Are you going to be able to say no to him if there's a higher bidder?"

"It's not a disadvantage because we're not selling."

"And I'm not running Eden's with you. Nor am I any

less financially strapped than I was the last time we talked about this."

"You know I'm not in a position to buy you out."

"Again, you're making my case for me. If we sell, you won't have to worry about it. All of our problems will be solved."

Sophie needed to put an end to this discussion. Her head and her heart couldn't take running in circles with her sister, especially with Jake Wheeler walking around the world, able to pull at her strings. "Look. Nothing can be done until the will is read. Can we just put this entire discussion on a shelf until then?"

"Only if you'll promise we'll have a real discussion then. A real one where you remember that not everything is about what you want."

"And you need to promise that you will talk to Sam Blackwell and get him to keep his mouth shut. And I'd like you to remember for just a few minutes that you are a member of the Eden family."

"As if I could ever, ever forget."

Sophie got off the phone with her sister, but she wasn't ready to call Jake right away. She needed time to think about everything Mindy had said. Maybe Sophie did put men on a pedestal. Maybe she shouldn't let him know how willing she was to make him happy. It took away all of her power. She could learn at least that much from her sister.

Minutes ticked by on her phone. She waited for ten, and then Sophie plucked it from her desk and dialed Jake's number.

"What did she say?" he answered right away, sounding desperate for anything but a romantic or flirtatious phone call with her.

"She said that he approached her in a bar and they had a drink. That was it."

"That's not what I'm hearing."

"I don't know what to tell you. That's what she told me. I don't tend to question my sister too much. She's never lied to me before and I don't think she has any reason to lie to me now."

"Okay."

"You don't sound convinced."

"I'm not, but I don't know what else I can do about it."

"Well, think of it this way. Nothing can happen without me, and I promised you that I will not agree to a single thing pertaining to the ownership of Eden's without first telling you."

"I know. And I appreciate that."

"That doesn't mean I'm going to sell to you. But it does mean that you'll know as much as I do."

"That's all I need for now."

Sophie couldn't help but feel once again that Jake was holding all the cards and she was holding none. How did she end up feeling this way? She was the one who owned half of a $4 billion property, after all. She wasn't without resources. "Well, good. Guess I'd better get back to work."

"Me, too. I'm swamped. In fact…" Ominous silence came from the other end of the line. "I don't think tonight is going to work. I'm sorry. I'm still catching up from being away on Friday."

Sophie pressed her lips together hard, fighting back the crush of disappointment. "I'm too busy, too." She *was* too busy. But she would have found a way to see him. She would have.

"Maybe tomorrow?"

"We'll see." She didn't want to play games. She was simply having a hard time keeping it together.

"Okay, then."

Sophie hung up, immediately launching into a lecture to herself. *Don't be sad. He's busy. You're busy. You can't live and die by his approval or how much he chooses to make himself available. You do your thing. He'll do his. And what happens, happens. Be a little more Mindy, and a little less Sophie.*

These were all apt and good words for her to internalize, but the truth was that as unsure as she'd been of Jake's motives over the last few weeks, she felt that doubly now. The instant there was even a glimmer of bad news, a small chance that he might not get his deal, he was no longer fun-and-flirty Jake. He was incredibly busy, noncommittal Jake. Well, two could play at that game.

Sophie got up from her desk, marched to the elevator and meandered through the store, talking with some of her salespeople and making sure everyone was happy and, most important, full of the Christmas spirit. She helped men choose cashmere gloves for their wives and girlfriends. She helped an elderly woman onto the escalator and accompanied her to housewares to find a set of pots and pans for her niece. She scooped up a young boy who was running through lingerie screaming at the top of his lungs—his mother was relieved someone had found him. With a reassuring pat on the back, she offered him a candy cane from behind the register and wished them both a merry Christmas. She did everything Gram would have done if she was feeling lost and unsure of what to do next. Sophie clung to the one thing she knew she could count on—the magic of Eden's, especially at Christmas.

It was past eight when she decided to head back to her office. Her foot, still not fully healed, was aching, and so was her pride. She hated that she was so disappointed she wouldn't see Jake tonight. As she walked among the flocked trees and life-size nutcrackers, the giant candy canes and swags of pine with wide velvet ribbon, she couldn't help but wonder what made him dislike these things so much. She wished Jake could see the world the way she did—mostly full of good things and good people. For her, Christmas was a reminder of those things, a time to take stock and be thankful. If only Jake loved it like she did, he might open his eyes and see that a woman who would love to have a chance with him was sitting right under his nose.

Seven

Jake hadn't talked to Sophie in two days, and it was eating away at him more and more with every passing minute. He hated the way they'd left things the other day. He didn't enjoy being the guy who doesn't trust, but that was exactly who he was. The mere idea of another buyer in the mix, the thought that Sophie might have gone back on her word, had made him so anxious he was practically sick.

That reaction was ingrained, planted in his childhood when the two people he counted on more than anyone, his mother and grandmother, had betrayed him. His mother by making an empty promise to find them a better life and come back for him. His grandmother by never extending a single loving or caring gesture, made all the worse when it was clear that Jake's mom would never return. Any hope of hugs and *I love you* were gone by then, replaced by reprimands and a never-ending guilt trip. He was a burden—a mouth to feed and more laundry to wash. He was no longer a boy. He was a creature. He was something to be tolerated, and he felt the shame and betrayal to this day. He'd learned to live with it, but it would always be there.

That was why he doubted his ability to live up to what Sophie wanted, needed and deserved. No matter how much he'd learned to ignore his scars, the aftershocks still turned up. Every time he made a knee-jerk reaction to feeling deceived or misled, he knew it had all started when he was a kid.

Still, he didn't want to make excuses for himself. His past might have made him skittish when he was younger, but he was thirty-two. He had to get his act together, and there was only one woman he could imagine doing that with—Sophie. If he wanted any chance at having a future that went beyond work, work and more work, he had to make things better with Sophie, even when the news of a second buyer for Eden's had knocked him back on his heels.

He was going to start with her assistant.

"Sophie Eden's office. This is Lizzie."

"Lizzie. Hi. It's Jake Wheeler." Jake rose from his desk and closed his office door. Audrey was a fantastic assistant, but she was nosy, and if she learned that his previous attempts to get Sophie's attention had turned into a romance, he'd never hear the end of it.

"Mr. Wheeler. Ms. Eden is on a call right now."

"Actually, I need to talk to you for a minute."

"Ms. Eden has instructed me to put you through if you're on the line. If you want to wait a moment, I can get her."

Jake grinned. This was the glimmer of hope he'd needed. Sophie had called off the guards at some point. Maybe not today or yesterday, but she'd still done it. "No, Lizzie, I don't think you're listening to me. I need to speak to you."

"Oh. Okay." She sounded genuinely surprised.

"Can you tell me when Sophie is leaving for the evening?"

"She'll be here until the store closes at ten. Possibly later. She works that late every night these days."

Poor Sophie. She worked longer hours than anyone he knew. "What about dinner? She has to eat."

"I typically order in for her and she eats at her desk around eight. She's having sushi tonight."

"Perfect. Can you tell me where you're ordering from and I'll pick it up?"

"I'm sorry, Mr. Wheeler. I'm confused."

"I just want to surprise her. I have a few things to apologize for."

As requested, Lizzie shared the information about Sophie's take-out order. Jake had Audrey pick up a bottle of Krug and put it on ice. He left the office at seven fifteen and arrived at Eden's, dinner in tow, just as Lizzie was packing up her things at her desk.

"Heading out for the night?" he asked Lizzie, craning his neck to see if he could catch a glimpse of Sophie, but her office door was closed.

"I am. I thought I was going to have to buzz you up. How'd you get past security?"

"I made friends with Duane. He's a real teddy bear when you get to know him."

Lizzie laughed. "It's sweet of you to bring her dinner. She's been so stressed. It'll be good for her to have a break."

"Exactly my thinking." Jake headed back to Sophie's office and knocked softly.

"Come in," she called from inside.

He opened the door, but Sophie was practically impossible to see. A mountain of paperwork sat on her desk. "Hello?"

From behind all that paper, Sophie's head popped up. "Jake? What are you doing here?"

The second he set eyes on her, a huge grin sprang up on his face. He couldn't have hid it if he tried. God, he'd missed everything about her—her voice, the sweet smell that filled her office. Her presence and spirit. "Hey there." He held up the take-out bag and the bottle of champagne. "I brought dinner. And something to help you relax."

Sophie rounded her desk in a red dress. He was immediately fond of the deep neckline. It showed off her cleavage in a way that left his body buzzing. "I thought you were swamped. I thought you were too busy for socializing." Suddenly her voice was clipped and cold.

"I was. But now I'm not. And this is my peace offering, too."

"I wasn't aware we were at war."

"Let's just say I'm not overly proud of the way I acted when the Sam Blackwell news popped up. I'm sorry. Very sorry."

She drew in a breath so deep her shoulders bunched up around her ears. "I would never lie to you, Jake. If you don't believe that, I can't spend time with you."

He nodded. Sophie was the exact test he needed. Although he was off to a slightly bumpy start, this had been the right thing to do. "I know that. I do."

"Thank you for saying you're sorry. I appreciate it." She reached for the bottle of champagne. "Apology accepted. Now let's break into this bad boy. I've had the worst day. I'll go find us some glasses."

Deeply relieved, Jake took off his coat and set out their meal on the coffee table in her office, which sat in front of a long velvety gray sofa. He took the liberty of flipping off the harsh overhead fluorescent lights and instead turning on two floor lamps on either end of the sofa. It gave the room a much softer and admittedly more romantic feel.

Sophie returned with a pair of coffee mugs. "Sorry. This is all I could find. We have real glassware somewhere, but only Lizzie knows where everything is." She padded over to him and sat.

"You're barefoot. That's not really your look."

Sophie did the honors with the champagne this time. "It isn't, but flats are surprisingly uncomfortable and my foot still isn't one hundred percent. Hopefully I'll be back in heels by tomorrow." She held up her mug and clinked it with his.

"To good friends who will accept apologies," he said.

"To good friends who show up with unexpected surprises."

They each took a sip, neither taking their eyes off the other. If Jake wasn't mistaken, the electricity was still here between them. The last two days hadn't cooled things off at all. Still, he knew he'd stupidly wasted that time. He should have been bringing Sophie dinner every night. He should have been bringing her lunch, too.

"I'm honestly surprised you aren't more annoyed with me than you are."

"I wasn't happy with you when I hung up the phone that day, but I thought about it and realized that was silly. You're a businessman. I'm not going to fault you for wanting to make sure you were getting your fair shake. You're also busy. I'm busy. These are just facts." She took a piece of sushi with chopsticks and popped it into her mouth.

"I should have given you the benefit of the doubt. I'm still sorry I jumped to the wrong conclusion."

Sophie dabbed at her lips with the napkin. "We've known each other for too long and we both work too hard to dwell on one conversation that didn't go great."

"Judging by your desk, I'd say you're really working too hard."

She glanced at the pile of papers threatening to topple onto the floor and shook her head. "It's ridiculous. I'm trying to analyze our sales and figure out where we can make some changes, but it's such a jumble. I should probably bring in a consultant, but I'll be honest. I don't want to spend the money."

Jake knew he could help her make sense of it. Perhaps not to the degree that an experienced retail consultant might be able to, but he could help. "I might have some insight."

"You don't strike me as a big shopper."

"I'm not. But I did a lot of research when my fellow investors and I decided to approach you and Mindy about purchasing the store. I might be able to help."

Sophie crossed her arms and sat back against the sofa cushions, her eyes full of skepticism. "Why would you do that? It's in your best interest if I fail."

He didn't have a rational answer to the question. What he wanted to do had no logical purpose in the scheme of his professional life. He was thinking with his heart and a few other body parts right now, not his brain. "I'd like to think it's in my best interest to make you happy."

Sophie stared at Jake for a possibly unreasonable amount of time, while her body was humming from what he'd said. "You want me to be happy?"

"I do. It's a beautiful thing to see." He took another slug of champagne from the coffee mug and cleared his throat. "Why don't you show me what you're looking at?"

Sophie went to her desk and gathered several binders of spreadsheets—detailed sales records spanning the last five years and projections based on the trends. In general, the news was not good. She brought them over to Jake and they spread them out on the coffee table.

He rolled his shoulders out of his suit jacket and tossed it over a chair. "Guess I'd better get comfortable if we're going to get to work." He began to roll up his shirt-sleeves. Firm and taut with the perfect amount of dark hair, his forearms were crazy sexy, probably because she knew where they led—to his shoulders. And then to his chest, and eventually every other inch of his extraordinary body. "Do you want me to turn the lights back on? I went for mood lighting for dinner."

Sophie shook her head and scooted closer to him on the couch, stealing this chance to breathe in his warm scent. "No. I hate those things. This is much better."

They sat nearly shoulder to shoulder as Sophie walked him through the somewhat grim picture of Eden's Department Store. Unfortunately, the deeper she dug, the more she realized that Gram had made some poor de-

cisions along the way, like not recognizing the impor-
tance of an online presence and putting enough money
into a website.

"Everything I've read has just confirmed my suspi-
cions," Jake said. "I'll be honest. This doesn't look great.
But I have some ideas."

He then proceeded to dazzle her with about a dozen
amazing concepts for changes she could make. Some
were short-term fixes; others were long-term strategies.
One involved nearly doubling the size of the women's
shoe department and making Eden's online a true destination for female shoe aficionados everywhere, not
just those who could make it to the store in New York.

"I'd be lying if I said that this idea isn't incredibly ap-
pealing to me."

"You do love your shoes."

She looked at him and smiled. "Thank you."

"For this? It's nothing. Just a few things I happened
to notice while doing my due diligence." He waved it off
and placed his arm across the back of the sofa.

Much like the moment at Eden House when they were
in the sitting room and he'd taken the same pose, all she
could do was think about kissing him. The only difference now was that she had the luxury of being less conflicted over it. "It's not nothing. There's a chance you
just sank a billion-dollar deal."

"What's money when you have friends?" There it
was—that extralow rumble of his voice that shook her
to her core. In the soft light of the room, his eyes were
dark and intense. "You are my friend, aren't you?" He
trailed his hand up and down Sophie's bare arm, sending ribbons of electricity through her body.

With zero hesitation, she grasped his shoulder and

shifted herself up onto her knees. "I'm whatever you want me to be, Jake." She leaned in, kissing him seductively so there could be no mistaking what she wanted. Him. Now. In her office. Lock the door. Things were about to get serious.

He returned the kiss, reining her into his arms and leaning back. Sophie hitched up her skirt and straddled his lap, resting her arms on his shoulders and digging both hands into his hair. Between her legs, heat blazed and Jake got hard—she felt it all even through layers of clothes. She ground her center against his length, wanting only one reaction from him, another of those sexy groans. When he made that exact noise, she laughed between their lips.

"What's so funny?" he asked, gathering her hair in his hands and kissing her neck.

"I just love it when you do that."

"Yeah?" He nuzzled his nose in the tender spot right below her ear. She drew her knees tighter against his hips, gripping his legs with hers.

"Yes. It makes me want you even more."

"Want to hear some good news? I have a condom in my wallet."

Sophie hummed in his ear. "Sounds like Christmas came early." She eased off his lap and let him reach into his pocket while she checked the outer office for employees. Thankfully, no one was around, but for privacy, she locked the door. When she turned around, Jake already had his shirt off and was standing there barefoot in his suit trousers.

Anticipation made her feel like she was flying as she rushed over to him. She stole a quick kiss while unbuttoning his pants and pushing them to the floor. She wrapped her fingers around him, stroking softly while she pressed her chin into his chest and gazed up at him. Full lips, stubble and the most intense eyes she'd ever seen, Jake was too handsome for words. He leaned down and kissed her, drawing down the zipper of her dress.

"I want you, Soph." His chest was heaving, his voice low and insistent.

"I want you, too." Not poetry, but it was all that came to mind.

He handed her the condom packet and she opened it, rolling it on him. He pulled her dress forward from her shoulders and it fell to the floor in a poof. Then they were in each other's arms, pressed tightly against each other, tongues mingling as they kissed and hands roved everywhere. Sophie was so overcome with want and need, she didn't know which way was up. Jake reached down and grabbed her bottom with both hands, lifting her up until she wrapped her legs around his waist. He plopped her down on the edge of her desk, right where all of those binders had been hours ago. This was going to be way more fun than work.

Jake grabbed one of her legs behind the knee and raised it to his hip. With his other hand, he moved himself inside her. Sophie rolled her neck, taking in the sensations. He was so hot. He was so perfect. She scooted herself to the very edge, grabbing on to him with both legs. Jake took deep thrusts while he lowered his head and drew her nipple into his mouth, rolling it gently between his teeth and giving it a tug. A flash of white zipped through her, leaving tension and heat between her legs. He was already on the brink. The pressure radiated from his hips and she felt it in his firm shoulders when she reached up to pull herself closer.

Her breaths were jagged. She couldn't draw in enough air. She was right on the edge, but she couldn't get there. She could feel the outer limits of her destination, but it was just out of reach. "I'm close, Jake. Keep going. Harder."

He was nothing but sheer determination, his fingers digging into the flesh of her bottom as his hips forcefully met hers. That was all she needed to tumble over the cliff and float off into bliss. She closed her eyes and gripped his shoulders as he reached his own climax, feeling more than merely physically gratified. There was an enormous sense of joy and relief that came with this moment. Jake had come back to her.

They both were still struggling for breath, clinging to each other. Sophie had her cheek flat against Jake's chest, but he lifted her chin with his finger and placed a soft kiss on her lips. "Remind me to visit you at work more often," he said, a smile spreading across his face.

"I'm glad I moved those binders. Now let's go sit on the sofa where we can be a bit more comfortable."

They parted for a moment, Jake cleaning up with some tissues he'd grabbed from the table next to her office door. He pulled on his boxer briefs, but left it at that, which Sophie loved. It was her favorite view.

From the end of the couch, she grabbed a throw blanket she used for late nights at the office. Still naked, she wedged herself between the sofa arm and Jake, draping her legs across his lap and covering them both with the blanket. She wanted to be able to see his face when she talked to him. She needed that connection.

"I've always been curious where you got this." She smoothed her thumb over the scar above his eyebrow, her knuckles resting on his cheek. She'd never asked about it before. Jake was not forthcoming about himself or his past. She'd learned by now that if she did bring up a question like this, he would change the subject. But something about this moment made her want to take the chance anyway.

He grumbled and pulled her closer. "It's from when I was a kid." He trailed his fingers up and down her spine. If this was his way of distracting or deflecting, she might have to think of more potentially uncomfortable questions to ask him.

"But what happened?"

"Just an accident. It was nothing."

There was an edge to his voice that made her think there was more to it. Deep down, she wanted nothing more than to know more about Jake. He knew so much about her, had been fully pulled into her life from time to time. He knew her sister. He'd even met her mom at business school graduation. She knew next to nothing about him. "Was this when you lived in San Diego? What kind of accident?"

"Skateboard. I got off balance and went flying into a metal railing. I was just a stupid kid goofing around with his friends. It really wasn't that big of a deal."

She knew enough not to ask any more about the scar. "Did you skateboard a lot? Is that what you were into when you were younger?"

"Most kids in San Diego either skateboard or surf. It's just a Southern California thing. I wasn't anything special."

She scanned his face for some sign of what he was feeling, of why he was getting so on edge about this subject. "I'm sure you were all kinds of special."

"You're the one who's special." He murmured the

words into her hair, his arm around her tight. "I don't think I should leave tonight without us making a real plan to see each other. I was thinking maybe even a date."

Sophie set aside her disappointment over his deflecting about his past. She could hardly believe what she was hearing. "I thought you wanted to keep things under your hat."

"That was a stupid suggestion. Especially since it was keeping me away from you. I don't care what people say or think."

Sophie didn't want to get too carried away, but she loved that he wanted to be a little reckless because of her. "What did you have in mind?"

"Whatever you want. Something fun."

Of course, in December, everything Sophie wanted to do in the city revolved around Christmas. Maybe this could be another chance to chip away at his grumpy holiday attitude and help him see the joy and merriment through her eyes. "I haven't been to the Holiday Market at Bryant Park yet this year. I love going. I usually end up buying a ton of gifts."

Jake laughed. "With all of the amazing restaurants, bars and theater productions in the city, you want to go to that?"

"Yes. It's fun." She sat back and eyed him. "Have you been?"

"I haven't, but I can see it from the windows of my office. I see it every day right now."

She sensed that he wasn't thrilled about the prospect, but she decided to ignore that. She'd have to prove to him that they could have fun doing something he would normally avoid. "Then perfect. I'll scoop you up from work tomorrow night and I'll show you what you've been missing."

"I already know what I've been missing." He kissed her shoulder and caressed her arm softly. "I missed you, Soph. Is that crazy? After only two days?"

Goose bumps raced over the surface of her skin. She'd missed him, too. So much. "It's not crazy. At all."

Eight

Jake's plan for the Holiday Market was to indulge Sophie for an hour or two. He'd let her work out her Christmas urges—retail therapy or whatever they called it. Then he would whisk her away to his penthouse apartment, open a bottle of incredible wine, feed her a fabulous meal and, if all was right, take her to bed. The tryst in her office had been super hot, but he didn't want her to think a quickie on a desk was all he was after. Sophie deserved a soft bed and fine bedding. She deserved the luxury of a man who would take his time with her, which was precisely what he intended to do.

He was busy answering an email when Audrey buzzed the line in his office. "Mr. Wheeler, Ms. Eden is here."

Jake sprang from his desk chair like it was the ejector seat in a fighter jet. "Great. Send her in."

"Knock, knock." Sophie appeared in his doorway,

grinning, wearing a light gray wool coat that was cinched in at the waist and flared out to her knees. Her beautiful red hair peeked out from beneath a white hat with an enormous fluffy pom-pom on top. She was...well, there weren't really words. Her face was one he wanted to look at forever. Sheer perfection. He was transfixed.

"Don't you look wintery? And gorgeous?" He tugged her into his arms and kissed her softly. It felt like the best reward after a long day at work. He could get used to this—seeing her every day. Being with her.

"We're going to be outside for hours. Despite my devotion to fashion, I have to stay warm." She stepped back and turned in a circle. "Look. Pants. And boots. I'm practically ready to take a dogsled into the Arctic."

"I see you couldn't give up on the heels."

She looked down at her feet, seeming nothing less than enormously pleased with her shoes. "Some compromises simply aren't worth making."

"Very chic. I love it." *I love you.* The words nearly tumbled out of his mouth. He had to steel himself for a moment, holding on to her shoulder for support.

Sophie's sights narrowed on him, brows furrowed. "Are you okay?"

Was he? With no earthly idea where those words had come from, he was inclined to think no. "Of course. Just admiring you. That's all." He leaned closer and kissed her cheek. "I'll get my coat."

As he threaded his arms into his black wool coat, he gathered himself, thankful he hadn't slipped and uttered those three little words. Yes, he cared about Sophie, but their relationship was all about small steps. There would be no leaps. *I love you* was months off. Maybe a year. And who knew if he and Sophie would even last that long? Right now, he was trying to simply enjoy every moment when he wasn't stricken with panic. He was savoring every instance when he didn't have the urge to run for the door.

But he couldn't deny that there had been a shift in his thinking over the past several days. First he'd missed her greatly, more than he'd ever missed anyone. Then there had been his immense relief that she was the sort of person simply willing to talk out a problem. She was willing to forgive him for having been less than pleasant. She was willing to forget those two days when he hadn't called. He not only hadn't experienced that in any relationship, he wasn't sure he was capable of the same thing. When you learn to hold on to someone else's mistakes, it's a hard habit to break.

But he was ready to be better than all of that. There was a lot at stake between Sophie and him, and it wasn't just a multibillion-dollar real-estate deal. The conversation in her office last night, the one that took place before clothes started to come off, had been extremely gratifying. She eagerly accepted his advice and insight, offering her own experience and taking his ideas to the next level. They'd fed off each other's enthusiasm to create a vision. It was the first time he'd thought that Eden's might actually succeed with Sophie at the helm. Yes, that threatened his potential big deal, but at this point, he had to be realistic. Sophie's devotion to Eden's wasn't going anywhere. In the end, it would likely all come down to practicality, money and the question of whether or not she could find common ground with her sister. He might need to do what he never did and leave that one up to fate.

"Ready?" he asked.

She popped up onto her toes like a cork out of a bottle of champagne. "Yes. I'm so excited."

"Let's go."

Hand in hand, they marched out of his office, past Audrey, who was packing up her things for the day. "Have fun," she called. Knowing her, she'd pepper him with questions tomorrow morning. He had to prepare for that.

They took the elevator down to the lobby and walked out into the brisk night air. Across the street, rows of glass and metal vendor kiosks ran along the terraces of the park. Even he had to admit the tiny buildings were enticing. Lit up, they each looked like a jewel box. Once they crossed over into this Christmas wonderland, it was hard not to get caught up in Sophie's sheer excitement.

"What do you want to do first?" Her cheeks were already bright pink, her eyes startlingly clear and bright. "We could get something to eat. They have these amazing Belgian waffles with little sugar pearls inside them."

"I thought you wanted to do some shopping." He squeezed her hand a little tighter.

"I do. If that's okay."

"Tonight is all about you. Lead the way."

And so she did, pulling him along until they arrived at a shop that mixed custom perfumes. "I got this for Mindy two years ago and she loved it. I want to do it again." Inside, the saleswoman and Sophie discussed her sister's personal preferences. Apparently she favored citrus over floral and sweet over woody notes. To Jake, it was all like a foreign language, but in the end, the pair concocted a fragrance that was surprisingly lovely. Jake was simply amazed at how much thought and care Sophie would put into a single gift. He had to wonder if Mindy knew how tuned in her sister was to what she wanted.

From there, they shopped for locally made hand-knit scarves, hammered silver earrings from Central America and women's silky robes made in India and trimmed in wide, embroidered sari ribbons. Jake was happily loaded down with the shopping bags. Watching Sophie enjoy herself made it all worth it.

"One more stop," Sophie said. "Then we can grab something hot to drink and watch the ice-skaters."

"Sounds like a plan."

She led him into a shop packed with people and stocked to the ceiling with every Christmas ornament you could imagine—jolly snowmen with stovepipe hats, glittery snowflakes, glass icicles and round-belly Santas hanging from metallic gold string. These were the trappings of Christmas that were most foreign to Jake. He knew they should make him feel happy and nostalgic, but he couldn't attach any meaning to them other than that they were the things he had missed out on.

"I always buy a new ornament every year. Gram did the same. She always bought hers at Eden's, but I think this place has a better selection."

"Remember that come next Christmas. You should be shopping at your own store and using what I'm guessing is a substantial employee discount." *Next Christmas.* Would Eden's still be there? Would he and Sophie last that long?

Sophie smiled and patted him on the chest, smoothing her hand up over his shoulder. Any worries about the future were quashed by the ripples of warmth she sent through him.

"You're so right," she said. "We need to step up our game for next year. We put so much effort into the stuff we don't sell, like the window displays and the decorations in each department."

"Well, that's an important part of it, too. People come to the store for the experience more than anything. You make them happy. That's what keeps them coming back."

She cocked her head and jutted out her lower lip. "That's so sweet. You're going to make me cry."

"Don't do that. You've been looking forward to this. You're having fun. Plus, I'm holding fifty pounds of Christmas gifts and could use a break. Let's get your ornament and get out of here."

Sophie made her selection—a happy snowman wearing a red stocking cap and sitting in a teacup. "What do you think?"

It was just as sweet and funny and unexpected as Sophie. "I think it's perfect."

Taking her place in line, she pointed to a gold star atop one of several Christmas trees displayed in the shop. "See that? That's what Gram's star looks like." Like many things at Eden House, the star was funky and unusual— 1960s era possibly, with gold tinsel and glitter. "I still haven't heard back from Barry about finding the one up at the house." The corners of her mouth drew down, a sight he disliked so much.

"I'm sure it'll turn up. Who loses a Christmas star?"

And just like that, the frown was gone. "You're right. I shouldn't worry so much."

She paid for the ornament and they strolled to a coffee stand, where Jake ordered a latte and Sophie chose a hot cocoa with extra whipped cream. From there they wound their way to the ice rink at the opposite corner of the park. An older couple got up from a bench at the perfect time, and Jake was quick to snag it for them, setting down the bags and enjoying the chance to sit. He put his arm around her and watched the masses circling the rink. Holiday music filled the air, as did the sound of chatter, laughter and the occasional shriek when someone slipped and fell on the ice. Maybe it was just being with Sophie, but Jake was surprised to find that he was actually enjoying himself.

"This was nice. Thank you for bringing me."

Sophie removed the lid from her cocoa and swiped at the whipped cream with her tongue. Jake had to stare. It was too damn sexy. "Careful, Jake. Someone might notice you actually enjoying something related to Christmas."

"Hey. I'm not eager to return. This is exhausting. I don't know how you do it."

"I'm running on pure adrenaline these days. Trust me, I'll fall into a coma on December 26."

Jake laughed and pressed a kiss to her forehead. "I call that day Christmas Leave."

Sophie reared back her head. "Seriously?"

"Well, yeah. It's a joke. Like Christmas Eve, but it's the day after. Get it?"

"I get it. But I don't. It just seems so…"

"So what? Negative?"

"Yes. Exactly. And you aren't entirely like that. I've been watching you, Jake Wheeler, and you are not only capable of having a lot of fun, you also enjoy smiling and laughing and a million other pleasant things. So I still don't get what exactly it is about this holiday that makes you cringe."

Jake returned his sights to the ice rink for a moment, watching a young boy learning to skate with his mother's patient guidance. The little guy held his arms wide to brace his fall, but something about his stance said that he knew she would be there to catch him or, at the very least, pick him back up. The center of Jake's chest ached. There was a time when he would have done anything for five minutes of what that little boy had.

"You want to know the real reason I don't like Christmas?"

Sophie took his hand in hers, squeezing it tight. "Yes. I do."

Even with hundreds of people milling about, there was a stillness to the air around Sophie and Jake. She squeezed his hand a little tighter, studying his handsome profile. Even when he wasn't making eye contact, she sensed his vulnerability. Something deep and painful radiated from him. A part of her was scared to hear it, worried that it might change her vision of him as the strong and unflappable Jake. But a much bigger part of her simply wanted to understand the mystery. She wanted to see inside that head of his. She wanted to know the good, but she needed to hear the bad. "It's okay. You can tell me."

"I'm not the only one, you know. For a lot of people, Christmas is incredibly depressing."

"I know. I know it's hard on some people. But I want to know why it's hard on you."

"Where do I start? The commercialism. The running around for no good reason. The music is everywhere. Nobody gets anything done those last two weeks of the year. It's nothing more than a big disruption." He shook his head and looked down at his lap.

"That's an argument against celebrating. That doesn't tell me what happened in your life that made you feel like this. Surely you loved Christmas when you were a kid. All kids love Christmas. You weren't born hating it. I know that much."

"Not all kids love Christmas."

The way he'd said it made Sophie's breath seize up in her chest. She'd known that getting Jake to open up would not be easy, but damn, he wasn't giving her much to work with. She had to keep pushing so she could understand what made him closed off sometimes. "Is that how you felt? As a kid?"

"I don't want you to think less of me. I don't want this to be what defines me." He turned and scanned her face, searching for something she desperately wanted to give him. If only he'd tell her.

She pulled him a little closer and kissed his cheek. "I will never think less of you. And the only thing that has to define you is your actions. You're more than your past. You're more than the bad things that have happened to you." Her brain whirred faster as she searched for the words that would get him to talk. "I'm sensing that you've never talked about this. And maybe that's why you're struggling. You've been carrying it around all this time. I think it might be good if you just let it go."

He swallowed so hard his Adam's apple bobbed up and down. "I don't know what I did to deserve having you come back into my life."

"Maybe I'm here because you need someone to listen."

He cracked just a fraction of a smile, but she would take what she could get. "Maybe." He looked skyward at the midnight blue void hanging over the city. "Gram was everything to you, but my grandmother was a nightmare. And it was just the two of us from the age of seven. She was mean, she didn't want me around and she definitely did not believe in celebrating Christmas."

"How did you end up living with her?"

He refocused his sights on Sophie. "I never knew my dad. My mom got pregnant in high school, which infuriated my grandmother. I was just another mouth to feed. My grandmother worked during the day cleaning at a hotel. My mom didn't have anyone to take care of me, so she couldn't really get a job, but that just made my grandmother lash out at her. She'd tell her she was lazy. It was an impossible situation." Now that he was talking, he seemed calmer, but the words were coming faster, like he was rushing to get them out.

"Once I went to school, and got a little older and was able to take care of myself, my mom decided that was her chance to make a different life for us. She told me she was going to find a job and get us a place to live on her own, and that she'd come back for me. But she never came back. She left me with my grandmother. Forever."

Sophie was so still she had to hold her breath. "I had no idea all of that had happened to you."

"I don't tell anyone about it. I'm very good at hiding it."

"Too good." She shook her head. It just didn't seem real. "All I can think about is that day I met you and how you just seemed like such a golden boy to me. You were so handsome and sexy and oozing with confidence. It was mesmerizing."

"And largely an act." His gaze connected with hers again. "Well, not the handsome and sexy part. That part I come by honestly."

She laughed. "And the funny, self-deprecating, deflecting part. Don't forget that."

He smiled, which she loved seeing. It was such a bittersweet moment. "Never."

"Your scar. It's not from skateboarding, is it?"

He shook his head. "No. It's not. I forgot to take out the trash one day and my grandmother pushed me. I fell headfirst into the edge of a door."

Sophie gasped. Tears shimmered in her eyes at the thought of a young Jake at this woman's mercy. "I am so incredibly sorry."

"I don't want you to feel sorry for me, Soph. Please don't. Of all the things I want from you, pity isn't one of them."

Sophie desperately wanted to know what those other things were, but that was a question for another time. "It's not pity. I promise. But it hurts me to hear that those things happened to you. I hate it."

He shrugged. "It's just the way things played out. The reality is that those experiences are part of me, like anything else. And you know, I might not have become so successful without having that for motivation. I didn't want that life for myself. I worked my butt off in school and I moved as far away as I possibly could, as soon as I could, which is what brought me to the East Coast. If I hadn't done that, I might not have met you. My life would be very different now."

"That's such a nice way to think about it. I'm sorry I ever thought of you as a pessimist."

He shook his head. "Well, I am sort of a pessimist. Maybe fifty percent. I'm confident some things will work out. Just not everything. I can't be like you. I can't be all sunshine and rainbows."

Sophie could've denied it, but Jake never would have let her get away with it. "That's all Gram's influence. She always gravitated toward the light. I just try to follow that philosophy. If something makes you happy, if it makes you feel good, you should pursue it. Don't hold back."

A sweet smile spread across Jake's face. "Maybe that's why I'm so drawn to you. You're the light." He tucked a tendril of her hair back inside her hat. "I'm falling for you, Sophie."

"You are?" Sophie's heart jumped up into her throat. This was a revelation for which she had not prepared. She had a good handle on her own feelings, but not nearly enough of a good sense of Jake's. He always played everything so close to the vest. Not today, apparently.

He nodded. "I am. Hard. You make me happy. Happier than I've been in a long time. And you make me feel good." He pulled her closer, gazing down at her. "Will you let me make you feel good?"

Heat blazed in her cheeks and chest. Would his effect on her ever lessen? Or would it only continue to grow? She couldn't imagine what that would be like, but she wanted it more than anything. "You have a very special talent for making me feel good."

"Tonight, that's all I want to do."

Nine

Life with Jake had become a whirlwind. Ever since the night in her office, and especially since the Holiday Market, they'd been inseparable. There had been countless dinners and late-night rendezvous, visits to each other's offices and hours of talking in bed, in the dark, holding each other tight. With every passing minute together, Sophie fell a little further for him. The only question was whether he was traveling on the same path.

The reading of Gram's will today was going to complicate things. There was no question about that. A considerable chunk of Sophie's future would be laid out before her. The rest of it was all in Jake's hands. If he didn't want her, if he didn't feel the way she did, she wasn't sure she could muster much enthusiasm for anything, not even claiming her birthright, Eden's. They were going to have to revisit the discussion with Jake—

the one she'd put on hold. It killed her to know that she was going to ultimately end up disappointing him. She didn't see another way. He would not get his big deal. He had to know that on some level. If he didn't, he was fooling himself. She just had to hope that, in the end, he would see that what they had between them was worth more than any money that might be made.

"Good morning," she whispered, curling into his naked chest and breathing in his smell. Like the last several nights, they had stayed over at his sumptuous penthouse apartment. Her place was really nice, but his was spectacular, high atop a skyscraper with the most stunning views of the city.

"Good morning, yourself," Jake mumbled, smoothing his hand around her bare hip and pulling her closer. "What time do we have to be at the lawyer's office?"

"Nine sharp. You know, you don't have to come with me if you don't want to. There could be drama with my mom. She and Gram never really got along, and I know for a fact that there were accounts that were supposed to go to my dad when Gram passed away. They never worked out what would happen with that money after my dad died. I'm worried my mom is counting on that money to survive."

"If you want me there, I want to be there for you. Plus, I'd like the chance to see Mindy and your mom. I'm sure I'll be fine with whatever family drama happens to come up."

Sophie smiled and kissed him on the nose. "Good. Because I do want you there. I always want you by my side." She stopped herself from saying the words that were waiting on her lips—everything about not wanting him to walk away from her today. How she hoped that he would eventually find a way to go from falling for her to actually loving her. Because the truth was that Sophie loved him. She absolutely loved him. She'd loved him eight years ago, and she loved him even more now. As to when she could share that confession, she had no idea when that day would come. She couldn't bring herself to say it if she wasn't reasonably sure it would be returned.

"I'll put coffee on if you want to get into the shower," Jake said, glossing over the weight of what she'd just said about always wanting him by her side. It felt like confirmation that they were still operating with two separate sets of rules.

"Great." Sophie watched as he traipsed out of the room in only his pajama pants. She might as well soak up every beautiful view she could.

She showered and dressed in a chic but subdued black dress with a princess-seamed bodice and a full skirt. Today's shoes were anything but quiet, though—pale-pink-and-black patent-leather spectator pumps, courtesy of Mr. Blahnik's divine skills. Gram had always commented on them. That felt important today.

"Ready?" Jake asked as he walked into the kitchen still tying his tie.

"Yes. Come here." Sophie straightened the Windsor knot and neatened his collar. Jake was always put together, but even the most polished man needed help when he didn't have the benefit of a mirror. She watched as he pulled on his jacket and fastened the top button. "You look very handsome today." He really did. His charcoal-gray suit brought out his mesmerizing green eyes.

"You look spectacular. But you probably already know that."

"I promise you I will never tire of hearing it."

Hand in hand, they made their way down to the elevator and then to the garage, where Jake's driver was waiting for them. It was about twenty blocks downtown and a few avenues west to Gram's attorney's office, so it was a good thirty-minute trip in morning traffic. Sophie had considered softening the eventual blow of her decision to keep Eden's while they were in the car, but Jake got a phone call as soon as they got settled in the back seat. She calmed herself by taking his hand and clutching it firmly. She couldn't let him get away. Not again. She would just have to help him see that they were in love, and that was the most important thing.

When they pulled up outside the lawyer's office, Mindy was climbing out of a black stretch SUV. This was not her normal mode of transportation. Her car was much smaller and more modest. She'd often said she hated those big ostentatious cars. They felt snobbish to her.

"Did you get a ride from someone?" Sophie asked when they met on the sidewalk. Jake had stepped inside the building vestibule, finishing up his phone call. Sophie tried to catch a glimpse of who was in the back seat, but the door had been closed too quickly for her to see.

"Oh. Just a friend." Mindy avoided eye contact, tugging at her red wool coat. Her normally tidy hair, a much darker shade of red than Sophie's, was anything but neat and polished this morning. Something was definitely up.

"What kind of friend?"

Mindy narrowed her stare, practically shooting daggers from her eyes. "Just a friend, okay? I don't want to talk about it."

Sophie kept quiet, but she couldn't help but notice how the skin around Mindy's mouth was red and her lipstick was only about half on. "Okay. I'm sorry."

Mindy stood a little straighter and cleared her throat. "You and I need to talk. Before we go in for the reading."

Sophie did not like that biting edge of her sister's voice. It sounded like bad news wrapped up in doom. She also didn't like being ordered around by Mindy. It was insulting. "Is something wrong?"

"I don't want to talk about it out on the street, okay?"

"Well, you could use a trip to the ladies' room to re-apply your lipstick and fix your hair. Whatever you were doing with that friend you don't want to talk about has taken its toll." Sophie hustled inside and over to Jake, who put his hand over the phone receiver. "Mindy and I need to talk. I'll see you upstairs? It's Suite 401."

"Got it. I'll be done in two minutes."

"Sophie. Come on," Mindy said.

"I'm coming." She and Mindy rode the elevator to the fourth floor in silence. This building was filled to the brim with lawyers' offices and as old-school as it got, with speckled polished stone floors and glass mail chutes that were still being used on the rare occasion that someone needed to mail a letter.

The ladies' room was right off the elevator. Sophie led the way inside. Mindy checked under the stalls as the door swooshed shut. Sophie felt like they were in a spy movie.

When she'd completed her survey, Mindy turned to her. "We agreed that we wouldn't make any decisions until the will is read. So now that we're about to find out what we already know, I need to tell you that I've made a decision and you might not like it."

Great. Sophie's shoulders wanted to drop, but she wouldn't let them. She wouldn't let her sister beat her down like this. "Just tell me, Mindy. I'm tired of you holding everything over my head."

Mindy's jaw tensed. "Fine. Tomorrow, you're going to get a letter from my lawyer saying that you have six months to buy me out of my half of Eden's."

Sophie couldn't believe what she was hearing. She blinked again and again as if that would wash away the horror of it. "So that's it. No discussion. You're just going to have your lawyer settle this between us? You're my sister. I can't believe you would do this."

"You gave me no choice. You refused to listen to what I want and need for myself."

Sophie was filled with such disgust right now she could hardly see straight. "I swear, you are the most selfish person I have ever met. Our grandmother died and I'm doing everything I can to keep her dream alive, and you're fighting me every step of the way."

Mindy stepped closer. Her eyes were so angry it was as if they were on fire. "Are you listening to yourself? It was *her* dream, Sophie. And you feel a sense of obligation to see that through, but I don't. It might have been her dream, but it's not mine. My company is my dream. It's my vision. And I'm not going to take all of the hard work I've done to reach my goals and throw it away. I won't do it."

Sophie felt as though she couldn't breathe. Jake had warned her this might happen. He'd even told her to prepare herself for it, but she'd never believed that Mindy would be cold-blooded enough to do it. "So we're not going to work together. And I have to figure out how to buy you out of your stake in the business? We're talking two billion dollars for half of the current valuation, Mindy. Billion with a *b*. I don't have that kind of cash lying around. And I can't even begin to think where I'm going to get it."

"Then let me sell my half to Jake."

Sophie had thought about that once or twice, but she knew that wasn't what he was after. He and his partners wanted to buy the property so they could see Eden's to what they felt was its rightful demise. They wanted the building and the land. They envisioned condos and big-chain retail and fancy restaurants. They would never go in on what they all saw as a failing business. And Sophie wasn't willing to give up. Not yet.

"I don't think that's going to work."

"Why not? Trouble in paradise?" Mindy stepped up to the mirror and reapplied her lipstick, not acknowledging the fact that she truly did look disheveled.

"It's complicated."

"That's a Facebook status, not an answer."

Sophie simply stared at her sister's reflection in the mirror. Some days it felt as though they would never get along. It frustrated the hell out of her. Not being able to count on Mindy only made Sophie realize that, aside from the loyal staff at Eden's, people who were paid to be on her side, Jake was the only person in her life who was truly supporting her. That had always been Gram's role, and he'd filled it. For that reason, she had to find him right now.

"Where are you going?" Mindy asked.

"To find Jake."

Jake was waiting in the hall outside the conference room where the will was to be read. A peculiar edginess was in the air, which caught him off guard. He hadn't expected to feel nervous today. This was Sophie's day, and although it would be momentous, it was supposed to be very straightforward. Everyone knew what was in Victoria Eden's will, at least as it pertained to Eden's Department Store.

Still, Sophie and Mindy had been in the bathroom for a while now. He'd listened for the sound of arguing but hadn't heard a thing. That was a relief. By all accounts, there had already been more than enough tension between those two. When Sophie finally came strolling down the hall, he smiled at her, hoping that things would be okay between them after this was all over. He was fairly certain she wasn't going to be willing to sell him the Eden's property. They hadn't discussed it, but nothing about her dedication or hardworking attitude had changed. That meant that it would fall on him to break the news to his fellow investors. It wouldn't be easy. They might kick him out of the group. That would mean an entire stream of exclusive business opportunities, gone.

"They're ready for us," he said, kissing Sophie on the cheek. "Everything okay with Mindy?"

"Nothing two billion dollars can't fix," she quipped.

"You're kidding, right?"

She shook her head. "Afraid not."

A woman in a black suit stepped out of the conference room. "If we could get everyone situated inside, we'd like to start."

Sophie and Jake filed in behind her. Sophie came to a dead stop and grabbed his arm as soon as she stepped into the conference room.

"What?" Jake asked. "You okay?"

"My cousin Emma is here," she whispered, pulling Jake farther into the room, but into a corner away from the other people who had gathered. "So is my aunt Jill."

"So? I thought the whole reason the reading was delayed was because they had to wait for the beneficiaries to be here."

She squeezed his arm even harder and her eyes flashed with confusion. "But Emma is on the other side of the family. Her mom and my mom are sisters. Gram was my paternal grandmother. I didn't even know Gram knew Jill or Emma."

A team of lawyers was assembling at the head of the table. "Please. Everyone. Find a seat. We're going to start in a moment," the woman in the black suit said.

"I'm sure it's fine. Probably one of those things where they met her through your parents and she wanted to give them something to remember her by."

Sophie scanned Jake's face, her eyes darting back and forth. He could see the gears turning as she tried to make sense of what he was saying. "Okay. You're right. I'm sure it's nothing."

He took this moment of relative quiet to pull her closer. He drew the back of his hand across the smooth skin of her cheek. "It will all be okay. I promise."

He had to say something to reassure her. He couldn't stand to see her upset, even when his own stomach was churning. Talk about being torn—he wasn't sure how he would feel once the will had been read and Sophie, this beautiful woman he couldn't get out of his system, had inherited the massive Eden's business and property. Every moment with Sophie was only pulling him closer to her.

"We'll go ahead and get started. I'm Leslie Adams and I'm lead counsel for the Eden estate," the woman said again. "If everyone could take a seat at the table, that would be great."

Sophie and Jake stepped forward and each pulled out a rolling chair. He sat on Sophie's left, and to Sophie's right, her mother, Jenny, took a seat. Mindy walked in and took the seat next to Jake, mumbling a quiet hello. Several of Sophie's grandmother's cousins were next, followed by Emma, the mysterious cousin, and Jill, the aunt. Jake could feel the tension in the air again, especially between Sophie and Mindy's mom and her sister. They didn't even look at each other.

Ms. Adams cleared her throat loudly, and that was enough to garner everyone's attention. "This will be a straightforward proceeding. The decedent, Victoria Jane Eden, asked that her last will and testament be read aloud to her family." She then launched into the legal preamble to the will, followed by a laundry list of antiques and jewelry, all of which went to various family members. None of it seemed to warrant much of a response from those in attendance, but perhaps that was because everyone was waiting for the big-ticket items.

Ms. Adams turned a page of the will and readjusted her reading glasses. "And finally, we move on to the major assets." Everyone seemed to sit a little straighter, bending their ears and hanging on every word. "'To my eldest granddaughter, Mindy Eden, I leave my apartment overlooking Central Park. I have had many happy years there and I hope she chooses to make it her permanent residence.'"

Mindy shifted in her seat, but made no indication as to whether or not she was happy about the news.

"'To my middle granddaughter, Sophie Eden, I leave Eden House, the family's vacation home outside the city limits of Scarsdale, New York. She loves the house even more than I do, and I know she will take good care of it.'"

Under the table, Sophie's hand found Jake's. She tugged on it hard. "Did you know that?" he whispered.

Sophie nodded. "Yes. But what does she mean middle granddaughter?"

There was no time to discuss it. The lawyer continued. "'And finally, the most important piece of my legacy, Eden's Department Store. The business and all its holdings, including the building and the property on which it stands, will go to my granddaughters, Mindy Eden, Sophie Eden and Emma Stewart.'"

There was an audible gasp in the room. Sophie's eyes flew back to Jake's, then over to Ms. Adams, who held a finger to her lips.

"Please allow me to continue." She looked down again and returned to the text. "'I promised my son, Mitchell, that I would not divulge this information, but now that he and I are both gone, I feel that the truth must come out. Emma is my granddaughter, the product of a brief dalliance between my son and his wife's sister, Jill Stewart. I was not proud that he had strayed, but that should in no way reflect poorly on Emma. She has spent her entire life caught up in an impossible situation. I felt it was only right for her to have her piece of my fortune, along with her half sisters.'"

You could have heard a pin drop in that room. Everyone was dead silent. Ms. Adams held up her finger. "'There is one stipulation to the ownership of Eden's, however. The three granddaughters must proceed in good faith to keep the store in business for two years by running the store together. If any of the three do not agree to this, they shall forfeit their share to the remaining heir or heirs, but the stipulation remains in place. The property and business may not be sold or handed over to any entity until after a period of two years. At that time, the three granddaughters must come to a mutual agreement regarding the fate of the store. It is my most sincere dying wish that Eden's be run by a new generation of women, and I hope that they will endeavor to make it as grand a success as it once was.'"

The words sank in and Jake could feel himself shrinking in his chair. The store had indeed gone to Sophie and Mindy. It had also gone to someone with whom he had zero relationship, someone he knew nothing about. Even worse, the heirs were required to keep the store running for another two years. There never was a deal for him to pursue. He'd never had a chance. And there was an excellent chance that this woman he'd fallen for, the one he couldn't get enough of, had known all along.

Ten

_____

Sophie was frozen in shock. What had just happened? And what was she supposed to do about it? Her eyes glazed over. The room started to spin. Everything her grandmother had ever said to her echoed in her head. *You'll run Eden's one day, Sophie. You will.* She felt lightheaded, as if she might faint. And then she heard a sound that yanked her back to her reality—her mother, sobbing.

"Mom. Mom. It's okay." Sophie reached out and rubbed her back. She had no reason to reassure her mom that anything would be okay, but it was her impulse to comfort her, if only to quiet her cries. It was adding an unbearable layer of awkward to the tension in the room.

Sophie's mom looked up at her with mascara streaming down her face. Something about her pained expression made her look even more like Mindy, which was quite a feat. They were already near picture-perfect duplicates of each other. "I never wanted this to come out. But your grandmother never liked me. She never thought I was good enough for your father." Her mom whipped around and shot her own sister, Sophie's aunt Jill, the most glaring look. "You always had to have everything that was mine, didn't you?"

"Excuse me?" Jill answered with venom in her voice, pushing her chair back from the table and standing up straight. "You got everything from your husband. Everything. Meanwhile, I was paid off to lie to my own daughter about who her father was."

Ms. Adams, the lawyer who'd been leading the proceedings, stood and made her way over to Jill. "Ladies. I need to ask for civil discourse or I'm going to have to ask you to leave the premises."

Sophie couldn't believe what she was hearing. Her heart would have been a little more broken by each new revelation if her brain wasn't struggling so hard to put it all into context. Everything she thought she knew about her family was wrong. What other secrets were lurking between her mom and her aunt Jill? What else had her father done in his lifetime that would come back to haunt them all?

"You knew this was going to come out today, didn't you?" Mom asked Jill.

"Ladies…" Ms. Adams interjected with the leading tone required for a situation as tense as this.

"I had a pretty good idea, yes. And I have been waiting a very long time for it. Emma hasn't had the life she deserved. Now she'll have her birthright."

Her birthright. Anger began to bubble under Sophie's skin, a reaction that shocked her. She wasn't an angry person, but Eden's was also Sophie's birthright, something Sophie had dreamed about since she was a little girl. She'd put in the time over the last several years. She'd been the one at Gram's side, helping with the day-to-day, doing everything in her power to keep her grandmother's vision alive. It was one thing to have to share it with Mindy, the one who didn't care about it at all, the one who always had to be right and never gave Sophie the respect she deserved. It was another to have to share it with someone who might as well be a stranger.

Sophie scanned the conference table, and when she looked up, Emma was staring at her. Sophie's breath wasn't merely stuck in her chest. It felt as though it was never going to leave her body again. The look in Emma's eyes could only be described as disgust. Maybe even plain and simple hatred. Emma might have come here today in the hopes that a wrong would be righted, but Sophie was still getting up to speed. Much of the emotion coursing through Sophie had to do with confusion. She and Emma had never been close, partly because her mother and her sister had always kept their distance. If anything, their mother was more prone to disparaging comments uttered after one too many dirty martinis.

None of the bitterness between her mom and Aunt Jill made sense when Sophie was growing up. Now it was all coming together. Her mother had been living with the knowledge that her husband and her own sister had an affair. That made Sophie's mind run off on yet another tangent. How long did it go on? Was it a one-time thing? Or was their mother made to suffer that indignity on a regular basis while Mindy and Sophie were none the wiser?

Emma rose from her seat and looked down at her mother. "Let's go. We've gotten what we came for today."

She then directed her sights at Sophie again. The fury in her eyes had faded, replaced by ice-cold determination. "Sophie. Mindy. I'll begin work at Eden's on the second of January. I expect to have an office. One that is no smaller or any less nice than either of yours. Please make the appropriate accommodations."

Sophie and Mindy exchanged glances. Sophie was surprised Mindy didn't lunge for her and tackle her right there in the conference room.

"Of course. That won't be a problem," Sophie replied, thinking that this was going to be nothing but a huge problem. Gram's office would have to become Emma's. That made Sophie's heart hurt. Still, she had to respect the wishes of the woman she loved and admired. If Gram wanted Emma to be part of the operation, there had to have been a reason for it. Gram must have believed that this could all work out. Sophie prayed that was true.

Sophie and Jake both got up from the table and wandered out into the hall. She sought comfort in his arms the instant they were alone, but he stood straight as a board, putting only one arm around her, and even that wasn't a true embrace.

"I need a hug, Jake. I need reassurance right now. That was a complete nightmare."

He didn't say anything, but she felt the rise of his chest as he drew in a deep breath.

"Jake. Hug me. Say something. Please. Can't you see that I'm upset?" She took a half step back. He wouldn't even look her in the eye. "What is going on?"

Finally, their gazes connected. "What's the one thing you always told me when you talked about your grandmother?"

Sophie shrugged, unsure of why he would even ask

this question. "I don't know. That I loved her more than anything?"

He nodded, slowly, but it wasn't so much agreement as it was confirmation that she was on the right track. "And?"

"That we were very close? That we talked all the time?"

"Exactly."

The air seemed to stand still as his one-word reply echoed in her head. "You think I knew about this business with my cousin being my half sister? Because I didn't. I am as shocked as anybody right now."

He rolled his eyes and turned away from her, running his hand through his hair. "Do you really expect me to believe that? What kind of family keeps that sort of thing a secret? All this time?"

"What kind of family? I don't know, Jake. Apparently mine. But don't act like this is somehow my fault. I knew nothing about it. Nothing."

A low grumble escaped Jake's lips. Suddenly that heavenly sound was no longer so pleasant. "Okay. Fine. I'll buy that much, but I am not about to buy the fact that you knew nothing about these stipulations about Eden's. You let me send you fruit baskets and bring you flowers and generally make a fool of myself when you knew that you were in no position to sell."

Sophie's eyebrows drew together. "I never asked you to do any of those things. If you acted foolishly, that was your doing, not mine. If you honestly think that I knew what was going to happen today, then I don't know what to say. If you think that little of me, we have a serious problem. A problem that goes well beyond flowers and fruit baskets."

"You talked about nothing but how close you and your grandmother were. It was the basis of your entire argument for not selling. I don't see any way you couldn't have known about this. All those years of working closely with her and she never said a thing to you about you having another sister? She never said anything about restricting the sale of the business when you inherited it? That seems like an awfully salient detail. I can't believe you didn't know about this. I don't see any way you didn't know."

Sophie wasn't sure she'd ever heard more hurtful words come out of Jake's mouth, aside from the morning after their first tryst eight years ago. "I can't believe you don't even care that I am deeply upset about what happened today."

"Why would you be upset? You got exactly what you wanted. Part ownership of a multibillion-dollar property, and two years to try to make it a success. You have an ironclad legal excuse to do exactly what you wanted all this time. You win, Sophie. You got everything you ever wanted today. The rest of us got screwed."

Hundreds of thoughts were colliding in Sophie's head. None of this made sense. The secrets. The will. Jake's anger. "You really think I got everything I ever wanted? Because that's not true." As her words left her mouth, the weight of what came next became unbearable. She would not get everything she wanted. Because what she truly wanted was Jake. And he thought she'd deceived him. He thought she was some sort of terrible conniving person when Sophie couldn't have been any less that if she tried.

"Just be honest about it, Soph. I can't stand the deception. You were never going to sell to me and you just let me believe there was still a chance."

That really got her blood boiling, even hotter than it had been when she started to think about Emma's claim on Sophie's birthright. "I told you from the beginning that I didn't want to sell. You just didn't want to listen. You knew that I was putty in your hands and you did everything you could to take advantage of that. If I'm guilty of letting you believe in anything, it's that I let you believe in us, Jake. And judging by this conversation, I guess I was wrong to do that."

"Why did you let me come here today, Sophie? To humiliate me? To make it that much worse when I call my business partners and tell them what an idiot I've been?" Jake's expression was unflinching. None of what Sophie was saying was making the slightest bit of an impression. That was the moment when she knew this was over.

"Do you honestly think I would do that? I'm not even capable of being that conniving." Sophie wrapped her arms around her waist. "You know what? You are just as much of a jerk now as you were eight years ago. You don't care about me. You don't care about my feelings or what I'm going through. I was just a foot in the door, wasn't I? A chance for you to make a big pile of money and be the big important man."

"Don't criticize me for being successful or good at what I do. That isn't what this conversation is about, okay? I need to know why you weren't honest with me. I need to know why you let me believe one thing when you knew all along that it was never going to happen."

An awkward and unexpected burst of laughter left Sophie's lips. She couldn't help it. The irony of this situation was not lost on her. In fact, it was slapping her in the face, and the sting was going to linger for a very long time. "Sort of what you did to me in school, isn't it?

Be sweet to me and flirt all day long and let me be the girl who makes you feel good about yourself, but never actually give anything back."

"That's not the same thing at all."

Now the irony was eating away at Sophie's insides, hollowing her out. Jake was never going to take a leap with her. Even when this was so much better than last time, it wasn't what she really wanted it to be. It wasn't love, returned and given freely. It was love one way. She'd allowed her stupid optimism to get in the way of rational thought. Jake Wheeler wasn't capable of an emotional investment. Money, yes. His heart? No.

And to think she'd been prepared to profess her affection for him today. The universe's timing was impeccable. Here she was being pulled back from the precipice in the nick of time.

A smaller laugh left Sophie's lips. "It's funny, you know."

His vision narrowed on her. It was such a waste of his incredible eyes. "There's nothing funny about this."

Sophie threaded her arms into her coat, straightening her spine and forcing her tears back down her throat with nothing but sheer will. "Perhaps we'll find it funny later. Years from now. When it doesn't hurt so much."

"Sophie, you've lost me. And honestly, I don't have the patience for your clever games right now. If you want to tell me something, just say it and get it over with."

His voice sliced through the air like a sharpened blade, destroying everything sweet and kind and beautiful between them. She was no longer sadly resigned to her fate. She was no longer going to be sweet, polite Sophie Eden. She'd had enough. "It's not a game, Jake. I was going to tell you today that I love you. But you have ruined that. For the second time in my life, actually. You have ripped it to hundreds of pieces. So instead, I'm going to say goodbye. Have a nice life. I never want to see you again."

She turned on her heel, the tears starting the instant she could afford to cry, when her face was turned away from Jake and she was marching down to the elevator.

"Sophie. Stop. Don't be so dramatic."

She couldn't turn back. She couldn't look at him. She couldn't see what she had so stupidly believed could be her future. Her life. It was just going to break her heart. She picked up her speed, turning the corner. The elevator door was closing. "Hold it, please!" she called out in desperation. A man stuck out his hand. With a lunge, Sophie's foot hit the inside of the car and she pulled the rest of herself through the narrow opening. She nearly collapsed against the back wall of the elevator. The doors closed.

"Are you okay, ma'am?"

Sophie straightened and smoothed down the front of her coat. She endeavored to keep her breaths even. She told herself that crying would have to be for later. Not now. She'd never be able to stop. "Oh, yes. I'm just fine. Thank you for holding the elevator." She turned and granted the man a small smile before opening her purse and rifling through it for a tissue.

The elevator dinged at the lobby floor. The man held the door for her. "No problem. Happy holidays."

"Happy holidays to you, too." For the first time ever, Sophie put no stock in the sentiments behind those words. As she strolled out into the biting-cold day, it felt as though the spirit of Christmas had not only been sucked out of her, it had been taken from the entire city.

She not only couldn't conjure the feeling she looked forward to all year long, it was as if she couldn't even remember what it felt like. It was simply one more damning detail in her history with Jake. She loved him and he wasn't capable of giving it back. This time, recovering from the loss might take forever.

Jake took the stairs. He couldn't get in the elevator that Sophie had just ridden in. He already knew that his nose would betray him and pick up on any traces of her sweet scent. That would just bring back a flood of memories that did nothing to help him out of his predicament. It would do nothing to fix what had transpired over the last hour—the utter dismantling of the most vital plan he'd ever had.

Jake's driver was waiting for him at the curb outside the lawyer's office. Jake had hoped Sophie would be waiting as well, having remembered that they'd arrived together.

"Sir, I saw Ms. Eden come outside, but she didn't say anything when I called out to her. She just kept going down the sidewalk."

"She had somewhere she had to be." Jake was quick with the excuse.

"I have never seen anyone walk so fast in heels. She was practically sprinting."

"It's in her DNA."

Just as fast and able in heels, Mindy stormed out of the building. The stretch SUV was back again. But Jake wanted a word with her before she got away.

"Mindy. Do you have a minute?"

She wrapped her arms around herself. "I have exactly that. I have to get back to my office."

"Did you know about all of this? Did you know all of that was going to happen?"

She shook her head so fast her hair went flying in the cold winter wind. "No, I didn't know. I was completely broadsided in there. And I'm furious with my sister. She had to have known that was going to happen. She was ridiculously close with our grandmother. I can't believe she never told me."

In any other situation, Jake would have felt vindicated by Mindy's statement. She was equally astounded by Sophie's deception. But he took no joy in the revelation. There was nothing good to get out of any of this. "I'm in shock. She definitely never gave me any indication that this would happen. Obviously, I never would have pursued the purchase if that were the case." Nor would he have pursued Sophie, which would have meant that his heart wouldn't be broken right now. "No wonder she was so willing to promise me she wouldn't cut a deal with any buyer without first talking to me. It meant nothing."

Mindy's eyes were wide as dinner plates. "She did what? She never told me that. How could she make that promise to you and not tell me?" Mindy looked over her shoulder at the car waiting for her. "I don't know what to tell you, Jake, other than today has been just as horrible for me as it has been for you. I'm going to have to sell my company or clone myself or something. I'm going to have to go to that store every day for the next two years and work with my sister, who I no longer trust, along with another sister I never even knew I had."

However upset he was with Sophie, Jake did realize that both she and Mindy had also taken a real beating today. "I'm sorry. I'm sorry for all of us."

Mindy returned her sights to him. "Yeah. Me, too. I

sort of thought you two might figure out your issues this time. Looks like Sophie was the one to mess it up on this go-around, huh?"

Jake nodded, but he hated every word out of Mindy's mouth. It felt like she was sealing his fate. His deal was gone, and so was any chance at a future with Sophie. "I guess so." Out of the corner of his eye, he saw a door on the SUV open and out came a man he immediately recognized—Sam Blackwell. His blood began to boil. Sophie had told him that Mindy knew him only casually. Apparently that was not the case. "I think your ride is waiting for you."

Mindy glanced at the car and didn't turn back. "Oh, yes. I have to go. Take care of yourself." She trotted off and Sam stood aside and helped her into the car. Then it sped off.

Jake just stood there on the sidewalk, wondering how many more shocks he was going to have to withstand today. He couldn't take many more. Sophie had lied to him about Sam Blackwell, too.

"Mr. Wheeler? You ready?" David, his driver, called out.

"Yes." Jake got settled in the back seat of the car as David rounded to his door. He started to run over everything that had just happened, if only to try to make sense of it. The vision most easily conjured was one he hadn't actually seen—Sophie running down the street, away from him. It troubled him that his mind had no problem imagining her wanting to distance herself from him, forever. He looked out the window and ran his hand through his hair. What future did he have now? The business deal of a decade was officially dead. And any prospect of love was gone, as well.

"Back to the office, sir?"

"Yes, please." Jake had phone calls to make as soon as he returned. Phone calls that he dreaded making. No matter how hard he had tried in the past to shrug off failure, it always bothered him. None of his investment partners was going to listen to an excuse. They weren't going to listen to him explain how hard he had worked to put this deal together. He knew this because he knew this of himself. If the roles had been reversed, if he had been counting on someone else, he wouldn't want to hear excuses.

"How did things go at the lawyer's office?" Audrey asked when he returned.

"They could have gone better."

Audrey frowned and cocked her head to one side. "You missed Stephanie in Accounting's birthday. Would you like me to get you a piece of cake?"

"No, thank you. I'm not sure sugar is going to help me out now." All he could think about was that day at Eden House, making Christmas cookies. Talk about a slice of life he'd thought was never meant for him. But that was Sophie. She filled in the gaps, the things he'd missed out on. He hadn't needed sugar that day. He'd only needed her. And they had fit together so perfectly, it was hard to stomach the realization that she was gone from his life now.

"Coffee, then?" Audrey asked.

"Yes, actually. That would be great."

"Go ahead. I'll bring it in."

Jake stepped into his office and forced himself to move quickly, to sit behind his desk and pull out his phone and prepare to get this over with. These calls would not be pleasant, but there was very little of Jake's job that was fun. Today was a day for eating crow. Tomorrow he'd get up in the morning and do it all over again, hopefully with his pride intact.

The first few phone calls were irksome, but ultimately it all came down to business. He endured a few moments of disgruntlement, followed by the sentiment that everyone still wanted to keep working together. There was always money to be made. They just had to find the next big deal. At least he had that much going for him.

More than one person expressed the hope that when the two years were up, Jake would still have the inside track. "Make sure you maintain that relationship," one of his fellow investors said. Jake wasn't about to get into it, but that relationship was gone. There would be no more Sophie in his life. Not after today.

He decided to reach out to Sawyer last. This call was going to be the most difficult, only because he admired Sawyer so much and they had become friends. "Hey, Jake. I was eagerly waiting for this phone call, but the truth is that I already heard through the grapevine about what happened with Victoria Eden's will."

Jake slumped back in his chair and raked his fingers through his hair. "News travels fast."

"Bad news travels fastest of all."

"So true."

"Are you holding up okay? I'm sure it's disappointing. You've put a lot of work into it."

"You know this game as well as anyone. Sometimes you work your tail off and it still doesn't work. This is just another of those instances." Except that it really wasn't. There was more to it. So much more. And he couldn't talk to anyone about it.

"Do you want to grab a beer after work? I'm over at

the hotel. We could go up to the speakeasy and hole up in a corner booth."

Jake was always eager to get a drink with a colleague, especially someone he liked as much as Sawyer. But he hesitated, knowing that a beer or two might turn to truth serum in his veins, which might cause him to talk about things that weren't appropriate. The blowup with Sophie was still so fresh in his head, but it was as if it hadn't truly sunk in yet. If he tried hard enough, it might never do that.

"Jake? Everything okay?"

"Yeah. Sorry. I've got a lot on my mind right now."

Eleven

After the day Jake threw away their future, Sophie did the only thing she knew how to do. She threw herself into work. Unfortunately, work right now was like jumping into the deepest part of the ocean without a life vest. The days were long and brutally tiring. She spent more than one night on the couch in her office. She tried to ignore her memories of being with Jake on that couch, but then again, she was doing her level best to forget everything she ever knew about Jake Wheeler. He'd returned to the category of people to leave in the past. Forever. She simply couldn't be dumb enough to let him break her heart again. She couldn't afford to be so self-destructive.

She wasn't quite sure how she made it through the five days from December 18, the reading of Gram's will, to December 23, also known at Eden's as The Hardest Day of the Year. Customers were desperate to be done with their shopping, but their choices had dwindled considerably. Employees were exhausted after many long days spent on their feet dealing with short fuses and endless demands. Tomorrow, Christmas Eve, would be much better. Eden's was open for only a few hours, the crowds were always much smaller that day and most people were officially in the Christmas spirit.

Which was why December 23 was a day where Gram always went the extra mile. Complimentary fresh-baked cookies, hot cocoa and mulled cider were available on each floor of the store. That alone made such a huge difference—everything smelled heavenly. Santa no longer sat on his regal chair waiting for children to share their Christmas wishes. Instead, he roamed the store with a photographer elf, delivering candy canes and candid Polaroids, while spreading good cheer. Breakfast, lunch and dinner were brought in for the employees. Everyone earned time and a half.

Sophie's handling of December 23 was a test of whether she could match her grandmother's greatness. Could she keep everyone at Eden's, customers and employees alike, happy on the worst shopping day of the year? She only knew that she had to try, and even if she failed, it would keep her mind off the person she missed so desperately—Jake.

Arriving at the store that morning, running on a scant five hours of sleep and too much coffee, Sophie immediately noticed that something was off. Normally, salespeople and the department managers were buzzing about, busy as bees. Not now. Only a handful of employees were at their stations and the store was set to open in ten minutes. She made her way up to women's shoes and spotted Lizzie waiting for her, perched on one of the sofas. She popped up from her seat the instant she saw Sophie.

"I'm afraid I have bad news." Lizzie walked double time with Sophie back to the elevator.

"Do I even want to know?"

"Santa called in sick. It's impossible to find a replacement this close to Christmas. I tried."

Sophie blew out a breath and jabbed the button for the elevator. "Do we have anyone who can fill in?"

"I'm not sure."

"Reginald? Duane?"

Lizzie peered at Sophie as if she'd lost her mind. "Can you really see Reginald in the fur-trimmed suit? I think he'd rather die. As for Duane, he's too big for it."

"What about Theo in men's shoes?"

Lizzie nodded eagerly. "Good idea. I'll go talk to him after we discuss the bagel disaster."

"Disaster?"

"Mary's Bagels lost our order. They never showed up, and when I called, they said it was too late for them to deliver now. People are not happy. Everyone's waiting in the employee lounge, wondering where their food is."

"So that's why nobody's in their department. The store opens in ten minutes. I'll call about the bagels. You tell everyone it's on the way."

"Got it."

Sophie and Lizzie stepped off the elevator and marched down the hall to Sophie's office. Sophie was already on the phone to Mary's.

"Mary's Bagels. This is Mary."

"Mary, hey. It's Sophie Eden. What happened?" Sophie tossed her purse onto her desk.

"When your grandmother passed away, one of my

guys canceled your standing order. I don't know what to tell you."

"There's nothing you can do? I have a ton of hungry employees. I can't let this happen today." *Please not today.* Sophie had to at least show herself that she was capable of living up to what Gram would have done. This job and Eden's were the only things Sophie had right now, and somebody had to be competent going into next year. Mindy was bound to be difficult, and Emma was a wild card. "I will owe you, big-time, if you can make this happen."

Mary grumbled over the line. "I can get you four dozen now and the rest in an hour. It's the best I can do."

Gram never would have stood for this. There would have been hell to pay. But Sophie didn't have the energy to yell at anyone. "Thank you so much. And please, reinstate our order for next year." She hung up her phone and looked at Lizzie, who had just walked in. "Food is on the way. Hopefully that will be the worst of it. Can you please confirm lunch and dinner?"

"I'm on it." Lizzie turned on her heel and disappeared through the door.

Sophie plopped down in her chair. Through one of her office windows, she glimpsed snow flurries fluttering. This might end up being the prettiest, snowiest Christmas yet. Too bad she might have no Christmas to speak of at all. Her family was in tatters over everything that had come to light the day the will was read. Her mother wanted no part of celebrating. She was still too upset. Instead, she'd jetted off to Grand Cayman to spend the holiday drinking rum cocktails and lounging by the pool at a friend's villa. Mindy wasn't speaking to her at all. More than a dozen phone calls in five days had gone unreturned.

At this rate, Sophie would end up going to Eden House by herself. Sophie's preparations could very well be down the drain. Jake was wrong about a lot, but he might end up being right about one thing—decorating Eden House could very well have been a waste of time.

The mere thought of Jake made Sophie's stomach sour. It wasn't that Sophie had been looking forward to the holiday with him. He'd made it clear how much he disliked it and didn't care to participate. It was more that she'd looked forward to his being a part of her life this Christmas. There had been joy in knowing that she and her handsome Grinch had somehow miraculously found their way back to each other. Their future had been anything but sewn up, but there were glimmers of hope, and that was all she'd ever asked for.

But no. That wasn't the way things had played out. Although she would have far preferred to have learned about Emma while Gram was still alive, Sophie refused to blame the Jake situation on the will. He'd used it as an excuse to cut her out of his life. He'd been waiting for her to betray him, just so he could reaffirm his deep-seated belief that the people who mean the most ultimately let you down.

She and Jake simply weren't meant to be together, however much she wanted him and cared about him. It didn't matter that the last few weeks had been the best of her life. Whatever he was feeling, it clearly wasn't enough to make him want to stay in her life. It was just as true now as it had been years ago, but far more painful. She'd never find another love like Jake. The sooner she got used to it, the better.

Burying herself in the business of Eden's was the only thing that could save her now, so Sophie decided to walk the store, helping as needed. It was the sort of hands-on thing that Gram would have done in a pinch, and honestly it was a godsend. It kept Sophie so occupied that she worked right through lunch and well into the afternoon. She lent a hand at the gift wrapping station on the third floor, and helped customers at the perfume counter. She restocked gloves and scarves in ladies' accessories, and folded sweaters in the men's department. She forced a smile and soothed unruly customers by doling out discount shopping passes. By four thirty, her stomach rumbled so loudly that a woman standing a good fifteen feet away from her must have heard it, because she shot her a look. She needed food.

She headed upstairs to the employee lounge, discovering that dinner had not yet been delivered and that lunch had largely been decimated. She grabbed a wheat roll and a pat of butter and scarfed it down. At least it would hold her over a bit longer.

She then trudged down the hall, so exhausted that she had to stop at Lizzie's desk and sit for a minute. "I don't know how my grandmother did it. I feel like I've been hit by a truck." Sophie kicked off her shoes, another of her favorite Blahniks, Mary Janes in turquoise suede with an adorable scalloped edge.

"I don't know how either of you managed a whole day in heels." Lizzie kicked her foot out from behind her desk to reveal a cute but sensible pair of black flats.

"Most days I don't even think about it." Sophie tapped her bare feet on the floor. "Lizzie, can I ask you a question?"

"Of course."

"You were at Eden's with my grandmother for five years before I worked here. You've seen a few of the ups and downs of the store. Do you think we can make it?"

Just then, Reginald breezed in from the elevator, wearing a kelly green suit that made him look like a towering, flamboyant elf. "Is it time to go home yet? I have had the worst day. A child climbed into one of the window displays and it took nearly an hour to convince him to come out."

Lizzie checked her phone. "Sorry. Another two hours until closing."

Reginald shook his head and took the seat next to Sophie. "What are we talking about? And please tell me we're gossiping about Barb and Mike in housewares. Those two? That's a love connection if ever I have seen one."

Sophie laughed. "Sorry. No gossip. In fact, I had to go and get serious on poor Lizzie."

"We were discussing whether or not Eden's can make it," Lizzie said.

Reginald crossed his legs and looked over at Sophie, past his glasses perched on the edge of his nose. "This business is a roller coaster. That is nothing new. The sooner you get used to it, the better."

Sophie nodded slowly, not sure if that made her feel any better at all. "I know. You're right."

"But let me tell you this. First off, I have a lot of friends who do what I do. People don't know it, but the world of window dressing is incredibly tight-knit." He gently rested his hand on Sophie's forearm. "None of my friends works in a store as special as Eden's. Your grandmother knew what she was doing. Her spirit is in every square inch of this place."

Sophie had to wonder if Reginald had any idea how unencouraging his pep talk was. This all seemed like more confirmation that Sophie would never live up to the specter of her grandmother.

"But I can also tell you that I've seen a big change in this store over the last three years. A big change. Lizzie, I'm sure you noticed it, too."

Lizzie nodded and looked at Sophie, seeming resigned. "I have."

Sophie's heart felt heavy. Would she ever be able to overcome the challenges facing the store? Especially now that she was going to have to work with Mindy, who would be digging in her heels the whole way? And what about Emma? Sophie hardly knew her. Now they were supposed to save the family business together? "I know. It's the downturn in retail. I don't know how we're going to get through it. It's not just the store. It's a market condition. I suppose we just have to ride it out."

Reginald pursed his lips. "Please. Downturn in retail. There have been a million of those. In the end, people will always love to shop. It's the hunter-gatherer in all of us. I wasn't talking about that. I was talking about you."

"Me?"

He nodded, and for an instant Sophie thought she saw his eyes mist up. "Your grandmother was a new woman when you came to work here. She was energized. It was like she was twenty years younger."

"I never noticed any difference in her," Sophie said.

"That's because you weren't here to see her at work in the years before that. She believed in you. She believed that there was a future for this store when you came to work here. You had ideas. You had enthusiasm. She loved every second of it."

Sophie remembered so clearly the day her grandmother finally asked her to come to work for the store. It had always been the plan for Sophie to start right after business school, but it hadn't played out that way. Gram had other employees in the role that Sophie would eventually play, so she had to wait until they moved on. Sophie spent three years aimlessly shuffling from corporate job to corporate job, waiting for her chance. When she got it, she leaped at it.

Unfortunately, having a job she'd been predestined for had made Sophie discount the times when her grandmother said she was lucky to have Sophie there. She'd assumed that was her grandmother speaking, not her boss. Now she knew that Gram had meant it.

"Why do you think she didn't tell me? About Emma or the stipulation about keeping the store open for two years?"

"My guess is she thought she had time. Everybody thinks they have time. And honestly, she had no reason to believe otherwise. She was so full of life. That's part of what made it such a shock."

Sophie nodded. She would have cried if she had the energy. She'd shed everything she had for Jake over the past few days. Still, it all made perfect sense. Gram would have eventually told her. But she thought she had time. Just then, Sophie's cell phone rang. She fished it out of the pocket of her dress. *Look who finally decided to call me back.* "I need to take this. It's my sister."

"Which one?" Reginald quipped.

Sophie started back to her office. "Funny. That's funny." She answered the call and shut her office door behind her. "Did you lose your phone? Or were you merely torturing me?"

"I needed time to think."

Skipping her desk, Sophie stretched out on her couch and put her feet up. "You could have called me and told me that, you know."

"I was angry. I didn't want to say something ugly."

"Gram's will is not my fault."

"I know that. But I was pretty sure you'd hidden those stipulations from me. You and Gram talked about everything."

Sophie kneaded her forehead. "Not everything."

"Really, Soph? Because I really want to believe you, but I still need to hear it from you."

"I did not know about any of it. I'll take a lie detector test if you want me to. I swear I didn't know."

Mindy blew out a breath. "Okay. I believe you. Thank you."

"I'm glad that's cleared up." It was then that Sophie realized just how much it might not have been ridiculous for Jake to arrive at the same conclusion as Mindy. Sophie and her sister had known each other for their entire lives, and Mindy still thought Sophie had pulled the wool over everyone's eyes. "Are you still coming up to Eden House tomorrow?"

Mindy sighed. "I'm not. I need a break from family, and I made plans to spend it with a friend."

Sophie's heart sank to her stomach. "What am I supposed to do with your gifts?"

"Give them to me for my birthday? I haven't even had time to shop for you, so I don't have the same problem. I'm sorry. I think we just need to pretend like Christmas doesn't even exist this year."

Christmas doesn't exist. Sophie couldn't have thought up a more depressing concept if she tried. "Fine. I'll celebrate by myself."

"What about Jake? Did you not patch things up?"

"No, we didn't patch things up. You would have known that if you'd called me back. We're done."

"Oh. Wow. I'm sorry. I just assumed you guys would get back together. You seemed so...happy."

A headache the size of the women's shoe department was now brewing in Sophie's head. "Funny, but he's holding the same grudge you were. Maybe you two should spend some time together."

"I'm so sorry. I, uh, well, I might not have made plans if I'd known. Please don't be mad."

"Don't be mad? I feel like I'm the only one trying to hold everything together. Our family. The store." Sophie could feel herself unraveling. Between her lack of sleep and everything that had gone wrong, she wasn't far from coming apart at the seams.

"I'll make it up to you next year. I'm sorry, but that's my decision. And I have to go. I'm meeting my friend. I'm going to be late."

Sophie didn't have the strength to argue. "Fine. Merry Christmas." It wasn't like her at all, but she hung up on Mindy and dropped her phone on the floor.

She rolled to her side and held her hand to her chest, her breaths coming out of her in fits. From across the room, the lights on her office Christmas tree were twinkling like everything in the world was okay. But it wasn't. The tears were coming now, and she couldn't do anything to stop them. Everything that was *wrong* in her life and *gone* from her life was too much. Gram. Jake. Now Christmas.

Twelve

Jake was typically alone in his office on Christmas Eve, and this year was no different. His employees were either traveling or already at home with their families. Jake used the day to catch up on projects he'd put off. He took some time to finish up his projections for the new year. Basically, anything that could keep his mind off Christmas.

He'd told himself that he wouldn't work a full day, but now that it was noon, he didn't really see any reason to go home. What was waiting for him there? Nothing. No Sophie, that was for sure. But he did need lunch, and for that he'd need to run down the block to the deli.

Outside, it was bitter cold. Yesterday's snow had been mostly swept from the sidewalks, but it remained along the curbs, piled up and waiting to melt. Across the street in the park, the holiday market was bustling as always, but it would be closed in an hour or two. Another reminder of this season he had to withstand every year would be gone. It would be worse next year because now Christmas would just remind him of Sophie. She had not only put her mark on him, but she would forever be inextricably linked to December 25.

He grabbed a turkey sandwich and was trekking back to the office when his phone rang. He had to wrestle his glove from his hand in order to dig his cell out of his pocket and answer.

"Hello?" His breath was a puff of white in the cold air as he continued to walk.

"Jake. It's Mindy Eden."

He came to a stop in the middle of the sidewalk. This was not a call he'd expected. "Mindy. Hi."

"Do you have a minute?"

Jake nearly laughed. Today, he had nothing but time. "Of course."

"Good. Because I talked to Sophie yesterday and I can't stop thinking about you two."

"What about us? Your sister and I are no longer involved."

"I know. And that's the problem."

"She told me she never wanted to see me again. I don't really know how I'm supposed to come back from that. She ran away in heels down a snowy New York street to prove her point."

"Sophie runs in heels all the time. That should not be the measure of whether or not she actually meant what she said."

The cold was getting to Jake, so he put his glove back on and resumed the walk back to his office. "I wasn't very kind to her that day, either. I accused her of lying, and I wish I could take it back. I was upset and I said some stupid things."

"Do you still think she lied?"

Jake strolled back into his building and wandered off to the side of the lobby. "Honestly? I don't believe that your sister has an insincere or dishonest bone in her body. I don't know what the hell I was thinking."

"I'm glad to know it's not just me who's feeling like a jerk for not believing her. I apologized yesterday, though. I'm wondering if you shouldn't do the same."

He shook his head. "Do you think she would actually listen to me?"

"Sounds to me like you're asking whether or not she'll take you back. That I can't answer. But I do think she would at least let you apologize, which could be just what she needs. It might make her Christmas less miserable."

Jake laughed. A miserable Christmas? For Sophie? That seemed as unlikely a scenario as a repeat of yesterday's snowstorm in July.

"I'm serious, Jake. She's going to be all alone unless she can convince Barry to come and hang out with her. She's going to Eden House by herself."

"Where are you going to be? What about your mom?"

Mindy explained that her mom had taken off for the Caribbean and Mindy was opting for Miami with a friend. In fact, they'd both already left the city. Neither of them was feeling either the Christmas spirit or the joy of being a member of the Eden family.

This was not adding up for Jake. The Edens were solid as a rock, or so he had thought. Sophie had painted visions of a Christmas filled with love and laughter, of a house where everyone was happy and safe. And she wouldn't have that this year. Her Christmas was going to be just as terrible as Jake's, except it meant so much more to her.

"Where's Sophie now? Has she left for Eden House already?"

"I think the store is open until two today. Knowing her, she'll stay until closing and then she'll leave."

Jake was certain of very little right now, but the mere thought of Sophie suffering and being unhappy made his chest ache, and that could mean only one thing. He wasn't merely falling for Sophie. He loved her. And the only way to prove it was to save the thing he'd once despised. He was going to have to save Christmas.

"Mindy. I have to go. I hope you have fun in Miami with Sam Blackwell. Just be careful. He's not my favorite person. You can tell him I said that, too."

"How do you know I'm with Sam?"

"I pay attention. That's how." Jake marched over to the security desk. "We'll have to talk about this later. If I'm going to catch your sister at the store, I need to go now."

"Thanks, Jake."

"For what?"

"For being a good enough guy to want to make my sister happy."

He laughed again, much more readily this time. If he was being honest, he'd always been that guy. He'd always wanted to make Sophie happy. He'd just been doing an exceptionally poor job of it. "No problem." Jake hung up the phone and offered his deli bag to the female security guard working today. "Turkey on rye? Kosher dill on the side?"

She eyed him with suspicion. "What's the catch?"

"No catch. Just spreading a little holiday cheer." He was surprised to learn it didn't sound nearly as corny as he'd feared.

The guard dropped her steely stare and she smiled. "Thank you so much. I hope you have a merry Christmas."

"Thanks. I'm hoping so, too."

With no time to waste, Jake rushed back outside and down Fifth Avenue to Fortieth Street and the south side of the park. He was nearly to the Sixth Avenue corner when he spied the shop where Sophie had bought her ornament. The star. There was no telling if Barry had ever tracked down Sophie's grandmother's tree topper. Even if Sophie might not accept his apology, she might accept one final gift from him. It couldn't be met with any worse a reaction than a fruit basket.

He sprinted to the corner and back along the walkway, squeezing past people doing their last-minute shopping. When he got to the kiosk, a man was locking up the door.

"Please don't close the store. I need something," Jake blurted.

The man rolled his eyes. "We're basically sold out of everything. Sorry. Come see us next year."

Jake stepped right in front of him and looked him square in the eye. "You don't understand. I have to save Christmas for a very special woman. And if I don't, well, I might end up living my entire life alone."

"I'm sure that whatever you want is gone."

Jake could see it through the window. "It's not gone. It's right there. The gold star on top of that tree."

"We don't sell those. It's just for display."

"I'll give you a hundred bucks for it."

"Sir…"

"Two hundred. Cash."

"I wouldn't even know how to ring it up."

"Three hundred. I don't need a receipt. Trust me, I'm not going to bring it back."

The man closed his eyes and shook his head, just long enough to make Jake sick to his stomach. "All right. Fine." He turned the key and opened the door. "I'll be right back."

Jake watched as the man got out a stepladder, climbed to the top and removed the star from the top of the tree. He returned with Jake's purchase.

"Do you have a bag or a gift box?"

"No. Sorry."

Jake fished the cash out of his wallet and handed it over. "No worries. Thanks for your help."

With the gold star tucked under his arm, he broke free of the holiday market crowd and started to jog down Fortieth. When he got to the corner of Seventh Avenue, he spotted people with arms loaded down with Eden's shopping bags. The store was only three blocks down the avenue. Jake hurried to get there, his breath coming out in lofty puffs of white while the brisk wind whipped at his cheeks. The massive stone structure with the signature black-and-white Eden's sign hanging from the corner of the building loomed larger. It looked exactly as it had weeks ago, except Jake realized that he no longer saw it the same way. It was no longer a deal to be had. This was Sophie's whole life. He had to wonder if she would make room in that life for him or if he'd used up all of his chances. She'd told him a week ago that she intended to tell him that she loved him. Did she still feel that way? Or had he ruined everything?

He tried to imagine that day from Sophie's side of things. If it had gone as Jake had presumed it would, that would have been a difficult day for her. Mindy had given her ultimatum, which meant Sophie would have been scrambling for $2 billion. Granted, Jake could have bought Mindy out, but that wasn't a solution, either. That wasn't what Sophie wanted. It wasn't what her grandmother had envisioned. She'd wanted the granddaughters to run the store together. As a team. Now that team had one more person, someone she didn't know or trust. He'd been much too hard on Sophie. He knew that now.

He was steps from the revolving door when he came to a stop. He hadn't looked at the window displays the other times he'd been to the store. Not once. But here were crowds of people admiring them, pointing, taking pictures and raving. Children rushed from one window to another. They jumped up and down. There was so much joy and happiness around him. You could feel it in the air. For a moment, he allowed himself to simply soak it up. To drink it in. He'd been missing out on this because he'd decided as a young boy that it wasn't meant for him. Money and prestige were the things he'd been dead set on acquiring, just to prove to himself that he was stronger than his lot in life. In the meantime, he'd forgotten the part about being happy.

But it had found him with Sophie. She was his ray of sunshine. She was the reason that those two years of business school had been some of the best in his entire life. She made him look forward to things, even if it was merely looking forward to the chance to see her. He couldn't postpone happiness anymore. He had to grab it now.

He burst through the revolving doors and ran back to the elevators that went up to the offices. When he reached the top floor, there was nobody there. It was eerily quiet. For a split second, he thought he was too late. But then he turned and saw the light filtering from her office. Taking long strides, he arrived at her door, but she wasn't at her desk. She was asleep on her couch.

He crept into the room and set the star on her desk, taking a second to admire how beautiful she was when she was peacefully sleeping. He couldn't believe the way his heart swelled in his chest just to see her. So this really was love. He'd done more than fall for her. He was head-to-toe in love.

Not wanting to scare her, he cleared his throat. She stirred, but then snuggled up with the pillow again. The second time, he coughed. That was enough to make her open one eye.

"Jake." Sophie sat up, blinking, adorably sleepy. Her vision narrowed on him. "Why are you here?"

It wasn't exactly the greeting he'd hoped for, but honestly, it just felt good to be near her. He sat on the edge of the sofa near her feet and looked into her beautiful eyes. "I'm here because I'm a jerk."

"You are?" She sat up straighter, waking up. "Actually, you're right. You are a jerk."

Again, not what he'd wanted to hear, but better to face the music than lose out on a second, or technically a third, chance with Sophie. "I never should have doubted that you were just as surprised as I was by what was in your grandmother's will. But more important than that, I never, ever should have put a deal before my friendship with you. I never should have let it matter when I had a chance at more with you."

"Then why did you do it?"

Still unsure how she was feeling, he fought his deep longing to take her hand. He needed her to understand how much he meant what he was about to say, but he'd have to let her decide on his sincerity for herself. "I did it because that was the part I knew I could make work. Give me numbers and a business or a piece of property and I will turn it into more. It was us that I didn't know how to turn into more. And frankly, I was terrified of more. I was scared of hurting you, or you hurting me, or something coming along and ruining everything. I played it safe, Sophie, and you know that's not me."

"I'm so happy to hear that you've figured it out. Really. I am. I'm happy for you."

"I was hoping you'd be happy for us." Jake looked into her warm eyes, hoping and praying that there was forgiveness in what she'd said. He wanted his third chance. More than anything. "Say something."

"It's kind of amazing that after all of that, I still missed you."

"You did?"

She gently swatted him on the arm and moved closer, her sweet scent making the moment that much more powerful. He wanted this more than anything.

"Of course I did. I missed you all those years we were apart. I missed you when I'd only known you for a day. That's what you do to me, Jake. You make me miss you, even when you're a jerk."

"Does that mean you'll give me a third chance?"

"That depends. Are you going to be needing a fourth one? Because if you are, I might have to pass. I can't do this again. It will kill me."

"I don't need a fourth chance. I promise." He bundled her in his arms and kissed her deeply. It was more than passion or heat; it was his chance to tell her without words that she was his world. "I love you, Sophie. I nearly said it weeks ago and I really wish I had."

"You do?" Tears welled in her eyes. He tried to kiss them away.

"I do."

"Thank God. I love you, too. And it has not been easy to convince myself otherwise. I have failed completely."

He smiled. "That's one thing I'd like to see you fail at."

Sophie glanced over at her desk and her brow furrowed. "What's that?"

Jake hopped up from the couch. "I brought you a gift."

"I told you that you didn't need to bring me presents every time you come to my office."

He picked up the tree topper and handed it to her. Her mouth went slack with surprise. "Oh, my God. The star from the market. You got it for me?"

"It's insurance. I didn't want to risk you not having a good Christmas, and I knew that having a star on the tree was important to you."

"That was so sweet of you, but you know, Christmas is already pretty much ruined. My mom and Mindy aren't coming."

"I know. I spoke to Mindy today."

"You did? Is that what finally made you get off your butt and get over here?"

Jake laughed. "Something like that." He put his arm around her and kissed her forehead. "And you know, we can save Christmas. Together."

"But you hate it."

He shook his head. "I am determined to change my thinking. But I'm going to need a few days at Eden House with you if I'm going to do it right."

Sophie's expression was one of happiness, delight and sheer thankfulness. "You'll come with me? You'll save Christmas?"

"As unlikely as that sounds, I don't want anything else."

Thirteen

The sky was pitch-black by the time Sophie and Jake made the trip down the driveway at Eden House. This was not how Sophie had envisioned arriving this year, in the car with Jake, looking forward to several days of just the two of them, alone. This holiday was going to be very different. There was no denying that. Nor was there any denying that it was a good thing. Everything else in her life was changing—why not Christmas, too?

"Good to be back?" Jake asked as he pulled under the porte cochere and parked the car.

She took a moment to look at him, still in awe that several hours ago she was out cold in her office, having lulled herself to sleep by trying to wish away the holiday she loved so much. Thank goodness Jake not only recognized the error of his ways, he had the nerve to show up at her office and apologize, just in the nick of time. There really were Christmas miracles.

"It's absolutely fantastic to be back."

Jake brought in their suitcases and took them up to Sophie's room while she unloaded the groceries they'd bought at the market in town for their Christmas Day feast. Luckily, they'd grabbed dinner during their drive up, so she wouldn't have to cook tonight. For tomorrow, she planned to prepare the same elegant meal Gram always made—beef tenderloin roasted with carrots and fresh herbs, along with a homemade potato gratin and sautéed green beans. For dessert, she needed only to reach into the freezer.

"Ooh. I forgot there were cookies." Jake wrapped his arms around her from behind as she placed the tin on the counter to thaw.

"Now you're happy I made you bake with me."

"I am." He kissed her neck. "I'm also wondering when we get to go upstairs and make up for real."

Sophie turned in his arms, fighting a smile. That smoldering look in his eyes was going to kill her. "There's a protocol to the Eden family Christmas, and that will have to wait just a little bit longer."

"Well, that might need to change if I have anything to say about it."

"I promise you the to-do list is much shorter now than it was the last time you were here."

Jake cast his sights up to the ceiling. "Thank God. So what do I need to do?"

"Nothing too arduous. It's tradition that we build a fire in the sitting room, drink champagne and talk about what we're thankful for."

"That's it?"

Sophie nodded. "Hardly any trouble at all. It'll mean

a lot to me, though. It's exactly what we would be doing if Gram was here."

"I'm on fire duty." Jake disappeared into the utility room.

Sophie pulled out a bottle of Krug and placed it on the silver serving tray along with two champagne flutes. She also took a handful of cookies from the tin and put them on a plate. Once the fire got going, she figured they'd no longer be frozen. By the time she reached the sitting room, Jake was already hard at work placing the logs and crumpling newspaper. Sophie sat and opened the champagne as the fire started to crackle and pop.

"It'll be going in no time," he said, joining her on the couch.

"You seem remarkably happy." She poured them each a glass of champagne.

He picked up his glass but didn't drink from it yet. He simply looked at her, scanning her face, breaking her down with his eyes. "I am happy. I think this is the one time in my life I've ever felt hopeful. Truly hopeful. I can't explain it. I guess it's just being in love." He leaned forward and kissed her softly on the lips. "Which really just means that it all comes down to you. You make me feel hopeful."

Sophie smiled and kissed him again before raising her glass. "To feeling hopeful." With a soft musical clink, they toasted, then each took a sip.

Jake predictably went for a cookie soon after. "These really are good. Is there some reason you can't have them year-round? I mean, are they just for Christmas?"

Sophie laughed. "If you like them that much, I will make them more often. Valentine's Day. Easter. Whatever you want."

"Thanksgiving. Arbor Day. There are a lot of holidays we could exploit in the interest of cookies."

She sat back on the couch and watched him as he happily polished off his treat. She loved seeing him like this—relaxed, fun Jake was the absolute best. "Do you feel like you already said what you're thankful for? Or is there more?"

He cast a look at her that was one-half genuine warmth and one-half seduction. It sent zaps of electricity down her legs. "I have a feeling there will always be more to be thankful for if I'm with you." He scooted closer to her on the couch. "What about you?"

Sophie sighed. This year had been crazy. A roller coaster unlike anything she'd ever experienced. Losing Gram, gaining a half sister, inheriting Eden's and having Jake return to her life. It was hard to believe she'd not only crammed it into twelve months, but this had been only the last three. And there was no sign of things slowing down anytime soon. Luckily, she'd have Jake by her side.

"I'm thankful for love. I'm thankful that I had my family's love and I'm thankful that I now have yours. That's the greatest gift of all. It's all I've ever wanted."

He put his arm around her and pulled her close. "That's so perfect."

"Yeah? It was pretty simple, but that's all it boils down to."

He nodded and looked off at the fire. "How are you feeling about the challenges ahead? Your sister. Emma. Eden's. It's a lot to think about."

She could only nod in agreement. "It is. I'd be lying if I said that I wasn't worried at least a little bit. The unknown is scary. I don't want to spend the next two years waging battle with Mindy. And Emma? There's no telling what that's going to be like. She sure didn't seem warm and fuzzy at the lawyer's office that day."

"Well, as someone with their fair share of family up-heaval, and a dad who wasn't in their life, I'm guessing there are probably some pretty big scars there. I'd try to give her the benefit of the doubt if you can."

Sophie didn't want to think about it too hard. She would just have to cling to optimism and hope that would get her through. "I can do that. For a little while, at least."

"Whatever happens, I want you to know I'll be with you every step of the way."

"What about two years from now? The building and the land will still be there, except then it will be ripe for the picking."

"I want what you want, Sophie. I am fully prepared to help you with the store in any way I can if that's what you want."

"It is what I want. More than almost anything. I mean, I don't want that more than I want you."

"I don't want anything more than you. And as for two years from now, I'm hoping we'll be in this exact spot talking about our future again, except maybe we'll be married by then and talking about kids."

Sophie was flat-out shocked. "That's quite the leap for you, Jake."

"It is. But I don't want to put off happiness anymore. We've both waited plenty long."

"A family? On top of the crazy lives we already have?"

"Don't you want this house to be full of love and laughter again? Like it was when you were a kid?"

"I do. Although one could argue that it's already full of love."

"That is the sweetest thing you could ever say. Now I just need to make you laugh." He tickled her on her sides and Sophie erupted into laughter, folding in half and trying to get away from his hands. She jerked, falling back onto the couch. Jake climbed on top of her and slid his hand under her sweater, still tickling, although it was quickly turning into more. He planted a hot kiss on her mouth, encouraging her lips apart with his tongue. She wanted him so badly she could hardly see straight. But there was one more thing that had to be done.

"Jake. We need to put the star on the tree before we can go up to bed."

"Who says we have to go up to bed? This couch is working great for me right now. We have all night, after all." He nuzzled her neck with his nose, driving her wild.

"I'm serious. Just this one thing. Then I promise you that clothes can come off."

She had never seen a human being hop off a piece of furniture so fast in her life. "The star on the tree and that's it?"

"Scout's honor." Sophie got up from the couch and took the star from the top of the bar, where Jake had left it. "I should probably get the stepladder. Unless you think you can reach it."

"First off, you should be the one to put the star on the tree. And second, I do not want to wait for one of us to get a stepladder. Come here." Jake wrapped his arms around her legs and hoisted her up.

It felt momentous to do this with him, with the star he had bought for her. It felt like a new beginning. "I love it. It's perfect. It might even be better than the old one. Gram would have approved."

"Good." He gently set her back down on her feet but

kept her in his arms. "Have I told you how happy I am to be here with you? To have you share this with me? It means the world. Truly."

"Does this mean you might start liking Christmas?"

"Are you kidding? With you, Christmas is going to become my favorite day of the year."

"You're saying that so I'll go upstairs with you." She rose up onto her tiptoes and gave him a kiss that said that upstairs was the only place she wanted to go.

"Whatever it takes, Sophie. Whatever it takes."

* * * * *

COMING SOON!

We really hope you enjoyed reading this book. If you're looking for more romance, be sure to head to the shops when new books are available on

Thursday 15th November

To see which titles are coming soon, please visit
millsandboon.co.uk

MILLS & BOON

LET'S TALK
Romance

For exclusive extracts, competitions
and special offers, find us online:

- facebook.com/millsandboon
- @MillsandBoon
- @MillsandBoonUK

Get in touch on 01413 063232

For all the latest titles coming soon, visit
millsandboon.co.uk/nextmonth